WE ARE !

BOOK I:

ROCK

BY

S A FIELD

WE ARE SOULS

Book 1: ROCK
Book 2: PAPER (due for release Winter 2017)
Book 3: KNIFE (due for release Spring 2018)

ISBN: 978-1-5495-0015-2
E-book ISBN: 978-1-5272-1252-7

A CIP catalogue record for this E-book is available from the British Library.

Without you,
I wouldn't have the ingrained love of history or books. That's not a platitude, it's plain fact.

For my Trojan

So the foundation of all of this is you.

love,
Your son

Steven.

CHAPTERS

CH 1: A FREE MAN

Central London, midsummer 1987, amidst the simmering gridlock of the evening rush hour, and the swiftly-rising-temperature of the eighties housing-market boom...

'KIIINNN-ARRSSSOLLLLE!!!'screamed Angrim Skull-splitter. Leaning out from the shabby box-van's juddering cabin, the huge barbarian warrior accompanied the spittle-flecked war-cry with the meaningful-waving of a battle axe; His face an even deeper shade of scarlet than the convertible Porsche, which had just verily cut him up a real-treat.

'Alexander-Freeman-Properties.' Unlike his conduct on the road, the driver of the sleek, red sports-car was polite as he answered the bleating phone. These primordial days of the mobile offered no such protection as displaying the caller's number. It was the wife.
'Missing you too bunny. No darling, I'll be tucked up early tonight in the hotel with whore-licks!' Alexander answered his wife truthfully, which was a novelty.
'Horlicks?'
'Yes, *whore-licks* darling.'
'I hope it'll be hot and frothy!'
'Oh, I'm sure it will be darling.'
The estate agent, a dark-haired slim-built man around thirty or so, ended the conversation by regrettably announcing to his true love that he was 'breaking-up' (a new and useful phrase which had only recently entered the English language), and further that he could hardly bear the thought of another twenty-four hours without her. But after all, annoying though it was, business was of course business.
'I ca bel—too-ne-si---------ye--mon' Alexander barked in well-practised staccato, before pushing the red-phone button and cutting his spouse off. Mr Freeman did not replace the unwieldy-handset in its breeze-block like power-pack immediately, due to the extremely attractive blonde in the VW Golf now alongside. Mobile phones being both a fairly-recent and expensive arrival, Alexander felt his expertly and coolly executed wink

was enhanced by the chunky, black-plastic piece of social-status pressed to his ear.

Indeed, the Vodafone VT1, released in 1985, cost £2,000, or £5,000 in today's money. This did not include the three-year contract for line-rental and calls, which were not cheap. Our younger generation would be astounded, but the beast weighed in at five kilograms including the power pack. *Five* bags of sugar.

From behind her sun glasses the young lady concerned briefly noted the leering wolfish features. Swept back Bryl-creamed hair. Wide red braces and loud bespoke silk tie. The smile full of teeth. She noted the revving of a powerful and extremely-expensive precision engine competing against the Blaupunkt at full blast.

Being in possession of a life she therefore extended an elegant hand, and in response performed an equally-well executed 'wanker' signal.

However, Alexander was no longer present, and in his universe, he had of course left the poor blonde-totty begging for more. Taking advantage of a sudden lack of traffic in the oncoming lane, with one eye on the road and one on the handset of the phone upon which he stabbed a number, Alexander veered onto the opposite carriageway, roaring past the queuing sheep, awaiting the gap some soft-touch member of the flock would surely provide on the correct side of the road. With the ringing phone clamped between ear and shoulder, Alexander nimbly flicked his Ray bans onto the bridge of his nose and a Dunhill International into his pursed lips.

Moments later, accompanied by a furious chorus of expletives, screeching breaks and the horn blasts of his fellow commuters, Alexander re-joined the northward bound traffic. Replacing the glowing car lighter in the dashboard, he exhaled smoke with satisfaction.

'Arsey you ol git, that's a tonne you owe me mate, I told you they'd fuckin go for it, asking price offer my son! Yee of little faith!'

Richard Cornell, a fellow seller of bricks and drinking buddy was known as 'arsey' within the trade due to both his initials and general attitude toward the world. The private number plate which adorned his BMW was aptly 'RC 1'.

'You evil tart Alex! You'll rot in hell matey!' The receiver erupted upper-middle-class braying laughter into Alexander's ear.

'What're you trying to say? I'm deeply hurt! That fine example of Edwardian architecture constitutes a solid long-term investment. I said as much to the punters', Alex exclaimed with mock effrontery. 'I also did the decent thing, old softy that I am, and told them everything will be 10K more by the end of the month, so best not to hang around in securing their first love-nest.' Further laughter.

'So, the word *subsidence* means bugger-all to you then chummy? That place is a frigging submarine! We've had it on the books for as long as your lot Alex; Three sales on it, three surveys, three stick it up your arses!' giggled Arsey.

'Well that's the difference between you girls and me!' laughed Alex. 'The trusting first-time-buyers are using my mortgage guy, so we all know which lender it's going to be, and more importantly of course therefore which surveyor...'

'BHJ I suppose?' (Back-Hander-Johnson) enquired Arsey.

'The very same! I can see that crystal clean survey report now! And so what about a bit of subsidence anyway? I don't know why everyone gets so emotional over the word! Today it's a three-up two-down, by the time the proud new owners are thinking of retiring, it'll be a bungalow with a fuck-off basement! See what I say? An investment for the future or what? Never have to move bless-em!'

'More like won't be able to', chuckled Arsey.

'Bollocks! They could come and see me!'

'They probably will Alex, in court!'

'Anyway, I haven't got time to talk shit with you Arsey. I've got the roses..' Alexander glanced down at the two extravagant bouquets resting on the passenger seat, '..I've got the night in town away from the missus, and most importantly I've got the expensive oral delights of suction-Suzie and her sister awaiting me as we speak just north of the river!'

'Ah shit Alex! You're in town all night and you're not coming out with the lads? You cheesing tosser!'

'Hmm, *let's* see?..' Alexander deliberated in mock-serious tone, '..spend the night with you and the piss-heads, or the very-high-class hired help of the female variety? Well it's a toughie Rich I gotta tell you!' On the other end, a now *very* arsey Richard found himself talking to a dead line.

Travelling swiftly up the gears, Alexander approached the roundabout where he intended to turn *left,* heading north toward Tower Bridge. He therefore of course approached at break neck speed in the *right*-hand lane due to its state of lesser congestion. In earlier days when Alexander had been lower down the car-brand pecking order, he had liked to give the impression he was lost on these occasions. That was then, now he entered the roundabout in the right-hand lane and completed a triumphant circuit, before smugly exiting with right-of-way over those who'd been foolish enough to patiently queue in the left.

Alexander believed there were two types of people in the world, wolves and sheep. By his estimation, the flock accounted for about ninety percent of the population, whilst the remainder were as he; the go-getters, the leaders, the achievers, the realists. Even amongst those wolves Alexander considered himself a pack-leader.

Alexander knew you had to make your own luck in this life and that you only had the one. He did not feel it necessary to delude himself with foolish notions of an after-life, or indeed of there being any mystical point to this one. That was for the sheep, milling around in the pathetic hope that some imagined being or fate was going to make everything better for them; Patiently queuing, awaiting their turn, lambs to the slaughter. Yet the sheep served their purpose, for if they did not exist the wolves would be without prey. Alexander believed in the survival of the slipperiest and did not burden or limit himself with any self-imposed moral code, that stuff only got in the way. One day he would die, so what? There it was. Shit happened. The point was to make the most of it whilst you could, *and what a life it could be!* As the twin spires of the bridge loomed into view, with heady thoughts of that evening's delights, the deals of the day and the bigger deals of tomorrow burning through his mind, Alexander threw back his head and howled like the alpha wolf proclaiming mastery of all he surveyed.

Angrim had just about fucking had it. He was a big man in a little man's job. He was a big man, in a little man's van. His was a misplaced destiny. A sorrowful tale of untapped potential and unfair knocks, and he was sick to the back teeth of being pushed around and having the piss taken out of him. The hulking champion threw himself back into the worn driver's seat of the rusty Fiat, flinging his battle-worn axe onto the passenger seat beside him. With a torrent of oaths to dark gods, he set off after the over-paid flash bastard in the red penis-substitute, amidst a pall of black diesel smoke.

The early evening sun awoke a bedazzling fire about the glossy crimson paintwork and the wind blasted over and around Alexander's head, as he sped under the first lofty stone arch of the grandiose Victorian span, at a speed worthy of the autobahn. Unlike his politics, he was middle of the road. As if savouring a vintage of the highest calibre, he deeply inhaled the intoxicating aroma of the Thames at high summer and the petrol fumes of EC3; *His* world.

Annoyingly enough, half way across the river the eager salesman's amorous charge was brought to an inglorious halt, in sight of the very smoked-glass tower which held his pair of coin-operated-slots (as he lovingly referred to the sisters). The twin drawbridges were clogged with the bleating sheep in their beeping heaps, some of which had astutely managed a tangled collision upon the apex of the bridge, several vehicles ahead of the frustrated estate agent.

Alexander did not sound his horn, that would be the ineffectual action of a trapped person; A person who'd given up, a person without either the will or power to change the situation they faced. A follower rather than the followed; A sheep, a bleater, a prisoner of life. That wasn't Alex, he was a free man. Indeed, he was *Mr* 'A Freeman', and it said so on his briefcase, office door and platinum American Express card. In life, he had started with little, and through shear tenacity and unhindered by morals or remorse had risen to his current standing. Obviously, marrying into daddy's-money and connections had also assisted, but then that relationship had been as cynically pursued as any other deal he'd gone after. As a hunting wolf crouched ready to spring, he awaited his opportunity.

The engine screamed and whined as Angrim savagely wrenched the wheel from side to side, shouting incoherent abuse at all who barred his way. Those who did not immediately make way before that manic, snarling visage found themselves looking down the business end of the gruesome battle axe. This wild man of the wilderness had been meant for better things than this life. In youth, he'd roared like a lion. He'd been proud and impatient to discover what great destiny the wide world had in store for him. He'd dreamed of walking in the wide-open spaces, and scaling the high-places of the roof of the world. Upon leaving boyhood he hadn't been sure exactly what he'd wanted to do, just that it would be something different, something exciting; Not run of the mill as all those around him seemed satisfied to accept. How the hell the wife, the two kids, and the average house in the slightly-below-average area had crept up on him he wasn't quite sure, but that was now his world. A world of mortgage repayments and school-catchment areas, and of course the lifetime sentence to the monotony of the slightly-below-average job. Angrim's bewilderment and bitterness toward his society was only compounded by

9

its infuriating habit of constantly rewarding those around him of lesser ability, integrity and intelligence with better jobs, flasher cars, bigger houses and sexier wives. In his envious view, Angrim was just unlucky. The muscle-rippling giant did not ponder the mysteries of a possible after-life, he was mystified enough by this one. One thing he did know for bloody-sure however, he'd had enough, and someone was going to pay... 'Gotcha-me-fuckin-beauty!' The purple faced barbarian grinned with insane, bestial delight, as his blood-shot eyes suddenly fixed on the red Porsche only a few vehicles ahead. The beserker reached for his axe with a bear-like paw, and then the door handle.

'Thank you, ladies.' As the Red Sea before Moses, the traffic in front of Alexander parted. Recovery vehicles were slowly making their way from either end of the bridge towards the pile-up under a flashing halo of amber light. The dutiful sheep were squeezing to the kerbside along the length of the bridge, to make an avenue for the pick-up trucks down the centre of the road. The very moment the black cab directly in front of him pulled out of the way, Alexander was gone. The estate agent was oblivious to the ranting barbarian left jumping up and down on the simmering tarmac behind him.

As he approached the knot of vehicles responsible for the hold-up, Alexander noted a clear passage to their left, partially obscured by a packed double-decker bus. The railings separating road from footpath had been ripped from their footings by the collision the entire length of the accident site, with a gap wide enough at either end for a slim-line sports car to slip through. The pathway beyond was empty, tourists and veteran commuters alike having fled. His escape route now before him, Alexander howled like the wolf who has found the scent-trail of its quarry. It *was* good to be alive! He was in his prime, looked sharp, *was* sharp. The only thing rising faster than house prices was his bank balance, and in the not-too-distant-future his manhood also. The hood was down, profits were up, life was fuck-tastically-good in the extreme.

Like a verbal Mexican wave, swear words accompanied by a variety of hand gestures burst from either side of the road as Alexander passed at reckless speed. In answer, he gave a royal wave and smiled benevolently, before accelerating toward the gap ahead. Several things then happened in quick succession. Firstly, the phone began to ring. Alexander, being a man never to miss either a possible opportunity of business or of talking to a lady, reached for the receiver instinctively. It would most-likely be the girls wanting to know if they were to order the Dom Perignon or Krug. However, before he could place it to his ear he dropped the handset into his lap. Alexander howled like the wolf who has bitten into a small curled up rodent, only to discover it is in fact the left testicle of a sleeping daddy-size grizzly-bear. If his concentration hadn't been broken by the ringing phone and Alex hadn't had to glance down for the split-second to answer, he would have seen what was coming just that bit earlier and may well have reacted to his predicament quicker. As the Porsche glided smoothly through the gap in the buckled and broken railings, and onto the pathway, its driver realized the way was not in fact clear at all.

Travelling in the same direction as Alex, one of the northward-bound vehicles involved in the incident had been towing an empty trailer. A metal-framed flat trailer for transporting a car with fold down ramps. A southward-bound double-decker bus had blown a tire causing it to veer across the roadway into the oncoming lane, hitting the trailer side-on with such force, that it was separated from the towing-car and shunted sideways through the iron railings. The trailer ended up wedged at an angle between the bus and the steel parapet on the very edge of the bridge. The coupling-end hung out over the brink into thin air, whilst the rear ramps were flung downward facing the pathway, into the path of the speeding estate agent... Alexander howled like the wolf moments after the grizzly has awoken to find himself short of a bollock ….

With a screech of brakes, rubber, a scraping of chrome and a shower of sparks, the sports car mounted the trailer as if in some meticulously planned Hollywood stunt. Alexander's spirits had been so high he had felt like he'd been flying all day. Now he was. For a brief moment, everything seemed to slow, all noise, all sense of motion was shut out. It was as if the car hung suspended in mid-air, supported by unseen means. In that surreal situation, the pilot who had begun his journey a driver, was treated to an unparalleled view of London's skyline under summer's golden dome. In an instant however, out of the blur of emotions streaming through Alexander's mind, terror arrived and claimed the whole of his consciousness for its own. Suddenly reality was taken off pause and Alexander said hello to vertigo. He felt his stomach rising as the nose of the car dipped, and the brown Thames hurtled up toward him.

'AAAAAGGHHHHHH-SSHHHIIIIIIIIIIIIITTTT!!!!' A shower of Property-detail sheets, roses and Alexander's earlier eaten lunch, flew up from the diving car. Alex's lifelong disdain of wearing a seat-belt saw him catapulted out and away from the plummeting car. Split-seconds later his scream was cut off, as bludgeoned and winded he hit the solid-feeling surface of the river. Suddenly to his side the water exploded and turned white with oxygen bubbles. There was a blur of red and a violent outwash of pressure buffeted him. Miraculously the car had landed without causing him injury! His stunned senses returning, a still groggy and battered Alexander felt relief even exuberance flood through him as he sank beneath the river's surface. He was a strong swimmer and although severely bruised indeed from the fall, he was still alive! Alexander peered skyward and kicked toward the glimmering light above. He'd be on the news! What a tale for the punters! What a tale for the lads! What a tale for the ladies! This would be good for bucks and fucks. He was going to be a celebrity to those who mattered. As he strove for the surface the estate agent smiled to himself. If he 'd been one of the sheep he'd be at bottom of the river still strapped in. It then struck him that he didn't appear to be making any headway against the water and wasn't rising at all. That was when he felt the restriction around his legs, and a weight pulling him down. In panic Alexander peered down through the green-brown mirk. In the fall and subsequent thrashing about in the water, the thick rubber cord of the not-so-mobile mobile-phone had become entangled around his thighs and waist. The heavy battery pack hung some feet below him, like an anchor.

In increasing terror, the man's fingers dug into his skin as he desperately tried to free himself, but to no avail. As long moments dragged without air-intake, Alex's attempts became weaker and weaker, until with a look of absolute surprise on his face, Alexander Freeman sank into the blackness below.

Alexander had always maintained an ardent belief that everything which happened in the world was complete coincidence and that any form of divine or universal justice simply did not exist. 'What goes around comes around' and 'You reap what you sow' meant nothing to him. He may well have felt his views somewhat urinated upon had he known that it was Faith, his wife, the lady whom he'd betrayed and lied-to for a living, who made the phone call which in all-probability killed him. On the other hand, he would have probably just thought it was a coincidence. Faith had called because she'd forgotten to say she loved him.

For a man who had none, Alexander was killed by Faith.

A shocked and breathless Angrim reached the parapet and stared down at the writhing surface of the river far below, just in time to witness the still-smoking exhaust pipe of the red sports car sink beneath the bubbling water. As the burning fury of road-rage left him (a rage which allows the wimpiest of us to believe we can slay any who stand before us irrespective of their size or numbers), Angrim shrank in stature returning once more to a sheepish Nigel Vickers, self-employed plumber. Six-pack returned to beer-belly, battle-axe became adjustable-spanner. Once back inside his cab, a shaken Nigel retrieved a grubby photo from behind the sun-shield. He studied the faces of his Lizzie and his two little diamonds (now not so little), Karen and Philip. The envious plumber's initials were 'NV', and if he could have afforded it, they would have made as apt a private number plate as Richard Cornell's were for him. Yet after placing the photo on his dashboard where he could see it and glancing once more at the crowd gathered at the side of the bridge, Nigel suddenly felt very lucky; Very lucky indeed. He turned the key in the ignition, and set out for home.

Amidst the glitter of the sun on the water, Alex's roses floated serenely downriver, moulded roughly into a circle by the current. Somewhat like a funerary wreath. Something emerged from the depths amidst the flowers, a yellow plaque, like a banner across a wreath. It was the front number plate from Alex's car, loosened by the impact. A3 MAN.

CH 2: A KEY

2017. A not so nice summer's day, and a not-so-posh district of London.

'Urrrrr-Ah wha! Oh-Naaa!' Allen Key tumbled from his bed in a panic, leaving the crumpled duvet on the bedroom floor amid the week's laundry. This was the third time in two weeks he'd slept through the alarm. Staring blankly through the grimy bus window, Allen grimaced as he slipped the phone back into his raincoat pocket. Everyone had raved about face-time and video-calls when they'd come out, especially his gran. Oh yeah, it was really cool to be able to see the person you were speaking to, everyone had said so. Oh yeah, *really* cool. Cool that is until you couldn't refuse the face-time call and had to bullshit your supervisor on a rainy Monday morning, about being late for work again and the hangover showed. 'Old-iron-knickers' wasn't happy. Not the best way to start appraisal day. Great…
Allen swapped the bus window for a tube window. Different glass, same stare.
Twenty-nine! Twenty-bloody-nine. How had that happened? Next he'd be thirty…. The death of his twenties.. One minute he was sixteen, leaving school and glad to be out. The next, here he was thirteen years later doing a bean-counting desk job that bored him shitless, all of it a blur and nothing to show for it. Not a house, car or girl-friend. Allen worked to pay the rent on his damp room, buy clothes (not as many as he'd have liked) and party with his mates as often as his inadequate budget allowed. The inadequateness of his monthly budget and his cavalier approach to personal finances generally saw Allen living it up for the first week after getting paid, followed by two weeks of frugal-living, followed by a week of living off everyone else or pay-day loans. Allen had no big plan, no vast ambitions. Clubs, pubs, parties, gigs, the usual music-festivals, get away see the sun once a year when he could afford it. That was Allen Key. For a long-time that'd been enough, but lately there had been an increasing sense of monotony. Allen's life was spent generally either looking forward to payday, a holiday, or the end of the working day.
Of course, he knew that in the planetary run of things he was lucky. He was lucky globally when compared with say the starving, the homeless, the afflicted and the persecuted. And you had to work, there it was. As his dad never tired of reminding him, 'better to have a shit-job than no job

mate'. To be fair, his dad had more years-in by far than Allen on hating his job.

Yet Allen still couldn't escape the feeling of being robbed; Robbed of twelve years of his life by the education system and now the seemingly never-ending daylight-robbery of the workplace. Having considered the fact that we all spend half of our lives asleep, Allen was feeling increasingly depressed by the realization that between birth and death, the average person appeared to get only a miniscule amount of time in which to do exactly as they desired. Sure, there were the vocations of life, scientists, doctors, nurses, priests, nuns, musicians and the like. He could understand that sort of dedication. But to Allen a job was a job, and people who either enjoyed theirs' too much or appeared not to notice there was anything else, gave him the sincere willies. Allen certainly couldn't get excited about paper which was a shame, bearing in mind this is what his present employer sold.

However, Allen had always loved drawing and writing on the stuff. From his earliest years, Allen's dad enthralled and entertained him with tales of dragons, wizards and knights; Vikings to ancient Romans, Greeks and Egyptians, or space-men and aliens. Always with Allen as the unexpected and overlooked pint-sized hero; All painted in the glorious infinite-spectrum of colour of the imagination. His dad told a mean story.

So as a skinny child and a skinnier early-teenager Allen had produced swathes of short-stories, cartoons and sketches, and had even daydreamed of being a future author or artist. But with the onset of spots and girls, he'd found himself increasingly embarrassed concerning his 'childish' pass times.

As a young man, Allen now considered himself average and ordinary, in both looks and destiny. He was of average build and had average brown hair. If you'd asked him about his IQ, he'd have said 'about average'. He considered his artistic efforts to be amateurish at best, and certainly not something from which he could realistically make a living. That sort of thing wasn't for normal, every-day ordinary people like him. In a cynical world, artistic success even for the talented was all too often down to luck. Too risky. Therefore, like so many ordinary people before him, Allen had put away his extraordinary childhood dreams and had ended up in an ordinary 'proper job'.

Allen was Milton Keynes born and bred. For the first half of his life he apparently came from somewhere really shit and embarrassing, known only for concrete cows and roundabouts. Surprisingly enough, for the second half of his life he apparently came from somewhere increasingly cool. So much so in fact that house prices, which always increase in line with apparent-coolness, meant that along with the greater part of his generation, he had bugger-all chance of affording to buy a house in his home-town for the foreseeable.

Allen had been brought up in one of the few older corners of Milton Keynes. An uncharacteristically picturesque hamlet pre-dating the town, yet now hemmed in by newbuild within one of the regimented grid-squares. For a family of four, whilst undeniably quaint and cosy, the two-bedroom terraced cottage offered more-cramped living-conditions than the Weasleys' house, if they'd had no magic and no money. It made Charlie's house (of Chocolate Factory fame) look positively spacious. It was an anti-Tardis, in that it was even smaller than it looked from the outside.

Now in their fifties, Allen's parents, Ray and Anna, bought the Victorian starter-home pre-kids in their care-free twenties, at which time it had been a cool and characterful home. A green and leafy quirky haven amidst the bustling ever-expanding uniform town.

Allen's dad had met his mum through selling her this very house.

Ray was an estate agent.

Alexander Freeman, he was not. He was the sort of estate agent who'd fallen into it at twenty just because he needed a job, and one was advertised. A child of the sixties, Ray had always viewed his career as a shelf-filling role to which he gave as little of himself as possible. Initially, this is what he'd done to party and go on holiday, then to pay the bills and later help keep a roof over the kids' heads. But one day, *one day* he'd escape and do something cool. Making and selling arty stuff or something... basically anything which didn't involve targets and greedy people. Now he was at the stage whereby the only thing he felt he'd escape to was retirement.

Most long-term estate agents generally at the very least used their experience and position to upsize or accrue the odd rental property by way of a pension.

With both being rubbish at forward-planning and money however, rather than upsize, Allen's parents had remortgaged repeatedly to pay for a spending-slightly-more-than-they-earned type life-style, until by their forties they had a mortgage more than twice what they'd paid for the house, and two unplanned boys with a ten-year age gap in bunk beds. That being said, there'd been plenty of love if not floor-space.

16

It wasn't as if Allen never had the encouragement to pursue his dreams. Anna was an unashamed hippy at heart, forever optimistic. She believed everyone was here for a reason, and no one else could tell you what that reason was, not a teacher, employer, priest or politician. She'd always told her son he could be anything he wanted to be. Allen's dad had always drummed it into him not to make the same mistake he had, in that Allen should pursue something he loved, rather than end up doing a job he hated out of necessity.

If he was honest, at the age of sixteen Allen certainly hadn't felt like a fully-fledged adult, able to go out into the working world and hold his own. If he was really-honest, he was also far too busy enjoying being sixteen to want to take mundane full-time work seriously. So, as an average academic except for art, when it came to sixth form or college, he'd chosen college. Moulton college, Northampton to be exact, on the advice of Mrs Bottomly the school careers advisor. A quirky place and a throw-back to the past, it specialised in the old traditional skills. Being creative with his hands, Allen had felt drawn to the three-year course in stone-masonry. He'd been taken to nearly every castle in the country throughout his childhood and had pretended to storm many a gateway or tower with his dad, and later his little brother, tooled up to the medieval-nines from the gift shop. He'd grown up on King Arthur, Lord of the Rings and later Game of Thrones. A lot of castles. So, from his perspective, the opportunity to work on historical restoration had really appealed. When he'd asked his parents' advice before applying, his mum had told him to follow his heart, as she would. His dad had told him he was one-thousand-percent behind him, and Ray always pulled people up for saying anything over one-hundred-percent as it wasn't possible, just sales-speaky-annoying. Ray had always told Allen that whenever he'd been involved in the sale of a period or listed property and a thatcher or mason was required to quote, their waiting list was always long and they always charged the earth.

His dad was elated that at last his son would break the mould of the last two generations. Ray had always wanted to do something arty and creative but had ended up an estate agent. His own dad, Allen's grandad, Mick, had been a talented drummer in the London sixties scene, but ended up a managing-director in the food industry, and a later a full-time alcoholic. For years, Ray had tortured himself that he'd been unable to provide a proper sized house for his children. He had fallen *into* rather than *planned* a family life. Allen's parents had been far too good at playing in the pre-children years to ever plan properly ahead, and for most of their childrens' lives had remained children financially. They were feast and famine merchants. Their children would have some damn cool memories as well as a good example of how not to manage their personal finances.

But now at least Ray believed he and Allen's mum had contributed to; and nurtured their son's creative side. He would now be going out into the world with the expectation of doing something fulfilling, both to the soul and pocket, in the real world rather than just dreaming about it. Allen's mum sold print but dreamed of being a psychic investigator or Reiki master.

When he'd been accepted on the course and they'd seen the amazing gargoyles and ornate stone-work in the college work shop, Allen's dad had cried. After the years of kicking his confidence had taken from the one-size-fits-all education system, Allen had beamed. This was something he knew he could do.

So, Allen had been extremely chuffed to have taken his first foot steps into a proper career in a solid and secure industry, which was also arty, interesting and well paid. Indeed, as a mason he would be as safe as houses.

However, three years later at the age of nineteen, when it actually came to gaining apprenticeship in the old-fashioned industry, Allen soon realised that being in Milton Keynes, renowned as one of the most modern purpose-built towns in the country, there were hardly any career opportunities on his door step in his chosen vocation. It had then dawned on him that it was no coincidence that most of his classmates had been from well-to-do backgrounds, whose parents were then funding them to go off to York Minster, Lincoln cathedral and such places, so they could survive the three years on nominal apprentice wages.

Needless to say, given his parents financial position this had not been an option for Allen. Though they'd paid for him to pass his driving test, his parents were unable to finance a car, let alone the small fortune to insure it for their teenage son. No car, no apprenticeship. Allen's dad had cried again. His mum had said 'everything happens for a reason, it'll all be fine my darling', as she would.

Allen loved his dad but had come to the realization that he was shit at careers advice.

His dad had often apologised for his and the previous generation's seeming lack of care for Allen's. For example, they themselves had taken home-ownership in early adulthood for granted, and being able to afford the insuring of a car even on lower wages in their youth. Through greed, they had not only put home ownership beyond most of Allen's generation but worse, were happy to charge them more-a-month as Dickensian-style private-landlords. They had voted to ensure there were no council houses for Allen's generation. Whilst young, the older generations had been considered responsible enough to get behind the wheel for a slightly higher premium. Apparently, Allen's generation were considered *sooo* dangerous that their premiums had to be *sooo* exorbitant, and be spied on and grassed-up by black-boxes invented by the older generation.

Allen's dad had also often said that it was therefore not surprising that the younger generation were happy to see the older farmed off to shit care homes.

Allen's dad did believe in 'goes around comes around'.

Throughout his college course Allen had part time jobs, and had worked in a succession of supermarkets and clothes shops. His last part time job had proved the most convenient as it was in the adjacent grid square, so he could walk there rather than relying on the bus, taxi, or mum and dad to get into the town centre. This turned into a full-time job on the realization that an apprenticeship as a mason wouldn't be possible any time soon. However, for the painfully self-conscious nineteen-year-old it was also the most embarrassing job given his name.

Allen Key worked in Timpson's, cutting keys. Verily did his mates and girls take the piss.

Just as Allen had been making the adult decision to stick it out at Timpson's, in the attempt to accrue enough money to finance a car to get to an apprenticeship, things had been turned upside down by Billy.

Allen had known Billy since he was six or so. Billy had lived off and on with his well-to-do grand-parents in their turn of the century cottage, which nestled in the parkland next to Allen's terrace. Bill could not be described as well-to-do. A couple of years older than Allen, and though a thoroughly lovely-bloke, Bill had always been a handful, and had been excluded from a succession of schools. However, not only was his heart in the right place, but being built like the proverbial brick shit-house, was also a handy mate to have in a scrape. At the age of twenty-one, Bill looked like a Viking, with fork beard, huge tribal-tattooed biceps, and a penchant for cannabis, shorts and heavy-metal.

One evening, just as Allen had put up a chart in his cramped man-cave loft-conversion (built by his dad so he could escape Jude, his nine-year old brother) noting how much money he'd need to put away each week to fund the all-important car, a very excited and animated Bill had turned up under his usual pall of pungent smoke.

Discussion swiftly moved to the treehouse situated in the communal wooded area fronting the terrace, where all matters of import were discussed. Allegedly the treehouse had been built for Allen when he was little. As usual with such projects, his dad had got carried away with what had initially been planned as the usual platform-type affair on a budget, but had ended up as a stout two-storey timber-turret, with iron-studded shutters and door, trees growing through it and the upstairs chamber referred to only half-jokingly as the biggest room in their diminutive house. All care of yet another consolidation remortgage. Whilst it had indeed been the venue for endless pretend dressing-up games, and had by turn been anything from a castle-tower to space-ship, it had also been increasingly commandeered by the adults of the street. Indeed, one morning when first built, A very-upset nine-year-old Allen had discovered what he innocently thought to be the remains of a black-feathered-bird killed by one of the street's cats, but was in actual-fact the feathers dropped from his mum's feather-boa following a somewhat amorous burlesque-style evening his parents had rounded off in the treehouse, it being the only private room of the house. His sheepish mum and dad had consoled their little man concerning the demise of the poor unfortunate said bird. A shoe-box burial of the feathers had even taken place.

Bifta in one hand, can of Stella in the other, and each-and-every sentence ending in 'man' or 'dude', Bill had then fervently put his plan to Allen. A plan that Allen apparently could only be 'a pussy', if he didn't go along with. Bill dismissed each-and-every one of Allen's concerns and misgivings, telling him that 'you're only young once man', and 'planning for the future is for boring oldies dude'.

Basically, his plan was for them both to leave behind drab and boring Milton Keynes and go to the entertainment centre of the country; excitement central; the most happening place in the UK; the very land of opportunity; London.

Allen did indeed love London. When they could afford it, He, Bill and their mates had attended the odd rave, gig, night and comedy club in the capital. The plan was simply to find any job with the least responsibility, rent the cheapest room possible and get on with enjoying the night life. By this stage, Allen was sick and tired of the pressure of trying to be mature and responsible by laying the foundations for a long-term career,

20

and so gave up without much of a fight. If he was honest with himself, Allen wanted to enjoy being nineteen too much to want to take work so seriously. Even though there was plenty of masonry work in London, apprentice wages wouldn't cover rent, and more-importantly partying.

He had also only very recently built up the nerve to finish his two-year relationship with Evelyn; Black-hair, china complexion, chillingly-pretty, chilling by nature; A girl his own age, but somehow fifty-nine at the same time.

Allen's mum was the proverbial easy-going, understanding soul. She firmly believed no one could be blamed for what their life-experience had made them. Yet having tried repeatedly to offer the olive-branch and get to know Eve, even she referred to her as a 'bunny-boiler'. Eve had always needed to know where Allen was, who he was with, and certainly didn't like him hanging out with his mates, etc etc. Since the break-up, the round-the-clock endless-barrage on social media, calls, texts and mails was doing his head in, and putting a good few miles between himself and his stalker also appealed.

Evelyn had been Allen's third serious girlfriend. She'd also been his third bunny-boiler. His dad nearly suffered a seizure from laughing, upon discovering Evelyn's surname was so-aptly 'Side'.

Evelyn-Side, though she of course pronounced her surname 'Seed-ay'. Allen's skill in being able to walk into a room of thirty girls, and unerringly walk out with the only nutter, always amazed his dad.

When Allen had broken the news of his travel plans to his parents, his mum's reaction had been along the lines of 'An adventure is always good for the soul. You're young enough to make mistakes and learn from them. I'm sure your journey will take you where you need to be, and you never know who or what will cross your path, etc, etc'. As she would. His dad had gone ape-shit.

So it was, having saved a nest egg over the following months and handed his keys in at Timpson's, Allen left home to travel to London just after his twentieth birthday, in 2008.

The first four years in lively-London were indeed a blast, and the boys would indeed amass a veritable swathe of hilarious and edgy-anecdotes for later life. Long hours in a succession of low-paid yet not-demanding jobs paid for the dingiest of rooms in the dodgiest of areas, in which the boys hardly spent a waking moment. Hangovers, or still being spaced-out generally ended each job due to lateness or complete failure to arrive at all, but each was replaced just in time to stave off eviction or starvation.

Bill received a financial life-line from his grandparents, and Allen's mum and dad transferred money as and when they could. The procession of jobs, addresses and night-time venues led to a wider and wider circle of social acquaintances and even some real mates. This proved handy for Allen, when at the end of that fourth year in 2012, Billy announced he was going home to Milton Keynes. The ageing grandparents were having a modern bungalow built for themselves within their rambling gardens, and Billy had inherited the cottage. Also, through a family connection, he'd managed to secure a job in Milton Keynes delivering top-end cars to clients, and Billy loved his cars. Allen couldn't blame Bill of course, they'd had a good run. He was happy for his mate and Bill had even suggested Allen lodge at his. However, Allen had at last stumbled unexpectedly on a job which he hoped might offer a more creative future. He even dared to believe there may have been some greater point in coming to London after all, other than just partying.

He'd met Tim that year in the chill-out room of a club, and the two had clicked immediately. Tim worked for a publishing house, and it all sounded very arty indeed, dealing with authors and artwork etc. In his inebriated state Allen had waxed lyrical concerning his childhood ambitions of becoming a writer, or at least something more artistic than a run-of-the-mill job. An equally-inebriated Tim had promised there and then to get him a job with his company. However, when it came to it, though the job was within the group for which Tim worked, the only role available was with a sister company who dealt with commercial print and paper, rather than publishing. Allen still enthusiastically took the job at the paper merchants in the firm belief he'd impress his employers and make the move across to publishing at some point.

However, five years later he'd become disillusioned and it was clear that his supervisor and line manager felt that the account manager job in paper sales was all he was good for, if that.

He'd travelled to London to be-free.

But had ended up selling A4.

There was no one special. Allen sternly believed any girl he thought was special wouldn't think he was. Sure, he could talk a good game under the influence on the dance floor or in the pub, and had a string of one-night-stands to his name, but nothing serious. His bunny-boiler hat-trick had left him not only cautious but confident he could only attract those with serious issues. He didn't think of himself as cynical or inferior in any way. He just thought he was normal, ordinary.

9.33AM
'Ah shit.' An extremely fragile Allen gingerly shrank into the turned-up
collar of his raincoat as he emerged from the tube station, and into the
rain, heading for the office.
5.33PM
'Yeah, can you believe it? Yeah, I'm not frigging joking Timmo, bugger
all money! More work! And a fucking written warning if I'm late again!
Total bastards! Fuck-em. You get the beers in - I'll be there in about
twenty, I'm gonna get blown my friend, you got the mandy yeah? You're
a lord! See ye inna minit' Allen returned the mobile to his pocket and
headed for the tube station.
3.33AM following morning
'Nnngggghhh' Allen lay face down on his bed, fully-dressed and utterly
wasted. After a number of attempts, he managed to roll over onto his back,
his eyes glazed slits, saliva trailing down his chin.
'Uuuuurghhh....ah f-fank f-uk' Allen felt relieved as he managed to
persuade the ceiling above him to cease the slow revolutions it had begun.
Experience had taught him that if you didn't deal with these things quickly
they soon got out of hand. If unchecked, it would not be long before Allen
would find himself on the old horizontal Wurlitzer, and then it'd be multi-
colour yawn time. Not nice to wake up in.
'Eh don thuckin beleeeve it, wha a stunna, what a sort!' Allen exhaled
blearily to the ceiling. Having reasonable confidence that he had control
over his stomach for the time being at least, Allen had allowed himself to
think about something else, something wonderful, a girl.
'Diddit rilly hap-n?' he asked himself. His brow wrinkled in
concentration. Then he giggled.
'Tooo fukkin-rite-it-did it did, yeh it did, uh huh.' The young clerk's
features were split by the widest and cheesiest of grins. Allen's world had
seemingly been a place of misery and woe, a place of disappointment and
unwarranted adversity. Yet just when everything had seemed at its darkest,
a light had appeared to illuminate the empty void of his life. Against all
odds, and in complete contradiction to all his previous experience with the
opposite sex, that night a goddess, an angel, had just walked up to him in
the club and started talking to him. And her name was.....
'Thuck, wozz-er-name?' Allen asked himself aloud. Due to the treatment
it had received that night, his sulking brain blatantly refused to cooperate.
'Ahhshit!' He attempted to think some more without the aid of his brain.

'Long-long luffly bran air, big-gize, bigga-titz. Legz too-er-neck, luvvly!! Luffly-lady. WOZZA-FUKINAME!!! C'MON FINK MAN!' Allen limply slapped himself across the face. The most beautiful girl in the world had come up to him; *Him*, could you believe it? And now he'd forgotten her bloody name! Relief suddenly washed abject desolation from his face.

'Magzeen I vuggin luv yoooooou', he slurred. Out of compassion, Allen's brain had at last begrudgingly and reluctantly decided to chip in. The man with three and-a-half hours left for sleep before he allegedly had to get up for work, basked in the warming glow of *his* Maxine, '*his wittle max*', and the fact that somewhere on his person (at that point he wasn't clear exactly where) he had her phone number! Again, the cheesy grin.

'Itzzz abbit f-kin-late innit?' Allen's head turned to the bedroom wall. Even Allen's liberal 'let's party all night' sensibilities were offended by the music which had begun to emanate from his neighbour's wall at this ungodly hour. Slight irritation increased in intensity with the volume, interrupting Allen's befuddled musings concerning the most divine creature in the entire world.

'Wha?' Allen's irritation was replaced with curiosity. Allen would readily admit his parents (oldies as they were) had quite a cool and eclectic musical taste, spanning some decades even to that of the present. Save for the odd embarrassing slip on his mum's part perhaps. As with many parents after a few drinks, Allen's had taken many a nostalgic musical trip during his childhood, lamenting their youthful love; Recalling a less complicated time before the children when they'd first met, which in their case was the early eighties. To his undulating state of mind, it seemed to Allen as if someone was playing a number of eighties-compilations at the same time, the tunes entwined and intermingling, yet each strangely distinct. He found himself humming along, and at one point even groggily-mouthing the words to some half-forgotten tracks.

As the volume continued to rise, Allen was taken by the uneasy feeling that something wasn't quite right. The music didn't just seem to be getting louder. Oddly it also appeared to be getting *nearer*.

And then in an explosion of sound, the car came through his bedroom wall.

CH 3: TALKING TO YOURSELF

Silence. Wedged upside-down in an ungainly heap in the narrow gap between his bed and the wall, Allen found himself having an extremely close and uncomfortable inspection of the bedroom carpet. His eyes were tightly closed. Was he injured? No pain registered, yet shock and the earlier-welcomed anaesthetic of a vast amount of alcohol and a number of other chemicals could now be cloaking the unthinkable. How many stories were there of those who'd lost all sorts of bits and pieces of themselves in war or sudden accidents, embarrassingly didn't appear to notice until it was pointed out to them? One minute you're lying there minding your own business, the next a bloody car comes through the fucking wall! What was all that about then? He was on the first floor for Christ's sake! What the hell was going on?

Allen was shaking violently and grimaced as he warily opened an eye. From the condition of the wallpaper against which his nose was pressed, seemingly no fire ball had enveloped the room. Doing the job also of its cowardly partner, the blood-shot eyeball darted wildly about. No blood. *Relief.* No debris appeared to be pressing down on him. There was no dust clogging his mouth or nostrils. Could he smell smoke? No. *Further relief.* But what could he smell? *Confusion.* It was sweet, pungent. *Aftershave?*

'Allen? Hello Allen-mate, come-out come-out wherever you are!'

A hollow thud was followed by a half-stifled cry of pain and fear. Behind the bed, Allen rubbed his head and silently cursed himself for having the kind of bed base that goes all the way down to the floor, and not an open one that could be crawled under; One which would allow you to shit yourself in private. Why was a car, and a deeply-resonant, honeyed voice in his bedroom at nearly four o'clock in the morning? A weird voice which somehow sounded of innumerable accents at once, all of which wanted to be liked and trusted, and said so. The tone was persuasive and would fit in equally-well with either the Chelsea set or the east-end geezers, a voice that was all things to all men. Like an oral chameleon, the voice tailored itself to please the listener. A voice which therefore obviously couldn't be trusted as far as it could be thrown.

How the hell did the owner of the voice know his name?

'Hey Alley-babes! You coming out to see me or what? I don't bite! Honest! Come on now don't be shy!' Silence.

'Rite I'm gonna sh-shtand up, an there's noh gonna be no soddin moata in ma room, you hear mi muffucka, an yor not gonna f-kin be ear eye-ver.

You ear me! No one's here sept me, I'm noh sked. Thissiz thissiz ma soddin bed-droom godammit! 'n' thissizz all in my ed'. Shock and sheer terror had galvanised Allen's stupefied senses into some semblance of coherent thinking. If a car had really crashed through his bedroom wall he'd be dead or close to it. With relief, it had then dawned on him that it was simply the accumulated cocktail of drink, drugs and lack of sleep over an extended weekend of 'having it large' three days after payday, which clearly accounted for this obviously hallucinogenic episode. He was going to cut down. To start with, he was going to dismiss this figment of his imagination from his bedroom.

'Calmdown-calmdown-calmdown-thissiz-notreal-notreal-notreal....' Allen slowly and unsteadily arose from behind the bed feverishly repeating the mantra, eyes once again tightly squeezed shut; his brow knit in deep concentration. Having reached a point of absolute confidence in his own sanity he inhaled and exhaled deeply, opened his eyes and panned slowly around the room. He then screamed, passed out, and collapsed once more behind the bed.

'Oh, for fuck's sake' said the deeply-resonant voice wearily.

Allen's exit from a state of consciousness had been due in part to the fact that beyond reason, a blood-red convertible sports car still stubbornly continued to occupy the entire room beyond the mattress. An odd car which seemed to writhe and flow under the eye, so that the intimidated onlooker was left with the impression that this car had all the best-flash-bits of all the best-flash-cars that had ever been made, or ever *would* be made. It hurt the eyes if you tried to look at it too hard.

Further, there appeared to be no hole in the wall or debris which might explain the vehicle's presence. Allen's feint was also largely due to the lean dark figure masked in shadow who nonchalantly reclined on the bonnet of the glossy low car; leaning back against the windscreen, ankles-crossed arms-folded. The silent figure coolly regarded him. As with his car, there was something *not quite right* about the driver. To Allen it was like looking at a man-shaped television screen with the channel not properly tuned in. A weaving vortex of moats of tiny points of light. Yet the overall impression was of the sharpest suit ever crafted, the label of which would have the entire host of designer names on it, and a face that although was cloaked in darkness, said *'trust me'*. That was of course shit-scary, no doubt about it. But what really caused his brain to say, 'sod this for a lark, I'm off', was the fact that there before him, he saw himself still lying face down on the bed.

'Wakey-wakey-Allen'.

'Uh-wha?' Allen returned from blissful oblivion, enjoyed an all too brief period of vagueness, before his short-term memory showed up to spoil things. Allen opened his eyes. Still obscured by the night, the tall dark figure towered over him, peering down through the blackest of sunglasses. Allen screamed before curling into a ball, his eyes screwed tightly shut.

'Thissiz-not-appnin, not-happnin-not-appnin,noh....been overdoo-in-it...thissiz-a-wakey-dream, a-dream-a-dream-a-dream. I'm juss gonna stay ere like thiz, wait it out till yer soddoff.' Long minutes stretched.

'This sort of thing happen to you regularly then does it?' asked the tall dark figure.

'No itsh mi firsht, Jush a bad-bad trip yeh. So I-I'm noh gonna talk to yer ye-know! Yer jussa figmnt ov ma-imadge-nation! D-y-hear-mi, jussa figmnt of mi wossname.'

'Do you have to talk like that Allen? It's very hard to understand you, and also bloody-annoying mate!'

'Yer wa? Tork like wa? Ohh-I-she. Dooo foggif me, you f-find me exi-dingly pisshd'n'shtoned'. Off-mi titz so-to-speak, outta–ma-tree.' Allen sniggered.

'Anywaze, not torkin t-yer, yer fig-mnt ov mi thingy', he added.

'No, you're not, and no I'm not' said the fuzzy man calmly.

'Yer wha?'

'I thought you weren't going to talk to me?'

'It's not sunni in ere ye know mista shades, Yer-twat!' spat Allen acidly.

'Charming Allen. What I said is *no* you're not drunk or stoned, and *no* I'm not a figment of your imagination.'

'I vink th-the fact that mi room's a car park, an we're avving thiz lil chatt would shay toomi, ELLO!! I'M OFF-MI-FAYSHE!!'

'No need to shout Allen, I'm here to help you - you know, now why don't you just try opening your eyes and standing up like a good little-fella?'

'How-dush fuck-off grab ya?'

'So you're just going to stay down there are you?' The figure asked curtly. A long pause followed.

'C-c-couldn't shtan even iffa wonnid tooo, I'm a lil tooo mashed.'

'Oh yes! That's right! You're out of it! Aren't you Allen?'

'Egshactly!'

'Allen, you are no longer tied to the collection of matter that you call a body. That piece of meat which you think is *all* of you. Your conscious-self is no longer chemically-affected by your squidgy bits. Your spirit is in

27

control, the matter doesn't matter. It's simply that you've experienced nothing in your life so far which allows you to believe that you could immediately sober up without having to sleep it off'.

'Bolloxsch.'

'So, you didn't recognize the bloke on the bed then? Well okay Allen, have it your way. I must say it's not the way I'd like to remember the golden moment I first heard the mind-blowing news that completely changed my perspective on life, death, the universe and everything. The moment that changed my life, sniffing my own arse I mean.'

'Oh dooo f-fuckin tel!' slurred Allen.

'My name is, *was,* Alexander Freeman…' said the figure. Somehow Allen couldn't escape the feeling that the name was familiar to him, though for the moment it remained beyond his addled senses to place it.

'I am the spirit of your last lifetime on this earth', continued the figure. 'And you Allen Neil Key, *you* me ol mate are *my* reincarnation. I have come to help you.'

CH 4: DYING TO MEET YOU

'Wha? Yoooz sayin yer afriggin angel?' Allen drunkenly sniggered.

'Oh, I wouldn't say that!' The figure's canine teeth showed as he smiled wolfishly. When the raucous drunken laughter had at last subsided, the tall figure continued unperturbed.

'Oh yes, I'm dead as dead can be bless-me! And I went out in style! Here, take a look at *this*....'

Allen half-opened his eyes and squinted at what appeared to be an old copy of 'The Sun', which had been thrust under his nose. It was as insubstantial as the hand which held it.

'D-D-De..' Allen gave up any attempt to read and sniggered again.

'Don't worry about the headline, it's *'The Sun'* after all! Hardly Shakespeare! Look, that's me!' A well-manicured finger of fizzing-light pointed to a magnified section of the poor-quality picture, which covered most of the tabloid's cover. His head sinking toward the page, Allen attempted to focus on the fuzzy scene. A still from some tourist's video. Even his dulled senses recognized the unmistakable silhouette of Tower Bridge. He studied the blown-up image. An orange, possibly *red* sports car plunging from the bridge.

'Yeah rite, wha-effer, my madge-nation's out-ray-jush', giggled Allen, though at the back of his mind something was trying to make itself heard. Something which was attempting to cut through the alcohol and drugs, and annoyingly was suggesting that the name Alexander Freeman and a red sports-car plunging from Tower Bridge, went together.

'See this Allen?' Bleary eyes followed the finger once again to a section of text at the bottom of the page.

'Notice the pronounced time of death?' The tall figure who said his name was Alexander Freeman, grinned like a wolf.

'Thix o'clock peee-emm, sithth orv jooon, n-eye n-eye teeen ay-*teee* seffen… yeh so-what?'

'The sixth hour of the sixth day of the sixth month, nineteen eighty-seven? Six-six-six. That not spooky to you then?'

'Sigs-sigs-sigsh, ooer skerry-man, ril skerry! Ooo! It's the aunty-chrisht! Eye b-bin watchin too-much t-telli! I'm not soup-tish, suppa-stisch, super… I don beleeev in thatsh sh-shite.'

'Allen.' There was something inexplicably persuasive in the figure's tone. Allen found his gaze rising involuntarily from the page to the face above.

'So, you don't think there's anything interesting at all in the sixth of the sixth of the sixth nineteen-eighty-seven then?' With a flourish, the figure removed his sunglasses. Allen suddenly found himself gripped by one of those emotions which are so overwhelming in intensity, that whilst it's screaming in your face it's also tapping you on the back of the shoulder at the same time. The old not knowing whether to shit shave or shower, as it has so eloquently been put.

'*You've got my eyes.*' Allen whispered, mesmerised. He had the uneasy feeling of looking into a mirror, without being able to tell who was the reflection. The face above him was intangible. Possibly an elegantly-sculpted jaw line, a hint of pronounced cheek bones perhaps, swept back dark hair maybe. But the eyes, they were another matter. Allen felt as if he were looking into his own, and that bent his head if he thought about it too much....

'Or rather you have mine', the figure replied. Allen was again visited by the equally-uneasy feeling that the deep, resonant voice was somehow familiar.

'So then, now that I have your attention, anything you'd like to add to the old sixth of the sixth of the sixth eighty-seven situation?' The figure asked. Allen continued to stare.

'Shit! That's nine months before I was born, to the day..', he whispered without thinking, almost as if someone else had spoken the words; His unblinking eyes never leaving those which returned his gaze. Usually he was crap with dates, and he knew it.

'That's nine months to the *hour*, from my time of death to your time of birth. But then you're not superstitious, are you?'

'Ah yeah, but all this has just been created by a particularly obscure part of my subconscious, let loose by booze 'n' mind-expanding drugs. Wow! The imagination is a mad thing! What will I think of next! This is mental gymnastics-arama! Hallucination city! One thing's for sure, I'm going to feel like shit in the morning! Another thing's for bloody-sure, I'll keep this to myself, I'll get myself locked up otherwise!' As if coming-to from a trance, Allen shook his head vigorously and began to laugh.

'Hang the fuck-on-a-minute!' he giggled suddenly, 'I think I dreamed about you! So *that's* where I'm getting all this from!' he added, relief flooding through him as a rational explanation for the nature of his hallucinatory-visitor presented itself at last. Of course, Allen couldn't recall the entire dream. Just snippets, glimpses and an overall feeling, like the memory of most dreams. However, there was no doubting the figure before him and the car had featured very prominently in it.

'You dreamed about me? Ah that's sweet!' replied Alex with a smile, before adding

with an evil grin, 'I do have to hand it to you, you can certainly hold your beer 'n' gear Al, because you're sounding pretty-damn-articulate for a pissed-up spaced-out bloke all of a sudden. Wouldn't you agree?'

Allen abruptly stopped laughing. Following a painful silence, a rather embarrassed Allen stood up with ease, coughing into his hand, eyes to the floor. After a while he sat down beside himself on the bed.

'So then, I'm just asleep and dreaming this right?'

'It is the fact that you are asleep, an *in-between* state, that allows me to make contact with your spirit at all, without your sceptical waking-consciousness being able to ignore or dismiss my presence', explained the figure.

'Well that's as clear as mud. As I was saying, the fact that oddly I'm consciously aware of being in a dream-state is something to do with the drugs and not taking care of myself yeah? Maybe I won't remember any of this shit in the morning! Hang on a minute! Maybe when you dream it's always like this? You just don't remember anything in the morning! Well bollocks to sitting up all night thinking about it! I'm off to sleep! Been nice knowing-ye Mr-nightmare but I've got work in the morning.' Allen waved a curt farewell to the figure before falling back onto the pillow, closing his eyes and curling into the spoons position with himself. Uncomfortable minutes crawled past.

'Allen, your body's already asleep.'

Allen listened to himself snoring.

'Look, will you just bugger off, *please?*' he pleaded.

'Not very polite to the dead, are you?'

'Look, you're not fucking dead, right! You don't exist! It's just a piggin dream!'

'And you dream like this a lot then do you?'

Allen rolled over, raising his hands to the ceiling in exasperation.

'Who knows how anyone dreams! It's just a mish-mash of memories, all your daily experiences and emotions, isn't it? Not to mention some way-out shit, take the car for example!' Allen laughed.

'What? You think it's too much?' The figure's voice and ever-changing features registered genuine concern and bemusement.

'*Ha ha,* very funny. I mean the fact that it's bloody *here at all.* Look, dreams are *never* consistent. For example, I believe you die, you rot. That's it. I wish it was different but there you go, it's just so bloody obvious!'

'Is it really?'

'I *certainly* don't believe in reincarnation yeah? All that coming-back as someone else or a bloody rabbit or whatever! But even if I did believe in that old pony, how could I meet you? If what you were telling me was true, you would have died and moved on to *be* me, yeah? You see, this isn't logical, there shouldn't be two of us here to have this conversation. A dream you see?'

'Well bugger me! And there I was thinking I'd had a whole life and died and everything, and all the time I was just a figment of your imagination, a bit of your *dream.*' The figure's voice dripped sarcasm, and was indignant to say the least.

'Look, it's very hard to explain to the cynical, narrow-minded living', he said at last.

'I thought it might be!' Allen chuckled.

'You think you're ready for a crash course in *"The-Big-One"* then do you?

'Try me', replied Allen, defiantly.

'Right, okay then. Imagine an energy, like electricity or something. Only this is a universal energy which animates and powers *everything*…It is the universal life-force energy..'

'Hang-on a bloody minute! Are we talking god here by any chance? Big bloke, beard, lots of smiting 'n' shit?'

'I said an *energy.*'

'Okeydokey! Just checking you weren't leading up to something. It's just that quite frankly, at this time of night I could do without the Jehovah's-Witness bit! I really could!'

'Odd you seeming disinterested in the spiritual. You sitting here I mean, talking to a spirit', smiled the figure.

'I'm not talking to a spirit, I'm talking to myself!' Allen's voice was a tight-lipped monotone.

'Well I suppose speaking to another one of your own incarnations is like talking to yourself in a sense.'

'Whatever.'

'Anyway, as I was saying, the energy acts on everything. It animates the matter, the body. The body is a vehicle, nothing more. How you treat it, is how it treats you. So, imagine the energy is the petrol, and the body is a car yeah?'

'Yeah.' Allen's voice was resigned, the back of his hand across his eyes.

'Well *you* and *me*, the bit that cares, worries, desires, fears, rejoices and hopes etcetera. Well you and me, are the five-day holiday at Weymouth that was only possible, *because* the petrol and car existed. The petrol and the car make experience possible, we *are* the experience. We are the feeling, the emotion. Once an emotion has been experienced, it has occurred, it cannot be undone, it is immortal.'

'Weymouth?'

'Yeah we're Weymouth.'

'Right. I wish I still felt stoned my dear Alex, I really do. I'd probably be lapping this up mate! But as it stands I've got to say Whoosh!' Allen made a sweeping-motion with his hand over his head.

'Look, each life time that is led inevitably gives rise to the need for another life afterward, to balance the mistakes that were made in the former one. The good from one life is the shoulder the next life stands upon, a head start if you like. The strand of life-energy which generates a living form in this world goes on to power the next life when one vehicle is worn out, like a snake continually shedding skins. The unique experiences of that life time still exist when the body dies. That is the spirit of that particular life time. You and I are connected by a strand of life-force energy, my life time has contributed to your existence, but we are yet individuals in our own right. Like everyone who has lived or will ever live, we're all one-offs, *we are souls*'.

'We *arse-oles* more like!' growled Allen, thinking about humanity in general.

'Hey! Give people a break! Sure! There *are* those with a lot to learn shall we say, the *young* souls. But there are those who've learnt a lot mate, the *old* souls. Young souls and old souls..'

'And Arse-oles!'

The figure desisted from further explanation upon noting the sullen expression of utter incomprehension and anger on Allen's face.

'Life-energy?' scowled Allen, 'Shedding skins? Spirits? Oh yes and Weymouth! Oh, do fucking stroll on!'

'You could try and be more respectful to a dead person you know' commented Alex.

'Oh, and so you've died have you? Well Mr Freeman what does it feel like to die then? Go on! dooo enlighten me? Dooo tell! Go on mate, in a word, what does it feel like to die!'

'In a word? Hmm that's a toughie, I suppose if I had to pick *the* word, the word would be *embarrassing*, yeah that's it'.

'Embarrassing?'

'Well yeah, especially for me, having been a non-believer and everything!' Shaking his head, the figure laughed before continuing.

'You see initially it's like rising up in a balloon' Mr Freeman's voice took on a faraway air. Allen thought he could almost hear the angelic tones of a harp.

'The old rising up bit eh' he said, giggling.

'Everything spreads out beneath you, and I don't just mean the landscape. When you're alive it's like being *in* the maze of life. You can only see the bit you're in, so lots of things occurring around, or to you, don't seem to make any sense. As you leave the world you can look down upon the maze with an ever-widening perspective, and see how it all fits together, how it's all connected, you see the pattern. You see all the conversations, all the lives. To me it was like it started with the last conversation I ever had, and it panned out from there. It's like you see what mood Mr 'X' was in when he left the house in the morning, which explained why he had the attitude he had when he bumped into Mrs 'Y'. You see Mrs 'Y's reaction, and how she takes that with her through her day. Her and billions like her, each making small ripples which make up the great current of life, the current we all get swept away in. Squillions of ants running blindly around bumping into each other, all occurring upon a tiny pin point of rock, amid trillions of others in an unending void. As you rise higher you see how those lives were connected to those that came before them. It all makes a *common* sense. The embarrassment arises from a sense of scale, because you truly *feel* your life in context. You realise that many of the things you had held to be *so* important whilst you were alive as not having been worth jack-shit, all the ideals, all the beliefs as petty. You get the picture? You get a lot of deceased opposing-politicians and opposing-sports-supporters having group-hugs. Lots of sheepish fanatics, suicide bombers and suchlike all turning up groaning like they've just realised they've been the victims of a *You've-been-framed* type programme; all slapping each other on the back and going '*you-guys! What were we thinking!*' Alex grinned, and despite himself Allen chuckled. Alex continued, 'But it's okay, because then you get a feeling of relief, like remembering something you can't believe you've forgotten. Like its fine that you're so insignificant, because then you're not so *responsible* for things as you'd held yourself to be; all the fuck-ups. Neither is anyone else. You let go. You also remember that all the little things are as important as the big things. Big things are made up of little things. Most importantly you remember that it's not embarrassing to be embarrassed. All-the-colours-in-all-the-sizes really'. Alexander finished with a smug grin.

'Yeah yeah, all very heavy, all very spiritual' Allen yawned. The harp music fell silent.

'Isn't it! No one was more surprised than me mate believe you me!' The sincerity in Alexander's voice unsettled Allen.

'Why oh why am I lying here talking to myself? I bloody hope I wake up soon because this is doing my head in!' Allen growled with agitation.

'Let me get this straight Allen-chap, you are being given a next-to-unique opportunity, proof of an afterlife in *your lifetime*. An opportunity to dispel the heaviest fears of most mortals, i.e. is there anything after I die? Is there a point at all to this life? To *me*? What happens to my loved ones? You are being handed on a plate an opportunity of enlightenment which most have to die to experience, and you prefer to think of it as a figment of your imagination?' asked Alex.

'You got it in a nut-shell Ally-babes' Allen replied, Ally babes glowered.

'Okay, okay! If I agree that this is a dream would you come with me?' pressed Alex.

'Come with you? Well if we can get this dream business agreed on I don't suppose it matters much, does it? It's only a bloody dream after-all! But come with you where?' asked Allen.

'To visit one of our past lives, a soul who had a far harsher start in life than either you or I.' Alex's tone seemed almost earnest.

'*Another* one of us! Oooh how cosy! The three amigos!' laughed Allen. The figure continued, unruffled, 'A soul who rose from the lowest station to the giddying heights of success; and when he lost it all, got it back! No matter how many times he was knocked down he picked himself right back up, and clawed his way up to the top of the tree again. Think of it as an educational experience that will help you in this lifetime when you wake up'.

'Visit the past with a ghost? Oh, very fucking *A-Christmas-Carol!* So, I'm Scrooge am I? Off to bleedin-Christmas-sodding-past am I? Hang on! Where's me bloody night-cap? Bah humbug!' Allen chuckled.

'Yeah I'll come with you' he added at last.

'So Allen, let me get this straight, for you to accompany me willingly, you want me to *lie* to you?' asked Alexander. The ex-estate-agent then fell silent and spent a quiet moment in reflection before continuing, 'Hmmm you've got a deal! I don't think I've got a problem with lying to you Allen, no problem whatsoever in fact. *This* Allen..' Alexander gestured to himself and his vehicle '..is all a dream. Alexander Freeman, pleased to meet you' he extended a hand.

'Allen Key, pleased to meet you' responded Allen, swinging into a seated position and instinctively reaching for the offered hand.

'I'm glad we've got that sorted out... Shit!' Allen gasped. As his hand travelled forward to grasp that of the fizzing apparition's, he'd oddly only just noticed that his own arm appeared to be made up of the same swirling currents of light as his visitor and the car.

'Wild dream!' giggled Allen, studying his arm and then the rest of himself in delight, he was almost transparent. Thankfully no internal organs showed, just bits of his room he shouldn't be able to see. The two shook hands. To Allen there was no physical sensation of contact, rather a faint heat and a tingling in the palm like a pulsing, prickling mild attack of pins and needles. An odd sensation, but then as he reminded himself, this was after all a dream.

'One more thing' Allen added.

'Just name it Mr Key'

'Put your sun-glasses back on please!' pleaded Allen.

With an amused smile and a deft flick of the wrist, Alexander once again veiled the source of Allen's deep discomfort.

'So, you'll come with me Allen? Great! Well as you say, it's only a dream! What've you got to lose eh chap?'

'Why?' asked Allen.

'Why what?'

'In this dream I'm having, *why* would you want to visit me and take me somewhere allegedly for my benefit? Why would you do that?'

'Well Allen, as I said with this reincarnation business, how one conducts oneself in life has a great bearing on the nature, fate and circumstances of one's next incarnation. We all get free choice in this life, but none in our beginnings. It's all this universal justice, the balance of nature, the inexorable tide of fate etcetera. It's very complicated, I won't bore you with all the bureaucratic details'

'No don't' sighed Allen.

'I suppose it's just that I feel a bit *responsible* for where you've ended up bless you. You see I was a bit of a bugger in my time, I was an *estate agent*.' Alexander coughed the word into his fist. Having confessed, the figure looked down at the floor, shuffling his feet.

'So what' replied Allen, 'so's my dad'.

'No Allen. An *extremely* successful estate agent.'

'Fuck off! Leave my dad alone!' there was true vehemence in Allen's voice. Ray Key had always prided himself on being straight and honest with everyone he dealt with in his often-despised job. He never wanted to rise above sales negotiator, never wanted to manage people, and certainly didn't have any inclination to run his own business. His approach had made him a popular person amongst clients to deal with, as opposed to some of his slimier stereotypical-estate-agent colleagues, delivering him a lot of repeat business, if not a fortune.

'I remember you weren't very successful with bridges from my dream!' giggled Allen.

'I'd describe what you saw as a past-life-memory rather than a dream' replied Alex.

'Er, remember the deal Alex?' asked Allen, raising his eyebrows with emphasis, 'this is *all* a dream, remember!'

'Sorry about that' apologised Alex sheepishly.

'And fuck me, this really is a nightmare of a dream, being descended from an extremely-successful-estate agent!' Allen chuckled, until his laughter abruptly ended. 'Hang on, what do you bloody mean? *Where I've ended up bless me,* what're you trying to say you cheeky-git?'

'Oh come on Allen! It's not exactly a penthouse in Mayfair is it?' replied the former estate agent, gesturing around Allen's modest home.

'Christ! I must be on a real-downer, to be having a pop at myself in a dream!'

'Look Allen, maybe I haven't helped matters spiritually-wise, but what're ye playing at mate? You're how old? Twenty-nine, right? I was on a right wedge at your age. I died at thirty, by which time I owned my own *very* lucrative business, had numerous investments, travelled the world regularly, ate at the best places, had a string of flash cars, had a posh missus and dirty mistresses, and was generally minted. Looked the nuts, *was* the nuts, so you're already *way* behind. Are you going to catch up in a year? If so, you've got a lot of work ahead of you sunshine!'

'*Sunshine?*' growled Allen, 'Who knows where I'll be a year from now? God! I don't know where I'll be this time next month!' Allen laughed his best 'devil-may-care' laugh.

'You'll be here mate, that's where you'll be' Alex replied flatly.

'Well maybe the big house and flash car isn't what I want out of life *Mr* estate agent. I do all right, and there's more to life than just money' spat Allen scornfully.

'Spoken like a man who's got none.'

'Fuck-you! You shallow tosser!' In the tense silence that followed Allen proceeded to sulk like a good-un.

'Look Allen, Al, Ally-babes! C'mon! we're family me ol mucka. Look, I'm sorry.' The ghost of Mr Freeman adopted a consolatory tone as he executed three 'buddy' punches on Allen's arm, again the slight tingling sensation like static electric. Allen was not amused.

'I get this dream, you're just my negative side. Here to tell me how crap I am!' he groaned.

'Look Allen, don't take it so personally! You see with this reincarnation business we're all in it together, we're a team.'

'You sound like my soddin-supervisor!'

'You come from a long line of great achievers Allen Key, just *how* great will become clear. We that have gone before you in the chain all have a lot riding on you. You've got a lot to live up to chap. You mate, are the current holder of the torch of life..'

'Torch-of-fucking-life-eh!' Allen sniggered.

'..but this relay-race is a marathon believe you me, and there's a long, long way to go yet. In the chain, we're each responsible for the start we give the next member of our team..'

'Oh *the-team!*' Allen's voice dripped mock-seriousness.

'..How you pass on that torch is of importance to all of us. I suppose I thought maybe I owed you a bit of a helping-hand, so here I am! But even with my contribution to your beginnings, you're letting the side down mate if I'm being brutally honest!'

'Well I'm sorry to be such a bleedin disappointment to you all!'

'Hey! Don't shoot the messenger'

'It's my bloody dream!' Allen growled, closing his eyes and trying to dream up a semi-automatic weapon. To his disappointment none materialised.

'Allen, you have a crappily-paid dead-end paper-pushing job you detest. You own a bus-pass, a rent book and are sadly lacking in the female department!'

'Ah-ha! Well that's where you're bloody wrong!' responded Allen with a smile, 'It just so happens that only tonight, well last night, a stunning, interesting girl came up to me and I ended up with her phone number! She wants to see me again! She asked me! So up yours mate! And she wasn't only interested in me for my money!'

'Ah, that would be the delightful Maxine? Ah this is going to be tricky..' Alexander's tone sounded genuinely uncomfortable.

'What is it?' Alexander's demeanour was making Allen increasingly nervous.

'What're you trying to say! I certainly didn't bloody dream *that* I can tell you! Go on, what is it?' he demanded of the grimacing ghost.

'Well I hate to be the one to break it to you mate, but I suppose it falls to me being close and everything..'

'Will you bloody get on with it!' demanded Allen angrily.

'Okay, Maxine really did like you, and yes she did give you her phone number, and yes she does want to see you again. It's just that, and I *really* am sorry to be the one to tell you this, it's just not going to be possible for you to get in touch with her again'.

'What do you mean! I've got her number, somewhere, I remember her writing it down for me, she *really* wanted me to have it!'

'Yes she did, she is *up for it* no doubt, but can you remember where she wrote it?' enquired Alex. Allen turned his thoughts to the blurry events of the evening. Instinctively he reached for his left fore-arm.

'She wrote it on my arm in eye-liner, neither of us had our phones or anything else to write with or on..' Allen's mobile had disappeared somewhere around the sixth beer and second-half of a pill if he recalled rightly. Allen noted with some concern that his ghostly fore-arm bore no marks whatsoever.

'*This* I'm afraid is the bad news..' coughed Alex nervously. Allen's eyes followed Alexander's gesture toward the bed. Allen looked back at his slumbering form. More specifically he stared at his bared left fore-arm. There was nothing on it except a muddy-brown smudge.

'Do you remember a certain visit to the toilets toward the end of the evening?' asked Alex softly, 'A rather hasty visit where you found yourself wishing that you hadn't downed as much laughing juice and other stimulants as you had before meeting Maxine?'

'I remember..' admitted Allen with a growing dread. He had indeed over-indulged the previous evening, as he had all weekend. After-all, he'd been paid on Friday. It was due to how much party-petrol he'd consumed in the last three days which had left him with no idea as to what Maxine's surname was, where she lived or worked. He remembered she was only visiting friends and like him, didn't come from London. He couldn't swear to it, but it was highly likely in his somewhat-out-of-it state, that he would have embellished upon the standing of both his address and job. He did recall neither did Face-book or twitter. It was yet another thing they shared. The one thing he was sure of however, was that she was gorgeous inside out.

'You blew your groceries big-time did you not?'

Allen nodded numbly.

'You sprayed that cubicle good-and-proper did you not?' pressed Alex, in the tone and manner of a barrister cross-examining the witness. Again, the answering nod.

'And in your panicked preparations to return in a reasonable timescale to the object of your desire, was there; or was there *not,* a lot of gargling and general water-splashing in the sink involved?' continued Alex. Another nod.

'Also, vigorous rubbing of splashed sleeves, hands and arms with a copious number of paper-towels?' This time the nod was accompanied by a trembling lip. Allen's form visibly sagged, the fight gone out of him. 'I don't fucking believe it' he sighed.

'That's just about my bloody luck that is, what an utter twat I am!' he spat, before jumping up and attempting to kick his sleeping body in the testicles. To his further rage, his foot went straight through himself. He then sat back down, his face in his hands. Alexander sat next to him, an arm around his shoulders.

'Look come with me on this accompanied viewing and it'll all make sense I promise you.' Alex urged. After a while Allen raised his head.

'What've I got to bloody lose!' he smiled grimly.

'Exactly Al, that's the spirit!' cried Alex, heartily slapping Allen on the back, before adding 'well strictly speaking I am. Hop in chap! Consider me your soul-agent! We'll have a ball mate!'

'I hope there're no bridges on the way!' Allen laughed, Alexander didn't.

CH 5: REVERSE PSYCHOLOGY

'Now you might find this somewhat *disconcerting..*'
'Bring it on!' Allen laughed in fey mood. The two sat in the shimmering
ghost-car, an ethereal engine purring, an ever-real Alexander at the wheel.
'Now Allen, we're going back down the chain a bit here, back in history.
When we get there, don't worry, no one will see or hear you, or be able to
touch you. Neither will you be able to interact with anyone or anything.
Nothing can touch you. This story has already happened, we're only going
along to view what took place. Except that to you it will actually feel like
you're there. It'll be like walking through the best virtual-reality
programme you could dream up.

Alexander put the gear-stick into 'reverse' but continued to hold the clutch
down.
'Now Allen, you may find this first leg of our little trip an odd experience
in the extreme. We're going to slide back through the channel of our
previous incarnations all the way back to our destination. A bit of
revisiting you might say. On-arrival you may have a few questions'.
'Yeah-yeah-yeah! Come on then flash-guy, impress me with your wheels'
Allen yawned.
As Alexander flicked on the stereo, a ghostly ready-lit cigarette appeared
in the region of his mouth. He half-turned in his seat, arm across the back
of Allen's head rest, staring at a point on the wardrobe door just beyond
the boot.
'Hang on!' he warned.
 Bobbing his head to the sound of the eighties, Allen continued to lounge
casually in his figure hugging seat. Alexander adjusted his grip on the
wheel, revved the engine and smiled a smile which made Allen, despite
his former nonchalance, reach for the seat belt. There weren't any.
Alexander flicked his foot off the clutch, and floored the accelerator. The
car exited the bedroom backwards in a blur to the accompaniment of
Allen's high-pitched scream.
On the bed, Allen snored. The clock ticked.

Allen sat frozen in the passenger seat, as he had for some time. Staring
straight ahead, eyes-wide. For the third time, Alexander clicked his fingers
in front of the unblinking gaze, but failed to raise any response. Not a
flinch from the ashen grey features.

41

'Allen, oh Allen' he cooed gently.

'Come on now Allen-buddy, you'll be fine mate. Come on, tell your uncle Alex all about it. It's been quite an experience for you I know. Come on, you can do it, just start talking and it'll all be rosy.' If it wasn't for the fact that the car now hung in mid-air, amid an endless black void where space and time meant nothing, one might have thought quite a lot of time passed before Allen spoke. When at last he did it was in a scarcely audible whisper.

'Wh-what just happened to me?'

'What can you remember? Start from when we left the bed-sit. You get the ball rolling and it'll all fall into place. You're just going through a bit of 'past-life-experience' overload, like jet-lag. It'll pass, trust me. Now come on Al.'

'I remember lifting off the bloody seat! I remember kissing the windscreen! What was I bloody thinking! Getting into a car with someone who thought their last one was a flying-submarine!' Although his voice had risen to an angry pitch, Allen remained staring fixedly ahead. His mouth moved, yet his drawn features were emotionless.

'I remember clawing my way back into my seat, and dragging my head around to look where we were going. I remember holding on for dear life, and then the strangest thing…'

'Go on'

'It was like I realised I was weightless and that there wasn't any feeling of momentum or speed or even any wind - even though we were obviously breaking aviation speed-limits at the time! There was no danger'.

A brief pause.

'I remember the walls…' Allen's hushed voice trailed back into silence. To begin with it had appeared to the disconcerted clerk that they were flying backwards through thin air, a brilliant blue and cloudless sky stretching out around them in all directions. Then out of the blurring distance a golden shimmering wall had appeared, a vast wall stretching from horizon to horizon, towering above and diminishing below into an impossible distance. As they careered toward it, Allen could see that the wall appeared to be a calm and rippling lake surface, seemingly of liquid gold. A *vertical* lake surface. His senses had become bewildered and confused by the feeling of weightlessness and the scale of the wall, so that it felt as if he was falling *downward* toward a vast ocean surface. And then they had hit it.

'Oh-shit-oh-shit-oh-shit-oh-shit…' said Allen as recollection began to return. Other than his ears popping and a faint '*Whomp!*' like noise there had been no sensation of impact, no explosion of golden water, no golden shower. Instead, as if passing through a smoke screen, they had broken back into endless blue heavens again, the great barrier shrinking behind them as they sped on. And then it had started…

Given the circumstances, Allen had been a little confused to find himself thinking about a leisurely walk in the woods. Although it was nothing more than a memory, he could keenly smell the leaf-mould smells of late Autumn in the forest. He could feel his feet sinking into the mulch with each pace and the crisp air upon his face. Only a file from his memory banks concerning a favourite walk, nothing more. What concerned Allen was the absolute knowledge that he had never been to this particular place. Yet at the same time he *knew* that he knew each and every hidden track and glade in this woodland. The fact of it being a forgotten childhood memory was instantly dismissed due to the three gleefully chattering small children running around him in the scene, all wellies, scarves and woolly hats; All a lot smaller than him. He knew that his perspective of the scene wasn't that of a child riding on an adult's shoulders, because he knew he was the adult and he *knew* that the children were his….

Before Allen could rally the practical and scientific division of his mental forces to remind himself that this was only a dream, another intense home-video type vision had burst within his mind's eye. A close-up of a young woman's face framed in darkness, the comfortable darkness of the bedroom. Allen knew that she farted like a trooper after spicy food, and could be a very naughty girl between the sheets, which was surprising given that he didn't recognise the woman at all. Allen had certainly not had that many sexual partners that he would have forgotten the intimate passion they had shared, a shared passion with a woman he'd never met. Yet again before he could even consider the impossible emotions rampaging through his mind, a further 'memory' arrived, and then another, and another. A day trip on a boat, an argument with a taxi driver, the old 'nodding field of corn in the sunshine'. The laughter of friends as they signed the plaster-cast on the leg that he had never broken, but which he could remember the pain of. Each vision appeared briefer than the last, yet felt greater in intensity, faster and faster, snap-shots flying through his head, gathering pace. A thousand sights, smells and sounds, none of them familiar yet all undoubtedly *his* memories.

Allen's eyes were squeezed shut in a silent agony, teeth gritted, hands clamped to his head as they broke through the second golden wall, new memories. By the third wall Allen had begun to scream again. Each wall brought a fresh sequence of visions different to those that had gone before. Yet as the walls were breached in ever faster succession, each speeding group appeared to be almost re-runs of the previous group with only slight and subtle differences, at least that's how it appeared to Allen. The walls had blurred into one and he had felt like a man drowning, overwhelmed, as if every computer in the world was attempting to download its content into his mind at once. Allen's conscious state had crashed.

'Allen! Allen! Come back to me now buddy, c'mon stay focused, you gotta concentrate here mate'.

'Wha?'

'Eh! Good man! Lost you again there for a minute, keep talking, c'mon get it all out'.

'The shining walls…' Allen whispered.

'Ah yes, big buggers right? That was just the margins between the different life times, nothing to worry about yeah?'

'The memories…'

'Yeah it's all a little troubling for you I should imagine' Alex said soothingly.

'TROUBLING! I remember kissing a man for fuck's sake! It's not every day I find myself having homosexual thoughts you know!'

'Homosexual? What did this bloke look like then?' Alex asked, Allen told him.

'No! Bless you that was 4765! We were a woman then! That was Francois! He was our husband! See? No worries! You're still *all man!*' Alex replied in geezer-voice.

'*Our husband?*' Allen's face was now very animated.

'Yep! Married! All legal, we were a respectable girl!' Alex smiled.

'4765?' asked Allen.

'Yes, do forgive me, I number our incarnations. Just my little system bless me! Makes it easier for me! Everyone's got their own system! No doubt you'll have yours when the time comes..'

'Oh bloody hell! I've just remembered remembering licking a dog's arse!'

'Oh yeah, 3744' Alexander looked very uncomfortable, 'Don't worry mate, we weren't bow-wow-worriers. Unfortunately, 3743 went a little bit off the old spiritual-track shall we say. We lost our way a bit. So much so in fact that in our next life-cycle we had to go right back to basics'

'Back to basics?' asked Allen.

'Yes, a black Labrador to be precise'

'Called?'

'Podkin-chops' replied Alexander, coughing and avoiding eye contact.

'Podkin-chops?'

'Yes Podkin-chops.'

'I should have bloody guessed'

'Hey! We were very devoted! Very loyal! Shit-hot in the stick-fetching department, and never dumped in the house! We were a good dog!' A long-embarrassed silence followed.

'Bloody 3743!' Alexander growled with feeling.

'Oh my lord' smiled Allen suddenly.

'Go on.'

'I've just remembered remembering having sex with the most amazing looking woman you can imagine, and hey was *she* having a great time! We must have been some sort of stud that time around!' Allen laughed, entering into the spirit of Alexander's insane ramblings. He then went on to describe the delectable female concerned and the numerous imaginative feats he remembered having performed upon her with great pride and in great detail.

'Er, that was 2891, we were a lesbian in that life'.

'Oh.'

'Well when I say lesbian, more 'bi' really. We did a lot of *riding* in that life-cycle! Well we had double the amount of opportunities! We *rode* that cycle for all it was worth! A bi-cycle!' Alex giggled.

Allen's own laughter gave way to a shudder.

'You all right Allen mate?'

'There's other stuff in my head too, eating nearly raw meat and other gross stuff, being dressed in rags, crapping in the bushes, and worse, much-much worse! Barbaric shit that I'd rather not talk about..'

'Ah that's just earlier incarnations'

'Of course it is' There were big helpings of sarcasm in Allen's voice.

'All of it mate honestly, it's just glimpses of our past lives, nothing to worry about, it's already happened' Alex explained. Allen stared into the nothing.

'So, how're you feeling now?' enquired Alex some moments later.

'Odd.'

'That's understandable chappy.'

'What I have to remember is *this*; No matter how real and freaky any of these experiences and weird thoughts seem, they're still nothing more than part of a dream, right?'

'Of course you do' replied Alex in sympathetic tone.

'And anyway! The whole point of reincarnation would be that you have to come back to live in the world each time yeah? To learn things for yourself, learn by your own mistakes right?'

'Bang-on!' Alex replied in a pleased, almost congratulatory tone.

'So if that's the case, you'd have thought that if *it, reincarnation, this, you..*' Allen gestured about himself and to Alexander. '..was really true, there'd be some kind of rule against a ghost coming back to spill the beans and give the game away to his next incarnation, about life I mean, creation and how it all works! I mean it'd rather piss on the whole point don't you think? You'd most certainly think there would be a rule against it! Well wouldn't you?'

'You would, wouldn't you?' replied Alex. 'Perhaps there is, but hey! Evolution has spent a long time in coming up with me, I'm an estate agent! Rules are often there for the breaking! I just thought nothing ventured, nothing gained! You never know what's possible until you try after all! So I gave it a bash, no one's tried to stop me! And here I am!'

'Dream or no dream, it'd be a pretty bloody irresponsible act to come back and tell someone all this stuff wouldn't it! I mean what a burden on the poor sod who was alive! They could've just got on with their life like everyone else! But that'd all be buggered wouldn't it! A bit much to deal with in one go! I'm bloody glad this is only a dream mate!' Allen laughed, Alexander didn't.

'I thought you'd bloody-well be happy to see me, you unadventurous git!' The sincerity in Alexander's voice halted Allen's mirth.

'Remember, we agreed this was a dream right?'

'Right' Alex grimaced out of the corner of his mouth.

'And also, imagine really putting some poor git through what I've just gone through, I mean bloody dangerous or what? You'd fry the poor bugger's sanity!'

'Oh c'mon Allen, you seem okay now' replied Alex defensively, before adding 'though to be honest, I'm not sure anyone's ever tried it with the living before'.

Allen gave Alexander a look that was blacker than even their surroundings. He surveyed the lightless nothingness around them. 'So anyway, where the hell are we supposed to be then?' he asked angrily.

'I thought it wise that we pull over into a lay-by so to speak for a bit of a debrief. It wouldn't really do for you to arrive at our final destination a gibbering-wreck, now would it? We're sort of in between time and space at the moment, we're not exactly anywhere or any-*when*, it's complicated'

'It's bloody dark' said Allen.

'Time and distance are irrelevant here' replied Alexander, reaching into an inside pocket of his ever-changing suit and pulling out a slim silver lighter. He held his arm out and dropped the lighter into the void. It plummeted into the darkness. Moments passed.

'It's all rather spooky really' he said, as the lighter dropped back into his hand from above.

'I see what you mean' agreed Allen.

'Now before we go, there's one last thing to mention. The other reason we're here is that there's no prying eyes, no one to tell tales shall we say' Alexander appeared genuinely nervous as he furtively looked around in all directions, before leaning across Allen to retrieve a dusty rectangular object from the glove compartment.

'A book?' enquired Allen somewhat deflated after the build-up.

'*The* Book' Intoned Alexander, reverence in his hushed voice as he gingerly placed the bulky leather-bound tome in his lap. '𝔉𝔬𝔯 𝕳𝕴𝕾 𝕮𝔶𝔢𝔰 𝕺𝔫𝔩𝔶' was inscribed in ornate Gothic script upon the dust-covered ancient hide.

'This is *The* Book, everything that has ever been written or ever *will* be written is in here. All the great scientific, philosophical and religious books that billions of people swear by are just shards of this big boy, pamphlets, hints. The power of words is limitless believe me, and they're all *in here*. This is the *Big-Man's* Book' Alexander's voice was a barely audible whisper as he pointed upward. His features became transformed by a wolfish manic leer as he leaned forward and took Allen by the lapels, staring into his eyes, their noses nearly touching.

'And I've only fuckin nicked it aint-I!' he grinned.

'And why may I ask would you do that old mad dream-mate-of-mine?' asked Allen, with the voice of the bus-passenger, who upon playing the seating-companions Russian-roulette that is public transport, humours the nutter they unfortunately find themselves sitting next to.

'You open this anywhere mate and it'll tell you all you need to know, trust me. Think of it as a kind of impartial guide for our little jaunt. This is going to be major culture shock for you chap. It's no good you just relying on me telling you what's going on, that'd just be my opinion. Sure, I'll

47

give you my side, but this little baby tells it as it *is*. It's the best travelling companion you'll ever have, it reads the reader, and then it writes for them. Now put it away somewhere safe.' Alexander attempted to pass the heavy volume to a very concerned looking Allen. But his passenger held up a palm, refusing to accept it.

'You want me to take it? After what you've just told me?'

'I thought you liked books?' asked Alex.

'I do, it's just that...'

'Hey Allen, what can go wrong? It's only a dream after-all!' there was amusement in Alexander's voice.

'Yeah I know...' Allen was still unsure. 'Anyway, I'm not lugging that bloody great big thing around with me. Hardly travel size for my convenience is it!'

'What do you mean?' replied Alexander. Allen looked quizzically at the object in the driver's hand. In keeping with the era of the car and its driver, it was now a Filofax. Being without an excuse, he nervously tucked it into his raincoat pocket.

'Bloody dream!' he grumbled.

'So, you're ready then Allen?'

'As I'll ever be.'

'Right let's go' Alexander took the gear-stick out of neutral and dropped it back into reverse. To Allen's relief there was no roaring engine, no blurring speed this time, simply a growing light and the rising sound of the sea...

CH 6: PATRIC

Allen shielded his eyes against the dazzling light, which diminished into nothing more than the daylight of an overcast afternoon as his sight adjusted.

'Whoaa!' Allen found himself standing upon the rise of a gentle slope carpeted in low wind-sculpted brackens and heathers, which swept down before him, abruptly ending on a precipitous cliff-edge overlooking a slate-grey, not-very-friendly looking ocean. Inland, broken heath land gave way to ferns and then dark forest. He could smell the damp vegetation and feel the moist breath of the sea on his face. Other than the wail of a solitary gull there was no sign of life or movement. Allen could feel that it was cold, but he didn't *feel* cold.

'Wow! This is amazing!' Allen walked forward, noting with delight that not only was the plant-life still visible through his striding legs, but that also his passage raised not a flicker of movement in the knee-high foliage. Coming to a halt some paces on, he stared upward at the brooding, low-lying underbelly of the sky, shaking his head in wonder at the creative abilities of his own mind. He turned back toward Alexander.

'Jesus!' He gasped.

'What?'

'You look different, somehow more solid, more *here*.'

'Ah bless you!' smiled Alex, 'that means you're getting more used to me, accepting me more.'

'Yes, accepting you as part of a dream' Allen reminded his guide.

'It goes without saying, you're the boss.'

'That's right! I'm in the driving seat. Hey! Where's the car?' asked Allen, looking around.

'I don't drive everywhere you know.'

'So, where's this supposed to be then?' asked Allen, gesturing about himself.

'You've never been to Ireland, right?'

'No.'

'You can say you have now mate, well what's going to be called Ireland one day. In the far north-east of the island to be more exact.'

'One day? When exactly might this be then?'

'Around two-thousand-six-hundred BC, give or take a decade or two.'

'Bloody hell! No point asking what time the pubs open then.'

'Very original Allen!'

'What *are* you wearing?' giggled Allen.

'Do you like it?' To Allen, Alexander appeared somehow less fuzzy, more defined than he had in his room, but still not completely clear. It was he decided, like looking at the reflection of a person in a gently rippling pool. Half bare-chested, the leanly built, dark-haired estate agent was now swathed in an elegant tartan robe fashioned from a single sheet, draped over one shoulder and wound about the waist in the fashion of a kilt. However, the actual pattern and colour of the Tartan was indistinct, leaving the viewer with the impression that numerous Tartans were somehow displayed.

At Alexander's throat and wrists were polished stones of differing colours, strung together on leathern chords. His hair was braided, and upon his feet he wore soft hide-skin boots. He gave Allen a twirl.

'Wearing any pants jock?' guffawed Allen.

'Jock? You ignorant git! I said this is Ireland yer fool! The Celts have already been here for ages by this time, just as they've populated Scotland and most of western Europe! *This* I'll have you know is the robe of a Celtic warrior chieftain sunny-Jim!' Alexander jutted out his chin, stuck his fists into his waist and struck what he thought to be a heroic warrior-type pose. 'Suits me don't you think?' he preened.

'Goes well with the sunglasses!' Allen laughed.

'I can take them off' Alex suggested, Allen stopped laughing.

'No, you're fine, honestly!' he answered quickly, before adding, 'but I thought you said no one would be able to see us?'

'They won't.'

'So why dress up then?'

'Because *I* can see me, and because well hey! I'm just getting into the mood so to speak. What's the problem?'

'Twat' exhaled Allen, still dressed in an extremely dishevelled suit and raincoat.

'I didn't realise you were a closet history-re-enactment-merchant' he added acidly.

'Yee of little imagination! Don't you try to fit into the culture, with the *natives* when you go abroad?' Alex asked.

'Hey! I'm in my twenties you old git...'

'Not for long you're not my old mate' Alex cut-in glibly, causing Allen to scowl, before continuing.

'Well aren't you the culture-vulture! And there was me thinking you liked your ancient history, your culture, your legends and mythology, the

Romans, Greeks, Egyptians, the Aztecs and all of that. You used to love all that in a big-way, didn't you? All those little stories and pictures? I mean! That's why I thought you'd be so up for the trip.'

'That was when I was a bloody kid!' Allen retorted.

'Oh, sorry *old* man! You're twenty-nine! I forgot! But do forgive me, didn't you just say you were young? A young man who I thought wanted to knock out some great novel about all that history bit; be a best seller, and just maybe live up to the standards of those who've gone before him. But then if I really believed that, I wouldn't be here at-all, now would I?'

'Oh, get stuffed!' Allen replied dejectedly. As unerringly as ever, Alexander had hit a raw-nerve.

'And anyway, who's to say I won't write a best seller one day!' he added defiantly.

'No one. But judging by *the* pad I don't think it's very likely in the foreseeable future, do you?'

'You know about *the* pad?' asked Allen nervously.

'I know about *everything,* remember I'm dead. And yes, I know about the Sparrow, and the thing when you were thirteen you mucky git!'

'Shit.'

A few months earlier, upon realising that the entire job-thing just didn't quite do it for him, Allen had once again decided to put pen to paper in a million-to-one attempt to free himself from his monotonous life. He needed to start making notes. With an extremely meagre budget he had gone out and spent a good while at the newsagents in the picking of *the* pad and pen which might possibly change his entire life. However, day-in day-out, week-in week-out *the* pad had remained empty, the new biro untouched. His ancient lap-top never came out of the case. Allen had found himself wholly without either inspiration or confidence, because after all *who'd* want to read what he wrote? It was, he had once again decided, nothing more than a childish fantasy. Who did he think he was?

'So, bearing in mind your current-lack of literary success Shakespeare, I think it prudent that we get on with our little tour, don't you? Maybe give you the inspiration to find a more practical means to make your way in the world. I must say I thought you'd be more intrigued about your surroundings. Now, if you wouldn't mind following me'. Alexander sounded genuinely disappointed.

'Lead on my good man, Oh Alex..'

'Yes?'

'Like the make-up mate!'

'They're woad tattoos *actually*, denoting status and physical prowess if you *must* know!'

'*Corse*-they-are-mate, *corse*-they-are, nothing wrong with a skirt and make-up!' Allen executed a conspiratorial wink.

'Are you coming or what?' growled Alex. Allen relished with satisfaction the annoyance in Alexander's voice.

'After you.' Allen whistled a tune as he followed his dream-guide along the crest of the slope, parallel to the coastline. He had decided that if this was indeed his dream, he was going to enjoy the experience. It was either that or go completely bloody insane.

Though he and Alex had taken what he thought to be only a few steps, a thin grey band in the distance materialised into a dark cliff-face, rearing menacingly above them in moments. As if the ground had simply slid beneath their pacing feet, the horizon seemingly gliding toward them. Allen looked questioningly at his rarely exercised feet and then back across the distance they had allegedly covered.

'Don't worry about that, it's just the boring bits speeded up', explained Alexander.

'Oh, I see.'

The rock wall emerged from the woodland on their right, running across to the cliff-edge below them on their left, barring their path. Alexander led them downhill toward the sea. About half way down the slope, Allen followed his guide around a buttress of rock that thrust forward from the main face, to discover a narrow opening hidden in the cliff behind it.

'Follow me.' Alexander stooped, beckoning Allen to follow suit, before disappearing into the blackness of the gash-like entrance. A nervous Allen found himself bent-double, shuffling sideways along a winding narrow passage, barely wide or tall enough to accommodate him. Thankfully only a short distance on, as grey daylight diminished behind, they emerged into a naturally-formed, low-ceilinged chamber, illuminated by flickering tongues of orange light.

'Allen key, meet Patric son of Hatric, of the clan O'Lant.' Alexander gestured to the far corner of the damp cavern. Allen peered into the writhing shadows.

'Jesus-Christ!' Startled, he realised that a few paces ahead a gangly young boy clothed in animal-skins, perhaps thirteen or fourteen or so, was squatting in front of the cave wall. Pale, feral features were partly obscured by a shaggy copper mane, shadow, grime, and the acrid, cloying smoke of the modest fire at his side. Allen clamped his hand over his mouth.

'Don't worry he can't see or hear you.' Alexander reassured his startled companion.

'I nearly shit myself then!' Allen whispered through clenched teeth, accompanied by clenched buttocks.

'It's okay he can't smell you either.'

'Ha-ha, *very* funny.'

'This is Patric, the eldest of the three sons of Hatric.'

'Three sons? Hat-trick?'

'Yes Hatric. Patric is an earlier incarnation of ours. It's his story that we are here to see.'

'We were a ginge?'

Alexander ignored him.

Oblivious to his visitors, the lad appeared to be intently drawing on the rock in front of his nose, tongue sticking out of the side of his mouth in concentration. Nimble fingers etched into the rock surface using a succession of flints, and fire-hardened sharpened sticks. The unused implements lay lovingly cradled in the boy's lap, nestling in a rabbit-skin pouch. At his knees were a group of sea-smoothed flat stones, each chosen for its concave surface, for each held a paste or powder of differing colour. Next to the fire a make-shift mortar and pestle in the shape of a much-stained larger flat stone, and a smaller spherical rock were surrounded by crushed berries, leaves and petals, explaining the origin of the painting materials.

Allen's eyes were drawn to the scene being depicted. Apparently, an empty-handed naked stick-man, surrounded by what appeared to be a number of skeletal dogs.

'What's all that about then do you think?' he asked.

'He calls it *My dad meets a pack of wolves without his lucky spear.*'

'Likes his dad then!' Allen laughed. Alexander made no response.

'These others, what's the story?' Allen indicated further murals around the cave.

'That's *My favourite stick.*' Alexander motioned to a simple tapering dark vertical line drawn on the curving wall.

'These are *My two favourite throwing stones.*' He indicated two circles scratched below the first picture.

'And this one?' Allen pointed toward a shaggy four-legged creature with curled horns.

'That's *Our goat.*'

'Not *Our favourite goat then?*'

'No, his clan can only afford the one.'

Suddenly, both men's attentions were grabbed by a sudden movement from the lad. With lightning speed the skinny boy's free hand snaked out and in one flowing motion retrieved *his favourite stick* from his side, before striking out with it in the semi-darkness. There was a dull thud, a crunching sound, and a high-pitched shriek as the bulbous head of the staff connected with something thankfully hidden in the shadows. The limp body of a rather large rat slid against the wall at the mens' feet. Without taking his gaze from the mural, Patric replaced his trusty stave at his side and returned to his work.

Some moments later he paused, wiping a finger across the broader end of the staff before holding it up to his eyes in the dull light. Patric then began to smear the rat's blood into the scene before him. He smiled, seemingly pleased with the effect of the sticky crimson substance.

'Oh choice! Nice place to live!' Allen's voice and face registered both distaste and disgust.

'He doesn't live here, he's not bloody stupid! I mean; it's wet, dark and bleedin freezing.'

'What do you mean? This is a cave man, well boy. A cave boy in a cave.'

'He's hiding.' explained Alex.

'Hiding?' asked Allen.

'Yes, from Hatric.' Allen, who was still standing with his back to the tunnel-entrance, wondered why Alexander was pointing at him. And then something very odd indeed happened.

Allen felt a tingling at the back of his head, which grew to a tickling sensation between his ears. Cross-eyed, he squinted down at his own nose which felt as if it was about to discharge the largest sneeze imaginable and possibly also the contents of his skull. Butterflies arose in the pit of his belly, rising until his stomach began to spasm and somersault. From the tip of his toes to his scalp, his skin itched and then began to crawl. Allen had an extreme case of the heebie-jeebies as the back of a man's head emerged in front of his eyes. The owner of the back of that head having just walked straight through him.

'Nnghhhhh.' Allen shuddered as he vigorously rubbed himself all over, raked his fingers through his hair, and spat repeatedly. He felt invaded in the nastiest sense of the word.

'I should avoid that happening if I were you', said Alex evenly.

'You're not friggin-wrong there mate!' grimaced Allen. The after-shock attacks of the judders were now thankfully beginning to recede.

'GAHA NAI ATTRI PATRISCHE! MI SCHALLA-NURA?' The shaggy red-haired, bearded man screamed. Violently shaking, eyes wide with terror, the boy now cowered, huddled into the deepest recess of the cave as if trying to burrow into the very rock to escape his ranting father. The formerly lovingly cared-for drawing implements were now strewn across the cave floor. An enraged kick from Hatric similarly sent the group of flat stones in all directions, spattering Patric's current work-in-progress with reddish-brown blotches, like dried blood.

'SHADDRA-TORL! LLANNOUGH SE-HEE-MAHA!' Hatric's eyes were wild and bloodshot, his face red with anger and the after-effects of the half-empty leathern-drinking-skin which was clasped in one hand. In the other hand was *his* favourite stick, Patric's terrified eyes were fixed on this dreadful object, *his least*-favourite stick.

'What's his bloody problem?' Allen was becoming more and more uneasy about the scene unfolding before his eyes.

'Just listen and it will become clear.'

'But I can't understand a word!' protested Allen.

'Look, it's like the realization in the car that you weren't at the mercy of the elements, or that you didn't really hurt your head when you banged it on the wall when I first turned up in your room. It takes a while to adjust to this higher level of consciousness for the living, you're not used to it. Open your mind and try to *forget* that you can't understand this language for a moment. Simply listen and you will intuit Hatric's intent, and therefore understand his words also. It's the *common* sense.'

'Will I really.'

'Go on, give it a try!'

'Okay whatever you say.' Allen shook his head, unconvinced.

'TORMA DRA! LLEL SHODRI HELGH-ADDARA!!' Hatric swung the staff in a wide humming arc, unknowingly scraping an orange and red scar across the figure of himself on the wall, and showering Patric with chips of stone. The lad cried out in terror.

'It's still all Neolithic to me!' Allen raised his hands in incomprehension, concern for the boy growing within him with every passing moment.

'Give it a chance.'

'KEMANI LLAN NOR!! YE WASTE 'O' FOOD! MI TORL! CURSE YER YE SCHLADADD!'

55

'Hang on! I think I'm getting some of this!' Surprise was apparent in Allen's voice.

'Shhh, keep listening.' Alex gestured to the surly, drunken Hatric.

'EH FEED YER! WIPE YER ARSE! DON'T-I? DORRONA LAZY REGA! WILL YE SCRATCHINGS FILL THE BELLY? WILL THEY WARM THE BONES ON A COL' EVE? WILL IT SLAY THOSE THAT ENVY THY LAND? WHY WILL YER LISTEN TO ME NOT! DAMN-YER! I'LL MAKE A PRETTY-PATTERN 'O' ME OWN UPON YER BACK WI' MINE ROD!'

'I'm getting it now', said an even more worried Allen.

'I understand the old *My dad meets a pack of wolves without his lucky spear* now! What a bastard!' said Allen nervously. Alexander didn't reply.

'The words are still hard to understand though, heavy-shit like old English, Shakespeare or Chaucer or something like that!'

'Make it easier for yourself Allen! Torque your will up a bit, give yourself a break! Understand it in a way that's easier for you, or this trip's going to be hard-bloody-going for you and no mistake!' smiled Alex. With a look of confusion Allen once more returned his attention to Hatric.

'HOW MANY BLOODY TIMES DO I HAF TI' TELL YER PAT! MAKING PRETTY PICTURES ISN'T FOR THE LIKES 'O' US! OURS' IS T' SCRATCH A LIFE FROM THIS-ERE MEAGRE SOIL! IT'S TIME YER WOKE UP T' IT SONNY!'

'Wow, it's working' giggled Allen. If someone had asked Allen to describe Hatric's voice he would have been hard put to describe the accent. All he knew was that he understood it and it fitted its speaker. Perhaps there was the subtle hint of an Irish accent, maybe a lyrical trace of French. Freakily enough even a splash of Geordie, with a side-dish of Swedish. It was rather like hearing the voices of characters as a book is being read. Indescribable and intangible yet somehow *real*, never to be faithfully reproduced when the book becomes the film.

'YOU'RE ME FIRST-BORN! FOR THE SUN-GOD'S SAKE! HERE T' INHERIT WHAT'S YOURS WHEN I'M GONE! YOU'RE A MAN NOW! IT'S ABOUT BLOODY-TIME YER STARTED T' ACT LIKE ONE! CALL YERSELF AN O'LANT?'

'A man? A bloody kid more like it!' Allen was enraged by the violent father. Cloaked in thick animal hides, the bullying Hatric resembled all too much a bull about to charge.

'Allen, their life expectancy is around thirty-five, many don't make it past childhood. If you make it to forty or fifty around here you're doing bloody well!' explained Alex.

'Oh. But still....'

'YOU BE A SORRY EXAMPLE TO YOUR BROTHERS! *FIRST-BORN?*...PAH!! IT'S A BLESSING YOUR POOR MOTHER'S NOT BREATHIN TO SEE IT! THE GREAT-MOTHER PROTECT HER!' The cavern reverberated to Hatric's roaring anger.

'This be for yer own good lad, if you've not the sense to heed the tongue then by-Domi you'll have t' learn by th' *other* way' Though no longer raised, the stone-age man's voice was as hard as granite, he raised the stick.

'AHHHHHH!' Allen raged as he charged headlong across the cavern, suffering another attack of the willies as he passed straight through Hatric, and utterly failing to prevent the swift succession of blows that fell upon the shrieking boy.

'NOW GET YEE BACK T'YER CHORES YER LAGGARD!'

Defiantly biting back sobs, the youth scrambled upright and fled from the cavern. Hatric took a prolonged gulp from the drinking-skin.

'You're here as an onlooker only' said Alex softly. Allen, who was standing facing the cave wall, took a couple of deep breaths before angrily turning to answer.

'I get the picture' he said, glaring at the swaying Hatric.

'ARGHH!' Hatric bellowed as he kicked the peat fire, raising a cascading waterfall of amber-glowing embers. He spat meaningfully over the nearest mural, span on his heel and followed his son.

Alexander was watching Allen, his features unreadable. Allen glowered at his feet, fists clenched at his sides. The remaining traces of flame in the overturned sods dwindled to a dull orange sprinkle before winking out, plunging the underground chamber into complete darkness. A tense silence followed.

CH 7: FAST FORWARD

'What the hell was that!'

'What-was-what Allen?'

'Just then, it fell like the ground shifted, didn't you feel it?'

'Oh, don't worry about that.' Further tense silence.

'Can we bloody go then or what?' asked Allen, agitation entering his voice.

'In a moment, listen Allen, I know it's hard for you, but you really must try and stay detached from all this. Try and distance yourself. Remember it's already happened, for good or bad! You can't do anything about it. I mean it's not like you kick the telly, is it? Or punch the radio when you see or hear bad stuff?'

'I feel like it sometimes!'

'You know what I mean. Look, it's like the world in general, often you can't change it, only how you feel about it. To us emotional beings how we feel is all that matters!'

'Well I feel pretty shitty about what just happened to *him*.'

'To *us* you mean, remember we're *his* reincarnations. That beating went toward what made us-*us*. Anyway, no point getting so worked up if this is all just a dream now is it?' A long silence followed.

'Okay, okay! I can deal with this, can we go now please? I feel just a little bit silly standing here in the dark!' The words said silly, the tone said scared.

'There's something more for you to see before we leave this place, something which I hope will go some way in starting to bring you around to my way of thinking. Give you a higher perspective on things shall we say. You are the product of modern society. Most of the instinctive abilities and awareness with which you were born, were educated out of you by the time you were three. You believe only in that which can be touched or seen, you believe only in that which can be *proved*. You are only half awake, half conscious. You are a follower of the so-called professionals, the scientists, the lofty academics and their facts and figures. You rely on others to tell you what you *are*. You limit yourself because you do not truly rely on your own instincts, hence you find it very hard to believe in anything I say.'

'Where *is* my head getting this shite from!' Allen laughed. 'And you reckon you've got something to show me? Well I hope you've got a bloody torch stuffed down that skirt of yours then!'

'Don't worry the lights will be coming on any second.'

'Lights?' As if he were a film director, Allen's question was followed by a metallic *clunk* sound, and an eruption of dazzling white light. Former anger was replaced with bewilderment as Allen, squinting under a raised palm, peered out at the circuit of bulky spot-lights now bolted around the cavern ceiling.

'Now mind your head here m 'dear, it's a bit tricky!' The well-educated middle-class English accent saw Allen well clear of the cave entrance as a bespectacled, slightly-built balding man in his early-sixties emerged from the low tunnel-mouth. Unusually for stone-age Ireland he was protected from the elements by a blue pack-a-mac, green chords and well-worn brown leather walking boots. His only weapon was a biro, attached to a clipboard by a shoe-string, which was clutched to him by a bony, fingerless-gloved hand. He winced, placing a hand in the small of his back as he straightened up. A wide-eyed mousey-haired, freckle-faced teenage-girl, also wearing glasses but far-more-shapely in her bright-yellow anorak, appeared behind him.

'Wow!' her excited whisper echoed around the cave.

'Shit!' said Allen. The cavern floor was now utterly bare. All traces of the overturned fire, the recently-deceased rat, and Patric's artistic paraphernalia had completely disappeared. The murals remained, but were very faint. The brilliant colours (where visible) now a uniform dull brown.

'Er Alexander?'

'We've just popped forward a bit in time.'

'*Popped* forward?'

'Yeah, to about nineteen-eighty-ish or so.'

'So, that's what I felt just after the fire went out!'

'Yeah, it's not so traumatic an experience when you're only moving in time and the lights are out! Before we left Patric's art-studio, I just thought it'd be educational for you to witness *this*.' Alexander gestured to their new companions.

'It's simply amazing professor!' The bookish frizzy-haired girl enthused. The accent implied ownership of a pony was highly probable.

'Yes Felicity, it is, isn't it! To think! This very cave was home to members of a culture in the closing stages of the Neolithic period. Analysis and Carbon-dating of materials shows that up to around four-and-a-half thousand years ago, people made-fire, prayed, ate, lived, slept and no doubt died here! In this very space! Right where we're standing now! It's quite a find! A remarkable window into the lives of our distant ancestors!'

'And weren't you on the team that first discovered and excavated it professor!'

'Well yes.' The professor seemed almost uncomfortable.

'I was its leader in fact', he added bashfully.

'Gosh!' There was something bordering on awe in the teenager's voice. The professor looked briefly down at his feet.

'And what is believed to be the significance of the murals?' asked the girl. Allen dived out of the way just before Felicity walked through him. Annoyingly to Allen's mind, in contrast Alexander remained leaning nonchalantly against the wall, in the same place he'd occupied since they'd first entered the cave. Felicity peered intently at the now faint vertical line which Patric had entitled *My-favourite-stick,* removing her partially steamed-up glasses momentarily, to wipe them on her red and white knitted scarf.

'Well this..' the professor gestured to the faded vertical line and the barely-visible pair of circles immediately beneath it, which Pat had entitled *My-two-favourite-throwing-stones.*

'..is of course a crude reproduction of the male sexual organ, a phallic symbol, a symbol of fertility.

'Gosh,' Felicity blushed. Allen and Alexander smiled, both shaking their heads.

'A completely intact skeleton of a rat was even discovered directly beneath it. Obviously a votive offerin, *a sacrifice!* Possibly this chamber was the abode of the local wise-man or shaman!'

'Fascinating! And is this a hunting scene?'

'Urrgh!' Allen wildly threw himself sideways to yet again avoid the curious girl as she re-crossed the cavern toward an extremely worn *My-dad-meets-a-pack-of-wolves-without-his-lucky-spear.*

'Well done m 'dear! Very astute! It's just that in fact!' The professor's attentive student positively beamed.

'Note the central figure; Obviously a hunter of great prowess, look at the numerous beasts he has bloodily slain.' The professor motioned toward Patric's much faded wolves which were still faintly splattered with the splotchy blood-like stains of Hatric's handy-work.

'Slain?' spat Allen, knowing that the picture was intended to show the man as the hunted, not the hunter.

'Further note the out-of-proportion spear.' The professor's biro now indicated the horizontal scar gouged across the stick-man by Hatric's staff thousands of years earlier.

'Its vast dimensions signify the great hunting ability of its bearer. This may well be the depiction of an actual person, a chieftain or such-like. Or it might well be iconic, a ritualistic symbol to be prayed to, in order to bring success in the hunt. This second theory, of which you'll no doubt be aware of course from my thesis on the matter, is supported by the fact that part of this pagan mural is drawn in *actual blood!*' The professor paused for effect, Felicity gasped.

'Wanker!' said Allen and Alexander together, shaking their heads in exact unison. Unsettled by the duet in which he had just unintentionally participated, Allen looked questioningly at his companion. Alexander shrugged his shoulders.

'What can I say? We're close', he replied.

'Professor, can I just say it's a privilege to have the opportunity to learn from your great intellect and experience. The university is very lucky to have you!'

'Why thank you m' dear, you know how it is when you've been around for as long as I have, you're sure to pick a few things up along the way! Like a bookend gathering dust!' The professor chuckled wryly.

'It's no great achievement really', he added.

'You're too modest professor!'

'No, he's bloody not', commented Allen.

'Anyway Felicity, let us not overlook your own abilities. You did extremely well in the mocks did you not? *Very* promising! I'm sure one day you'll have your own students, and I'm sure they'll be very glad to be under your tutelage!'

'Gosh!'

'Now Felicity, I'm sure you could stay here all day! But we really must press on m' dear, there's much more to see!' The clipboard was held aloft for emphasis. 'Now remember! mind y' head on the way out.' A reluctant Felicity was ushered from the chamber, echoing conversation receded. There was another metallic *clunk*, an electrical crackle, and utter blackness returned.

'So, there you are Allen, one of the so-called *professionals,* a great academic! A professor no less! A well-educated man with letters after his name! An *authority* on his subject! And like many of the scientific-thinking shapers of the modern society in which you've grown up...bloody clueless! Well, now that you've witnessed this little side-show, let's be getting back to the main event, follow me!'

'*Hello!* I can't actually see bugger all!' spat Allen acidly.

'You've really no faith in yourself have you!' Alex sighed.

'I beg your bleedin-pardon?'

'Never mind, look, take my hand you'll be fine.' Allen felt the tingling grasp of Alexander's hand in his.

'Duck!' his guide cried.

Bent nearly double in the oppressive blackness of the low tunnel, Allen was revisited by the sensation of movement beneath his feet. Moments later, growing daylight enabled him to relinquish Alex's hand. Blinking against the comparative glare of a dismal afternoon, Allen emerged from the tunnel behind Alexander. Hatric stood a few paces ahead, his back to them, staring downhill toward the sea, and the swiftly diminishing figure of his fleeing son.

'Bastard!' Allen growled with feeling. If looks could kill, Hatric would have decorated much of the visible landscape.

'Maybe you should come here' suggested Alexander, who now stood beside the non-cave man. He beckoned to Allen, who approached warily.

'What?'

Alexander gestured toward Hatric's face. Allen's angry glare failed. Tears streamed from the Celt's bleary eyes, the rugged wind-chiselled features reddened and pinched with raw emotion. Hatric cried out like a wounded animal, flinging his staff from him. Sobbing, he let the drinking skin fall at his feet and buried his face in his hands. Allen looked extremely uncomfortable with himself.

'Allen-mate, life is generally a complicated place. I think at this point it might be prudent for you to consult the oracle.'

'You what?'

'*The* Book.' Alexander indicated Allen's fizzing raincoat pocket.

Following some hesitation, grimacing and using only his fingertips, Allen slid the dark-grey rectangular object out into the daylight as if it were a primed mousetrap. It now appeared that he had been carrying around a flat piece of slate.

CH 8: HEAVY READING

'And what *exactly* do I do with this then?' asked Allen.

'Read it.'

'Read it?' Allen turned the slate over in his hand, it was unmarked. 'Read what?'

'No bloody patience! That's the living!' Alexander shook his head in exasperation.

'Okay! Calm-down! Keep yer skirt on!' Allen held out a pacifying hand, turned his back to his companions so that he faced the sea, and returned his gaze to the brittle slice of stone.

'Oh, I see!' Allen's face split into a grin.

'Happy reading!' said Alexander over his shoulder.

As Allen watched, an indented dot appeared on the grey surface. The dot became an etched line, which in turn began sprouting branches like a growing sapling, as if invisible hands were engraving the stone. There was no sound, no residue of powdered-slate as the lines smoothly spread out, criss-crossing and coiling about the flat stone. In moments an obscure design, perhaps some sort of insect enclosed within a square, adorned the small tablet. Even as a frowning Allen pondered the illustration it began to fade until it vanished, only to be replaced with another dot, which again began to steadily grow into a crude picture.

The speed of the phantom engraving increased, so that the second design, similar to a noughts-and-crosses grid, was completed in moments. Rather than fading away, the simplistic image appeared to slide smoothly to the right, vanishing as it slipped off the stone. Further one-dimensional pictures followed, scrolling across the slate, groups of wavy lines, crosses, series of dots and simple shapes. As the river of images flowed past Allen's uncomprehending eyes with increasing pace, the depictions seemed to steadily evolve in diversity and sophistication. Streaming images reminiscent of Egyptian hieroglyphs, Aztec pictograms and Viking runes rushed by, until they too gave way to Greek, Latin and Arabic characters. As the script blurred a fascinated Allen began to feel almost mesmerised, his head beginning to nod, as if being drawn down toward the stone-age page by some compelling magnetic force.

Whether it was truly within the flickering ribbon of letters before him, or whether it existed only within his mind's eye, Allen couldn't be certain; but a pin-point of growing light was emerging from the writhing surface of the slate. The whirring text dissolved as the light spread out across the stone. Waves of differing colours began to emanate from the tablet, rippling outward, washing over the darkening landscape near at hand so that it became obscured, as if being viewed through the waters of a shallow pool.

'Whoa!' Though he had not been able to decipher any of the rushing text due to both its nature and speed, Allen was somehow aware that a picture or scene was growing before his eyes, a scene that was being described by the unintelligible words of *The* Book. It was as if understanding was arriving in some dark back room of his mind, without having had the common decency of knocking on the front door of his conscious state. Though he'd been unable to derive meaning from one single word or phrase of the literary onslaught, he could yet *see* the picture they were describing.

As the outwash of greys, browns and greens climbed toward the horizons Allen realised that it was a growing depiction of the very landscape within which he stood. What had begun as a postcard-size portrait of the rugged coastline was now approaching a full-size reproduction. With an almost inaudible popping sound the liquid-like image seemed to solidify, overlaying the view exactly. The vision had also added a tapering headland which thrust out into the ocean from what had been a crumbling cliff-edge only moments earlier. The chords of dramatic classical music arose out of the very voices of the sea and air. Allen felt himself gripped by an inexplicable but growing feeling of anticipation and exhilaration. To the foreground, hanging in mid-air, the words *'IT IS WRITTEN...'* appeared momentarily before fading away. Allen felt almost as if he were sitting in the cinema, an epic block-buster about to begin.

'Wha-hey! Where's the popcorn then! Bloody-hell Alex, are you getting this?' Allen turned back toward his companion.

'ALEX!' Allen nearly dropped the tablet in fright, behind him there was an impenetrable black wall of fog. Alexander, Hatric and basically *inland* had vanished.

'ALEX-BLOODY-ANDER!!'

'Ee-easy mate! I'm right here.'

'AHH!' Allen nearly jumped out of his insubstantial skin. Alexander's calm and collected voice had come from right behind him. Allen span around, his head whipping from side to side, but there was only the uninhabited landscape of *The* Book's vision.

'WHERE?!'

'Calm-down! I'm just where you left me before you started reading. It's like with any book, you're in a world of your own at the moment. That which is being described within the page fills your reality. Don't worry! I'll be right here waiting for you when you've finished'.

'Rrright' Allen, a man who had already been one world removed from his own before he had even looked upon *The* Book, sounded extremely unsure.

'Now if you wouldn't mind Allen-chap, the sooner you get back to it, the page I mean, the sooner you'll find yourself back here with me.'

'Er...Alex, This is still all a dream right?'

'You're asking me? Not having doubts are you?'

'Of course not! Okay-okay' Allen looked into the vision, allowing it to envelope him.

Without knowing how, Allen knew this to be an era long before that of Patric. However apart from the additional geography and a slightly-colder edge to the buffeting sea air, everything appeared and felt much the same. There was still the distant muffled boom of crashing waves, the waning and waxing drone of the wind, the baleful cry of a gull, the incessant rustle of wind-stunted plants. Then unfortunately, as is so often the case with the remote and savagely beautiful unconquered corners of this world, there came the sound of the arrival of a lot of people, and all else was drowned out.

From either side of the foreground, two lines of chattering heavily-laden humans clad in animal skins filed past. Moving downhill, they cried out excitedly, pointing toward the headland below. The O'Lants had arrived. The raging river of unseen words flowing through Allen's mind went into flood, sending the unfolding scene before him into overdrive. The low vault of the heavens raced past overhead, night followed day in rapid succession as did the seasons. A timber palisade of sharpened stakes sprang up across the narrow neck connecting the rock promontory to the mainland. Within, out of bow-shot, toward the sea-end of the peninsula, a cluster of small dome-like shelters popped up like a rash, seemingly in moments. The words and years sped on.

The O'Lants prospered and multiplied. Ever larger hunting-parties issued forth from the stout gates bound for the great forest, and ever larger warbands popped out to make unannounced visits on neighbouring clans. Both returned bearing an ever-richer bount, and ever more blood on their hands. In stone-age terms, the O'Lants were tooled up the nines, and not very big on the agriculture front. Others could sow, reaping was their

The home of the O'Lants

forte. They were hunter-gatherers, that is; they hunted the gatherers, as wolves pursue the sheep. A ravening wolf's head in black, upon a blood-red background was their emblem, their war-cry a chilling wolf's howl. The rude collection of huts disappeared and a great hall rose up in their stead, surrounded by sturdy roundhouses. Drab furs and course garb gave way to robes of fine-weave and many hues, similar to Alexander's in style (if not as pretentious).

The height of the timber battlement increased with the number of enemies, and an earthen embankment with a ditch before it appeared for good measure. As warrior chieftains and rowdy generations passed, the clan became a wealthy and influential force in the region.

Many amongst the clan, especially the high-born, soon had time for pursuits other than that of simple survival. Through the gates there came a growing succession of wandering entertainers and traders, bringing the culture, news and wondrous goods of a wider world. The towering beams of the lofty hall were entwined by intricate, richly coloured designs. Beneath their great span there was ever music, revelry, or the echoing poetic verses of the great sagas of the bards. Over the years there were also of course quite a number of damn good brawls.

Luckily for neighbouring clans, the ever more comfortable O'Lants mellowed with the millennia. As the years rolled on there was thankfully more trade and less slayed. However, it was well known to all that the O'Lants sold high and bought cheap. Woe betide those tribes that did not either buy in bulk from the clan, or weren't prepared to sell five of their goats for one O'Lant twig. However, the neighbours still preferred the O'Lants' 'demanding-goods-with-menaces', to their earlier 'demanding-goods-with-your-relative's-head-in-their-hands' approach.

The chieftain Vattric lived up to his name when he introduced an extortionate rate of VAT (Violence-Abatement-Tax) upon the already vastly overpriced shabby trading stock of the O'Lants, managing the TRICK of doubling tribal revenue. 'Vat-trick' was a great reformer, and in the very height of civilised and sophisticated living, a domed all-weathers twelve-holer outdoors latrine appeared just outside the gates. Far safer and less messy than attempting a number-two in a force-ten off the edge of a hundred-foot cliff.

So it was, that Hatric son of Vattric was born into a proud and powerful society. From his earliest days, the lad was groomed to succeed his father as chieftain of the O'Lants. He was therefore schooled in the mastery of both men and weapons, and in the hunt. An image-conscious Vattric was

67

keen that the future head of the family business should be perceived as a well-rounded modern-man of the Stone-age, and so Hatric was also tutored in the arts. To the great frustration and disappointment of his father, Hatric however appeared to possess little taste for arms or warfare at all, yet excelled in all manner of creative expression, from dancing to drawing. Especially in drawing...

To the fury and shame of Vattric, the sniggers and whispered mutterings of 'kilt-lifter' about the great hall concerning his son were many. Hatric endured many a beating as his father attempted to make a true man of him. Vattric consoled himself that the necessary beatings he meted out were as nothing to those that he had experienced as a lad at the hands of his own father.

As the young Celt grew toward manhood so grew also his distaste for the O'Lant's grizzly and parasitic lifestyle. The 'proppa-edge-cation-I-nevva-ad' which Vattric had paid for, had assisted Hatric to see things somewhat differently from his father. Things would change when the mantle of the chieftain rested upon his brow. Yes indeed, things would be mellower, the business was going straight. Wisely the youth kept his musings to himself.
 *Hatric was betrothed in his early teenage years as was custom, to the beauteous and alluring Kara. Feeling sure he had met his soul-mate, Hatric patiently awaited his golden destiny. He believed the most-rosiest of futures to be ahead of him. When one arrived, Hatric knew that he would **never** beat a son of his..*

However, as the power of the O'Lants had increased over the many centuries, their lands had in fact unfortunately decreased. The unpopular light-fingered ancestors of the clan had chosen the precarious, thin sliver of land due to its easily defensible nature. Just like everyone else around them at the time, the early O'Lants would stitch their distant descendants up like kippers.

The great ocean, the author of this broken coastline, had continued its inexorable assault upon the land, undercutting the very foundations of the O'Lant's home, ceaselessly gnawing away unnoticeable yet incessant inches with each passing generation. Successive ignorant chieftains had simply celebrated an ever increasingly better sea-view from the giddying height of their great hall. The generations had mounted, the inches had added up, and then amidst the screaming blackness of a storm-wracked night, the clan's bloody history had abruptly caught up with them.
 Above the shrieking gale and the bludgeoning violence of the waves, there came a deep and unearthly subterranean rumble. The entire precipitous

finger of rock had shuddered, before the greater part of it fell into the furious sea in a thunderous and reverberating tidal-wave of rolling sound, mercifully crushing and drowning out the wails of the crushed and drowning.

Hatric and Kara were amongst a pathetic handful of survivors who miraculously clawed their way back into the land of the living that dark night. Vattric was amongst the many who perished. The young Hatric had of course previously envisaged his inauguration somewhat differently.

Most of the new chieftain's few-remaining grief-stricken subjects departed in the vain hope of escaping the fates, for they believed themselves to be cursed by the gods. Some cast themselves over the brink in order to follow their loved ones.

Though gripped by utter despair, Hatric could not follow their suit for he was now chieftain. He was tied to the land, even if most of it now lay a hundred feet below him. More importantly, Kara was heavy with their first child. Hatric was tortured daily by the life into which his formerly eagerly-anticipated child would now be born.

The impressive timber and earth bulwark yet remained, and in a fit of manic-hysteria Hatric had even paced the sturdy battlements, crying out that if they kept the gates closed no one would be any the wiser. Ten of the holes were filled in, and the few shattered survivors of the once-proud tribe took up residence in the outside latrine. The clan was in the shit-house, literally. Patric arrived shortly afterward.

Being without resources or manpower, the powerless O'Lants could no longer enforce their hunting rights in the great forest, neither could they exact revenge for the taunts and jibes of a seemingly never-ending procession of celebratory, formerly-cautious neighbouring clans, come to gloat on the richly-deserved fate of their tormentors. With the blurring passage of but a handful of seasons, the palisade disappeared, being the only readily available source of firewood, and the stubby remainder of the peninsula collapsed into the sea.

Two summers following Patric's birth, Kara died in childbirth to his twin younger brothers, Peeta and Porl. By the time all three boys had mastered walking, the last of Hatric's few dejected subjects had deserted him. Three male toddlers in a confined space after all is no picnic.

So it was, that the skilled and well-educated chieftain of the O'Lants, having seen barely a score of winters, found himself an embittered lone single parent, and a simple tiller of the soil. Hatric, a man who had been used to vast amounts of time for recreation and contemplation, now found

In the shit-house.

the entirety of his existence absolutely owned by the basic need for food, heat, shelter, and the never-ending demands of his little ones. He hit the grain-beer big time.

Thus would it be, that by the time Patric had entered the emotional minefield that is adolescence, his inheritance was but a narrow strip which clung cat-like upon the brink of a great cliff, beneath which gaped the ravening maw of the sea, and the greater part of what had once been O'Lant land. The three brothers remained more or less ignorant of their eventful past. For apart from the odd drunken ramblings, the once extrovert Hatric had become man of very few words indeed, most of which were unprintable.

So it was also that Patric, from his earliest years, would find he harboured an inexplicable yet inescapable belief that Domi the Sun god (due to a heavy workload) had inadvertently dropped him into creation at a station far below that which had obviously been intended. He certainly did not feel like a farmer, and so he slipped away at every opportunity to spend golden, yet all too brief moments with his beloved charcoals and dyes. He had also endured many beatings from an understandably demoralized father who now firmly believed that for such as they, there would only be endless toil. Their lot was to eke out a sparse existence from the near-barren earth. The best that could be hoped for was to be supported by one's children in the doting years. A disillusioned and despondent father would therefore discourage a daydreaming offspring of fanciful ideas above his station. Ideas which would only lead to later pain and disappointment. Life was shit and Hatric knew it.

The chieftain of the four-man-tribe, perhaps understandably, was possessed by a great phobia of loved ones abandoning him. He was therefore fearful of any thoughts of betterment his heir might harbour; thoughts that might lead to said-heir going for a long-term wander, thus also setting a very bad, and very dangerous example to his two younger brothers. Patric would follow in the footsteps of both his father and his long-dead forefathers, and inherit the land that was his birth right, whether he liked it or not. O'Lants had dwelt on this land for generations, and Hatric would not be the one to allow that chain to be broken. He would not be the weakest link, even if it meant him acting like the missing one.

Yet even when his father had both found and destroyed his secret cache of slate-sketches, Patric would steal away to local caves, and thus hidden would etch upon the very walls....

71

'Jesus-bloody-Christ!' Allen's expression was somewhat harrowed as he looked up from the ordinary piece of blank slate in his hand. Sliding *The* Book into his pocket, he turned toward Hatric, but he and Alexander now stood alone amidst the stirring heather. The Celt had followed his son's route, and was now nearing the cliff-edge below. Allen felt relief when Hatric halted upon the brink rather than jumping, stooping as he disappeared from view into the diminutive turf-covered hillock that was the family seat. A sputtering broken plume now arose into the fading light from the smoke-hole of the low domed shelter.

'I didn't even notice it before we went into the cave!' said Allen, shaking his head.

'Yep, in the old property game it's always wise to remember that there's snakes as well as ladders. Down-sizing time-arama for the clan bless-em! Wednesday night the O'Lants are on the throne, Thursday morning it's all down the toilet and they're living in a *real* shit-house!'

'It's no bloody wonder Hatric's a tad off the rails!'

'As I said, life's generally a complicated place, the living see to that!'

'That was weird-on-toast mate, reading *The* Book I mean.'

'Weird? What, you consider this as normal then now do you?' Alexander gestured around them chuckling.

'Ha-ha! Ver-ry funny! Hardly! I know what I mean' Allen laughed, taking in a deep breath and the dramatic sea view under a darkening sky.

'It's just that I could really *feel* what the poor sods were going through.' Allen visibly shuddered as dark memories briefly returned.

'Admittedly Alex, you and all of this is odd-on-a-fucking-stick no doubt about it! No offence intended you understand Al.'

'None-taken Al' replied Alex with a smile.

'It's just that this part of the dream feels very much like being awake to me, don't get me wrong now! Awake in bloody wonderland! But still similar to what I know, if you understand me.'

'I hear you brother.'

'But when I was reading *The* Book it was *odder,* somehow *more.* It was like watching the film of a story I already knew really well.'

'That's *The* Book for you!'

'I can't explain it..'

'Then don't try.'

'Oh cheers mate!'

'Look there'll be plenty to see, plenty to ponder believe you me, this is just the beginning of the journey Allen. You've been given enough background for now. It's time to get going or we'll miss Patric. Follow me!' Alexander pointed toward the O'Lant's toilet of a home, before setting off downhill at a brisk pace. A thoughtful Allen followed after him.

CH 9: NO GOING BACK

The two figures lightly strode beneath a speeded-up sky, the clouds scudding by overhead as if driven by some silent hurricane. By the time Alex and Allen had covered the relatively short distance to the O'Lant's door-step it was the dead of night. The sky slowed as time began to behave itself again. The heavy canopy had dissipated, silver starlight now gloomily illuminating the scenery near at hand. Allen grinned inanely upward at the bejewelled light-pollution-free view, and what a view it was, and it was free.

On closer inspection, the squat overgrown shelter rose to shoulder height, a boil on the cliff-face. A low arched portal faced seaward, screened by oiled-skins stretched over a tightly woven stout wicker-frame.

'This is *really* what you call living on the edge!' Allen peered down between his feet into inky oblivion below. Feeling the ominous power of the sea through his feet, he shuddered.

'Yep! A big case of mind-the-step! Now do as I do..' the end of Alexander's sentence was muffled, somehow distant.

Allen turned from the brink to discover that he was alone on the cliff edge.

'Alexander?' he whispered.

'Yes.'

'Shit!' Allen laughed nervously, hands held to his chest as he attempted to regain his breath and composure before continuing. 'You should see yourself! You look like the bloody Cheshire-cat!' he laughed. The estate agent's disembodied, grinning face had materialised from the woven door, as if impaled there or like some ostentatious door-knocker.

'London-wolf more-like mate! You coming in or what?' A beckoning hand and forearm emerged from the door. Allen remained hesitant

'Come on Allen, remember you're not *really* part of this scenery, it's not your scene man! Now come on!'

'Whaaa!' Expecting a flattened nose Allen grimaced, but there was only a brief blurring before his eyes as he walked straight-through the apparently solid door. The squinting clerk found himself standing beside Alexander, ankle-deep in muddied, half-rotten straw, within a darkened circular-chamber fashioned from interwoven blackened timbers. A slender spiral of smoke lazily coiled upward from the remnants of a peat fire, ringed by begrimed stones at the centre of the sunken domed room. On either side of the circular fire-pit, two mounds (one larger than the other) huddled under heavy shaggy pelts.

'Urrrgh!' Allen felt extremely relieved that he was only in the humble abode of the O'Lants in mind rather than in body. 'Phew-eee! It smells like someone's died in here!' he complained. The stagnant, fetid air was almost chewy.

'It's a bit gamey I must say!' Alexander chuckled, waving a hand in front of his nose. 'But hey! It's only cosmetic! Think of the potential!' he added, seemingly unable to help himself.

'Yeah right! Bags of potential with the aid of a match and a gallon of petrol!'

Sporadic guttural snoring, a grunted belch followed by the extremely loud breaking of wind, emanated from the slumbering forms.

'Oh quality!' Allen grimaced. He fancied that he could almost hear the infinitesimal munching of mites and the *'twang'* of a legion of tiny flea legs jumping for joy.

Patric silently emerged from the shadows, wearing his entire thread-bare wardrobe on his back and a look of grim determination on his grimy face. In true offspring-doing-a-runner style, the lad's favourite stick was across a scrawny shoulder, a meagre bundle of worldly possessions hooked over its end.

'One beating too-many me-thinks' intoned Alexander.

Patric appeared to make for the doorway, which was cloaked on the inside by flea-bitten furs, but halted before the fire. He looked down at his inebriated father, and then turned to stare at his brothers upon the other side of the hearth. Patric spent long moments looking upon his sleeping family, a life's worth of shared experiences and memories rushing through his mind. The young Celt then looked down at his feet before he quietly laid down his burden. Straightening, Patric lifted his kilt over the water-filled squat, earthenware pot before him. Allen looked questioningly at his companion.

'Ah that would be the family drinking pot, in fact's it's the family's only pot. They can't even afford one to piss in!' explained Alex.

'Er..it would appear they do now' said Allen. The unmistakable sound that is urinating into a receptacle of water joined the unsavoury nightly overture of the O'Lants, and the muffled lowing of the rising wind outside.

'Well you know what Pat thinks of his dear-ol dad Allen-mate, and as for the twins, well you've read *The* Book'. Allen had indeed seen that many of the beatings Patric had received were due to the tale-telling-twins. Peeta and Porl were thick as thieves and O'Lants of the old school in nature. Allen smiled.

'Well I suppose he feels they've been taking the piss out of him for so long that they may as well take it in a more literal form!' he chuckled.

'Exactly, that's our Pat! Good-ol-boy!' applauded Alex.

'Amen!'

Having retrieved his pitiful belongings, the Celt turned his back on the family in more ways than one, gingerly lifted the door ajar, and shrank through the narrow gap. Beckoning to Allen, Alex followed.

'BOO! Wa-hey!'

'It's not big and it's not clever' sighed Alexander, unimpressed. He shook his head as he walked straight past a somewhat crest-fallen Allen; who'd been quite chuffed with jumping straight through the wall of the ex-public convenience in front of his guide. Feeling a little silly, the clerk hung his head, stuck his fizzing hands into his transparent pockets and unsuccessfully attempted to kick a rock at his feet, before following after the deceased estate agent.

Allen joined Alex in a sheltered natural hollow to the rear of the bijou residence, roofed over by an ancient entanglement of bracken, and floored with a deep bedding of hay which was far more fragrant than indoors.

'Farewell Adwi' whispered Patric, as he knelt beside the tethered black and white goat, arms flung about her neck, head nestled against the nuzzling beast's. Within the blurring history of the O'Lants Allen had watched a devoted Patric, a lad starved of companionship, more or less single-handedly raise the nanny from a feeble kid. The two had grown up together, and Pat often shared both his meagre rations and free time with his charge.

Patric had therefore received the goat's unquestioning trust and affection, whilst Hatric by contrast received a pair of horns, hooves or teeth whenever opportunity arose. Often the goat's bouts of violence followed on the heels of Pat's own beatings. Allen had joined a bruised Patric in laughter upon one particularly amusing incident when an inebriated Hatric, who had been bending over a manure-filled furrow to retrieve his fallen drinking-skin, suffered bruised buttocks and a dung-sandwich care of Adwi. Patric's father's fury had been such, that it was only the beast's milk, an irreplaceable staple source of nutrition which had saved her life.

'I thought the goat didn't have a name' Allen's voice was perplexed. *The Book* had shown that the heart-broken Hatric had always expressly forbidden the naming of any O'Lant livestock, for experience of life had taught him that greater attachment only led to greater pain on separation.

When the goat's milk ran out so also would the tenuous tenancy of its own body, and it would be time to get the bar-b going.

'Patric is naming the goat because he knows he'll never see her again' Alexander explained.

'Why Adwi?'

'Adwi is from the great myths of his forefathers, vast poetic sagas handed down by word of mouth alone. Adwi was one of the many fire goddesses imprisoned in the beginning beneath the rock by the gods of stone and soil, enslaved to maintain the life of men upon this earth. Yet ever does she attempt to break free, rending the earth and spouting beacons that might be seen by the great sun god, she awaits her time when the earth is no more and she is once again free'.

'Big name for a little goat' giggled Allen.

'The size and nature of the body does not reflect the size and nature of the soul within it.'

'Yeah, whatever vicar' replied Allen wearily.

'I've got ti go now Ad' Patric's burring Gaelic accent was a muffled half-choked whisper, wrung with emotion. Having seen the lad care for Adwi in all weathers; Having watched the two rough and tumble; Having witnessed Patric spend numerous hours airing his views on the world to the goat, Allen felt his own eyes moisten.

The Celt straightened, dragging the back of a ragged sleeve across his face. Allen stepped backward as Patric turned to leave, but instead of abandoning Adwi to a certain death the boy remained standing frozen. After some moments Patric spun on his heel, took the goat's leash in his hands and began to undo it.

'Gooo-on boy!' cheered Allen.

Patric's fingers ceased their feverish work with only one loose knot remaining between Adwi and freedom. Screwing his eyes shut, gritting his teeth and exhaling a groan of anguish, Patric retied the leash, his tears falling upon the upward-turned face of the nanny-goat. Patric left Allen and Alexander alone with Adwi, who tilted her head to one side and let out an enquiring muted bleat.

'He'd have been sentencing his family to certain serious malnutrition, maybe even starvation if he'd have let the goat go and the weather turns *real*-nasty, and he knew it' explained Alex. 'Come on Allen.' Before following, Allen coughed a number of times into his fist.

Back out in the wind, Allen joined Alexander and Patric beside a boulder-like rocky outcrop on the cliff edge to one side of the domed shelter.

In *The* Book, Allen had seen a youthful Hatric spend many hours sitting cross-legged in contemplation upon this very rock, as he looked up at the great stronghold that he believed would be his one day. Similarly seated, Patric had also spent many stolen moments crouched upon the same boulder. Yet unlike his dad, the younger O'Lant of course now stared out at an unhampered view of the sea, and a dark shadow on the far horizon that one day would be called the western coast of Scotland.

In his earliest years Patric had become used to the infrequent arrival of wondrous and outlandish visitors, many leading beasts burdened with all manner of goods for trade. To the lad's bewilderment all would perform more-or-less the same ceremony. Firstly, the travellers would gaze around in bemused fashion or look back upon their route with a confused expression. Many would then pace to the cliff edge, shaking their heads in incomprehension as they stared down into the inconspicuous foaming rocky jumble below. All would then hastily depart, pursued by the hairy, stick-waving, slavering and ranting mad man whom Patric called dad. As the years passed, the frequency of these inexplicable visitations lessened, until by Patric's ninth summer they had ceased completely. However, it would be one of the last of these visitors, a lone hooded and cloaked wizened old man, who would make the greatest impression on the boy.

On that day Hatric had thankfully taken the twins to the foot of the cliff at low tide, to collect limpets and mussels amongst the rock-pools that were the ancestral graveyard, leaving his eldest son to protect the modest homestead. Patric had been enjoying the rare opportunity of freedom and was seated upon his rock sketching the view, when the bent figure had arrived, performed the ceremony of the visitor, before asking him for directions. The youth of course new nothing of; and was unable to direct the old man to, the great citadel for which he searched.

Due to the waist-length beard, the tapering staff, the tattoos covering the dark and leathery wrinkled features, the piercing gaze from gimlet eyes, and the fact that the old man was able or dared to travel alone, Patric took the stranger to be a wandering holy man, a shaman.

Patric had known all about shamans, for his somewhat jaded and dispirited father had little time for the gods or their preaching after-life insurance salesmen upon this earth. Indeed, it was one of the few subjects upon which Hatric waxed lyrical. It was also the source of many of his most imaginative expletives.

The inquisitive youth had nervously enquired of the obviously worldly traveller as to what the dark line on the horizon might be, a question which had long troubled him. The old man had studied both Patric and his sketch for some time, as if pondering whether it was worth expending further words on the ignorant urchin. All except the uneducated, impudent boy it seemed knew that it was unwise to trouble the wielders of the dark magic with uninvited questions.

'That is a larger land than this' he'd said at last.

'A larger land?' Pat's voice had been awestruck, his young mental horizons having suddenly been broadened somewhat.

'Lad, you see before you the very gates to the lands of opportunity. Beyond that larger land there lay even larger lands, and larger lands beyond those' the stranger had intoned solemnly.

'Domi's-Bollocks!' the lad had exhaled emphatically. The old wise man had chuckled.

'And the larger the land tis said, the larger the opportunity!'

'*Lands of opportunity..*' Patric had repeated the words to himself in a hushed rapturous whisper.

'Lands indeed through which I have passed on an arduous pilgrimage.' The shaman's heavily accented voice had taken on a slightly peeved tone as he massaged weary and aching limbs.

'It has been an often-perilous journey over many, many cycles of the seasons that I have undertaken to reach this very spot, on a mission of great-great import, much have I sacrificed in life' peeved had given way to slightly pissed off.

'Oh' Patric had said.

'Can't bloody understand it really, last night was the third zenith of this cycle of sister moon, the Great Bear was directly overhead. The citadel should be *here. HE should be here!*' the hooded stranger had added, staring along the coast and then up at the sky obviously perplexed. The mystified lad had remained silent.

'Someone got the sums wrong in the brotherhood it would seem! Oh well that's that prophecy buggered then, but what can you do?' The old man's voice had been resigned, as raising a hand in farewell, he'd hobbled off in the direction from which he had come.

So it had been that the youth had received his first insight into the existence of a wider world beyond the narrow confines of his homeland, and further that it was possible to go there...

To Allen, the old man's voice had been that of Gandalf and Merlin at the same time. Having read of the elderly druid in *The* Book, unlike Patric, Allen knew that his name was Nella, Allen's own name backwards.

79

'Grooo-vy dream man!' he had thought to himself.

'Shame about the ol-goat'.
'Yeah, real-bummer' replied Alex, his tone non-committal.
Patric's copper hair flailed about his face in the now broad moonlight, his hand laid lovingly upon the stone as he stared out across glinting waves into the deeper darkness, toward his intended destination and destiny. Of the three that stood upon the cliff edge he alone was unaware that his father still infrequently visited the rock, usually in the early hours after he had watched his three slumbering sons; Hatric's only quality time with his children. The intoxicated Celt would then sit upon the rock as he had in childhood, lost in painful memories, raging against the cruel fates and begging forgiveness from his beloved Kara for his own worthlessness in turn.
'Looks like we're off then' commented Allen, stepping out of the way as Patric turned from the sea and set off up-hill, reddened eyes staring straight ahead. Falling into step with Alexander, Allen followed after him. Patric's humble home, the only one he'd known since birth, shrank into the night.

The surrounding clans had not allowed the last of the O'Lants to live out of any sense of pity or compassion. Indeed, it was believed that a quick death was far too good for any of the hated wolf's head clan. Following the quite literal collapse of the O'Lant family business there had followed a period of celebration, feast and excess amongst the clans of that region which would be unrivalled for many generations to come. At the height of the drunken festivities the vertically-challenged chieftains there-gathered had gleefully ordained that the vile name of O'Lant would die out over a degrading lifetime of shameful imprisonment, and public humiliation.
On pain of death, the O'Lant's who had not fled were to be confined to the pitiful remainder of their precious lands, never again allowed to leave. They would dine on berries rather than boar, root vegetables rather than venison. Never again would the O'Lants re-join the arms race and bear Stone-age weapons or tools. They were to be cast back into the Wood age. The impotent brothers and their father would serve as a reminder and warning to all, of the dangers of allowing any one-clan to grow too-powerful.
The neighbouring clans would take it in turns to keep watch over the O'Lants, and in the warmer seasons many would even picnic upon the

slopes overlooking the fetid dwelling, as if viewing the exhibited captives of a zoo or freak show.

As they had for generations, parents continued to warn their children that if they didn't behave themselves then the O'Lants would come and get them in the night.

So it was that the blameless young Patric, as many both before and after him in this world of ours, found himself the proud owner of a seemingly doomed and accursed future, all because of a few letters, just a word, a name...

Being a child however, and therefore possessing an unquenchable curiosity and irrepressible spirit, Patric was still sensible enough not to take such ridiculous things seriously. Therefore, apart from his clandestine field-trips in search of artistic solitude, Patric had also begun to venture further and further afield.

Slipping away unnoticed from his father and past the watchful sentries had become a game, a challenge and an adventure to the small boy. A game in which he increasingly excelled. The lithe and stealthy child had explored the depths of the forest and the heights of the cliffs. He'd wandered far along the craggy coast and amongst the undulating heath lands. Patric's most exhilarating (and most dangerous) discovery had however been the few scattered settlements near at hand. If discovered, the child knew he would at best be severely beaten.

By the time of Nella's visit, Patric had already become quite well versed in the ways of men, due to many hours of secretive eves-dropping and observation. Now having some basis upon which to make a comparison, he had decided that he was (without a shadow of doubt) a member of the Celtic-dysfunctional-family-unit-of-the-year.

So had been born the dream, a dream of one day journeying to a land where no one had heard of the name O'Lant.

'So Alex mate, what's this little episode supposed to be teaching me then?' Allen gestured ahead to the trudging young Celt.

'Well he's not happy with his life at the moment, right? Not unlike someone else I can think of not a million miles away from me...'

'Yeah? And...?'

'Well *he's* getting off his arse and doing something about it'

'Oh! And so that's what you're saying I should do then is it? I already moved to London, the alleged land of opportunity, if you hadn't forgotten.'

'I'm saying watch the story mate, this is just the first chapter of a fat-boy-saga. And there's a difference between setting out on a journey to pursue one's destiny, and running away from it.'

Allen continued the journey back up to the crest of the slope in an angry silence. Alexander by contrast whistled a jaunty tune, compounding his companion's dark mood.

On reaching the head of the rise Patric halted, turned and peered back down into the darkness. Carried on the chill wind, above the sound of the ever-present sea, there came a distant and plaintive bleat.

'Bye Adwi, may the grass be greener on t'other side. Bye Peeta, Porl. Bye Da. All-knowing Domi protect-ye, though bastards ye be.' Patric whispered, through tears not wholly due to the stinging, blustery night air.

By now, the lad was well used to being out and about in the night. He knew that as time had passed not only had the guards posted by the clans become less in number, but that they had also degenerated in calibre; from elite hand-picked warriors to cairn-dodgers who could just about lift a spear, and not see far past the end of one. If chilly, like tonight, often there was no guard at all; they were either at home by the hearth (whingeing that they could only afford to have one log on the fire) or too busy being buried.

The O'Lants had become less and less of a priority or public attraction with the passage of the years. The able-bodied clans-men were now of course needed to settle the inevitable fresh disputes between the formerly friendly tribes.

However, as Patric looked along the barely discernible trail that wound between the heather into the cold night, his expression had grown pensive and uncertain. Certainly, he'd made many daring nocturnal journeys, yet he had always set out with the knowledge that he would be coming home afterward. Patric's gaze returned to his birthplace, indecision upon his face. Moments dragged into minutes.

'Young Pat having second thoughts d'yer think?' enquired Allen.

Alexander remained silent, as in apparent answer a broad smile suddenly broke upon the boy's face.

Patric had reminded himself that he would indeed be coming home one day.

He had learnt much from his long study of the neighbours. The boy had realised that if his artistic talents were indeed worthless, then there existed an infinite number of professions in the world that offered the possibility of great reward for those unafraid of hard labour, and who were willing to

82

dedicate themselves. As a reviled O'Lant, Patric was of course unemployable locally. However, the confident lad intended not only to journey to the distant fabled lands of opportunity; but also gain himself apprenticeship to the most vaulted of all trades of the times; a 'proppa-job' at the very cutting edge of Stone-age technology. The IT industry of the time. He was going to become a mason.

By gaining employment within this esteemed occupation, Patric ardently believed that he would make his fortune, and one day be able to return home as a grown man and reap revenge on the cruel surrounding clans. More importantly the lad would then be able to look his father square in the eyes, disproving the assertions of many years that he was a worthless waste of space. Patric would make his father proud of him, whether Hatric liked it or not.

One day he'd show all of them, until then there would be no going back.

CH 10: OF STICKS AND STONES

'Fancy a paddle?' enquired Allen, standing upon the wet shingle in the dreary half-light of pre-dawn. Icy, foaming sea water washed around and through his transparent ankles. The narrow pebble beach was crescent shaped and rose out of the surf in an even slope. Gigantic boulders which had grown bored of being part of the surrounding cliff-face over the millennia littered the ground, like a beached shoal of whales.
'Come on Alex yer miserable git! You can't beat the seaside!' cried Allen.
'Don't mind me, you fill your boots Allen-mate! Oh, I see you have.' The estate agent remained perched upon the limpet-encrusted rock just above the tide-line, intently watching the dull orange lights clustered within the gloom of the cliff's foot.

Beneath an overhang which protruded from the knees of the rock face, a dozen or so rectangular timber huts sheltered from the elements, shielded from both rock-fall, and prying eyes above. The hidden dwellings were elevated on a natural shelf, three-men's' height above beach-level. At each door-post a dying torch glowed amber in the semi-darkness. Between the diminutive fishing village and the shoreline, a number of primitive vessels lay in line. Most were long and slender, fashioned from a single hollowed-out tree trunk, lashed with timber out-rigging for stability. Each was richly engraved with intricate Celtic designs imploring the gods to allow the owner to eat fish, not the fish eat the owner. There were also a number of wide, single-mast rafts. Here and there were skilfully-woven overturned coracles, like a grazing brood of giant beetles.

Hemp fishing nets weighted with stones were draped over posts in front of the dwellings, and eau-de-kipper arose from dried fish, hung from lines over a still-smouldering charcoal bed.

To one side of the huddled community a shallow brook issued from a fissure in the rock, to wend its babbling way down to the sea. Stout logs bridged the stream just below its source, and a few paces beyond, a narrow, precipitous path zig-zagged up the cliff face.

Deflated drinking skins and earthenware beakers, the remains of many a fish supper, and the contents of not-a-few stomachs, littered the length of the beach. No one, it seemed, was out of bed yet.
'Well this is a quaint little place.' Amongst the dawn chorus of the gulls, Allen leisurely strolled back up the beach to re-join Alexander at the sea-

A quaint little place.

smoothed boulder. Behind, the first light of the rising sun broke upon the rolling waves.

'Yeah quaint' echoed Alexander distractedly, without taking his eyes from the settlement above.

'Shame the inhabitants aren't so quaint! Is he awake yet?' Allen, hands in pockets, dipped his head toward a bloodied and bruised Patric, who was slumped face down in the wet gravel behind the boulder.

'Phew-eeee! They certainly beat the living-shit out of him, didn't they?!' Allen whistled through his teeth, shaking his head with a wry chuckle.

'They certainly did. You seem to be getting the hang of the ol' *staying detached* bit all of a sudden.'

'Yeah well yer know, I took your advice. What's the point in getting worked-up over a dream? Eh?'

'Exactly' Alex continued to watch the village.

There was a groan from the curled, drenched form.

'Looks like Laughing-boy's ready to re-join the land of the living'.

Grimacing, Allen knelt, as with macabre-curiosity, he intently studied the numerous welts, grazes and bruises that covered more-or-less every visible part of Patric's body.

'Well that didn't quite work out as the poor sod intended' he said over his shoulder.

'Perhaps.'

Allen and Alexander had followed the gleeful young Celt along the coastal path through a black, windswept night, until with the coming of grey dawn, they had (luckily for Patric) put a good few miles between themselves, and what would be (by then) a somewhat furious Hatric. Seemingly driven by the possibilities of that which lay ahead, and that which lay behind, Patric had pressed on through the growing rainy-day without rest. Until, by mid-morning the travellers had reached the cliff-edge overlooking the high-walled cove, and its concealed settlement. At last the downpour had stopped.

Furtive and wary, the lad had kept low, peering over the precipice, obviously intent on being unobserved. Below, a small bustling community, clothed in hooded, oiled skins, busied themselves with the daily tasks of the Stone-age fishing world.

Patric had taken a handful of dark berries from his bundle. Crushing them in his hands, he had smeared the black mess into his hair, masking the distinctive fiery-red of the O'Lants. A layer of grime already hid the fair complexion of his hated clan, but Patric had also pulled the folds of his cloak up to his nose just in case. This done, the lad had arisen, taken a deep breath, before setting off down the cliff path, his two invisible companions following behind.

At the cliff's foot, Patric had raised his palm in greeting as he was welcomed by the hearty cries of the fisher-folk. The villagers were a squat, broad-shouldered breed, top-heavy from a life spent hauling on oars and heavy nets. They were fair or mousy-haired, and wore jewellery fashioned from sea-shells and fishbone.

Accepting a skin of the locals' strongest beer, the young Celt had introduced himself as one of the O'Hoohalarahan clan, a tribe whose lands lay many days' march beyond the great forest. The raven-haired O'Hoohalarahans were seldom seen in these parts, and Patric had hoped there would be little chance of a real one inconveniently turning up to drop him in it.

To a delighted chorus of encouraging whoops and howls, Patric had thrown his head back, and taken deep gulps from the skin.

Alexander had wandered amongst the villagers without a care, as they tended their catch and nets. He moved casually between the chattering fishwives, the labouring men and darting children, without a single collision. By contrast, an anxious-Allen had found himself performing a spasmodic, cavorting dance as he fruitlessly attempted to prevent anyone walking through him.

As the afternoon wore on a constant stream of Celtic visitors had arrived at the normally quiet and secluded hamlet. For this was a special day in the village calendar, the day of Onni-Okki. Work had lessened, beer-drinking, frivolity and the volume had increased. There had been a few jigs and a little bit of complimentary fisticuffs.

Allen had seen Patric secretly observe the tiny fishing village for three years in *The* Book, and had known that the reason for the lad's flight here was threefold.

Firstly, it was from here that the fabled ferryman departed for the-gates-to-the-lands-of-opportunity. Secondly, the destitute Patric had hoped that this particularly-special day would provide him with the means to pay the fare, and thirdly there was another important figure in his life to say goodbye to.

Onni-Okki was an annual stone-throwing competition, and had been a traditional event hosted by the fishing village for many, many generations. First prize was five men's' weight in fish. A valuable-asset in an age of barter, especially if traded with inlanders and surely more than enough for passage across the water.

Every year, men from all the nearby Clans would come to try their hand, and get a free belly-full of beer. Predominantly it was the broader, middle-aged variety of man who generally participated, and who were indeed the most consistent winners. Any that entered had to be able to hold their beer, for it was not without reason that the villagers plied their visitors with booze.

The villagers' own champion was without fail, a stout, hardened drinker. For of course they wished to keep the prize within the community, and more-often-than-not, they succeeded.

In a culture which attached a deity to each and every aspect of human life, emotion or geographical feature, Onni was a god of accuracy and hand-eye coordination, Okki the god of still being able to be as Onni himself when extremely pissed-up.

As Patric was lacking in both years and belly, and stood a head shorter than any of his fellow competitors, he was openly considered with derision and as little cause for concern.

Whilst the young Celt had joined the other competitors upon the beach, Alexander had continued to leisurely mingle as if he were enjoying a holiday rustic-excursion, and Allen had retired to the surf, in order to escape yet another unpleasant invasion of his body.

'Hey! I'm only bloody walking on water!' he'd cried, whist moon-walking the waves.

'Yeah, yeah JC! Coming to watch the important stuff or what?' Alex had replied irritably. After a quick jog around the bay, Allen had reluctantly joined his guide at the side of the limbering-up, beery and belchy contestants.

At one end of the cove, before the cliff wall, a line of y-shaped cleft-sticks had been set into the shingle, a sliced-section of a log wedged atop each. 'C'MON PAT MY SON!!' Alexander had added a shrill whistle through his fingers. A jeering and cheering crowd of Celts had gathered, lining the landward side of the beach between the throwers and their targets.

From *The* Book, Allen knew that the great sagas told that in the earliest age of men, he who is known by the Celts simply as *The Dark One* had envied the harmonious lives of a then innocent mankind. In his jealousy, he had set loose the great sky bull, who's nose and eyes poured flame 'as a burning wind upon the earth', and who's hoof-falls 'rent the very mountains asunder' no less. The bellowing vast beast had apparently charged across the heavens, unleashing from its rear a vast outpouring of bull-shit which covered the lands of men, turning many a formerly upstanding soul into an extremely dodgy character.

At the behest of the great sun god Domi (the all-knowing), Onni had deftly cast a stone into the monster's rear end, plugging the stinking avalanche, and causing the rampaging beast to explode across the vault of the skies, leaving only the pattern of stars which was to be named 'The great bull' by the Celts, and by later civilizations as Taurus.

Unfortunately however, the sagas attested that bull-shit was to remain with humankind as an integral feature thereafter.

During this particular celestial emergency, it was written that Okki (he who drinketh verily as the whale) had thankfully been on hand to supply a copious amount of alcohol, enough to get a god wasted. For the sensitive Onni did not possess the courage to face the dreadful creature, even from behind, without being off his face.

Onni-Okki involved propelling a Celtic-throwing-stone from twenty-one paces, into the narrow, y-shaped aperture of a stick, known as 'the bull's-eye', a crude reproduction of the great bull's back-passage. The object of the game being to knock 'the log' back through 'the crack'. Participants threw in turn, and were disqualified by their first miss. Often when the competitors were of a high standard, the matches could last hours and a good deal of beer got drunk. As vision blurred, it could be a dangerous spectator-sport in the extreme. The only stringent rule was that each contestant must hold a full beaker of beer in their free hand whilst throwing. Pride demanded not a drop was to be spilt, and that the pot must be drained before the next throw.

Since humanity first felt fear, hunger, or pissed-off, there has existed the instinctive urge to pick up a stone and throw it at something or somebody. Due to a healthy local-population of wolves, bears, boar and aggressive clans, the Celts of the time learnt stone throwing in infancy. The Celtic throwing-stone was traditionally palm-sized, circular, and flat. Carried in pairs (one with a honed edge, the other blunt), they were generally painted in rich and bright designs, intended to imbue them with greater lethalness, and making them easier to find after being thrown.

At a gesture from the wrinkled, snowy-bearded headman of the village, Patric's competitors had thrown one after the other. Each throw was accompanied by raucous adulation or heart-felt curses. Due to his age and shabby attire, the lad had been left to throw last.

The Celts wagered heavily on Onni-Okki, yet the only bets that had been placed on Patric that day related to whether he would pass out before his first throw.

Apart from a solitary cry of encouragement from a young girl, insults, cat-calls and mocking laughter had erupted from the crowd as the sheepish, obviously ignorant youngster took up an untutored throwing stance. There had been much shaking of heads, giggling, and wry chuckles at the skinny lad's undecorated stones.

However, Allen had seen Patric stun many a leaping rabbit or swooping bird at some distance, with the aid of his two favourite throwing stones, forbidden Stone-age weapons for an O'Lant. Further, due to Hatric's dubious fathering skills, Patric was also no stranger to alcohol. Both he and his brothers had often sampled the potent homebrew after their father had passed out.

The O'Lants had never decorated their throwing stones. For they believed that if after being thrown, the stone was not stained bright crimson with blood and therefore easy to find, then the thrower did not deserve the right to bear either the stone or the name O'Lant.

'GOOD OL BOY!!!' Alex's loud cry had joined the muted appreciation of a somewhat surprised audience, as Patric's first blurring, humming cast, though unorthodox in style, had been bang on target.

'YEAH! C'MON PAT!' Despite himself, Allen had been caught up in the moment, jumping up and down, he'd let out loud whoops of delight.

'YEAH! UP YOURS!' Allen had presented his finger to the crowd in general. Alexander had laughed.

Although an able athlete at school, and even having made it into a number of the school-teams, Allen wasn't normally into the whole *sport*-thing at all. He didn't follow it, didn't give a monkey's about *the results*, and didn't support a team. Allen's childhood had included little or no sport on the TV or radio, as his dad, Ray, had been brought up with sport as an endless topic of conversation between his sports-mad dad, Mick, and oddly-likewise older-sister, Martine. Family outings, even holidays, had revolved around the sporting calendar. All in all, it had put him off the subject for life. Allen's mum certainly wasn't into sport. Allen's dad had played every kind of ball, bat and racquet game imaginable with him throughout his childhood. They were both good at sport, they enjoyed it. They just didn't get the concept of watching or discussing other people doing it.

Many a bloke, many a geezer, had found Allen's sporting disinterest an annoying oddity, and his interest in writing and things artistic, as even more cause for masculine concern. There had been many a patronising or sarcastic comment when he'd told people that he was attempting to write a novel, so that very soon he hadn't mentioned it.

Well one day Allen would show them all! Just like Patric was showing these disbelieving gits!

'WANKERS!' he'd cried not only at the Celts, with feeling. Alexander had smiled at his oblivious companion.

Patric had bathed in the glow of unusually being the centre of friendly attention, of being *a success*. People were all around him, and for the first time in his life he wasn't hiding from them. However, not wishing to draw too much attention to himself or his hasty disguise, he'd kept his head low and ducked back into the group of remaining contestants. The stones of the successful throwers were collected by the village children, who had beamed with pride at their important role. Unsuccessful throwers could get their own.

'GIVE ME A P! **P!** GIVE ME AN A! **A!** GIVE ME A T! **T!**' Allen performed a little cheer-leader number, as with his second successful throw Patric had dispelled the onlookers' assumption that he'd simply been experiencing beginners-luck.

Grinning inanely, a very bashful Patric had also raised his hand to accept the enthusiastic cries of the crowd, seemingly now beginning to enjoy his first public appearance.

Afternoon had worn on to early evening, torches and bonfires were lit under a darkening sky.

The beer had flowed, the competitors had dwindled, and nine spectators had hilariously gone down to alcoholically-impaired throws. Patric's confidence however, increased with each throw. An earlier uncomfortable ness with praise had dissipated with success, drink, and the many adoring expressions of the female members of the audience. Patric, a lad who through no choice of his own had led an almost solitary life, had become the unexpected darling of the crowd.

As each round passed, the cleft sticks were rearranged so that some faced the throwers obliquely, or were obscured by others, increasing the difficulty of a successful strike. Patric's fellow contestants' initial scorn had grown into embarrassment, then anger, and at last to a grudging respect. Compared to his hellish daily life, the competition was a breeze for the lad.

After numerous rounds, only Patric and the village's own champion, a purple-faced, glassy-eyed bloater, had remained. The novel turn of events had led to wagers even greater in number and amount than usual. All had held their breath.

'YERRRRRR-ESSSSS!!!!' Allen had gone wild as the reigning champion of four cycles of the seasons missed his throw. 'YOU-FAT-BASTARD! YOU-FAT-BASTARD! YOU'RE NOT SINGING ANYMORE!' He'd chanted with glee, amongst the celebratory cries and anguished sighs of those around him.

'Into our sport all of a sudden, aren't we?' Alex had commented, putting his best geezer voice on.

'Sincerely up yours Alex!'

'Oo-oooo! Aren't we the touchy one!' Alexander had sniggered to himself.

When only two remained in an Onni-Okki match, the ancient rules dictated that both throwers must take their turn. If both missed, they must throw again and again, until one made a successful cast and the other did not.

As Patric had taken his place to throw, apart from the foaming water upon the shingle, and the crackle of burning timbers, all that could be heard were the lisping whispered incantations of the toothless village shaman, as he did his expected civic duty and cursed the lad by every dark god he could think of.

'YOU-FUCKIN-DIAMOND!' Allen's fist had punched the air, an arm around Alex's shoulder, as the crowd had erupted into wild jubilation or angry disappointment (dependent upon which way they had wagered). Patric's stone had hit its mark, annoyingly for the loser, the trickiest of the remaining targets. The defeated village champion had stood with his head in his podgy hands, beaten by a young upstart, and soon no doubt to be beaten by his lord's men.

'WE DE-MEN!' Allen had screamed into Alexander's ear.

'Oh, so it's *we* now is it?' the estate agent had laughed.

'YEAH! WHAT THE HELL! WE'RE THE BOYS! WE'RE THE INCARNATIONS THAT MATTER!'

'I think you'd better come with me'.

'Wha..?'

Alexander had reached under Allen's armpits as the roaring crowd had surged forward.

The crowd were willing to trample their brethren for a chance of touching one obviously blessed by the gods, vainly hoping some of it might rub off on them. Just for the chance to be able to boast *they* were there, *they* had seen or even touched *him*, a celebrity.

'Whoa…nice one!' Allen had looked down between his feet at the tightly pressed throng beneath. He and Alexander were now floating a few feet above the chanting crowd.

'That could've been very nasty for you Allen-mate. Now I'm gonna let go of you in a second. You're going to be fine, just believe that there's no reason why you can't stay up here, you understand me yeah?'

'I'll give it a try, WHAA! Bloody hell!' As Alexander had released him, Allen had dipped slightly, sending his stomach into somersault. Thankfully he had bobbed upwards moments later, to re-join his hovering companion.

'Wow! This is mad!'

'Oh, for buggery's-sake!' Alexander's tone had been brassed-off, as Allen, who'd obviously been enjoying this latest revelatory experience of his dream, had sprinted out across the bay, gaining altitude as he went.

'AA-LLLENNNN!!! WILL YOU GET YOUR BLEEDIN-ARSE BACK ERE SHARPISH!'

'Okay! Okay! Don't have a baby!' The distant answer had come from just below cloud level.

Alexander had waited, arms crossed, foot tapping in mid-air. Not happy.

'Missing me or something Alex? No need to lose your rag ye know matey!' an elated Allen had lain back in the air next to his guide, hands cradling his head.

'Look Allen, I've brought you here for a reason yeah? And it's all gonna be a just *a little bit* of a waste of SODDIN-time if you're having-it-away-on-yer-toes during the important bits! YER FOLLOW?!'

'ALRIGHT! Alright! Keep yer hair on! Christ! Whose dream is this anyway?'

Below, Patric had found himself surrounded by a tight press of jostling, beered-up Celtic fans. A ring of the headman's largest men strained against the crowd with arms locked, preventing the new Onni-Okki champion from being crushed.

Buffeted and bewildered, the rather unsteady lad had looked about himself, grinning and shaking his head in disbelief. He'd drained the remnants of his beaker, froth pouring down his face, before wiping his mouth on the back of his sleeve and tossing the drinking vessel into the waiting sea of hands. Where it had landed, fervent fists and throwing-stones had flown over ownership. Patric had cried out with sheer glee. All agreed (even the loyal home crowd) that the game had not seen the lad's like for generations. None had witnessed a throwing style of such ferocity or accuracy.

The boy threw as if hunting or at war, not the 'it's-all-in-the-wrist' deft toss that was the accepted style of the game. Out of necessity, Patric had always looked after himself and only knew one way to throw a stone, and that was to kill. With a charging territorial boar or a hungry wolf, you only got one throw.

Under a shower of beer, ecstatic oaths and stone-age female undergarments, Patric had been ushered from the shore by his burly bodyguards toward the village. The triumphal procession barged and elbowed its way through rowdy Celtic-frivolity, and good-natured violence, until Patric had found himself beneath the rocky shelf, his retinue forming a protective horseshoe around him. Before Patric, upon a mat of ferns, lay five-men's weight in dried-fish, heavy-dosh indeed for a lad of such humble background. From above, drowned in the folds of his bear-skin robe, the skeletal headman looked down upon him from his ceremonial chair. The seat was fashioned from twisting silvered drift-wood and its high back from the rib-cage of a dolphin, crested by the leering skull of the creature.

In claw-like, liver-spotted, mottled hands, the beak-nosed headman held a carrot and a stick, his tokens of office. At his side, dressed (unfortunately) in nothing but a fishing-net, and leaning on a tall-staff fashioned from a hollowed whale-bone, the elderly tattooed and shaven-headed village shaman stood. Though both were miffed, the lord at having lost out on a valuable commodity, and the humiliated witch-doctor at having been publicly ignored by the gods, both smiled broadly. After all, it was many days' journey back to the lands of the O'Hoohalarahans. The forest was indeed a dangerous place, and sadly much harm could unfortunately befall a young unwary lone traveller…

'Ah, there she is' Alex had said as he and Allen had lightly stepped onto the rock shelf next to the bone-throne, and the bonier dodgy-duo.

'Who?'

'Enixam of course' Alex had pointed down into the forefront of the undulating crowd below.

'Oh yes' Allen had smiled warmly at the waving, cheering teenage girl. An extremely attractive girl with full red lips, a wild cascade of dark tresses, and piercing green eyes hooded under long lashes. She was four-summers older than Patric, was born in the same season, and was blossoming into shapely womanhood. The very same curvaceous girl in fact, who'd given Patric the solitary, enthusiastic cry of encouragement as he'd attempted his first throw earlier that afternoon, when everyone else had doubted his ability.

'Enixam..' Allen had repeated the name (Maxine backwards) quietly to himself, his glazed expression far away. Enixam was exactly as he imagined Maxine to have looked at that age. She had Maxine's eyes, as Alexander had his.

Max was four years older than Allen and born in the same month. In the club, the night before (*the night before?* The whole time-thing had 'gone-west' on Allen) amongst millions of other things, he'd uncharacteristically told Maxine that he was a closet-writer. She was just *so* easy to talk to…she hadn't taken the piss, hadn't patronised him, she'd simply told him to go for it. She'd believed in him.

'Maybe this dream's all right after all Alex-mate' the still staring, smiling Allen had said.

'Glad you're beginning to think so ol' reincarnation-mate of mine.'

In *The* Book, Allen had seen Patric's spying missions increasingly centre upon this particular fishing village. Initially of course, the travel-hungry Celt had been primarily interested in the mysterious ferryman, but very soon however, Enixam had become an equally enticing draw...

In his attempt to gain a greater and greater knowledge of the arrivals and departures of the ferryman, Patric had become increasingly daring, and had even begun to sneak down to the beach, hiding amongst the tumbled boulders and rock pools at the cliff's foot.

It had been on a mild spring afternoon, whilst crouched behind a large rock, ankle deep in salt-water, that he'd been startled by a girl's voice from behind.

'Bit shy, are we?' the husky tone had been cheeky yet friendly. To Allen, Enixam's voice was like the bawdiest of experienced wenches, to the heavenly tones of a childlike angel at the same time. It was Maxine's voice.

Patric had nearly jumped out of his skin. Like a cornered beast, spinning around, his back and hands splayed against the barnacled rock, heart pounding, he'd stared wide-eyed at the smiling, dark haired girl. Her complexion was flawless and golden, darker than the Celtic women of the region.

'I love yer hair, it burns like fire under the sun!' she had said with genuine warmth, her head cocked to one side. Patric had made no answer, remaining frozen, still terrified but now also captivated.

'Not from round here are ye? Don't worry, neither am I' she'd laughed. Although he'd always been petrified of discovery with very good reason, Patric had grinned, his cheeks flushing at the girl's compliment. He was completely disarmed by the broad rosy-lipped smile and striking eyes of the full-figured girl, as she stood with one slender hand on a curvy, cocked hip, dark curls falling about her smooth shoulders. She wore only a figure-hugging leathern sleeveless vest, which restrained a buxom-chest and finished at her upper thighs, leaving the long, tapering legs naked.

At this point it is worthy of mention that Patric was an extremely hormonal, hyper-sensitive thirteen-year-old who didn't get out much, enough said.

'Ur....' He'd said, his eyes fixed on the girl, but most certainly not her face. The girl's smile had broadened with amusement. Moments had dragged.

'Don't worry, I won't tell a soul yer here if that's what's worryin ye' she had said softly, obviously having taken in Patric's panicked state. Further long moments had dragged.

'Ur..' awe-struck, Patric had at last forcibly dragged his eyes back up to meet the smirking girl's knowing gaze. She'd laughed, he'd blushed until his face had matched his red hair.

'Yer safe with me, honest' the languid girl had chuckled naughtily. Patric had swallowed hard. She had then reached into the netted bag at her side, from which protruded the clawing appendages of half a dozen or so squirming crabs, before disentangling two of the glistening occupants and offering them to Patric.

'Here, accept these as gifts of welcome'. So had been the first meeting of Patric and Enixam. He had given her his adolescent heart, she'd given him crabs.

Thereafter, whenever his father had departed on a poaching trip into the forest (usually Hatric would return with a hangover rather than meat, with slurred sagas concerning 'the one that got away' and reminding his sons for the millionth time that 'y-lil shites d-yer-no eye cudda bin shumwun'); Or if he was too drunk to make it back up the cliff for a day or two after

96

going winkling; Or was simply out-to-lunch on a week-long bender, Patric would return to the narrow cove.

He would delight in attempting to sneak up on, and surprise Enixam as she collected shell-fish. Yet more-often-than-not the quick-witted girl would jump out on him, causing him more than one near-heart-attack. It should be remembered that Patric risked serious harm, even possible death, with each-and-every visit. Though opportunity for the secretive meetings amongst the rock-pools was infrequent, Patric and Enixam had soon become fast friends. They'd talked endlessly of every subject under the sun, and had laughed and cried over each other's life story. Patric had learnt, after much scalding from Enix, to take part in a conversation where every third word wasn't 'bollocks' or worse. Enixam had learnt of a world that thankfully didn't involve fish.

For his part, Patric had found not just a friend, but also a goddess to place upon a pedestal and worship, (from his youthful perspective) an *older woman*. For hers, though he was but a boy, Enixam had found a fellow outsider with whom she felt an affinity. She had explained to the lad (who hung on her every word) that she'd been brought to this land by her then pregnant mother. However, her mother had suddenly passed away with a fever in Enixam's fifth summer, leaving behind but a handful of memories and a blurred-vision of a doe-eyed, beauteous face framed by long dark hair. Enixam was also left without the knowledge as to why she was there at all, alone in a strange culture. A culture which although had begrudgingly adopted her as some black-sheep of the family, still regarded her (even after many winters) as not truly one of their own. She was considered as somehow different, odd. To this day, often it can take generations to truly be accepted into a village's life.

Even the name O'Lant did not put Enixam off (though of course she knew it well) for she had been only a toddler when the clan's rule had ended, and in any case believed that you should learn things for yourself rather than listen to stories. Enix hadn't laughed at Patric's aspirations and travel plans, she hadn't patronised him; she had simply told him to go for it. Patric had told Enixam all about his goat, and his goat all about her. As the seasons had passed, though he would now find it harder to leave, Patric had found in the girl an even greater reason to return from the lands of opportunity a success. One day, though he dared not mention it then, he would ask Enixam to wed.

Enixam had delighted in Patric's slate-sketches, which he would bring with him each visit; From the well-executed images of the beasts of the forest, and landscapes that she'd never seen in life, to uncomplimentary comical scenes generally involving Hatric and Patric's brothers. In return, the girl had done a little drawing of her own. Using a small conical shell filled with a sea-weed dye, she had etched simple characters upon his left forearm, explaining that they were part of the scant memory of her mother and long distant people. The tattoo was comprised of two wading birds with long tapering beaks, three parallel lines, and a circle with a dot in the middle of it. As she had drawn, she'd sounded out the syllables 'En-ix-am', explaining that she drew a picture of her name. Though Patric was utterly mystified by the concept of the written word, he'd vowed on the spot that he would never wash his arm again. Bearing in mind Patric's general hygiene regime, this was however no great hardship.

As Dyloch the headman had brought a rather abrupt and half-hearted, mumbled congratulatory speech to a close, a fine rain had begun to descend out of a now dark sky. A vaporous cloud arose from the heaving, sweating throng below, as an unearthly host of writhing spirits in the firelight. A carpet of faces squinted upward into the refreshing light spray. Upon the beach and amongst the crowd, the torches had spat and hissed. Upon Dyloch's final word, he'd nodded curtly to Sarak, his shaman. Silhouetted as a giant against the rear cavern wall behind, Sarak had held his whale-bone staff aloft and gestured theatrically toward the audience before him with an outstretched hand.
'ONNI-ONNI-ONNI! He barked, pointing toward the lad below.
'OI-OI-OI!' the crowd responded as was customary, before (for the most part) falling into respectful silence.
'OKKI-OKKI-OKKI! Sarak had cried.
'OI-OI-OI!'
The old shaman had then dramatically taken in a great breath, before screwing his sunken, rheumy eyes tightly-shut. Then in exaggerated manner, he'd placed a hand to his chest and began a series of very loud, hacking coughs. The phlegmy, barking overture had echoed loudly within the wide cavern, before reverberating out over the crowd, and was interspersed by the puffing out of hollow cheeks and the gyrating of a bony jaw. To the obvious anticipation of the crowd, the shaman had then drawn back his angular head on a scrawny, turkey-like neck and gargled. All eyes had been on Sarak, as suddenly he had bugged out his bloodshot eyes, and with a violent whip-like motion, sent forth a flying globule of saliva which arced out into the night. Moments later, some twenty feet or

so below, the crowd had erupted into wild jubilation, as the glutinous projectile had wetly exploded on Patric's forehead with an audible 'splat!' Allen had grimaced. Sarak had raised a palm, acknowledging with pride the many cries of praise from the crowd. It was a shaman thing.

The fish were officially Patric's. The formalities out of the way, the Celts had commenced with the serious celebrating.

Amongst the clamour and the many faces, Patric had eyes for one alone, Enixam. As she uselessly wrestled against the tree-trunk arm of one of Dyloch's men, the girl's adoring eyes had streamed with emotion and pride. Her broad, quivering smile had caused Patric's heart to catch.

'Ah bless-im' Allen had said, giving Alexander a static gentle nudge. He'd then fallen silent, a questioning look on his face.

'He's got our eyes' he'd whispered, oddly only just seeming to have noticed for the first time. 'How the hell did I miss that before?'

Alex had smiled 'Ah! The ol' windows of the soul! It just means that you're seeing him more as a real person, accepting him more'.

'Yeah!' Allen had laughed, 'remember though! Only accepting him more…'

'…as part of a dream, yeah-yeah I know the speech' Alexander had finished.

'Odd though…' Allen again looked perplexed.

'What is?'

'Well his eyes don't give me the willies like yours do'

Alexander had laughed 'He's just further removed from you, that's all. Whereas I'm just a bit *too* close for comfort shall we say. The living often have a problem with having a *really* close look at themselves'.

Patric had raised his palms to the heavens, his eyes never leaving Enixam's, and silently praised Domi, and all the other deities of a great and beautiful creation who his father had lost faith in. Gods! It was good to be alive! If Hatric could only see him now! Even if the miserable bugger really did turn up and attempt to drag him off, Patric now seemingly had a lot of new friends who worshipped him, and who'd beat the living-daylights out of anyone messing with him. He was safe. He'd achieved, through his own efforts, the means to embark upon the first leg of his quest well provisioned; a first leg which his boyhood-dreams assured him would one day lead him back to Enixam in a position to ask for her hand. Though he was at the bottom of a cliff and at sea-level, the elated Patric had felt on top of the world. It was as if he stood alone, sure-footed, upon the giddying pinnacle of a mountain, above all those around him. He was master of the game, top-dog, instead of being kicked like one. For the first time in his life he felt truly proud of himself, and the elation of feeling like a winner for a change burned through him like an all-consuming fire.

He couldn't put a foot wrong.

He was untouchable.

He was in love.

He suddenly felt sure that a rosy future lay ahead of him.

He wouldn't, as his father would think, fuck it up.

He couldn't fuck it up, he was on fire.

Drunk on alcohol and the heady moment, the almost delirious boy threw back his head and howled like a wolf, an alpha wolf proclaiming mastery of all that he surveyed. Similar indeed to that of a particularly-wolfish estate agent, four and-a-half thousand years later, as he sped across Tower Bridge in a red Porsche.

'Ooops! He's fucked it up' said Alex quietly, almost as if he was speaking to himself.

'That's the O'Lantic war-cry, isn't it?' Allen had enquired, somewhat confused.

'Yep' Alex had replied in a somewhat sheepish, even embarrassed tone.

'Well, is it me or is that not very clever then?'

'Nope, not clever at all'

'Oh shit'

'Oh Shit-on-a-stick-*arama* mate'

The last resounding echoes of the bestial cry had finally died upon the cliff walls, to be met by a grim silence. The entire recently-raucous, cavorting crowd had been frozen in shock. Those old enough to remember that fearful and now-forbidden howl had felt their blood run cold, and the hairs on the back of their necks rise. The high walls of the cove had amplified the cry a hundred-fold so that many in the crowd had cried out in fear and cowered, their terrified gaze to the cliff-tops, as if expecting to see a host of the O'Lants, returned from their watery grave, baying for blood. All eyes had at last sternly fallen on Patric, a skinny boy who'd put the fear of the gods into all of them, and caused many to soil their kilts.

Enixam had sagged against the body-guard's bicep, dread and horror etched painfully upon her face.

From his lofty seat, Dyloch had arched a wrinkled eyebrow 'well that's handy'.

'I've still got it!' Sarak had chuckled, a gummy grin spreading across his face. Allen had eyed the two with distaste.

Cringingly for Allen, a euphoric and addled Patric had taken some moments to take in the fact that the party had died. Still in his 'reach-for-the-stars' swaying pose, he'd opened an eye, which after a brief roving journey, closed tightly as groggy realization of what he'd just done sank in.

'Oh crap' he'd said quietly.

To compound matters, the strengthening drizzle had begun to rinse the berry-juice from Patric's hair, sending dark rivulets down his face, and revealing his red flowing mane for all to see in the firelight.

He'd then punched himself in the face.

'We'll just forget about the fish then shall we?' Patric's wavering voice had been answered only by a low and growing reverberating growl from the encircling crowd. Celebrity being a fickle thing indeed, Patric's former fans now only wanted to tear him limb-from-limb.

'I'll be getting back then, it's been nice to get out' Patric had begun to slowly back away from the piled fish, a quivering smile fixed upon his face, eyes darting from side to side in the hope of an escape route.

'It's been great, really!' Patric had waved jovially at the snarling faces with one hand, the other sliding into his robe for the throwing stones, he was surrounded.

As one, the onlookers' furious gaze had risen to their enthroned master above.

By contrast, Dyloch's expression had been compassionate, almost kindly as he'd stared down at the slowly retreating lad. He'd smiled warmly.

'Kill him' he'd suggested.

From *The* Book, Allen knew that the inhabitants of the village had as much reason to hate the O'Lants as any clan of the region. The tribe's ancestors had been renowned fishermen, so much so in fact that it was said that they saw with the very eyes of the gull. A gull's eye had become their emblem, and was painted upon the prow of their vessels as they sped over the roof of the ocean. The catch of the Bird's-eye clan was said to be the freshest and greatest in variety of any tribe thereabouts, so that soon the neighbouring Celts had flocked from near and far to acquire their succulent wares. The village of the prosperous Bird's-eye clan had originally been located upon the cliff-top, proudly overlooking their rich fishing grounds. In front of their lodges had been wide stalls laden with the bounty of the sea packed in ice, thronged by the many travellers of the coastal path.

Unfortunately for the clan, it was their very reputation for having 'fish-fingers' (like green-fingers only smellier) which had at last brought them to the attention of the O'Lants. After a number of devastating raids, the Bird's-eye clan had abandoned their airy homes to take up residence in the concealed but very damp cavern below. Due to the fishy nature of their trade however, the O'Lants had soon sniffed them out. It was also due to the marauding O'Lants that travellers upon the coastal paths had dwindled, depriving the fishermen of their marketplace. Within a few generations, the standing of the Bird's-eye had diminished greatly. Indeed, it was in an effort simply to remain on friendly terms with the larger tribes of the area, that the weakened Birds-eye clan had begun hosting the Onni-Okki tournament. Even with the end of the O'Lants' tyranny, the Birds-eye never rose to the cliff-top again, for the largest neighbouring clan had claimed the vacated land above for their own. In the summer months, to add insult to injury, enterprising whores of the dominant clan had even begun to set up a tented-brothel upon the cliff-top, to catch the passing-trade, which had become known as 'The Fish Market'.

Patric had nervously loosened his favourite stick, which was slung across his back on a twine strap, and took a stone in each sweating palm. All around, a hundred stones were raised against him. The crowd closed in, at their forefront Dyloch's men, with death in their eyes and big sticks in their hands.

'Any of yer throws or strikes and I bleed on the fish!' Patric had cried, leaping backward to land ankle-deep in the pungent Onni-Okki prize. The fish would be inedible and therefore worthless, should they be defiled by accursed O'Lant blood. There were too many witnesses from other clans around to try and knock them out on-the-quiet after a bit of sluicing down. They'd have to be publicly destroyed.

Struggling to keep his balance, Patric had waded backwards deeper into the fleshy mound.

Dyloch had sighed and nodded to his shaman. Sarak had gestured to the brutish bodyguards below 'REMOVE THE UNCLEAN-ONE FROM MY LORD'S PROPERTY!'

'Oooh this is going to be *nasty*' Allen had closed one eye, only squinting through the other.

However, just as the ring of henchmen had reached the piled fish, a dark-haired young girl (obviously in a zealous attempt to be the first to injure the loathsome O'Lant) had slipped between two of the advancing beef-cakes, before screaming a high-pitched war-cry and launching herself at the lad. But to the dismay of the crowd, the enthusiastic maiden had seemingly lost her footing in the oily pile, and had taken an undignified headlong dive into the fish between the lad's legs, to then surface abruptly in his evil clutches.

'Wha-by-Domi's-big-one d'yer think ye playin at Enix?' Patric had hissed through clenched teeth.

'HE'S GOT ME SO HE HAS!' Enixam had wailed forlornly, ignoring Patric and reaching out imploringly to her audience. *'Tell em to let yer'* *go, or you'll kill me'* she'd whispered. Patric's expression had been incredulous, after a moment Enixam had elbowed him painfully in the ribs *'well!'*

'Er, MAKE WAY OR THE GIRL GETS IT!' Patric had cried with more confidence than he'd felt, and shakily raised his sharp-edged stone as if to strike.

'OH I BEG YER! PLEASE DON'T LET IM DO F'ME!' Near swooning, Enixam had continued to play her part well. Sympathetic and anguished cries had arisen from many amongst the crowd.

'OH GREAT LORD DYLOCH! M'MOTHER PUT HER TRUST IN YE, AND THE BRAVE MEN O'YER CLAN! CAPTAIN OF THE BIRDS-EYE! I PRAY YE! PROVE HER TRUST NOT IN VAIN!' SAVE ME!'

'Ye don't normally talk like that'

'Yer have to be more assertive Pat'

'IF YOU DON'T LET ME PASS I'LL KILL ER! I MEAN IT!'

'HE MEANS IT!' Enixam had turned the waterworks up to full output. In the crowd a girl had feinted, men had clenched their fists and growled dark oaths. From somewhere near the back had come a cry 'FOR GODS' SAKES! WILL SOMEONE DO SOMETHING!' Dyloch's men had looked to their lord before advancing further.

'That's our gel' Alex had said. Allen had taken a furtive peek through laced fingers.

Though she was of little concern to Dyloch, it was indeed true that following the death of her mother, the girl was a ward of the tribe. With so many visiting clansmen present, pride demanded that the Birds-Eye must be seen capable of protecting their own. With a caring and concerned expression, the headman had held out placating hands to the throng 'Get them away from the goods would you' he'd said quietly out of the corner of his mouth.

The shaman had stepped forward and made a parting gesture with his hands 'LET THE BLACK-HEARTED O'LANT PASS' he'd cried. With meaningful glances at the lad, Dyloch's men had obediently about-faced and proceeded to make an avenue through the enraged crowd.

'Don't go so fast!' Patric had hissed. Though the opposite had appeared to be the case, Enixam had half dragged the petrified boy through a narrow corridor in the scowling mob, to emerge upon the shingled crest of the beach. Beyond the quivering light of the bonfires there lay only inky-blackness.

'What now then? We can't get ti th' path from here'. With Enixam still in his embrace, Patric had turned with his back to the beached fishing vessels and the sea, attempting the impossible task of keeping an eye on everyone at the same time.

'Take a boat Pat, it looks like you'll be rowing yourself to the other side'.

'Wha? I've never been in a boat, nor handled one.'

'Don't worry! You'll learn fast with this lot behind you, and anyway I'll show you the ropes.'

'Wha d' ye think yer sayin, I'll not lead ye inta the unknown Nix.'

'It's the only way you'll get out of here alive Pat!' Despite his predicament, a future involving the close companionship of his beloved had been enticing. Especially bearing in mind that moments before Patric had thought he was dead, now seemingly he could have his future dreams made flesh there and then. However, he'd also reminded himself that he might very well, still end up dead at any moment, and if not on this shore, then perhaps on the further one, or most likely between the two.

'I can't do it. It'd not be right, to lead ye inta danger Eni. You're safe here, you're looked after. I've nothing to offer yer. And anyway no one goes to sea when Domi's not in the heavens! Not even the ferryman! Everyone knows that!'

'You've no choice Pat.'

'I dunno En.' Under the vengeful eyes of the crowd, the two had slowly retreated backwards, until they were amidst the boats.

From his birds-eye view of the unfolding scene below, Dyloch had noted that the fish were now safely out of blood-spatter range 'now, I think' he'd suggested. In answer Sarak had nodded to the head bully-boy, who'd been awaiting his signal.

At the sound of the first foot-fall upon the pebbles, Patric had instinctively shoved a protesting Enixam to one side, where she'd fallen backwards into one of the slender vessels, her bottom wedging firmly in the narrow aperture. Hopefully out of the firing line.

Grabbing at their groins and Pitching to the ground in silent agony, the first two henchmen who'd suddenly broken from the crowd to rush the lad, had fallen prey to Patric's two favourite throwing stones. Though Pat had received several sickening blows, the next three assailants were downed by his blurring favourite stick, as he'd performed the O'Lantic patterns-of-war-for-the-staff, learned over many years of watching his father drunkenly repeat the ingrained lessons of a hated childhood.

Having learnt caution, the half-dozen or so remaining thugs had looked to their master.

'Fiery-bugger that one!' Dyloch had grimaced. 'He's certainly an O'Lant, there's no doubting it!'

'A pity we couldn't be seen to hire him really, he'd be *very* useful' Sarak had commented.

'Indeed he would! Oh well, let it be ended.'

Sarak had signalled to the hulking head-bruiser once again, who in response had raised his palm. The entire crowd had screamed their rage and made ready to throw.

Allen had once again closed his remaining squinting eye.

A hail of stones had thundered down upon the overturned coracle under which Patric had dived for cover. As the infuriated Celts had broken into a wild charge, the low wicker-dome had lifted slightly off the beach, scuttling for the surf under a bludgeoning and continuous rain of stones.

'RUN PAT! RUN!' a trapped Enixam had cried out as she'd wriggled and squirmed to free herself, seemingly now forgotten by the blood-thirsty rabble intent on its quarry.

'GOO-ON! GOOO-N PAT! YOU CAN MAKE IT SON!' Allen had cried, peering over the top of his cupped hands, willing his dream former self on. Alex had looked on in silence.

Though bruised and beaten, running bent half-double under his protective shell, Patric had luckily made it to the water just before the crowd had made it to him. Flipping onto his back amid the icy surf, Patric had landed in the bowl-like boat, which had pitched and tilted wildly beneath him, threatening to capsize at any moment. The nimble lad however, had thankfully managed to stay upright in the tiny circular craft. Fortunately for Patric, the sea floor fell away steeply just beyond the water's edge, and a dragging rip-tide had drawn the spinning boat swiftly out into the blackness and away from the screaming crowd, as they recklessly plunged headlong into the breakers after him.

A pain-wracked and gasping Patric had curled foetal-like within the shallow hollow of the boat, his bloodied stick still clutched to him, as a hail of stones, sticks, and the odd spear fell in, and all around the boat. Luckily for the young Celt the throwers were pissed-up to a man, so that most of the projectiles overshot, fell short, or went wide of their target. However, Patric had groaned or cried out in agony time and again as the throws of those blessed by Okki had found their mark. Fortunately, Patric had not been struck by a single spear, for few clansmen had them to hand, and those that were carried at such an event were generally the showy, ceremonial-heirloom type, carried to impress rather than to be cast. There would be a few former antique-spear-owners who would wake upon the following morning with both a hangover and regret at having chucked their much-prized, bird-pulling, bloke-intimidating weapon into the sea in the heat of the moment.

A further stroke of luck for Patric was that due to the Celtic nature following a few bevvies too many, bows were banned at all such beery-gatherings.

Patric's grimacing, terrified features had been intermittently illuminated by thrown torches which had hissed as they'd winked out, extinguished in the waves. Yet much to his relief, the baying of the crowd had soon become muffled by the sea and the last half-hearted sticks and stones had plopped into the water behind him, as he'd been carried beyond their range by the outwash.

'Well bugger me! He's made it! Nice one Pat!' Allen had laughed, giving Alexander a static-slap on the back. Alex hadn't replied.

Though beyond the reach of the crowd, Patric's fear had been replaced by that of being an inexperienced mariner, alone in a glorified bucket at the mercy of the sea at night time. The roar of his pursuers had been replaced by that of the ominous boom of the ocean against rocks hidden in the darkness, the drizzle by salty-spray. None went to sea after sun-down, as none (except the ferrymen) ventured beyond the coastal waters even during daylight. For it was said that when Domi the great sun god did not look down from the heavens, the terrible giant beasts of The Dark One arose from their bottomless watery home, to devour any foolish enough to ride the waves under the stars. On certain still nights, their unearthly and haunting wails were carried across the ocean to the lands of quailing men.

'I think we'd better catch up with Pat, let's go.'

'Right behind you.' Allen had replied as he'd stepped off the ledge, following Alex out into the night. 'I'm glad to get away from those two I can tell you!' he'd added, gesturing back to the headman and his shaman, 'they give me the bloody creeps!'

As they'd passed over the heads of the frustrated crowd, Allen had noted that there appeared to be frantic activity going on below.

'It's a bit dark out here' Allen had commented, after they'd passed beyond the firelight of the beach. 'Where's Pat then?' he'd added, peering down into the darkness.

'Right below us, don't worry, they'll be some light along any moment.'

Still attempting to remain wedged rigid within the shallow frame, Patric had craned his neck and dared a furtive peek over the rim of the boat. In what must have been the direction of the shore, a dull band of orange light amidst the darkness was revealed and concealed in turn, as the boat climbed and slid down the waves. The distance between him and the light had been both reassuring and alarming at the same time.

'I'd rather the fish or the dark-one hisself av mi th'n youse basss-tuds!' he'd said aloud, to keep himself company, but without much conviction.

'AHH! WHA-the?..' Patric had then cried out, his head disappearing once more within the lurching boat. Suddenly the darkness had been banished as a crackling torch had sailed overhead.

A terrified, suddenly-sober three-man-crew had set out upon their long slender craft, under the stern eye of Dyloch's head-heavy and his bruised bully-boys. It had been pointed out to the reluctant and superstitious fishermen that a near-certain death upon the waves at night, was still better than an absolutely-certain one, right there and then on the beach. Under the eyes of the other clans, Dyloch wanted a body, or some form of evidence that the fearsome O'Lant had indeed perished, and that it was the Bird's-Eye who'd accomplished his end.

The boat had been tethered with a line, which had been taken up by the crowd. The knotted rope was fed out hand over fist as the narrow boat was poled into the darkness, torches burning upon its pitching prow and stern. Laying down their poles across the out-rigging, two of the nervous crew had squatted, striving against the spray-crested breakers with narrow-bladed oars, whilst the third had stood between them at a burning earthenware brazier, slender harpoon in hand.

Experienced hands had steadily driven the sleek craft through the black ocean, whilst the frightened look-out had lit, and then cast, a succession of torches out into the darkness ahead, afraid of what he might see. No one went to sea after dark.

'Bloody-Hell!' Allen had gasped as Patric briefly appeared in the amber glow some feet beneath his.

Fear heightening his senses, the look-out had lived up to his clan's name. His sharp eyes had immediately picked out the tiny boat and its occupant amid the rolling walls of water.

Struggling to keep his balance, Patric had gingerly knelt upright in the unstable coracle, as the brightly-lit craft hove into view and bore down on him.

'C'MON I'M NOR SKED O'YER! C'MON! BIRD'S-EYE IS IT? YEAH I'VE GOT FISH-FINGERS TOO! COZ YER WIVES ARE KINDA-FRENNLY! IF-YE-GET-MI-MEANIN! C'MON NOW YER WIMMIN! IF YER GOT THE STOMACH T'FACE AN O'LANT THAT IS!' At this point it had seemed to Allen that Patric's voice had gone very 'drunken-Irishman-down-the-pub'. In an effort to keep his own terror at bay and hopefully also annoy his enemy into making poor casts, Patric had embarked upon a torrent of verbal-abuse. The traditional Celtic opening of hostilities. He'd held his trusty splintered staff ready to deliver a blow or deflect a throw. His equally terrified enemy had remained silent.

When still at some distance from the screaming lad, the front oarsman had laid aside his paddle, and had taken over from his fellow with the torch-hurling. The formerly-jittery harpoon-thrower, had appeared to calm as he crouched, taking his stance to cast.

'YER EEJUTS YER!..OH SHITE!!' still hurling a barrage of insults in the flickering weak light, Patric had seen the tell-tale tiny white splash upon the back of the wave in front of him too late. The lad had been expecting a harpoon cast, yet the wily fisherman had loosed a throwing stone with his free hand, using 'the skimmer', an ancient throw used to stun leaping dolphin and seals in the oceans, or trout and salmon in the rivers. A throw known even to this day by the same name, yet the modern equivalent is but a weak reminder of its skilful and lethal ancestor.

The fisherman had unleashed a beautifully-judged, curving three-bouncer with extra under-spin. Even as Patric had realized his error, the wickedly spinning rock-disk had leapt up from the ocean beneath his guard, and struck him hard upon the temple.

'UH!' Patric's eyes had glassed over as the bloodied stone had dropped into the boat with a dull thud. His favourite stick had clattered against the side of the boat before falling into the dark ocean. Moments later an unconscious Patric had followed it.

Upon the fishing boat there had been no cheer, no cry of celebration. Not wishing to proceed further into the blackness, the panicky crew had hastily harpooned and retrieved the capsized coracle, before making for the shore with grim determination, crying to the crowd to pull harder.

'Is that it then? Patric drowns? What a way to go! Poor bloody sod! Not much of a life was it?' Allen's shocked voice had been shaky in the blackness.

'Don't talk to me about drowning mate' Alex's voice had been matter-of-fact 'been-there-done-that, got the bloody-body-bag son!'

'Oh yes, sorry, I forgot..' Though Allen constantly reminded himself that he was dreaming, he'd still been unable to prevent himself from feeling a little tactless.

'No worries Allen. Don't get me wrong now, it'd be nice to leave the world under a lady sure! But if it's your time, drowning's as good a way to go as any other! Better than some! Though it all adds up to the same thing at the end of the day.' Alexander had chuckled before continuing. 'Not that it really matters you understand, but I must say watching my own dissection afterward was odd! The cheeky buggers only had mi-ticker didn't they! I was fished out of dear-ol father Thames the same day you see? I only got that piggin-donor's card to impress the birds that go for the conscientious-type-bloke! I arrived in the hereafter singing 'EYE-EE LEFT MY-YY HEART-TAH! INNA PAPWORTH-GENERALLL!' Alex had adopted the 'pub-singer' style. Allen had nervously joined Alex in laughter.

'So, some poor-sod ended up with the heart of an estate-agent!' Allen commented, his own laughter increasing.

'Yeah-yeah-yeah, ha-dee-bloody-ha. Actually a vicar did, a perfect match apparently!' replied Alex, 'kept the randy ol' goat going for another ten years bless-im. He died of pneumonia, his lungs filled with fluid, he drowned. You see what I say? One heart, two drownings? It's all the same in the end.'

'Alex-mate, I swear, you give me the fucking-willies.'

109

'That's what I'm here for Allen. C'mon, let's be getting back to the beach.'

'So that's it? We just walk away? It doesn't seem right somehow, like maybe we should stay here with him for a little while, out of respect or something? Ah shit I don't know..' Long moments had passed in the blackness, with only the sound of the ocean below. *'Alexander?'* There had been no answer. Allen was alone in the night. 'Hey! ALEX! WAIT UP WILL YER!'

'A very satisfying conclusion to the evening's proceedings I'd say, wouldn't you?' Dyloch had reclined in his macabre chair, as below, Patric's battered coracle had bounced above the heads of the jubilant, chanting crowd. The beer was flowing again, and five-men's weight in fish now lay safely back in the cold-store. At the centre of the wild frivolity, the three fishermen (all now heroes to the crowd) partied the wildest.

'Indeed my lord', Sarak had agreed.

'Ah! Before I retire, tell me, what *was* the name of the feisty lass earlier? I've noticed her before'.

'Ah, I believe she is known as *Inegs-im* my lord, or some such foreign name. A spirited child indeed, if perhaps of course a little rash,' the old shaman had chuckled.

'Rash? Enthusiastic certainly'

'*Enthusiastic,* of course my lord, the very word I was searching for, the blessing of the young.' The shaman had not managed to remain at his master's side for so many years by disagreeing with him.

'Yes Sarak, a *very* spirited *woman* indeed! Inegs-im is it?' Dyloch's old eyes had scanned the crowd. 'And a pretty little thing to boot.'

'My lord unerringly as ever, has an eye for beauty.'

'Odd, I've not seen the wench since the O'Lant was slain, her bravery should be rewarded Sarak.'

'Er, yes my lord, of course. I believe the maiden lodges with Moch the weaver'.

'Ah, the estimable and dependable Moch, but tell me does he not already have three daughters of his own to support?'

'As ever, my lord is once again right'.

'It seems to me an unfair burden on the poor man.'

'That I believe, if you'll forgive me, were his very words my lord, these many summers past when you decreed that he should shelter the girl.'

'Were they indeed?' Dyloch had cackled, 'Upon the morrow you shall go to the weaver with my words and two-men's' weight in fish. Advise the goodly Moch to send the girl to me. His burden shall be lessened, and my wives, and in time my sons, shall be increased.'

'Two men's weight my lord? Surely would not one-goat's-weight be sufficient?'

'Two men's-weight shall it be Sarak! I am captain of the Birds-eye! Let it be seen that I have fish to spare! That's what the young-beauties *really* like! A bit of affluence! Not some snotty-whelp with half-a-kipper in his kilt! I am besotted and wish to make a gesture that reflects the depth of my feelings!'

'As you wish my lord Dyloch, so shall it be done.'

Below, the celebrations were building to a crescendo, and in true Celtic style, the embracing, fighting and dancing had merged seamlessly. Though he raised a hand in farewell to the crowd, Dyloch had smiled, noting that hardly anyone noticed his departure. 'The mark of a good party', he'd said as he allowed his shaman to help him to his feet.

'Indeed my lord', agreed Sarak.

Leaning on a stick and his shaman's bony shoulder, Dyloch had gingerly hobbled to the fresh-hold of his modest hall, before halting and turning to his equally-ancient advisor. 'Ah, there is one more thing my faithful Sarak'.

'My lord?' enquired the shaman.

'Have you heard whispers that over this last cycle of the seasons, on two occasions boats have put to sea only to discover that their holed deep-sea net had not been mended?'

'That is a grave matter my lord, for it takes the food from our peoples' mouths', replied Sarak darkly.

'Indeed, a *very* grave matter.'

'Do these whispers tell of which of the weavers is responsible for such a grave dereliction of duty?' Sarak had enquired, before adding 'for I have not heard these whispers'.

'Then see to it that you and others do.'

'Yes, my lord.'

'And then see to it that I do.'

'Yes, my lord.'

'And Sarak, it is my understanding that it is Moch whom mainly weaves our strongest nets for deep-sea fishing'

'Oh dear my lord.'

'Oh-dear *indeed* my good Sarak, of course Moch is a valued member of the community! He has rendered many years of loyal, and-until-now, faultless service. Indeed, has he not raised my beloved Anig-som as one of his own?'

'Certainly a man of good-character my lord!' agreed Sarak.

'Indeed! So, I shall levy only the lightest of penalties for each of the two offences as is decreed by our forefathers'.

'That being a man's-weight in fish for each net?' Sarak had intoned.

'The very same! Now Sarak, you'd need not bother yourself with this matter for a couple of days or so, no need to put a dampener on the conjugal-festivities after all!'

'Indeed, my lord.'

'Goodnight my shaman.'

'Goodnight my lord'.

'You could've bleedin waited yer know.' Allen's voice had been extremely irritable and edgy as he'd emerged from the deeper blackness, and joined Alexander at Enixam's side. The forlorn girl sat alone upon the water's edge, beyond the firelight of the wild and abandoned celebration. Alex had remained silent.

'Poor cow.' Allen's anger had dissolved instantly, as he'd seen the tear-streaked, wretched expression of the girl who looked like a younger Maxine. Enixam stared woodenly into the darkness, hands outstretched to the heavens, her trembling lips moving soundlessly in prayer to her gods. As the early hours of the morning had slowly passed, the two men had remained in silence at the sobbing girl's side. Behind, the sounds of revelry had diminished until at last they had ceased all together, the bonfires and torches reducing to glowing embers one by one. By the arrival of the cold black hours heralding the approach of dawn, the three had been left completely alone upon the pebbles.

'Well Alex, all I can say is, if this dream is meant to be teaching me something, it's to bloody-well stay put and know when you're well off, and don't be too adventurous! Look where *going-for-it* has got the pair of you silly-sods! frigging drowned! That's where!'

Once again, Alexander had made no reply. Instead, Allen's words had been answered by a sudden gasp from Enixam. With a whoop of delight, she'd jumped up and sprinted into the surf, joyously proclaiming heart-felt thanks to a string of deities.

For in those moments, a nearly-full moon had sunk beneath the sullen canopy as it merged with the far horizon, crowning the crests of the waves before the trio with dim milky ribbons, and revealing a sprawled, boy-sized form beached upon the shingle only a few paces ahead.

'Who said Patric had drowned?' Alex had smiled wolfishly in the moonlight.

'You bastard!' Allen had replied, before following after Enixam.

Patric had his father to thank for both his ability to swim, and for being able to hold his breath underwater for some time. In *The* Book, Allen had witnessed an infuriated Hatric chase his son into the sea on a number of occasions. Raised as a coastal dweller, Hatric could swim, yet had found himself unable to enter the sea ever since the terrifying night of the O'Lants' downfall. Though he knew nothing of its cause, Patric was aware of his father's deep aversion to entering the waves, and therefore the ocean had often become the boy's sanctuary. Both in calm and heavy seas, many was the time a self-taught Patric had found himself treading water, often for hours on end, as his father ranted and raved upon the beach. But drunk or sober, Hatric could throw a mean skimmer with the best of them, and hence Patric had been given much practice in remaining submerged.

Luckily for Patric, he'd only been momentarily stunned by the fisherman's cunning throw, and the sudden embrace of icy water had actually revived him. Thankfully, the fishermen had returned to the shore almost immediately, albeit with Patric's boat, allowing him to gratefully resurface.

Struggling at times to remain conscious, a numbed, bruised and battered, yet stubborn Patric had remained afloat in the shallows of the cove, only to be returned to shore upon the incoming tide in the early hours, sometime after the last reveller had collapsed.

'Ah! Domi be praised!' Enixam's beaming face had been stained by fresh tears, this time of relief, as she'd crushed a still-breathing Patric to her bosom. Then, with the aid of the advancing breakers, she had at last managed to drag the half-conscious, mumbling boy behind a boulder, just below the beached fishing-vessels, hidden from the village above.

'He's resilient! I'll give him that!' Allen had exhaled, impressed at Patric's endurance. 'Of course, if this wasn't a dream though, he'd be dead-as-you-like, wouldn't he?' he'd added.

113

'People are often capable of great feats when it really matters' Alexander had replied quietly.

'Oh! My Pat! What've they done t'yer?' Enixam had whispered, with pain in both her voice and expression, as she'd tenderly inspected, and attempted to treat, Patric's many wounds.

'Can ye hear me Pat m'darlin?' Patric had remained incoherent, his gargled breathing shallow and uneven.

'C'mon Patric, it's Enix, come back to me now!' The girl had pummelled the slumped boy repeatedly upon the back. Suddenly Patric had broken into retching coughs and splutters, before violently ejecting a stomach-full of beer and sea over Enixam.

'Very nice! He's got a way with the women that one!' Allen had sniggered. To his surprise however, though covered in vomit, Enixam had cried out with joy and thrown her arms around a groggy Patric, covering his bruised face in kisses.

'You're not wrong there matey' Alex had replied.

When at last she'd seemed happier with his condition, Enixam had gently laid Patric back upon the shingle, a torn strip of her flowing tartan-robe cushioning his head.

'Urr..' Patric had half-opened an eye, and shakily tried to lift a hand to his beloved's face, before falling back into exhausted-slumber.

'Now you lay still there my Pat, I'll be back for ye in no time, and don't worry, I'm going to getcha outta here. I've got a plan!' Planting a further kiss on Patric's forehead, Enixam had risen before vanishing into the darkness, heading toward the further end of the cove. As dawn drew closer, and pitch black gave way to a steely-grey, Alexander had taken up a seated position on the boulder, whilst Allen had gone for a paddle.

'Ah here they come now' Alexander said, gesturing along the beach.

'They?' Allen replied from behind the boulder. With a final shake of his head at the extent of Patric's injuries, he stood up. In the early morning sun, Enixam reappeared from the jumble of boulders under the cliff face. She clutched a bundle to her, and a tall figure hooded and cloaked in black, carrying a long staff, trudged over the pebbles behind. 'She's got the ferryman with her.'

'Indeed she has' replied Alexander, before adding 'She's a star that one!'

'She is, isn't she' said Allen with a smile, thinking of Maxine.

Some moments after, Allen stepped out of the way as Enix crouched at Patric's side. After covering him in a wolf-skin pelt which she'd brought with her, she cradled Patric's head, before pouring drops of water between his swollen lips from a drinking-skin.

'Patti, oh Pat m'luv' the girl cooed whilst gently patting the boy's cheek. For a moment, a bleary-eye half-opened, before closing again.

'Nix?' Patric's voice was a croaked whisper.

'Now Pat, I've bought the ferryman to ye'

'verry-min?'

'Yes Pat that's right, n' he seeks an apprentice! He'll take you with him!' In response Patric only groaned, returning to delirium.

'It must be the boy's choice, for the way of the ferryman is not to be taken lightly.' The low, hissing voice of the cloaked figure was harsh and rasping.

'Looks like the grim-reaper, sounds like the grim-reaper' Allen commented with a shiver.

From *The* Book, Allen knew that the ferrymen were a strange and solitary breed, surrounded in occult myth and legend. Their emblem, which Allen had seen for himself placed at the top of the path leading down to the cove, was a freshly cut sod of lush turf, denoting that the grass was always greener on the other side, and that a ferryman awaited to take you there. They carried people from the land of the dead, to the land of the living; That is, they carried people whom believed their own land held no future for them, to a land where a new life could be lived. More often than not, the ferrymen also brought them back again.

Up and down the coastline which faced the lands of opportunity, during the spring, summer and early autumn months, the ferrymen repeatedly made the crossing, never tarrying long on either shore, always departing at daybreak, so as to make landfall before dusk.

The role was handed down from father to son, as were the hooded black robes, and apparently-magical staff. If an elderly ferryman was without heir, he would take an apprentice, who would be treated like a son. No one ever saw a ferryman's face, for they wore skeletal-masks which hid their features. It was well known that the masks were in fact the front portion of their dead father's skull, worn so that the son could look out through the more experienced eyes of the father upon the treacherous waves.

The ferrymen were said to understand the voices of the gulls, for it was believed they shared an affinity. The seabirds were beloved by the boatmen, for the seabirds warned of impending foul weather, and ensured that the ferrymen never lost their way upon the ocean.

The ferrymen spoke seldom, unless it concerned a fare. They were judges of men and set their fee according to the nature of the passenger. As to how the figure was arrived at was a closely guarded secret within the trade, and was a constant source of irritation to travellers. The ferrymen saw it as their duty to ensure a would-be migrant had really thought about the great step they were about to take, and therefore had to ensure they charged enough to make it hurt. During a crossing, a ferryman would never speak, and their nervous passengers were generally happy to let them concentrate on the job in hand. None dared slay a ferryman, for they were believed to be akin to the shamans. Before each departure, they would perform strange rituals in a trance-like state, involving much chanting, gesturing and spitting, to ward off evil and ensure a safe passage.

Each day the ferrymen faced death upon the uncertain ocean, and no other dared to venture beyond the sheltered coastal-waters. For the ancestors of the Celts of the region had made their migrations many generations before, and sea-travel had become a lost and unnecessary art.

Though they were thought of as outlandish and strange by the coastal-dwellers, the ferrymen yet bought a prosperous traffic through the villages from which they sailed, and were therefore tolerated. However, the population in general shunned those who wore the black robe, thinking of them with contempt, though none would dare show it openly.

During the winter months, the ferrymen lived a solitary life apart from the coastal-dwellers, often upon uninhabited tiny off-shore islands, or lonely hill-tops. All in all, the way of the ferryman was indeed not to be taken lightly.

Enixam gave a dazzling smile 'Ah tis what he's always dreamed of oh noble ferryman! Never stops goin on about it in fact! Bores me senseless with it so he does! Always goin on about tides and what-not! Drives me to distraction sometimes! Why else d'yer think he travelled all the way here?'

'Why else indeed?' there was wry mirth in the ferryman's dry voice, as he stared down at the animated curvaceous beauty, seeing reason enough before him for any red-blooded lad to make a journey.

'G'on now Pat! Tell the man!' Enix dug Patric sharply in the ribs, raising a groan.

'You see! Itching to go so he is' the girl implored in earnest.

'So it's nothing to do with him being an O'Lant then? An O'Lant who'd best disappear sharpish if he's not to meet Domi just a little bit earlier than expected?'

'She's been rumbled' Allen sighed.

'Please sir, you're his only hope! Though I know the name of his clan, he's always been a loyal and true friend to me! He'll prove to be an asset to ye I'm sure! He even has experience!'

'Experience you say?'

Enix gestured to a sodden Patric, who was festooned with seaweed 'well you can see he's already been to sea.'

The ferryman chuckled before enquiring 'Now why would I wish to help one of the wolf's-head clan m 'dear? Tell me that?'

'Cos he's kind of soul, that's why! Cos all he's ever known is hatred and anger! And why? All because of a name he didn't even pick! That's what's brought him here to this sorry state! He deserves a chance!' There were tears once again in Enixam's eyes as she gestured to the brutally-beaten lad.

'Alright-alright' the ferryman placed an arm around the now sobbing girl's shoulder, shrouding her in the folds of his dusty cloak. 'So it is in the world I'm afraid my child, as you will learn, sticks and stones may break your bones, but a name can *really* hurt you.

117

CH 11: CROSSING THE WATER

'Young lady, do you have *any* idea how much it would upset the Birds-eye and other clans hereabouts, if it were known that a ferryman had rescued an O'Lant?' Enixam's expression fell at the ferryman's words. The ferryman looked thoughtful for a moment, as if contemplating his own words, before adding 'well that's as good a reason as any to give the lad a chance I suppose!' He spat in the direction of the village.

'Oh thank you! Thank you, most noble and honourable ferryman! Thank you!' Enixam jumped up, flinging her arms gratefully around the gruesome figure.

The ferryman's usually-authoritative tone took on a higher, reedy pitch 'Er, it is not usual etiquette to embrace a ferryman you know.'

'Sorry' Enixam gave him a final squeeze before relinquishing her grip, and wiping tears from her eyes. The ferryman coughed into his fist a couple of times before continuing. 'As it would appear that everyone's a little worse for wear this morn..' he looked toward the still-quiet fishing-village above, which ordinarily would already be a hive of activity even by this early hour '..this matter shall remain between you and I young maiden.' The ferryman's tone was once again stern.

'I shall never tell a living-soul my lord, I shall take it with me to Domi.'

'Good-girl'. The ferryman turned from Enixam and sank to his knees, the tattered folds of his black cloak falling about him, until he was almost nose to nose with Patric. 'Well son, is it to be the way o' the ferryman for ye?' moments passed with nothing but incoherent, slurred mumbles from the lad.

'C'mon now, Pat is it? If yer t' go with me, it must be by yer own word' a bony, mottled and weathered hand gently shook Patric's shoulder. 'D'yer understand me boy?'

Enixam joined the crouching figure at the boy's side, before leaning forward and placing a warm kiss on Patric's blood-encrusted forehead. Unfocused, blood-shot eyes slowly opened *'Aye, I understan-ye ferri-m'n, I- I'll go wi-yer, if ye'll av me'*

'Then settled it is! Good!' The ferryman slid an arm under Patric's shoulder, and using his staff for support, lifted the lad into a seated position. 'Come now lass, help me get him to the boat, we must catch the tide, and miss the gaze o' the Bird's-eye. Hurry now!' Though he'd regained groggy consciousness, Patric's legs were like jelly, and he hung limply between Enixam and the ferryman as they half-carried, half-dragged him across the glistening pebbles upon the water's edge, toward the further end of the beach. Anxious minutes dragged with many furtive upward glances to the sleeping village. Adding to the pressure, many of the long, slender fishing-vessels which they passed were occupied by a snoring Celt. Allen and Alex followed after.

To their relief however, the scrambling group made it to the towering far-wall of the cove without the alarm being raised.

'They really have got the luck of the Irish this lot!' Allen laughed.

The ferryman and Enixam carried Patric through a gap between the cliff-wall and a leaning giant slab of rock jutting from the surf, to emerge on a narrow-shingled strip, walled off and concealed from the main beach and sloping into the sea.

Perched upon the crest of the slope lay the ferry, resting on two beams sunk into the wet gravel. It was a wide, low-sided, flat-bottomed vessel, with a single tall mast, suitable for transporting men, beasts or goods. Too small to be called a ship, too big to be described as just a boat, the vessel was fashioned from supple planks, pegged and lashed together. The tapering prow and stern curved upward in a graceful arc, and the entire hull of the craft glistened with black pitch. Further beams, greased with animal fat, were laid end-to-end in two lines in the shingle, forming a slip-way down into the water.

'Right! Let's be gettin im aboard then.' The ferryman's voice echoed under the overhanging wall of the cliff, as he and the girl mounted wide timber steps leading to a stout wooden platform level with the ferry's deck. Patric groaned in pain as he was lowered upon a large black pelt, draped over bulging sacks of grain.

'Yer safe now mi darlin, never you fear Pat!' Enix whispered 'You'll be mended in no time! Ye see if yer not! You'll be back after the wintering, hailing me as you come in t' land, a ferryman's apprentice no less!'

Luckily for Patric the job would come with the apprentice's uniform, a brown hooded-cloak which would hide his features from the Bird's-eye, otherwise of course he would enjoy an extremely short career. Enix's hair and tears fell about Patric's face as she lent down, hugging him in farewell.

'Come now lassie, for we must be away.' The ferryman placed a gentle but firm hand on the girl's shoulder.

'I'll let yer be on ye way now Pat, may th' grass be green on t'other side' Enix's voice was hushed as she placed a gentle kiss on Patric's bruised cheek. Once again only semi-conscious, Patric made no response. The ferryman offered his arm to the tearful girl as she stepped back onto the log-platform.

'I'm forever in your debt ferryman' she said hoarsely.

'No my child, do not imagine that I do this as any favour.' The dark figure looked back to the lad 'for there are no free rides in this life' he said, repeating the motto of the ferrymen. 'And anyway my dear,' he continued, 'you are not indebted to me, rather we are nearer even'. Enixam looked at the masked figure with confusion, but he turned from her without further explanation, pacing swiftly to the rear of his craft. Once there, he took up a sure-footed stance facing the prow, one hand gripping a hempen-rope which ran from the stern-post up to the cross-beam atop the mast, the other holding his staff over the side of the ferry. Peering intently into the waves below, the skeletal-masked figure waited.

'Ferryman! Are ye not to perform yer rites of protection?' Enix asked, confused.

'D'yer see an audience?' the ferryman laughed. Enixam looked shocked. 'Now stand clear girl!' he cried as he raised the black stave, before bringing it down in a single, well-practiced blow, dislodging the timber stake wedged under the hull as a brake. There was a dull grinding sound followed by a screeching of tortured-timber, as the craft began to inch ponderously forward. Upon the deck, the ferryman took his staff in both hands, and drove it into the gravel to increase momentum.

'Fare-thee well Patric! May all-knowing-Domi smile down on yer till our next meeting!' Enix whispered as the ferry rumbled past, gathering speed as it slid toward the surf.

With the well-honed experience of a lifetime, the ferryman had timed the release of his vessel with exquisite accuracy, so that as the ferry dove headlong into the sea, it rode the backwash of a wave which had broken upon the pebbles only moments before. As the swift craft was carried out into the bay, the ferryman yanked sharply upon the rope running up to the mast, and a single rectangular black sail unfurled with a sharp snap, drawing the vessel with greater speed out of the shallows.

With her invisible companions following behind her, Enixam rushed back down the steps, under the stone arch, and scrambled down to the sea edge below the village, just in time to see the vessel pass between the gates of the cove and out into the wider ocean.

'Well there he goes. You were right Alex, looks like Pat caught the ferry in the end after all' smiled Allen 'shouldn't we be catching up with him though?'

'In a while' replied Alex.

Behind and above, Dyloch's head-henchman groggily emerged from his master's hall, and shuffled slowly to the ledge's edge. He blearily noted the diminishing black sail with a grunt, before being noisily and violently sick. From below, disgusted and indignant cries erupted from someone who'd obviously been in no fit state to climb back up to the village the night before.

Enixam sat upon the pebbles, as she had in the dark hours before dawn, staring fixedly out to sea through tearful eyes. The single black sail was now a shrinking finger on the horizon. She remained so as the morning grew, until at last the ferry passed beyond view.

'Looks like we've got company' Allen turned, as he heard the sound of trudging feet in the shingle behind.

'Er Enix, I've some news for yer..' Moch the weaver could not meet the girl's eyes as she turned toward him. 'Sarak has paid me a visit this morn..' he began, his voice unsteady, 'it seems our lord Dyloch wishes to honour our family...' Over the years, an initially-indignant Moch had grown to love the fiery child as one of his own. However, none dared question the will of Dyloch.

'Dirty-ol'-coffin-dodger! He's old enough to be her bloody granddad! Poor bloody Enix!' Allen growled angrily, shaking his head with disgust, as he and Alex strode some feet above the foaming waves in pursuit of Patric. 'Bloody-hell! Poor bloody Patric! He'll lose it when he finds out!' In answer, his guide only gestured toward the fast-approaching arching stern of the vessel. As they drew alongside the pitching ferry, the two took up seated positions in mid-air, keeping pace with the rising and falling deck.

It was now approaching midday. Above, framed by broken cloud, windows of deepest- blue sailed across the heavens, born on the invigorating sea air. Below, Autumnal sunlight transformed the slate-grey waves into glinting rolling walls of darkest-blue.

'Uh? Ah mi ed!' Patric groaned as he awoke, placing a now-bandaged hand to his throbbing temple. 'Agh, b-by the gods'-*kin*-knackers!' As he raised himself up onto a grazed elbow, the lad grimaced, his eyes screwed shut against an explosion of sharp-pains, twinges and dull aches throughout his protesting body.

'Ah! The sleeper awakes!' The ferryman cried jovially as he lent casually against the curving stern-post, his hand upon the steering-oar.

121

Patric shielded his eyes against the sunlight, 'w-water!' he croaked.

'My! You're a pretty-un this day, and no mistake!' the ferryman erupted into hoarse laughter at Patric's swollen, purple and black features. 'You'll find the water just there son' he added in a kinder tone, gesturing to a lidded earthenware-urn lashed to the mast next to Patric's makeshift sick-bed.

Wincing in pain, and only half-awake, Patric struggled into a hunched seated position. He then gratefully ladled water between his cracked, bloated lips, and over his aching head. Still exhausted, he blearily stared past the ferryman's shoulder at the rising and falling horizon in the distance. After some time, he was rather noisily sick over the side.

'Oh bloody choice! Cheers Pat!' complained Allen, a man whose former-self had just vomited *through* him. Alexander chuckled.

When at last Patric was able to sit upright without retching at the motion of the sea, he dragged himself to the water urn once more, submersed his head for long moments, before rising for air and shaking his shaggy mane like a dog. At last he raised his head to stare back at the broadly smiling ferryman. Patric knew the ferryman was smiling because the black hood was pushed back, and the gruesome mask removed, revealing a scalp and chin of white-stubble, weathered yet-strong, lean features, and twinkling blue eyes. Though well past his prime, and in the autumn of life, the ferryman was yet ruggedly handsome.

'Er? Y-Yer mask ferryman' the boy stammered 'Yer not wearin it!'

'No lad, that's for the punters, you'll learn'.

Patric's puffy expression was one of confusion 'But what of the *looking through the eyes of yer father* bit?' he asked. 'It's well known by all to be the custom amongst you ferrymen, part of your power over the waves I mean'.

'*Power over the waves?*' the ferryman chuckled before continuing 'Oh you mean the ol' wearing-yer-dead-dad's-face bit.'

'Well yeah?' Patric's voice was uncertain.

'So you think me some kinda fuckin-sicko then do ye boy?' the ferryman's tone was harsh with annoyance. Allen and Alex chuckled.

'No, no not at all good master!' Patric's voice piped with fear, he held up a consolatory hand. No one messed with a ferryman, everyone knew that. If you did, then death, the great ferryman, would come for you, to take you to the *other* side.

'Oh yeah! That's right son!' the ferryman spat '*Oh hang on there dad, seeing as how you don't need it now, don't mind if I just saw yer face off*

*before we pop yer body under the cairn do yer? Hold his head mum would
yer.* Yeah that's fuckin-right boy!' Shaking his head with disgust, the
ferryman ceased his rant, before meaningfully spitting over the side, never
taking his eyes from the horizon ahead.

'Look, I'm sorry! I didn't mean to offend ye, it's just that's what everyone
says,' the young Celt protested with sincerity. There was only the creaking
of the hull and the sound of the sea for some time, until the ferryman burst
into laughter.

'It's okay lad, I'm only having you on!' the old man's face split into a
wide grin. 'That's what we like others t' think.'

'So, whose face is it then?'

'It's no one's son, each apprentice must fashion their own. Some carve the
drift-wood that salt and sea have burned chalk-white, some use a flat
animal-bone, some mould their mask from clay. As long as it deceives the
eye, it matters not'.

'But why d'yer wear a mask at all then?'

'Ah! An inquisitive lad! That's good, that's *very* good! Attempting to
cross the water is a hazardous affair m' boy. For folk to put their very lives
in our hands requires a sense that we are apart from other men. The mask
adds a required air of mystery..' The ferryman paused as he lent hard
against the steering-oar '..and helps keep the prices up!'

'Oh' said Patric.

'Also lad, the merchant doesn't like to see the face of he who witnesses
their greed, for we know how much he can afford to pay. The pauper who
seeks his fortune in the lands of opportunity, only to return a worn-out
pauper, doesn't like to see the face of he who witnesses his failure. The
brave warrior who cries like a babe, or the lord who loses his lunch amid
the towering waves, does not wish to see the face of he who witnesses his
shame.'

'Oh I see..' Patric's tone was unsure. After some contemplation, the young
Celt's face broke into a lop-sided smile. 'Ah! I get it! Yer powers lay not
in the mask, but in the staff!' Patric pointed to the ferryman's staff, which
was tied securely against the inner hull. He knew, as all did, that you'd
have to be mad to try and cross the sea once, let alone regularly, unless
you were under magical protection.

'No-lad!' said the ferryman slowly with resignation 'that's just for getting
the ferry off and on the beach. It's for unhooking driftwood and other such
flotsam from the hull. It's for stopping those thieving-bastard-gulls having

it away wi me lunch. It's for all manner o' boring day-t'-day jobs too
numerous and mundane to mention.'

'Ye sure it's not magical? Everyone thinks it is ye know' Patric stared at
the eldritch tapering pole, which curved at one end like a scythe.

'It's also for clouting those who persist in asking annoying questions' the
ferryman growled and spat once more into the brine.

'Don't you mind me' Allen's tone was terse as the globule of saliva was
whipped by the wind up between his eyes, and through his skull.

'Hang on!' said Patric, 'thieving-bastard-gulls? I thought the winged
messengers of the sea-gods were beloved by the ferryman? I thought they
were yer guides upon the ocean?'

'Ha! One o' the hardest parts of the job for a ferryman is trying to keep a
civil-tongue in yer head in front of the punters, when those vermin-on-
wings are having it away with half yer brekky! We hate the buggers!' the
ferryman scowled.

'Oh' said Patric, another illusion shattered.

'Look son' the ferryman said kindly, 'as you go through life you'll soon
realise many a bugger likes to shroud their job in mystery! It makes em
feel wiser and more important, and makes others think the job's harder
than it really is! The truth is; most people can do most jobs!'

'So, what *is* the source of your power over the waves then?' Pat asked,
seemingly oblivious to his new master's earlier reference to clouting.

'The source? I'll tell yer what the bloody source is sonny! It's a lifetime
spent in crossing and re-crossing this same stretch of bleedin water, that's
what it is! Long afore yer was even born! From the time I could first walk,
through countless gales and storms t' this very day, I've made this-ere
crossing. I was taught the turning of the tides, the ways of the waves, and
the signs of the storm by my father as he was by his. As ferrymen have
always been taught, down through the generations! Yes, we ferrymen have
a power, that power is knowledge, a hard-earned knowledge. Knowledge
is power son.'

'Knowledge is power' echoed Patric, listening intently.

'But be aware boy..' the ferryman continued '..our knowledge, though it
be amassed over the lives of many, many men, is no true shield against the
sea, against the elements. None can ever know all there is to know'. The
ferryman paused, and leaned forward in conspiratorial manner. 'I'll let ye
inta a little trade-secret boy, seeing as how yer wish to don the brown robe
n' all'. Patric strained to hear the next words over the sound of the waves,
and the cry of a solitary thieving-bastard-gull.

The ferryman's voice was hushed, 'We ferrymen have no power over the waves, no one does. Many of us perish upon the sea, to be replaced by others that wear the mask, without another soul even noticing that there has been a change of ferryman'.

'Shi-it!' Patric exhaled, looking nervously about himself at the vast surrounding expanse of undulating water. No one would travel beyond the coastal waters unless they had magical power over the sea. Everyone knew that. He was all at sea, alone with a nutter.

'Perhaps today son, somewhere out there is the wave with my name on it!' the ferryman pointed out across the sea.

'What *is* yer name ferryman?' asked Patric.

'It's Ferryman'.

'Oh'.

'And so will your name be, upon the very day that the great ferryman comes for me'.

'Oh' said Patric, not expecting a name-change to be part of the job description. 'A bit confusing I'd imagine at ferryman gatherings and celebrations, all having the same name I mean' he added, unable to prevent himself giggling.

'We don't have any' the ferryman replied dryly.

'Oh' said Patric, a teenager who'd just been told parties were out, and who suddenly felt less than safe. The ferryman smiled broadly at his passenger's obvious discomfort.

'Don't worry boy! I'll get ye safe t' the other side never-yer-fear, tis mild and gentle for the season, and we'll make landfall afore nightfall.' The ferryman laughed at Patric's anxious expression.

'Afore nightfall yer say? But the lands of opportunity still seem so far off! As far off as ever they have!' Patric pointed past the ferryman's shoulder, to the thin slither of darker-grey land which lay on the far horizon, a thin slither of land that the boy instantly recognised, because he had gazed upon it, and dreamt about it all his life. The ferryman looked at the boy with bemusement, before glancing backward. He returned his gaze to Patric 'That's yer homeland yer damn fool!' he guffawed. The cloaked man then nodded ahead, gesturing for Patric to turn around 'There lies our destination boy!' he cried. Patric painfully turned, the black-dyed hide sail billowing just above his head. 'Domi-save-me' he whispered. Beyond the high prow of the ferry, a craggy mountainous coastline rose upon the near horizon. Though still some way off, individual peaks and ridges could be discerned.

'But it looks like home!' said Patric, confused.

'Of course it does lad, what did ye expect?'

'I-I suppose I just thought it'd be different somehow, I dunno..' Patric lapsed into an embarrassed and thoughtful silence. Following some contemplation, Patric's eyes glazed over and his mouth turned upward in an uneven smile 'So there lie the lands of opportunity' he whispered, shaking his head, almost in disbelief at the evidence of his own eyes.

'It is said amongst us ferrymen,' the old man's words interrupted Patric's daydream 'that *where* the lands of opportunity lie, depends upon *which* coast you stand. For is it not said amongst men that the grass is always greener on the *other* side?'

'Indeed it is' agreed Patric, a devout lifetime follower of the greener-grass philosophy.

'But it is also said amongst us ferrymen that the greenest grass may never be seen, for in truth it lies beneath your feet, for who truly knows if they shall see another dawn?' The ferryman raised his silvered eyebrows for emphasis. But Patric's mind was elsewhere, thinking of the sickly wind-blasted grass he had grown up on, grass upon which his father had beaten him, grass that had instilled within him a deep-held belief that the grass anywhere else would be hell-of-a-lot greener. *'That sounds like bollocks'* Patric thought to himself, as he considered the ferryman's last words. 'That sounds *very* wise' he answered diplomatically. The ferryman chuckled.

'Yer think ye could manage some food now do yer lad?'

'Aye! That I could!' Though in pain, exhausted, and still feeling a little queasy at the motion of the sea, the teenager suddenly realised he was famished, for he'd eaten nothing but a knuckle-sandwich for over a day.

'Good!' The ferryman said, securing the steering-oar with a leather strap. 'Then we shall eat and talk together'. The old man strode across the rolling deck with ease, before bending to retrieve an oiled-skin bag from behind the swaying mast.

Taking a seat at Patric's side, the ferryman untied the bag at his feet, delved into it, and retrieved a succession of small leaf-wrapped parcels, a wooden platter, and a flint knife.

'GAAN-YER-WHORE-SON!' the ferryman cried, and the thieving-bastard-gull which had alighted upon the prow at the aroma of fish, launched itself back into the air with a defiant shriek.

'Have yer anything else at all master?' enquired Patric, who although starving, had seen quite enough of fish.

'Bit picky are we now lad?'

'No master, it's just that somehow I'm off fish today'.

'Understandable I suppose, it's not every day five-men's'-weight slips through yer fingers, now is it?' The ferryman patted Patric's back in sympathy before continuing, 'An' yer damn-near got away with it as well lad! Pity really. That Dyloch's slipperier than his fish. It would've been nice to see someone get one over on the oily bugger!' The old man chuckled, replacing the charcoal-dried mackerel upon the platter in his lap.

'Ye saw the match then?' Patric smiled.

'Aye that I did son, but not from the crowd mark ye, we ferrymen keep ourselves to ourselves as you'll learn, we sail and sleep in our boats, it's less complicated that way, trust me. I watched from the cliff-top'. The ferryman paused as he lifted a sardine to his mouth.

'And what did yer think?' enquired the young Celt.

'That yer throw... as Onni... hisself!' said the ferryman between bites. Patric beamed.

The ferryman finished his mouthful before continuing '..and that yerv wasted too much o' yer time learning to throw stones! Time that could've been spent doing something far more useful son'. The ferryman burped, and tossed the stripped bones over his shoulder.

'Sod this! I'm moving!' Allen glowered as the fishy mess sailed through him. Rising, he moved toward the stern, before once more taking a seat in mid-air above the waves. Alex chuckled.

'Well there were many last night who thought me blessed by the gods for my throwing!' Protested Patric indignantly, his bruised cheeks flushing red.

'Wha? These would be the same fine folk who tried to kill yer straight afterward would it now?' The ferryman asked in mock-innocent tone, whilst unwrapping a further leafy parcel. Patric didn't answer.

'Here lad, take no offence now' the old man said warmly, offering Patric strips of roasted-rabbit, a selection of berries, and a somewhat wrinkled apple. Despite his bruised feelings, Patric greedily accepted the food, and ravenously began to devour it.

'Oh for fu..' Allen cried, jumping up in fury as the berry-stone which Patric had just violently spat out over the sea, inevitably passed through both his ears. 'How bloody-comes nothing ever hits you Alex?' he demanded.

'Because I'm not as pessimistic as you are mate, that's why! You expect bad things to happen to you, so they do'

'Oh up yours!'

'Charming mate! If this is your dream..' Alex gestured around them, '...as you keep insisting it is, then it's you who's imagining *that* for example', the dead estate agent nodded his head toward the second fish bone the ferryman had just thrown straight through Allen, even though the annoyed clerk had moved yet again. Alex smiled an annoying smile, Allen sulked in silence. Patric and the ferryman ate.

The meal was punctuated with loud verbal outbursts and violent gestures from the old man, as a succession of seagulls alighted upon the deck, lured by the chance of food. Patric was impressed with the boatman's obviously intimate knowledge concerning the differing breeds of seabirds, for apparently, they had been visited by a number of species including an 'effing-bleeder,' a 'robbin-bugger', and a 'fetid-puss-sucker'. A 'bollocks-on-wings' had apparently enraged the ferryman to such a degree that he even threw a pebble at the screeching creature, only just missing it. Patric had smiled to himself as the bird retreated into the air. The lad was well versed in throwing technique, and noted the old man had deliberately pulled his shot at the last moment, intentionally missing his target. *'So not so gruff as you like make out old man'* he thought to himself.

'I must say lad..' the ferryman began to chuckle, wiping juices from his lips with a sleeve, '..there's no doubting mi highlight of last evening..' he paused as the chuckles became laughter '..was yer sh-shrieking out the ol' family w-war-cry!' The ferryman's laughter grew to hysterics, until, with tears in his eyes and struggling to draw breath, he repeatedly slammed his fist against the hull in an effort to regain control of himself.

Patric's earlier red cheeks had now turned a deep purple, as he sat simmering in silence. Wheezing and coughing, the ferryman shook his head and hugged his aching ribs before asking 'What in the many-hells were yer thinking of boy?'

'When you're still suffering from the hangover, there's nothing more excruciating and annoying than some smug-bastard going over your antics from the night before!' Alex said, shaking his head.

'Amen to that' agreed Allen, before pointing at the ferryman 'Oi! Leave the poor sod alone!' he cried with empathy for his former self, knowing full well that when he awoke from this dream, he'd be nursing a gargantuan hangover of his own.

'It's that stinking piss-for-beer those swine gave me!' Patric spat angrily, 'it had some devilry put on it by that bastard-shaman I tell yer! M'Da always tol' me, nevva-trust-a-shaman!'

'Oh, a dodgy beer' said the ferryman gravely, only just managing to prevent himself slipping back into the giggles.

'The ol' fabled dodgy-pint!' interjected Alex 'the mystical bane of the hung-over'.

'By Domi though lad!..' the ferryman gave a still-glowering-Patric a hearty slap on the back '..it did mi heart good to see those buggers near-shit their selves!' he added, laughing once again. Patric didn't answer.

'By the dark-one's cavernous-arse! I even had a look over mi shoulder misself when yer cry went up!' the ferryman exclaimed. 'We all remember the days o' the O'Lants!' he added, shivering noticeably.

'Everyone does! Except me so it seems!' replied Patric angrily, throwing his hands and the remainder of his lunch into the air. Allen refused to let his annoyance show as the shower of food rained down on him alone. Alex diplomatically pretended not to notice.

'Sure enough I suppose, yer being but a whelp n' all' said the ferryman 'yer da never boasted to ye of the ol' days then?' he enquired. In answer Patric only shook his head and laughed bitterly, as he recalled the nature of the education he'd received from his father. The ferryman winced, reading the pain in the boy's eyes.

'Yeah, I know sod-all about the O'Lants!' Patric growled 'but it don't seem to stop everyone hating me guts for bein one!'

'C'mon now lad! Take a jest will ye!' the ferryman cajoled 'Would I have taken yer under mi wing if I truly thought bad of yer! Well would I now? Would I have saved yer from the Bird's-eye?'

After some moments Patric raised his head 'I suppose not master' he said, a smile returning to his face at last. The ferryman retrieved a drinking-skin from his bag, which he offered to Patric.

'Shall we drink to it then lad?' he enquired, untying the chord.

'I think I'll stick with the water for now if yer don't mind' said Patric, looking a little green as the musky aroma of beer reached his nostrils. The ferryman laughed before taking a deep draught from the skin.

'So yer truly know nothing of yer folks' ways then lad?' the old man asked.

'My da wasn't the talking kind.'

'It must be said young Patric, that despite their many faults, your kin were good for business'. There was a glint in the ferryman's eyes as he rubbed his hands together, 'folks made the crossing in droves to get away from the mad-fuckers!' he then fell silent, lost in reminiscence.

129

'So yer don't live by *the nick-knack* then lad?' the ferryman suddenly asked, staring intently into the boy's eyes, as if to read any deceit in his answer.

'The nick-*what?*' asked Patric, genuinely mystified.

'Never mind boy' said the old man, satisfied that the boy was sincere. He then gave Patric a brief account of the gory history of the O'Lants, as he knew it.

Allen knew all about *the nick-knack* from *The* Book. The nick-knack, paddy-whack, give-the-dog-a-bone, had been the O'Lants' clan motto, the code by which they'd lived their violent and dishonest lives. O'Lantic warriors had to possess the knack of stealing, or nicking. *The Nick-knack.* They had to be able to deliver a punch as hard as only a true-blooded Celt can. *The paddy-whack.* And in a raid, they had to be prepared to rape even the extremely ugly.....

'Shit! That explains a bloody lot!' said Patric, his mind reeling as the ferryman brought his brief account to a close.

'Well lad, I can't chatter all day! The wind's a changing!' the ferryman said, rising and hastily replacing the remaining food and drinking-skin in the bag, before stowing it back behind the mast.

'She's a beauty' the old man said, lovingly stroking the upright post as he straightened, 'but she needs her master's hand' he added, striding back to the steering oar.

His thirst and hunger satisfied, Patric yawned deeply, the sea air and the rocking motion of the boat lulling him back toward sleep.

'Yer get ye rest boy, I'll wake ye when we make land, yer done in, and t' be honest ye look like boar-shit'.

'I-I'm fine, honest' Patric shook his head, in an attempt to stave off impending slumber.

'If yer say so lad' the ferryman smiled.

'So why did ye..' Patric stifled another yawn '..why *did* ye take me on then ferryman? Me being of O'Lant blood I mean'.

'Well lad, after last night's performance there's no doubting you possess talent. Secondly, this is the last crossing of the season and it's high-time I took an apprentice, an if I don't oblige Domi and take up this chance he's offered me, I'll have ti wait till after the wintering t' look for another. Finally, the young lass vouched for ye, an I've known her since she was in her mother's belly..'

130

'Ye knew Enixam's ma?' interrupted Patric, his senses suddenly alive.

'Aye, that I did son'.

'But how? Enix remembers little of her'

'We ferrymen never talk of those we've carried'.

'Then it was you that brought her to our land?!' Patric cried, 'In truth ferryman, I'm indebted to yer!'

'Is that so? Taken with the lass are ye then by any chance m' boy?'

'Aye ferryman, that I am' Patric said, almost bashfully. 'One day we'll wed!' he added, with greater confidence. For was he not now apprenticed to a worthy trade?

'Will yer now indeed?' the ferryman mused.

'Shit, Pat's in for a shock' said Allen, who knew that the betrothal of the young girl to Dyloch was being announced to the Bird's-eye this very day.

'Indeed we will wed master!' repeated Patric, 'I'll not let yer down! I'll work hard, and be as good a ferryman as has ever crossed these waters! So I'll be able to offer Enix a good life, as wife to a boatman!'

The ferryman made no reply. Allen cringed, Sarak was probably practising the wedding-ceremony as they spoke.

'Yer truly have love for her then boy?' the ferryman asked.

'Aye master, I do'.

'And she you?'

'Yes, I believe she does' Patric stroked his left fore-arm, as he'd become accustomed to doing, ever since Enix had tattooed her name on him.

'I am hers' he stated simply, 'Look master, this is token that she thinks of me as her property, she's put her very name on me so she has'. Patric removed his hand and held up his bared forearm.

The ferryman looked up from the boy's arm in confusion 'these ol' eyes are perhaps not as sharp as once they were, but you'll forgive me, I'm not quite clear about what I'm supposed to be looking at son.'

Patric looked to his outstretched arm, there was nothing there except a brown smudge. A night spent in the sea had erased Enixam's handy-work.

'Ah no!' He gasped in anguish. For long moments he hugged himself, eyes glazed, his mind back across the sea with his beloved. 'A bad omen' he whispered to himself, wondering if this was some dark token of the fates, signifying that he would never see Enix again.

Allen looked down at the brownish smudge on his own arm, and then to Alexander, his expression questioning.

'That's the reincarnation game for ya, same cast, same script, just different scenery, what can I say mate?' Alex said with a shrug. Allen looked uncomfortable 'freaky-dream' he said quietly, thinking of Maxine, and whether he'd see her again.

After a while, Patric seemed to come to, a resolve now in his eyes 'Yes she loves me' he said simply.

'Well lad, perhaps it's not my place to say..' The old man paused before continuing, as if deciding upon the right words to use '..But if I truly loved a lass, I'd never wish her to wed a ferryman, have yer not wondered as to why it is I have no son?'

'What d'yer mean master?'

'I've no son, because I've no wife Patric. I've no wife, because to be wedded to one our kind, is to live a life of solitude apart from others. A life of being politely shunned and feared by those around yer, a life of yer husband being away most of the time, and wondering if he'll return each time he puts to sea..'

'But I love her!' Patric interrupted, his voice raised.

'Then maybe ye should consider letting her go boy, it's a harsh and lonely life that she would have'

'NEVER!' there was fire in Patric's eyes 'we don't need anyone sept us!'

'Calm yerself lad, calm yerself now! It's yer own life after all! You'll do as you'll do I'm sure, like all of us!' In answer, Patric remained silent, his mood black. Again, there was only the sound of wind and wave for some time.

'Come now Pat! Forgive an old fool, and his scorn of young love. I was simply asking ye to consider the life yer choosing for yer intended, that's all' the ferryman said in a consolatory tone.

'Aye master I hear yer, but I'd rather not talk of the matter!' said Patric irritably.

'As yer wish boy, an I don't blame yer for carryin a torch for that fine lass! She must be a very old-soul of much understanding, to have love for one whose kin made her an orphan!' The ferryman returned his gaze to the approaching horizon.

'Yer addled so yer are ol' man!' spat Patric angrily, rising to his feet, bruised fists clenched at his sides 'Enix's ma was taken by the fever!'

'So she was' agreed the ferryman 'but it was the O'Lants who came and took most of the village's store of fish as winter was comin-on. Many starved or fell sick, the girl's mother bein among them! As I recall yer grandda paid with one half-dead goat, said he was feelin generous.' The ferryman shook his head in disgust at the memory.

132

As understanding registered, Patric slumped under the weight of what he was being told, the fight gone out of him. Pulling the wolf-skin tightly about him, he turned his back to the ferryman, facing the prow. Huddled, he sat with his knees tucked under his chin, shivering amid the spray, his expression haunted.

'Families eh?' said Alex wryly.

'Yer sure she knows?' Patric asked after a while.

'Aye, the Bird's-eye remember that winter well, as so they should. They recall the sorrow of their loss with solemn ceremony, and celebrate the fact that later the very same winter, the gods wrought terrible destruction upon your clan.'

'But Enix never said anything!' Patric's voice was shaky.

'As I said, a *very* special girl.'

'Yeah..' said the lad, his mind in turmoil. The ferry drove on through the waves.

'AGH! URRRR! For Usar's sake!' Patric squinted angrily up into the afternoon sky, as the yellowy-white sticky mess seeped into his hair and ran down his face. As the offending seagull wheeled overhead, its cry sounded like taunting laughter. Allen and Alex sniggered.

'HE THREW THE STONE!' Patric shouted up at the bird, pointing to the ferryman.

'That's very lucky yer know!' the old man said, smiling broadly, 'It's a token that the gods smile on ye' he chuckled.

'Is it really' A dejected Patric wiped at his face and hair with a corner of the pelt. The voyage continued in silence. By the approach of mid-afternoon, Patric had once again slipped into a deep slumber.

'Wha?' Patric awoke with a start and sat bolt upright, jarred from uneasy dreams by some loud noise. As another horn-blast arose from behind him, Patric span around, rubbing the sleep from his eyes. Still at the steering-oar, the ferryman stood with a black ram's horn pressed to his lips, his eyes squinting into the mist which now encircled the boat.

Daylight had diminished into the sombre grey of approaching dusk. Flickering torches burned upon the high stern and prow, casting weak dancing shadows across the deck.

The ferryman cupped a hand to his ear, straining to hear over the muffled sound of waves breaking on treacherous rocks. Patric's head whipped around to face the front, as a distant answering horn call came. The ferryman smiled as he heaved against the steering oar, turning the vessel toward the lowing sound.

'Yer woke just in time t' see journey's end lad!'

'*See?*' said Patric, shivering in the chill air of evening 'I can't *see* anything!' The enshrouding mist appeared to be thickening.

'SHI-IIT!' cried Patric in abject terror, as a towering dark shadow suddenly loomed out of the billowing greyness directly ahead of the ferry. 'Ah! Hab's finger!' cried the ferryman gleefully, as he wrenched violently upon the steering-oar, causing the vessel to pitch sharply to one side, and Patric's stomach to lurch. The ferry veered past the foam-wreathed jutting pillar of black rock with only inches to spare. Clinging to the mast, Patric turned white.

'Y' alright lad?' the old man laughed amid the suddenly wilder-water and drenching spray. Feeling his lunch rising to his mouth, a petrified Patric was unable to answer as the ferry bucked and dived.

'And now for Amrin's-gate!' the ferryman shouted as a wave broke over the side of the railing, raising a scream of terror from the quailing lad. Patric buried his head in the sodden pelt, as out of the fog two further great giants materialised in their path.

'Whaa-haa!' the exhilarated ferryman laughed manically, as the boat was washed between the jagged twin cliff-faces. Allen and Alex followed, Alex sliding through the air above the churning white water in surfing pose, Allen strolling along behind, hands in pockets, shaking his head in embarrassment at his companion.

As the speeding craft emerged from the narrow gateway, the ferryman winded his horn once again. Again an answering call came, now audibly closer, even over the growing boom and roar of the sea.

'*Domi-save-us-Domi-save-us-Domi-save-us..*' Tightening his arm-lock on the mast, Patric fervently repeated the prayer, his eyes screwed shut.

'Brace yerself lad!' the ferryman cried, over the sound of crashing waves and the suddenly-loud hiss of foaming water on sea-smoothed stones. Grimacing, Patric half-opened his eyes and squinted into the coiling mist ahead. Out of the thickening grey wall a faint amber glow appeared momentarily between wave crests.

'Uofff! Argh!' Patric's head bounced off the mast with an audible thud, as the scudding vessel mounted the pebbles with a jarring jolt and a grinding of timbers.

'Yer see lad! Tol yer I'd get yer here safe as can be!' His vessel now at rest, the ferryman raised the steering oar, and held out a hand to the crouching lad.

Patric emerged from the wolf's-pelt rubbing his forehead. 'We're really *there* then?' he whispered nervously. Seemingly the lad had achieved his lifetime's ambition of reaching the gateway to the lands of opportunity. 'Oh yes lad, we're *there*' the ferryman said with mock solemnity, before replacing his macabre mask with a chuckle.

CH 12: THE OTHER SIDE

'Ah, the rugged majesty that is the western coast of Scotland!' Alexander cried, throwing his head back and spreading his arms wide, as he stepped down onto the wet shingle beside the beached ferry.

'Well it's a foggy rugged-majesty I must say! We could be any-soddin-where!' Allen replied, seemingly unimpressed, peering inland into the uniform grey blanket. Ahead, under growing darkness, only a few feet of wet pebbles were visible.

'HALLA-HOCH! HALLA-HOCH!' a man's voice rang out from somewhere near at hand within the thick fog.

'Halla-what?' said Allen.

'Oh come on Allen mate, concentrate will you! It's just another Celtic dialect! Very close to the one you've understood perfectly well up till now mate!' Alexander's voice had taken on the tone of the disappointed primary-school teacher.

'Well do-oo excuse me why don't you!' Allen stuck his tongue out at his companion, before returning his attention to unfolding events.

'OVER HERE LADS!' the ferryman cried in answer, leaning from the prow and waving a torch in the air above his head. A nervous Patric peeped out into the impenetrable fog from behind his master.

'Understanding it now are we!' asked Alexander.

'Yes thank you' Allen replied, raising two fingers.

Suddenly from within the fog an orange glow appeared, which grew until the shadowy forms of trudging men emerged. The eight bearded Celts were taller than those of Patric's region. Their shaggy dark manes hung to their shoulders, and they wore heavy furs. Two held torches aloft, whilst their kinsmen each carried a greased-log nearly as large as themselves.

'Ah Kimah! Reliable as ever!' the ferryman greeted the men's leader using his business voice. Kimah nodded his head curtly in response, 'master' he intoned, without meeting the old man's gaze.

'Your payment's aboard as is usual', the ferryman nodded toward the sacks of grain upon the deck, 'I'll leave her with you' he added, patting the tapering prow. 'Take good care of her, I'll return upon the morrow to see she's settled in for the wintering.'

'Aye master' replied Kimah.

'Right lad! Let's get yer bones afore the fire!' The ferryman turned, retrieved his staff, and assisted a limping Patric to the side of the ship. Demonstrating the agility of a much younger man, the ferryman leapt overboard, and landed sure-footed upon the pebbles. He turned and gestured for a hesitant Patric to follow.

'Yer sure it's safe master?' the dubious lad eyed the foreign pebbles below with wary suspicion.

'Come now lad' the ferryman said softly in his own voice, 'yerv nothing t'fear', under his cold mask the old man's face wrinkled warmly in a grin. Grimacing in pain, the lad straddled the low timber railing, and allowed the ferryman to grasp him about the waist. As his feet neared the frothing pebbles, Patric inhaled deeply and grimaced.

'Ye can open yer eyes now son' the ferryman said kindly. Patric clenched his fists before daring a downward glance. Despite his worst fears, Patrics' trembling feet and ankles apparently hadn't been devoured by this alien land.

'Wait ere, I'll just be a moment' the ferryman whispered, before striding purposefully toward the prow where Kimah and his men stood waiting. The boatman halted in front of the vessel, facing it. He then knelt, and reverently placed his staff upon the pebbles at his feet. Rising, he delved into his robe. He then urinated upon his ferry.

After having adjusted himself, the ferryman retrieved his staff, and gesturing to Kimah, re-joined Patric.

'Yerl excuse me lad, just some more of the bullshit that goes wi this game' the ferryman whispered quietly to the frowning lad. The ceremony completed, the Celts busied themselves with laying the timber rollers in front of the ferry, in preparation for drawing the vessel up the beach.

'Follow, apprentice' the ferryman said loudly, once again using the business voice, before setting off into the enveloping fog, vanishing in moments. Patric hobbled painfully after his master. Alex gestured Allen to follow. Some paces on, a terrified Patric thankfully found the old man waiting for him.

'Jus for appearances yer understand?' the ferryman whispered, 'we boatmen must be seen to be above all hurt' he explained as he reached under Patric's shoulder, 'lean on me lad'. The two set off inland once again, though in the fog and near-darkness, Patric had lost all sense of direction, as had Allen. After some time, a cluster of dull orange lights emerged out of the coiling darkness ahead.

'Master?'

'Ah, that's just the fisher-village, that's not for us lad.' The ferryman guided Patric past the inviting pale amber glow, until in moments it was swallowed by the cold darkness.

137

'Ferryman?' ahead, a man's voice came out of the fog, causing Patric to start.

'Aye' replied the old man in his business voice.

'I seek passage master' a cloaked lone figure materialized out of the greyness, a bulging sack slung over one shoulder.

'The last crossing of this cycle of the seasons has been made, seek me again in the Spring'.

'But master! I cannot bear another sunrise on this gods-forsaken rock! Domi smiles not upon me here, I must cross to the land of opportunity yonder! I can pay well!' The stranger's tone was desperate, and edged with fear.

'I thought the fog dulled the eyes not the ears! Did yer hear me not my son' said the ferryman curtly, drawing himself up to full height and fingering his staff menacingly. The stranger stepped back, bowing his head, before turning and disappearing once more into the fog. Allen thought he heard sobbing.

'But *these* are the lands of opportunity' whispered Patric, confused.

'As I said lad' chuckled the ferryman, 'where the lands of opportunity lie, depends upon which coast yer stand!' Patric didn't answer, but looked back toward where he thought his homeland lay, his expression unsettled.

'Oh yes, people always think they can move away from their problems, without realising that most times they're taking them along' Alex commented. 'It's part of what keeps yer dad's and my old-game going!' the ex-estate agent added.

'Let's be on our way' said the ferryman in the thickening fog.

'D'yer need no torch master?'

'Lad, I've trod this path times uncounted, I'd know my way blindfolded'.

'That's good master' said Patric nervously, finding himself at the foot of vertical rock face. Before the group, a narrow path rose steeply into the fog. But true to his word, the ferryman unerringly led the shuffling boy up the precipitous track, even though the last light of dusk had now departed.

'Wow!' whistled Allen, emerging from the fog onto the crest of the cliff top, as if rising from beneath the steaming surface of a pool of water. He turned back toward the sea. At ankle height, the billowing, almost luminous carpet rolled out into the blackness before him, floodlit from above by the near-full moon and a star-strung jet heaven.

Catching up with Alex, Allen followed Patric and the ferryman inland. What had begun as a gradual rise of grassy tussocks and ground hugging vegetation soon steepened into the barer slopes of a towering solitary hill.

As the incline increased, a rough track appeared that climbed to and fro across the hillside between rocky ledges. Thankfully for an exhausted and pain-wracked Patric, the path levelled out at last just below the narrow-domed summit, coiling about the shoulders of the hill, leading around toward its landward side.

As the fog-bound sea disappeared from view, the travellers emerged on a natural shelf some forty paces or so across, facing inland. The flat, grassy area was sheltered from ocean gales by the stubby rocky hill-top to its seaward side, which rose above it to some four-men's height. Silhouetted against the night sky, it reminded Allen of a nipple, crowning the vast breast of the hill. He said as much to Alex, chuckling.

'Indeed' laughed Alex, pointing to a similar proportioned hill further down the coast, 'this and its twin are known locally as *Um-Karra-Lae'*

'Big-Pair-of-tits?' giggled Allen, bilingually.

'You got it!'

'This guy sure likes his solitude!' chuckled Allen from the ledge's edge, peering down an extremely steep slope into the blackness below. Beyond, across a misty, densely-forested valley, a range of hills marched off into the icy moonlight.

'Certainly no problems with neighbours!' agreed Alex.

The ferryman helped an ashen-faced and wheezing Patric to the rock-face of the giant nipple, before seating his charge against it. In the middle of the cliff-face, a cave entrance, roughly ten-paces across and a head higher than a man, opened onto the ledge. The opening was walled up with broad timbers, and at its centre there was a heavy wooden door set in stout posts. On either side of the doorway, a ram's skull leered. The ferryman deftly untied the thick hempen rope that held the door closed and pushed with his shoulder.

'Ah' he said with satisfaction, removing his mask. From within, the welcoming orange glow of a hearth fire illuminated the doorway, and an outwash of warm air caused the old man's face to break into a grin.

'Come now lad! Let's get yer weary self warmed through!' The ferryman helped Patric to his feet and led him across the smoothed stone slab of the threshold. Alex and Allen followed. To his surprise, Allen found himself in a pleasant chamber. The roomy, yet cosy cavern was floored with heavy beams covered in glossy thick pelts. The curving stone walls and ceiling had been white-washed with lime, and heavy furs hung upon the timber outer wall, shutting out the night's chill. At the rear of the cave, in a natural alcove at knee-height, a roaring fire of thick logs burned and crackled merrily, the smoke winding upward into some natural hidden-fissure in the rock. The fragrant aroma of freshly-burnt dried-sage pervaded the air. On the left-hand wall, a drawn curtain of heavy hide hung from a beam, revealing a further chamber beyond. The small sleeping-recess was roughly the floor space of a double bed and was floored with piled furs.

'How is it that the fire is set' breathed Patric in awe, sure that he had indeed at last witnessed an example of true ferryman magic.

'Ah, that would be her-as-does-for-me from down the village. There's always a fire upon the hearth and the furs have been freshly beaten whenever I return home', the ferryman chuckled at Patric's disappointed expression. The boatman assisted the lad to a low, high-backed bench set before the fire, fashioned from split logs and draped in pelts. Then, striding to a waist-height, flat-topped boulder at the centre of the chamber, which seemingly served as a table, he lifted the lid of an earthenware pot. 'She's a treasure' he added. The rich aroma of roasted meat and boiled vegetables wafted around the room.

'Well lad!' exhaled the ferryman with a satisfied belch, 'd'yer feel a little closer to the living for that?'

'Aye indeed I do master, my thanks' replied an equally bloated Patric, placing his platter at his feet. The two reclined side-by-side on the stone-age sofa, their feet warming before the fire, each sipping from a beaker of warmed beer. Minutes passed in comfortable silence, the fire crackled. Outside came the drone of a rising gale, adding to the cosiness.

'Well isn't this cosy' commented Allen, sitting in mid-air at one end of the sofa, hands behind his head, staring into the mesmerising fire.

'Indeed it is' replied Alex, similarly seated, from the other end.

'Better in the nostrils than in the belly' commented the ferryman sagely, breaking wind loudly, before enquiring 'so what did ye think t' the crossin then lad? Think yerl find yer sea-legs do yer?'

'Er great master, very er *exciting*' said Patric with a fixed grin, and an inward shudder as he recalled the terrifying climax of the sea voyage. 'Can't wait for the waves to be beneath mi feet again, to be sure master' he lied.

'So Patric, what *was* yer intention then son, if not to be a ferryman, that yer watched mi comings and goings over so many seasons?'

'Y-Yer spied me then?' stammered Patric, shocked.

'Of course, the eyes of the ferryman miss little. It comes with the long watching of the waves'.

'An yer never gave me away?'

'Twas not my affair that yer were on the land of the Bird's-eye lad. So why was it yer watched me so closely? Travel plans perhaps?'

'Perhaps' echoed Patric nervously.

'Come now Pat, yer can tell me son'.

For long moments Patric remained silent, before answering sheepishly, 'Well, it was a boyish dream I had, to travel to the lands of opportunity..'

'Ah! The fabled lands of opportunity!' the ferryman chuckled, shaking his head with obvious amusement, 'te seek yer fortune I suppose?'

'Well yes....' Patric trailed into embarrassed silence, before hastily adding 'But of course now I've a worthy trade master! I've no need of such childish fancies!'

'Indeed not' agreed the old man, staring into the flames. Again, there was a period of thoughtful silence before the ferryman spoke again, 'Be not ashamed lad, I've carried many across the water from your homeland who searched for the lands of opportunity. Many who wished to follow the white serpent over the hills, four days march toward the rising sun, and then twenty or so, toward Baloth'.

'White-serpent? Baloth?' enquired Allen, perplexed.

'The serpent is a chalk hill-path, Baloth is their name for Aquarius, which is on the southern horizon this time of year' explained Alex. 'So that's four days east, and twenty south to you'.

'Oh'.

'Four days toward arising Domi, and twenty toward Baloth, to the land of opportunity you say?' murmured Patric quietly, almost as if he'd meant to think it rather than say it out loud.

'So they believed lad' confirmed the ferryman without taking his eyes from the dancing flames. After some minutes the old man arose with a yawn, 'well it's time we were both a-bed lad, yer need yer rest if yer to mend, and I must be up at sunrise to make sure Kimah has bedded the ol-gel in for the wintering correctly, help yerself t' breakfast when ye awake, I'll be back for midday, sleep well boy'.

'An you master' Patric replied. With that the ferryman retired to his sleeping chamber, pulling the heavy curtain-to behind him. Within minutes, muffled snoring joined the low howl of the wind and the crackle of the fire. Pulling the furs over him, an exhausted Patric curled up on the bench, and with groggy thoughts of Enixam, was soon asleep himself.

CH 13: OF CHALK AND CHEESE

At the sound of Patric's first snore, Allen experienced the rushing sensation which he'd now begun to recognize as time speeding up. In moments the fire had reduced to ash, as if it had suddenly been snuffed out, and a faint crack of light grew beneath the door. As if he were superman, the ferryman appeared in a blur, buzzing around the cavern before zipping through the door. Moments later, time put the brakes on as Patric yawned into life.

'Ugh-*shit!*' complained the Celt, as with saying hello to the day, he also said hello to a body-full of dull, throbbing aches.

'Rise n' shine luvva boy' chuckled Alex.

'F-ferryman?' Patric received no answer. Beyond the now-open curtain, the old man's bed chamber was empty. The front door was now ajar, letting in the morning light and fresh sea air. After some moments contemplation, the boy threw aside the heavy fur and following a string of oaths (of which even Hatric would have been proud), hauled himself up.

'Ferryman!' Patric called again, louder, toward the doorway. When still no reply came, Patric's eyes began to rove around the room, before he painfully limped to the rear wall as quickly as he was able. Wincing, he started to explore the contents of a number of large stoneware storage-urns lining the wall, either side of the freshly-swept hearth.

'Well that's a fat-brekky and-a-half!' whistled Allen, laughing, as Patric dropped an armful of fruit, meat and vegetables onto the flat-topped boulder at the centre of the small cavern.

'I think that's intended to be Patric's three square meals for the next few days mate!' commented Alex.

'You what?'

'Well what do you bloody-think he's up to then Allen?' Alex's voice was exasperated as he gestured to Patric, who was now hastily placing the food in a hide sack.

'What? he's off?'

'Certainly looks like it' replied Alex, as Patric swung the sack over his shoulder with a grimace, before grabbing a thick pelt and making for the door. Outside, under a clear autumnal sky, Alex and Allen joined Patric at the abrupt edge of the green.

'Ah! There ye be!' whispered Patric, smiling as he peered inland over the wooded valley far below, to the bare hillside beyond. In the bright morning sunlight, a dazzling white line arced up the steep slope, to reappear, fainter and fainter into the distance on the slopes behind. Patric turned from the giddying drop, and headed toward the path leading down to the sea-cliff.

However, as he reached the narrow track the lad came to a halt and remained standing still for some minutes, staring down at his feet. Suddenly he turned on his heel with a sigh and limped back to the cavern, disappearing through the doorway. Alex motioned for Allen to wait.

'Something he forgot to nick off the poor old sod?' Allen said tartly, shaking his head. Alex didn't reply.

Moments later, Patric reappeared in the doorway, now without the sack or pelt, and only a chunk of white, slimy cheese grasped in one hand.

'I think you owe our Pat an apology' commented Alex evenly. Allen looked uncomfortable as he stepped back to allow the lad to pass.

Before stepping onto the path Patric halted, staring upward into the clear blue heavens above. 'By Domi!' he whispered quietly, 'I swear, one day I'll return with such riches to right this wrong I've done yer ferryman', he then spat into his palm and placed it over his heart, sealing the oath.

Without a backward glance, the lad limped onto the path and disappeared from view behind the giant nipple. Alex strolled back out onto the green.

'We're not going with him then?' enquired Allen.

'We'll follow along in a little while don't worry'.

'Ah' commented Allen as the mid-morning sun suddenly jumped high into the sky and tattered cloud zipped into view overhead, 'it's old fast-forward-time-again'.

As the advancing clouds slowed the ferryman appeared from the hill path. He was whistling quietly to himself, as he ambled up to the cave entrance in relaxed manner.

'He's gonna go ape-shit!' commented Allen. Alex didn't. Moments later, the old man strode back out into the sunlight looking unruffled and calm.

'Well you'd have thought the daft lad would've taken more provisions wouldn't you?' he said out loud, seemingly to himself. Above there came the cry of a gull.

'It's almost like he was expecting it' said Allen, his expression confused.

'He *was!*' sighed Alex, his tone incredulous. 'The ol boy was trying to put Pat off the whole ferryman game from the start, hadn't you gathered that? He couldn't have painted a blacker picture for the lad if he'd tried, and do you really think he normally approaches land through those shit-scary rocks when there's open sea all around? Bloody-hell! He even gave Pat directions on how to get to the lands of opportunity!'

'But I thought he wanted an apprentice?'

'He does, but only one born to it.'

'But why did he bring Pat across at all?'

'Come on Allen-mate, we'd better catch up to the lad now, I'll tell you on the way' Alex stepped off the ledge into thin air, and headed off toward the distant white-serpent. Allen followed.

The old man paced to the edge of the grassy ledge, looking out toward the white serpent, his expression glazed. In his mind's-eye he saw Niari, Enixam's mother. Though she didn't know it, Enixam was now the living image of Niari, as she had looked upon the very day the old man had first laid eyes upon her.

Though he'd deemed her beauty to be more than sufficient fare to make the crossing, the ferryman had yet pleaded with Niari, a lone expectant mother, not to venture into the dangerous lands ruled by the evil O'Lants. However, Enixam had received her own fiery nature from her mother. Niari would not be persuaded from her course, saying only that she went to fulfil a prophecy. Captivated by the spirited, gorgeous girl, the ferryman had lost his heart and granted her passage against his better judgement. From that time on, the boatman knew he would love no other. However, due to his occupation and the fact that he was some twenty years the girl's senior, the ferryman would never reveal the depth of his feelings to Niari, yet he kept a close interest in the fortunes of the girl and her daughter from a distance.

When upon the ferryman had learnt of Niari's death on his return to the Bird's-eye after the wintering that year, he thought he would die from both the pain of his broken heart, and the guilt of knowing that it was he who had carried her to that land. The ferryman had therefore felt he owed Enixam a great debt also, and hoped that in rescuing Patric at her bidding, he had repaid some small part of it. Though he'd worshipped Niari, the ferryman had seen too much of life to blame Patric for the wrongdoings of his grandfather, and indeed, if Enixam held no malice for the young O'Lant, what right did he have?

'May Domi smile down on ye Patric O'Lant' he said quietly, before turning from the brink and heading toward the cavern. As he approached the open door, a large sea gull gently alighted upon his shoulder, folding its wings and shrieking loudly.

'Oh shut it Alf, yer talking bollocks!' the ferryman laughed, before disappearing into the doorway.

'So the ferryman had the hots for Enix's mum! I see! Now it all makes sense!' said Allen, as he and Alex stepped out of mid-air and onto the chalk-path beside Patric, upon the crest of the steep slope. Leaning heavily on a wooden stave, the sweating lad stared back at the ferryman's hill, now on the other side of the wooded valley. His bruised face was streaked with tears of shame.

The ferryman had rescued Patric from certain death, and had offered the boy a job for life (even if, as Patric suspected, that might not be very long). In the short space Patric had known him, the old man had offered more fatherly advice than Hatric had in a lifetime. And what had Patric given in return for the ferryman's help, trust and generosity?

'Sorry master' Patric whispered under the late-afternoon sun, his voice cracking.

Since the moment he'd first heard the old man's dark words concerning the lot of a ferryman's wife, Patric had known he would be unable to subject his beloved Enixam to such a solitary half-life. Though it shamed him, the terror of the crossing had further convinced the lad that a sea-going career was most certainly not for him. Also, the revelations concerning his family history, and the news that it was his own clan which had been responsible for Enix being an orphan, had filled him with guilt and self-loathing, so that he'd felt unworthy of her. So he had resolved to resume his journey to the lands of opportunity. Either he would make it big, allowing him return to Enix and give her such a life of joy that he repaid some small part of the sorrow his clan had caused her, or he would not return at all.

Patric's gaze went beyond the ferryman's hill, and the iron-grey ribbon of the sea, to his homeland. Though Enixam had never spoken of her love for Patric, he felt sure her feelings were as strong as his. Though she was expecting his return in the spring, Patric felt sure that she would understand that the acquisition of a fortune in the lands of opportunity might prolong their joyous reunion somewhat. He was sure Enixam would wait for him.

'I'll see ye again soon Eni m' love' Patric said softly to the horizon, before turning and beginning a limping descent of the slope beyond.

'Shit!' Alex exhaled with an evil grin, glancing at the fizzing Rolex which momentarily appeared on his wrist before vanishing, 'Enix just got married!' He threw a handful of ghostly confetti into the air which disappeared as it touched the ground.

'Poor bastard!' Allen replied in sympathetic tone, watching the injured Patric struggling downhill, but also thinking of the horde of blokes who would be flocking around his Maxine, whilst he himself would be unable to contact her.

'Right! Let's get this show on the road!' Alex beckoned for Allen to follow.

As he took his first step, Allen once again felt time speeding up, and the ground began to slip beneath his feet faster and faster. Patric's legs became a blur.

'I don't suppose you remember Benny Hill' Alex laughed pointing to the lad.

'Weeeeee!' Allen giggled in answer, as their speeding journey along the climbing and plunging white ribbon of the chalk path began to feel like a roller-coaster ride. He took up a seated position and punched the air with both fists. Alex took up a skate-boarding pose. Night zipped by with Patric collapsed in a ditch just off the path, at the bottom of a narrow valley. The abrupt arrival of day saw the boy resume his lightening journey after finishing off the last of the cheese. Patric left the path a number of times, seemingly only for fleeting moments, to forage for berries and roots in the valleys, to answer the call of nature, and to drink from natural springs, marked by standing stones at the side of the path. Heralded by a blanket of chill mist, night returned only minutes after it had departed. Seemingly without the energy to find a more sheltered sleeping place, Patric collapsed on a hill-top.

'Wow! This chalk-path idea is a cool thing, you can see it in the fog and at night-time' commented Allen, before adding 'but where does all this chalk come from?'

'*The ground*' Alex replied, bugging out his eyes and pulling an expression that suggested his companion might well be a divvy.

'Yeah-yeah, very bleedin-funny! I mean we're in Scotland, right?'

'Right.'

'So it's all granite and hard stuff this far north isn't it?'

'Allen, it's the bloody *Stone*-age yeah! It's what people trade in. The Stone-age is the longest of all the ages so far, people have had tens of thousands of years to perfect transport routes and techniques. The stuff is moving around the place all the time! These paths criss-cross the entire country using the high land.'

'But why over the hills? I mean, talk about make life hard for yourself!'
'Allen mate, most of the island is one bloody great big forest at this time yeah? It's easier to take the high way than try to cut down a few hundred miles of densely packed trees and undergrowth that's just as densely packed with bears, boars and wolves! When the lowlands are eventually cleared, most of these paths fall out of use and the chalk is washed away, but the routes of some, like the Pennine way, or the Ridgeway path, still exist in our time!'
'Oh I see' replied Allen sheepishly, feeling like a naughty school-boy who hadn't done his homework.
'And anyway' Alex continued, 'this is just for foot-traffic, the heavy stuff goes by other routes'
'What, like rivers?'
'You'll see Al, you'll see. Each tribe is responsible for the upkeep of the chalk-path that runs through their territory, and believe-me it's not cheap! Chalk is a very valuable commodity in Patric's time, as an implement for drawing, for its 'be-seen-at-night' properties like this!' Alex pointed to the path, 'And it can be heated to make lime. The southerners send it north and in return the northerners send the weapons-grade and building hard-stuff back'.
'Oh'
'The northerners think their hard-rock is more manly, and that the southerners are as soft as their stone. The southerners think both themselves and their stone to be more sophisticated, and the northerners to be as dense as their rock' Alex shrugged his shoulders before adding 'You see nothing changes!' In response, Allen chuckled.
The sun arose and set a further three times, as Patric, slowed by his injuries, led on eastward, through a dramatic landscape of towering hills and snow-capped peaks that crushed deep valleys between them, until upon the sixth evening since they'd set out from the ferryman's cave, the travellers arrived at a cross roads.
Having spied the desired group of stars on the southern horizon, Patric took the path that led downhill toward them.

CH 14: MONUMENTAL MISUNDERSTANDINGS

'The Lake District!' cried Alex at the close of the next day, as the white serpent began to wind about the knees of scree-strewn barren slopes, just above the heads of dense conifer forest.

'Ah' said Alex, gesturing ahead as evening once again raced into the sky, 'I think you'll find this interesting.' Time slowed to its usual pace.

'What the hell is that?' asked Allen, bemused.

The white-serpent had descended into an uneven, grassed plain encircled by hills. Set at its centre was a sight which caused a fearful Patric to nervously leave the path, before re-joining it further on so he wouldn't come too close.

Allen found himself standing before what appeared to be a gigantic circular wooden plate, about thirty metres or so in diameter. It was fashioned from ancient blackened oak timbers pegged together. The sagging great disk was supported on an inner ring of half-rotten timber posts, and an outer ring of standing stones at just over head-height.

'Well?' asked Allen, 'What's this supposed to be then? Domi's dinner-plate I suppose?'

'This is a relic of the wood-age Allen, have a look in *The* Book.'

Recalling his last emotional *little-read,* Allen dubiously reached into his pocket and brought out what now appeared to be flat piece of bark. As Allen turned it over in his hand he found that the smooth inner surface was alive with whirring characters…

The words *IT IS WRITTEN* arose once again within his mind's eye.

Allen didn't know exactly what the date was, but somehow knew it was ye-olde-and-a-half, very early-days indeed for mankind. Before him under the early-evening stars, the plain, surrounded by its ring of hills appeared very much the same, but the path and the vast platter had disappeared. In their place seven old men sat in a circle around a crackling camp fire. Allen knew these to be the shamans of the surrounding Wood-age tribes, gathered for an emergency meeting following a prolonged period of natural catastrophes, pestilence, famine and warfare. Though their peoples had often been involved in sporadic conflicts over resources, beliefs and territory with each other, their spiritual leaders had always maintained a secretive alliance. Much blood-letting and hardship had been averted over the generations by the clandestine negotiations of the group, each of whom had the ear of their chieftain, and tribal god.

However, none could recall a time as dark as this. When misfortune had descended on one or more of the tribes previously, their shaman had always sought the council of his counterparts, and given sacrifice or performed ceremonies according to the advice of those shamans whose tribes were doing well. On certain desperate occasions shamans had even persuaded their chieftains to change gods all together, to one who obviously looked after his or her devotees a little bit better.

Yet in these dire times, the seven tribes had all tried each other's gods with no sign of things improving. So it was that this terrible meeting had been called at last, to ask the dread question, were there any gods at all?..

Suddenly, the council's baleful discussions were interrupted, as first one, then another and another fell silent, their shocked gaze tilting upward toward the stars above. Out of the black heaven, one of the brightest stars appeared to have detached itself from the firmament and had begun a smooth descent. As it neared the earth, the pinpoint of light grew in size and intensity, until a luminous disk, about thirty-metres or so across, and so bright that the shamans had to shield their eyes, hovered just above them. The incandescent circle of light gave out a low, throbbing hum, and the old men beneath it felt the air thicken causing their ears to pop, and found a metallic taste in their mouths (though of course they didn't have a clue what metal was).

Four spoke-like legs of glowing light emerged from the underside of the disk, and the shamans scattered, as the dazzling disk settled upon the ground with a hiss of expelled air, extinguishing the camp-fire. Within moments the light faded and silence returned to the plain, to reveal what Allen could only describe as a flying-saucer. In the moonlight, the craft appeared to be fashioned from some mirror-like, silvery glossy metal, without any joins or portals visible. The shamans prostrated themselves upon the ground in obeisance, each begging what they took to be the divine being, to forgive their lapse in faith, each of course using a different name.

For long moments, the imploring men received no response, until one or two dared a furtive peek. Suddenly, with liquid-like fluidity, a doorway appeared on the rim of the saucer, and a thin gantry slid to earth. Back-lit by a soft green glow, vapour, like dry-ice billowed from the portal. The shamans looked from one to the other in abject fear and bewilderment. And then, silhouetted in the doorway, a tall human-shaped figure appeared.

149

Dressed in a figure-hugging silver suit, a fair-skinned, shaven-headed man emerged from the billowing cloud, and slowly strode down the sleek walkway toward the sprawled group of old men. As he reached the ground, Allen could see that the extremely handsome, well-proportioned man was nearly seven-feet-tall. Holding up a silver-gloved hand, the towering blue-eyed figure gestured for the chorus of prayers and pleas for mercy to cease, which they did immediately.

'Oo-sil a marra ura mianelle' the figure said in a silken and harmonious voice.

With their noses still firmly pressed to the soil, the shamans nervously glanced at each other in incomprehension.

The giant-like man waited in silence. After a while, he raised a hand to his chest and swiped a hand across a sensor on his suit.

'We come in peace' he said in his clear, ringing voice. The shamans again exchanged concerned and confused glances. Most of the tribes' gods had more than one head, or were made up of the body parts of more than one species. All of them were vengeful by nature and extremely unlikely to "come-in-peace" to those who had dared question their existence. None of the seven tribes believed that their gods had made them in their own image, due to the fact of how crap they were prepared to treat them on occasion. Overcoming his fear, the oldest of the wise-men shakily arose on one knee, daring a brief upward glance. If this was indeed not one of their deities, then perhaps he was their messenger. The terrified old shaman quickly checked to make sure nothing animal-headed or append-aged had appeared in the doorway, before nervously asking 'Th-There is a god then?'

The tall space traveller looked down on the old man with a piercing gaze, his expression unreadable. However, after some moments his silver-padded shoulders sagged and a look of extreme-disappointment entered his handsome features, 'Oh for fuck's-sake!' he exhaled dejectedly, 'We were hoping you'd know!'

*Turning from the old shaman, the tall figure trudged back to the gantry of his ship, before angrily turning to the old men. 'Do you have **any** idea how bloody far we've come!' he spat. As he disappeared through the doorway, the slender walkway slid back up into the ship, and the portal closed. The mirror-like metal again became transfused with a growing light, until the old men had to cover their eyes once more. In near-silence the craft arose from the ground, its glowing legs smoothly retracting. There was a low humming sound, before the ship disappeared into the heavens in a blur.*

After a while the old men picked themselves up off the ground, dusted themselves down, before silently resuming their seated circle. No one looked at each other or said anything for the remainder of the night.
The Book went into overdrive, speeding up the scene before Allen's eyes. Seemingly in moments the timber monument to the disquieting-event popped up, the years blurred on.
Within a few generations most of the seven tribes had either abandoned their apparently cursed lands or had been overrun by invaders.
Knowledge as to what the timber saucer represented was lost with the unfolding of time, but due to its scale and obviously-mystical nature, later Stone-age inhabitants of the land treated it as a sacred sight. As the timber posts began to rot with age, a ring of stone-scaffolding was erected to support the mouldering disk.
However, with the passage of the millennia the entire timber structure would at last collapse, most would be carried off to be used on the fire, or would simply rot into the ground. By modern times all that would remain would be a circle of standing stones, which would become known as Castlerigg, just outside of Keswick, in the Lake District, England.

Historians and archaeologists would come up with numerous theories concerning the number and positioning of the stones. Hippies, new-age druids and various stone-huggers alike would have a lot to say about ley-lines and attending the circle on certain auspicious dates.
Though the ring was of course the sight of a most momentous event, all concerned, both the scientific and the spiritual, would remain blissfully unaware that they only studied and worshipped scaffolding...

'The ol' visitors from outer-space and bloody Scaffolding eh?' Allen chuckled dismissively, as he slid the piece of bark back into his pocket. However, his laughter was only half-hearted due to the uncanny way in which *The* Book worked.
'Yeah' responded Alex. 'Space travel's only about distance after all. The Aztecs thought the Spanish conquistadors were from another world when they rocked up in America only some five hundred years-ago. In our time, we know there's billions of stars surrounded by trillions of planets, yet alien visitation is still oddly thought to be cloud-cuckoo-land by many' replied Alex, as if he'd been reading over Allen's shoulder.
'Fair enough', conceded Allen.

'What that little episode was meant to show is that technological advancement is not the same thing as enlightenment, and as for the scaffolding chummy, I think you'd better wait till you've seen a little more of this story before passing judgement!'

'*Ner-ner-ner*-technological-advancement, *ner-ner*-enlighten-bloody-ment..' Allen whined in the most annoying voice he could come up with.

'Alex-mate, how comes half the time you sound like Mister-materialistic, and the other half you sound like some bleedin hippy-guru! Eh?'

'Coz like all of us Allen-mate, I'm a right friggin conundrum', Alex replied with an equally-annoying smile, before turning to follow Patric. Allen stared at the odd monument for some moments before following. Time speeded up again.

CH 15: THE ROCK OF AGES

The white serpent led eastward out of the plain, and two rainy-days later, turned southward onto what Alex explained was now known as the Pennine way. Having crossed the rolling Yorkshire Dales in sleet and driving winds, the travellers followed the path ever southward down through a snow-laden Peak District, where again the path veered toward the east, at modern-day Matlock. In the early evening of the following day, now passing through less mountainous terrain, the chalk-path again turned southward over the crests of undulating hills surrounded by forest, just west of modern-Mansfield.

The white serpent now overlooked, and ran parallel to, a wide valley which stretched north-to-south, from horizon to horizon.

'Christ! If he carries on like this much longer, he's going to peg it!' exclaimed Allen, as he looked down on Patric, who was curled up under a deep covering of ferns and Autumn leaves in the shelter of a tree, just below the path. It was over two weeks since the lad had left the ferryman's cave, and though he was behind the schedule the old man had given for the journey, he had battled-on relentlessly through the elements in his injured state. Though most of his cuts, bruises and other superficial injuries had healed, Patric was now suffering the effects of malnutrition and mild hyperthermia. The lad had eaten nothing but the odd rodent, roots, berries, mushrooms, worms and insects since he'd set out on the long march south, and though he was an able hunter, and though he had chosen new throwing-stones along the way, his weakened state had prevented him from benefiting from his hunting-skills. The lad had picked up flint along the more rugged leg of his journey, and had added a spear-head to his new favourite-stick, and fashioned a flint-knife also. Luckily, he had not had cause to need them so far.

Though, as all people of his time, Patric knew the art of making fire, either with sticks or flint, the fact that he travelled through the lands of possibly hostile tribes, had prevented him from receiving the warmth of the flame for a great part of his journey.

Patric's soft leather footwear had long since given up the ghost, and his bloodied and blistered feet were now wrapped in moss and autumnal leaves, soled with bark, and bound with nettles. Due to the time of year, Patric had encountered only a few fellow travellers upon the path, yet he'd not sought their aid, but had hidden from them all. Yet despite his failing strength and the arduous nature of his journey, the twin pictures of a smiling Enixam, and a gob-smacked Hatric, when Patric returned home a wealthy man, had driven him on.

'Ah, he's young and strong, he'll be fine mate!' replied Alex, as a speeded-up dawn banished night, and Patric stirred into groggy-life. A short distance on, time slowed, and the lad, who'd been trudging along, staring down at his feet, suddenly cried out in fear and dived off the path, rolling downhill into the cover of the bracken.

The source of the boy's terror had come in the form of an initially muffled, but ever loudening repetitive thumping noise, which as it neared, increased in volume, until it sounded as if the very gods were hammering on the hillsides. Allen began to feel a reverberating shudder through his feet.

'What is *that*?' asked Allen staring wildly about him, listening intently as the thunderous noise grew louder, and nearer.

'That my ol-chummy is the *Em-Wun*' chuckled an amused Alex, as the growing thumping noise was joined by a dull clonking-sound, similar to heavy-stone repeatedly hitting stone.

'*Em-Wun, Stone-Way?*' translated a bemused Allen.

'Yes indeed Allen, and this..' Alex gestured to the wooded valley below them to their east, '..is the Em-Wun corridor'.

As it neared, Allen realised that the heavy beats were echoing up to the path from the valley floor. As his gaze traced the path of the valley northward, there amongst the far-off tree tops he saw a trail of approaching faint puffs of what appeared to be smoke or dust, almost as if he were watching the distant approach of a steam-train. Whatever it was, it was travelling nearer at speed. As the small emerging clouds drew level with their vantage point, Allen could see that there was a cleared path through the forest running along the bottom of the valley, only now visible at this distance due to the smoky wisps erupting along it. Soon the sound and dust receded southward, until silence returned once more to the hill-top, and the valley floor was again an unblemished blanket of autumnal reds and golden browns.

Sure he'd witnessed the passage of some giant beast, Patric didn't emerge back onto the path for some minutes. However, as he furtively peered down into the valley, he once again shrieked in terror and scrambled back into hiding. Judging by the growing noise, whatever it was, was returning from the south.

'So what the buggery *is* the Stone-Way then?' asked Allen, once the dust and noise had retreated into the north, and all was once again peaceful.

154

'*The* Book I think?' suggested Alex.

'What do we have this time then?' mused Allen as he drew out a small rectangular tablet of worked stone from his pocket.

IT IS WRITTEN...

Though his visual view remained that of the valley below, Allen found (with little surprise, now that he was becoming used to The Book) that his brain had somehow been uploaded with all the relevant background information concerning the current culture, so that he knew exactly what he was looking at in context. He giggled.

This was an age of stone, where by Patric's time the masons ruled nearly every aspect of life with a fist of granite 1970's-union style. Masons were free to do as they wished; they were Free-Masons. But their services certainly were not.

Hills with underlying rock, escarpments, mountains and cliff-faces weren't just geographical features, they were prized sources of wealth and therefore power. As they had travelled southward, Allen had noted that nearly every slope and hillside bore a vast chalk-mural, denoting ownership or dire warnings to stay off. Indeed, apart from the many depictions of animals and suchlike which were the tribal-emblems, Allen had noted many were representations of the more-tender parts of the human anatomy. These giant pictures would be headed by an equally-large picture of a flint knife or axe, denoting trespassers and thieves would have the body part/s, as pictured below, cut off. Many of the pictures were accompanied by chalk renderings of a pair of watering eyes. Allen had smiled to himself, having visited one such huge chalk image as a child, the ancient White Horse of Uffington in Wiltshire, whilst on a family holiday. And most knew of the more-risqué Cerne Abbas giant in Dorset; Big naked bloke, waving a club over his head, and of course, the huge stiffy. The modern perception being of course that in their time, such murals would have been few and far between, so it tickled Allen to view a landscape literally covered in them.

Care of The Book, Allen had seen that in Stone-age high finance, hills and mountains were traded between tribes for large scale transactions, such as in the hiring of a mercenary army, or the purchase of herds of livestock. Of course, the geographic feature couldn't be moved, the mural simply changed.

The Book showed that there was a vast array of Masonic clans, known as lodges, each specialising in a different field of the trade, and each with a

155

different device upon their leather masonic-apron. Though the abodes of the time were generally of timber construction, the main support beam would always be set into a hollowed boulder, known as a home-stone. Home-stones were cherished family-heirlooms which moved with their owners, the loss or destruction of which were thought to bring about catastrophe. Therefore, the expensive services of a mason were required in each-and-every house-build, demolition or move. Though many did, woe-betide the layman who fashioned his own spear-head, axe-head, or flint fishing-hook, and the masons got wind of it. Due to its clay or other stone content, any form of earthenware pottery or stoneware could only be produced by a masonic-lodge. From the stones used to grind flour, to the stones needed to weight fishing nets or ploughs, you needed a mason, and boy it was going to cost you.

Whilst most people of the era looked to the heavens to a sun god, the Masonic lodges kept their feet firmly on the ground, and gazed downward to worship the subterranean god of stone, Geezer the great. The vast array of differing Masonic-jobs was matched by an equally-vast array of accompanying secret rituals, designed to illustrate to the masses that Masonry was no ordinary occupation. Those who broke the Masonic code and divulged any aspect of these rituals to someone outside the industry would be fitted with a pair of stone-shoes, and taken for a walk in the river..

Wood and cloth rotted, but stone was immortal. You could trust in stone, it was solid, it was safe. Those who practised the way of the stone-wright believed themselves to be above others, and liked to remind all concerned of this fact at every opportunity.

Arguably, the greatest feats of the masons were performed by the stone-herders. Allen saw that modern archaeology had rightly surmised that some great-stones were transported overland using ropes and timber rollers, and some were indeed taken by river using huge rafts. However, he also saw that condescending modern-humans like to congratulate themselves on how far they've come, and vastly underestimate the capabilities of their long-distant forefathers. Even though they survived quite-nicely, thank-you-very-much, in a far more hostile environment without gadgets.

In the early days of the Stone-age, masons had sought a practical and consistent way of transporting large volumes of trading-stone over long distances. For they were constantly reminded by their shamans, known as Druids, that their gods expected great things of them. For were the masonic not the very hands of the gods on this earth? The mystified-masons had therefore begged the council of their holy men as to how this great task might be accomplished. Apparently, after an in-depth chat with Domi, Geezer, and other gods, the wise men had directed the masons as to what they should do. But they had also warned the stone-wrights that they themselves would not benefit from their labours in this life-time, but would in their later incarnations.

The stone-way was the creation of many thousands of years, and luckily due to a belief in reincarnation, people had a much longer-term view of things than they do today. So it was, that as the large stones were quarried, instead of being immediately carried off, they were stood in an upright position, in a line, leading away from the quarry in the desired direction. The standing stones were placed one in front of the other, the gaps between them being only fractionally smaller than the height of each stone. Once a day, the stone nearest the quarry would be toppled forwards, so that it clipped the bottom of the one in front of it, causing it to topple forward, which in turn would topple the next stone, and so on and so on. Once a day, the stones would then be pulled back up into an upright position, but with the end that had been up in the air, now down in the ground, so that the entire line of stones had moved forward three-to-four metres or so, with new stones being added to the rear of the line from the quarry.

The great Stone-way was intended to link the masons of the north with those of the south, and so whilst one line began its few-metres-a-day journey from the quarries of the south, another began its journey from the north. Both avenues used the same route, chosen for its gradual incline, and avoidance of natural barriers. Often, where slopes were encountered, the stone-herders would deviate from a straight line and stand the stones in zig-zags and loops, to increase momentum uphill. As the lines extended, the generations of stone-herders became ever more adept at up-righting the stones, so that soon they could be toppled twice, and sometimes even three times a day.

Many, many generations later, the lines reached their destinations, and forever after would deliver two-to-three huge stones a day, day in day out, at either end; Stones from hundreds of miles away. For the generations who lived after its completion, the Stone-way was a labour-saving device, because the momentum of the stones did the work, and it's a lot easier to lever and pull a couple of tonnes of stone upright, than it is to try and drag it along the ground, or up a hill. Seemingly not put off by

157

the noise-pollution, violence and general bustle, communities would spring up all along the Em-Wun corridor, serving the needs of the army who worked on the Stone-way.

The masons of the south herded their sedimentary stones north, whilst their northern counterparts herded their igneous rock southward. There was great competition and regional pride involved in which side could move the greatest volume of stone the quickest. If the southerners managed three tilts in a day, and their northern rivals had only managed two, then the smug chants of 'three-two, three-two, three-twooooo' from the northbound lane would be very loud indeed that evening after a few beers. Generally after a few more beers, things would get nasty.

In an attempt to stop the highly-competitive stone-herders of the north and south killing each other, the druids introduced a game up and down the Em-Wun. The game involved two teams of eleven players, each of whom carried a full beaker of beer, and was played on a grassed rectangular field. The goal of the game was for a player to reach the back line of the opposition's half with a full beaker of beer, without having been kicked in the balls. Foot-ball. A point was awarded each time this was achieved, and play normally stopped when no one could walk anymore. If a player tried to claim a point, but was found to have spilled his beer, then the best kicker of the opposing side would be entitled to kick him in the penal region. This free-kick was known as a 'penal-ty'.

The Em-Wun had also given rise to another extremely-popular game. Upon the winter solstice, when the economy was slack due to the weather, and the great stone-way was silent, the most skilled of the herders of both sides would take part in an annual contest, attended by many thousands. The contest had been held for generations, since the earliest days of the Stone-way, at the order of the druids. The competition was allegedly intended to give thanks to the gods for their inspiration in the building of the Em-Wun, and to celebrate the economic benefits which the Stone-way had brought. However, to northerners and southerners alike, it had become an opportunity to publicly rub each other's noses in defeat.

Generations earlier, after consultation with the gods, the druids had ordained that a great stadium should be built upon hallowed ground, to house this holiest of contests. The sacred site chosen by the druids was in the lands of the southerners.

Upon its completion, the stadium took the form of a great chalk-covered embankment, built in the form of a ring, enclosing a circular, thirty-acre grassed arena within it. Inside the encircling embankment there was a

158

great ditch, also lined in chalk so that the whole edifice shone a dazzling white in the sunlight. The embankment was over four hundred and thirty metres in diameter. Of such a scale that thirty thousand spectators could stand upon it, and the ditch was ten metres deep. Deep enough to accommodate the toilet and vomiting requirements of thirty thousand beer-swilling people. There was a single break in the bank and ditch on its south-east side.

The competition involved the two teams of stone-herders each having to topple a line of great-stones. The two parallel-rock-lines, reminiscent of the Stone-way, began a mile and a half away from the stadium, upon the crest of a hill, to add momentum and therefore excitement. The two stone-avenues crossed a plain before entering the arena through the gap in the bank and ditch. Both lines then completed a circuit of the arena before spiralling inwards to its centre. At the very centre of the arena stood a single great stone, whichever line toppled it first was the winner.

Both teams would take a great deal of time walking the course, and care in the setting up and ordering of their stones. There was much secrecy involved, and a temporary high timber palisade was erected between the two lines during the setting up process, only to be dismantled on the morning of the contest when all the stones were erected.

All great stones were weighed when quarried, and daubed with two sets of white dots, the first pattern denoting weight, and the second as to what type of stone it was. Though both teams would be provided with stones of equal weight and mix of rock types, it was a notoriously hard game to predict. Indeed, it was said only all-knowing-Domi himself knew what the outcome would be, and hence this game became known as 'Domi-knows'. Team members of the game became household names and were treated and paid like gods, and the peoples of both sides would flock to the site just for a glimpse of them. So, the entire course and not just the arena, would be lined by a screaming, chanting throng. Many lived their lives in the hope that they would be reincarnated a player. It was an annoyance to all concerned that the masons hogged the entire stadium. In the stadium, the northerners would stand on the north half of the bank, and the southerners on the south, truly a game of two halves. Woe betide those accidentally wandering onto the wrong side following too much beer. The contest was begun upon the hill by a ceremonial whistle from the high-druid, upon the setting of the solstice sun, and both team captains would topple their first stone in earnest. Each year the two sides competed for a

much-coveted stone-cup. The victory beer drunk from it, being the
sweetest ever tasted.
It was the custom for the victorious captain to growl like a powerful bear
before the ecstatic screams of his supporters and the downcast faces of the
vanquished. The entire stadium would then take up the guttural-growl,
until it reverberated around the arena; When the growling-roar reached
deafening-crescendo, the captain would drain the stone-beaker of
ceremonial ale in one. and cry 'ALE!' in honour of beer. Hence this cup
was known as the Grrrr-ale.

.

'I've said it before, but I'll say it again!' sniggered Allen, 'I've seriously
got to knock the hard-stuff on the head!' He chuckled as he slid the stone
leaf back into his pocket, 'Footy and Dominoes indeed! M1 bloody-
corridor no less!'
Alex only smiled in answer. A nervous Patric returned to the path some
moments later, and scuttled southward. Time speeded up once more.
'Hey!' Alex cried four days later, pointing to the right of the blurring path,
'it's your home town Allen-mate!'
'What, good ol' MK?' replied Allen., as a group of low slopes zipped by
just beyond the pathway, each daubed with a chalk-mural of a cow.
'Looks about as exciting as when I live here'.
Three days later, the white-serpent came to an abrupt end.

CH 16: OPPORTUNITY KNOCKS

Patric was a mess. He'd walked nearly four hundred miles and by the time he arrived in the Thames valley, just north of the river, he was an exhausted and emaciated wreck. He swayed between the two standing-stones marking the end of the serpent, staggered a few paces out into a sparsely wooded plain, and collapsed unconscious into a bush.

'Good ol'Lundin-Taan! Ah, it's good to be back!' cried Alex, gesturing enthusiastically to the east, where distant smoke coiled into the cloud-strewn early-evening sky.

'Yeah-great' replied Allen despondently, reminded of the dreary life he'd wake up to in the morning. A life without Maxine's phone number.

'Or Cha-Hi-Nae as it's known here-abouts' Alex added.

'The-Big-Smoke?'

'Indeed'.

Next morning, a bedraggled Patric crawled out of the foliage and dragged himself to a nearby stream to drink. Following a breakfast of grubs and nuts, the near-delirious lad hauled himself upright and slowly began to follow a wide shingled track, marked on one side by standing stones every half-mile or so. The pocked and rutted path was criss-crossed by churned mud-tracks at regular intervals, showing it to be a much-used thoroughfare, and it was not long before Patric was joined by other travellers upon the way. However, seemingly only half-conscious, the weaving boy seemed oblivious to the growing number of fellow road-users, or the fact that he'd reached the lands of opportunity at last.

The locals were a stocky-built breed, of middling height for the era, and were cloaked and hooded against the chill and incessant drizzle. They were dark haired, and for the most part the men were bearded. Unlike the Celts, the men wore trousers of soft hide or leather, and belted woollen long-sleeved vests, which hung to just above the knee. Most wore supple boots. The women wore ankle-length woollen tunics and hooded cloaks, tied at the throat.

Many carried bundles or sacks. Some led oxen, and either side of the track, goats, a scrawny breed of sheep, and small squealing hairy pigs were driven before their masters.

'Ah the beaker-people!' smiled Alex, wandering amongst the foot traffic and bowing before the more attractive of the women.

'Hey! Like the threads!' commented Allen from the safety of the air. Alex was now dressed in the trousers and tunic of the locals, the cut and design of which, were of course far sharper than anyone else's on the road.

Historians have named the inhabitants of the greater part of England during this period 'The Beaker-People', due to the large number of pottery and earthenware vessels found in the grave-goods of their turf covered tombs, known as barrows. From *The* Book, Allen knew however, that modern-man has never understood the true importance of these beakers. For it was with these, rather than with spear, bow or axe, that this people had managed to invade the island from mainland Europe, thousands of years earlier at the end of the ice age.

The ice sheets had retreated from Europe much earlier than in Britain. Therefore, the beaker-people had perfected agriculture, and more importantly fermentation whilst their British counterparts were still isolated groups of hunter-gatherers. During the last glacial period, which lasted nearly a hundred thousand years in northern Europe, a sun god of course had not been very popular at all. However, with sunnier climes, the beaker-people had given thanks to the sun-god who was now clearly upping his game at last, and melting all the bloody ice. They named the golden disk Domi and worshipped it above all else. For Domi gave life to plants, and from plants, the beaker-people had discovered the secret of beer.

Between the end of the last ice age around 11,500BC and the resulting drowning of the land-bridge between Europe and thawing England in 6000BC, the beaker-people followed the retreating walls of ice. Yet if they were to take their beer with them, the beaker-people would need a means to transport it, hence the interest in all things pottery.

The beaker-people arrived in southern-England, bringing Domi with them and enough beer in beakers to carry out an invasion of persuasion, by getting the scattered indigenous tribes off their faces for the first time. When they arrived thousands of years later, even the Celts of Scotland and Ireland would be so impressed by the quality of the beaker-people's brew and pint-pots, they would begin to worship Domi themselves. The importance of the beaker would always remain with the beaker-people, so that it was not by chance the Domi-knows teams competed for a beaker of beer, or a warrior who allegedly could down fifteen beakers and still stand, would be buried with fifteen beakers in commemoration of this fact.

Archaeologists and historians, who don't really understand the importance of stone in the Stone-age would also misunderstand the nature of the beaker-people's tombs. Barrows were made up of a stone box-like structure, in which the body and grave-goods were placed. The whole lot was then covered in a hillock of earth and turf. Academics mistakenly think the stone is simply a building material, when in fact it was symbolic of the occupant's wealth in stone, intended to be taken to the other side.

'Oi! Carrot-top! Atta-th-bleedin way would-ya!'
'Oof' Patric rebounded off the large, burly man and staggered backwards.
'C'mon son! Walk on the right side!' An old man carrying a sack over one shoulder shook his head as he barged passed the lad. Allen could see that travellers on the busy pathway walked on the left, and that the half-conscious Patric had stumbled onto the wrong side, seemingly not knowing where he was. The red-haired boy's progress was marked by repeated oaths and cries of 'Bloody-Celts!' as the irate west-bound travellers either moved aside, or refused to give-way, repeatedly knocking Patric to the wet, muddied gravel.
'You tend to get a lot of knocks when you're searching for opportunity!' Alex commented.
Time and again Patric struggled back up to his feet, now covered from head to foot in the wet mud and slime of the road, and trudged on into the rain and oncoming traffic.
'Ye in mi way yer ginger-tosser! Lookin for a slap are ye mate or what?' the spotty-faced young man demanded of Patric, menacingly holding a half-full beaker of beer up to the oblivious-lad's face, before looking back to his four fellow-members of the five-a-side-foot-ball team with a grin.
'Well! D-ye wannit son!' The bully-with-an-audience spat, leaning forward until he was nose to nose with the lad. Patric blearily stared back through uncomprehending half-open eyes.
'Ye stink like shite! Ye uplander-granite-headed scumbag!' The team-captain drew his face back with a look of abject disgust, as if Patric was something nasty he'd stepped in, and waved his free hand in front of his nose. The Celtic lad remained silent, swaying slightly.
'Go-on Dhuna! Av-im!' came the chorus of cries from the rest of the team.
'Your sort shouldn't be dan ere in civ-lized lands' Dhuna snarled, turning away from Patric, before whirling around and viciously bringing his

booted foot up between the lad's legs. Patric crumpled to the floor with a groan, amidst the delighted whoops and howls of the whole team.

'Ye need t' learn some down-lander manners boy! Now fuck-off back to ginge-land!' Dhuna laughed, spitting on Patric's back, before continuing his journey, and accepting his compatriots' enthusiastic cheers of 'ONE-NIL!' with a raised palm.

'He was brave!' Allen spat disgustedly, angrily watching the jubilant football team until it was swallowed amongst the bustling traffic of the road.

'Wasn't he just' agreed Alex. Patric crawled through the muck and his vomited breakfast, to the side of the pathway, whilst his fellow travellers either stepped on or over him. The path was now raised on a causeway, a man's height above meadow and marshy bog. As Patric reached the brink he tumbled over, rolling down the bank, and landed unconscious in a bedraggled heap at the bottom.

Alex and Allen sat down to wait.

Rainy afternoon turned into soggy evening. Chilly night came and left, and when sunny, dew-laden morning arrived, Patric at last shivered back into some semblance of life.

'P-Praise-b-be-ti-Domi!' he croaked weakly. For as his squinting, bloodshot eyes focused under the dazzling radiance of his sun god, Patric saw before him a scene he had long dreamt of. He had gone through the pain and starvation barrier, and now felt numbed, almost serene under the warming touch of Domi. Across the small meadow bejewelled with twinkling dew was a wondrous sight. He knew that at last he'd stumbled upon his golden moment of opportunity.

'So ow much then?' The old carpenter asked, his tone tight-lipped and resigned.

'Phworr! It's not gonna be cheap mate!' Brother Baldor, the middle-aged, pot-bellied leader of the group of masons intoned solemnly, rubbing his stubbled cheek, as he considered the apparently numerous complications of the obviously tricky job.

The four-man Masonic-demolition team and the old carpenter stood in front of a dilapidated, rotting timber hall with bulging walls and sagging, holed roof, some yards from the now once-again busy highway, and an unnoticed Patric. The carpenter, whose hall it was, had the air of a man who is under sentence of death, and only waits to find out if he's to be beheaded or hung.

164

'Well! How much then!' He repeated as calmly as he could. Brother Baldor told him.

'Sure yer don't wanna av mi daughters while yer at it!' the old man gasped, unable to help himself. 'I said I want it pulled dan! Not bleedin rebuilt as well!'

'I think you'll find it's the go-in rate for a job of this complexity wood-chopper!' Brother Baldor sighed, hooking his thumbs in his leather apron with a confident air, 'Eh brother Norbin?'

'Indeed brother Baldor, a very reasonable price I'd say, given the difficulties in a job like this' agreed the well-built mason who stood just behind his gaffer, meaningfully patting his stone-hammer into a bear-like paw.

'Alright-alright!' exhaled the old carpenter, his shoulders sagging, 'when can yer start? An ow long is it gonna take yer?' Having not believed the first three estimates he'd been given for the works, the old man now knew he had little choice.

'Brother Rillet?' brother Baldor enquired of another member of his team.

'We might be able to fit it in just before the turning of spring brother Baldor' replied brother Rillet, the keeper of the records, 'but it's tight' he added.

'SPRING?! Ain't you-lot got anythin earlier?' cried the old man, raising his hands to the heavens in exasperation. 'I can't av the new hall started till the bloody home-stone's out o' this one now can I!'

'It's very busy' explained brother Baldor. 'Business is exceptionally good' he added, without attempting to remove the smugness in his voice. 'Now if you'd av given us a shout earlier in the year...' Brother Baldor raised his hands, shrugged, and shook his head seemingly in wonder at those who failed to plan ahead. The old man stood with his head hung low in dejected silence.

'Look, tell ya what I'll do' said brother Baldor after some moments in more sympathetic manor. 'I feel sorry for yer, I really do! What with high winter comin on 'n' all. Maybe we can shuffle some bits around and come up with somethin a little bit earlier for yer'. He looked to brother Rillet, who waggled a palm intimating that it was a faint possibility. 'But obviously' brother Baldor added 'I couldn't do it for the same price..'

A price was agreed on.

'So when *can* yer start?' the old man implored, fearing the worst.

'Tomorrow' smiled brother Baldor. The old man arched his eyebrows.

'And how long will it take?' enquired the carpenter, almost afraid to ask. Brother Baldor told him. The old man swore a lot.

'You lot outside the brotherhood!' brother Baldor chuckled wryly. 'You've got no idea what's involved in our work bless-yer!' This was indeed true, because masons erected high wicker hoardings around all their sites of work. For none outside the brotherhood were allowed to witness what a mason actually did for their pay. That would be an affront to Geezer, sacrilege.

Their business concluded, the old carpenter walked away. A soul who was now a lot less burdened by material wealth than he had been earlier that morning. The masons settled down on the grass for their early-morning beer break, the first of six that masons observed throughout their working day. Someone got the miniature Domi-knows out, and the wagers were placed.

'Eh, look what the white-serpent's dragged in' brother Norbin chuckled, his gaze rising from his frothing beaker. The skeletal, foul-smelling and looking Patric stared down at the squatting apron-wearing group, an inane grin on his black-slimed face.

'Whacked on berries looks like!' commented the balding, middle-aged brother Dendram with disgust, 'just like most o' the young-uns these days, it's disgusting!' he added, before taking deep gulps of beer and burping loudly.

'What's he up to?' enquired brother Norbin. Patric was making vague gestures with his hands. After a number of attempts, the glassy-eyed lad at last managed to perform the universally-known hand-sign for chiselling stone, followed by the hand to mouth gesture for eating.

'I think the cheeky-sod's looking for work!' laughed an incredulous brother Rillet, amazed that such a bedraggled, lowly urchin would dare think himself worthy of serving Geezer the great.

'Be on yer way lad!' brother Baldor growled, who was far more interested in the not-insubstantial amount of flint he had riding on the current game. All eyes returned to the grass.

'Ah by Neblik's-giant-nob!' exclaimed the disappointed leader of the masons some moments later.

'That's five-weight yer owe me brother Baldor!' chuckled the victorious brother Rillet gleefully, as he started to stand his line of diminutive stones up again, ready for the next contender.

'D'yer not understand the lingo boy? NOW BUGGER-OFF!' The not-happy brother Baldor shouted at Patric, who still stood just outside the ring of squatting men. The boy appeared oblivious to the threatening tone, and continued to grin down at the men.

'You erd!' barked brother Norbin, digging a huge hand into the soft soil and launching a clod of earth at the boy. The wet clump struck Patric in the face, whipping his head backward and filling his mouth, eyes and nose with mud. There was a chorus of laughter as the lad staggered about, spitting soil and weakly attempting to wipe the grit out of his eyes. After a while he stumbled off and the men returned to their game.

'Charmin bunch' commented Allen. Alex smiled.

'Where's he bleedin got to then?' Asked brother Norbin some moments later, looking around. Certainly, given the state he was in, the boy hadn't had time to climb the bank and return to the causeway, and yet he wasn't to be seen anywhere upon the meadow either.

'Who cares?' Said brother Rillet, taking a satisfying swig from his beaker, and mentally totting up the winnings of his second victory.

'It's just odd, that's all' replied brother Norbin. Play continued.

'What was that?' asked brother Baldor, looking up from the game some minutes later.

'It came from in there' a concerned brother Rillet pointed toward the crumbling hall, as a second growl of grinding timbers emanated from the dark open doorway. The brothers exchanged meaningful glances.

'He's having a laugh!' giggled Allen in disbelief, as Patric staggered back from the main support beam, which stood at the centre of the musty, disintegrating hall. Though obviously once of immense strength, the great timber-trunk rising to the apex of the vaulted ceiling high above, was now bowed and rotten.

'The lad's got a lot to prove' commented Alex, as Patric stumbled back across the sun-dappled, timber-strewn floor, before turning to take a second limping charge at the beam.

'He's bloody mad!' laughed Allen, as Patric's shoulder once more barged into the brittle post, slotted into a large boulder set in the floor. Nothing happened.

Now completely spent, Patric hung onto the crumbling timber for support, eyes closed, panting and wheezing. After a while he opened a bleary eye. *'Ah f-Domi's sake'.* His voice a croaking whisper, as he limply thumped his fist into the

wood before of his nose. For long-moments all that could be heard was Patric's rasping, wheezing breaths.

And then it started.

Patric's head rose, his eyes suddenly wide. A splintering sound arose next to his ears, which travelled up the post to the roof above, where it was joined by the louder noise of cracking timbers. Next came the high-pitched squeal of rotten support beams giving up the ghost, to be followed by a menacing growing rumble.

'*Shit*' whispered Patric peering upward, without the strength to run or even scream.

And then the roof fell in.

In a shower of beer, and with a string of oaths, the masons sprang to their feet and scrambled for safety, as the dilapidated hall folded inwards with a deafening roar.

Dazed and bewildered, the four dust-covered men at last turned to survey the scene of devastation. Huge timbers now lay where only moments before they had sat. Each man gave praise to Geezer, and delved into their pockets to touch stone.

A pall of brown dust still hung in the morning air, cloaking the scene. After some minutes the dust settled, revealing a jumble of mangled carpentry. At its centre, like a brown statue, a dust-covered Patric stood seemingly unharmed. For miraculously the roof directly above the lad had been holed, so that the it had fallen around, rather than on him. Patric still clung to the lower remaining shard of the main support post, the only piece of timber still standing. Then very slowly, the six-foot-or-so stub fell over, taking Patric with it, and leaving the home stone open to the air.

'Well lads!' chuckled brother Baldor dryly, beating the dust from his masonic apron, 'Best get the whicker screens up sharpish! Looks like we've got the next few days off!' Nervous chuckles from his men became raucous laughter.

'More lives than a cat this one!' marvelled Allen, peering down at the groaning boy, who was weakly attempting to rise.

'Here they come' commented Alex, gesturing to the approaching masons. Following a brief discussion, Brother Baldor and his men paced to the edge of the demolition site, their faces stern and set. They halted as one, forming a rank facing Patric.

'*Shall he be given entry through the doorway brothers?*' brother Baldor intoned solemnly in his best formal-speaking-voice.

168

'Yea verily' came the chorused reply of all four men, before each bent forward in exact unison, and grasped the hem of his apron with both hands.

'For has he not balls of granite?' the four recited in well-practised manner, before straightening and revealing what it is that a mason wears under his apron. From the belt of each man, two lumps of granite hung to their groin region on twine. The underside of each mason's apron bore a mural of a circle of stick-men, all scratching the back of the man in front of him.

'I wandered what was going on there for a minute' giggled Allen, as the masons lowered their aprons once more with well-drilled precision.

'GEEZER!' cried brother Baldor, pointing at Patric.

'GEEZER!' echoed the brothers loudly.

'So mote it be!' finished brother Baldor, bringing the apparent ritual to an end.

'He's in!' chuckled Alex, 'good ol Pat!'

'I'll say one thing for him' Allen laughed, 'when Patric attends an interview, he really brings the house down!'

'crap pun mate'.

'Sorry mate.'

'So our Pat's a mason at last! Just what he always wanted bless-im!' smiled Allen from the air above the causeway, as he and Alex followed the four masons west toward The-Big-Smoke. A senseless Patric draped over one of brother Norbin's broad shoulders.

Alex chuckled 'Yer see! That kick in the bollocks was the best thing that'd happened to Pat for ages! Otherwise he'd never have stumbled on that golden opportunity! The world often works like that!'

'He's certainly has earned it!' replied Allen, looking down with affection on the emaciated boy.

'Yer see Allen mate! Hard work really does pay off if in the end if you stick at it!' said Alex, gesturing emphatically to Pat, 'But you've got to make the right choices yeah?' he added, 'Pat realised early on that a few scribbles weren't gonna give him the life he wanted! So he got off his arse, got himself here, and now he's got a real job in the IT industry of the time, you see?'

'Yeah-yeah' sighed Allen, in no mood for a sermon.

'You gotta be a realist if you want to get on in this life Allen' Alex continued, seemingly unperturbed by Allen's indifference, 'it takes bollocks' he added.

'Must be why you did so well in life Alex-mate, coz you're full o' that!' Allen responded with a smile. The march continued for some time in silence.

'Well Allen' remarked Alex some time later, 'I think you've had quite enough of an introduction into how our Pat got started. We're still at the beginning of his tale, and there's only so much a cynical-git like you will accept being able to *dream* in one night, so I think we'd best speed it up for a while'.

Time blurred.

CH 17: OLDER

Seven years flashed by, seemingly in as many seconds before time slowed, leaving Allen feeling mentally bloated. Similar to the physical sensation of just having eaten too much too quickly.

'Christ! You could've bloody warned me!' he exclaimed, pummelling the sides of his pounding head with both hands, 'That was a bit much to take in one go!'

'Whinge-whinge-bloody-whinge! Do you *ever* stop Allen?' replied Alex, shaking his head. The two now stood on a pleasant shingled, tree-lined avenue of almost-identical well-kept circular houses. Each had white-washed wattle walls and well-trimmed, domed thatched rooves. Each property was fronted by a wicker-fenced herb garden, and each had a single or double stable attached to its side.

'C'mon Natti-luv! We've gotta get a move on darlin yeah! You can do yer eyes on the way can't yer?' A taller, cleaner, and leanly-built Patric emerged from the doorway of the nearest round-house, dressed in well-tailored woollen vest, heavy riding-cloak, soft hide trousers, and best ceremonial leather apron. The twenty-one-year-old was now clean shaven, as was his skull. Patric's eye-brows were now dyed brown, completely eradicating his tell-tale Celtic origins. To Allen, Patric's accent was now about as cockney as you can get.

'Oh that's right Ricky! I'll just go looking like a right-bleedin-dog's-dinner shall I?' came a piping female Essex-accented response. A petite and extremely-attractive, dark-haired girl emerged into the morning summer-sunshine some moments afterward, applying some dark powder to her long-lashed eyes with a delicate horse-hair brush. The buxom-girl was attired in what amounted to not much more than a soft-hide bikini, and knee-high boots. Every visible inch of skin was orange. From *The Book*, Allen knew that following the end of the ice age and the rise of Domi, the novelty of a sun-tan was considered to be the physical proof of the sun-god's favour toward a person. In dreary Briton, it was customary amongst certain types to rub ochre into their skin to show how apparently blessed by the gods they were. Over one shoulder, a wolf-pelt riding cloak, and in her free hand was clutched a hand-bag with complimentary pet rat.

'Rush-rush fackin-rush, that's all we ever seem t' fackin do these days Ric, it's a fackin-nightmare!' Nattarra's complaining voice had risen a further annoying-octave. 'I fackin-said we shoulda gone yesterday, but would yer ave it? Would yer bollocks!'

'That one's gorgeous' chuckled Alex, 'until she opens her gob that is, bless-er!'

'Poor-ol-Pat' Allen sniggered, joining Alex in evil laughter.

'C'mon Tarra-luv' Patric's tone was consolatory as he strode to the double doors of the stable. 'Yer know it's been mad! But it'll all be worth it luv! You'll see! This job's the big one! When it's sorted we'll be able to sit back and take it easy! Granite-arama Yeah?'

'Where av I erd that one before Ricky eh?'

'Look Nat, this one's different, and you bloody know it!' Patric's own voice was harsher as he untied the stable door and disappeared inside. 'You should be bleedin prad o' me instead of bloody moanin all th' time!' he added angrily as he emerged back into the sunlight, leading a stocky black pony. A tense silence followed as Patric threw a heavy blanket over the sturdy beast's back, and secured the leather saddle bag containing bedding and provisions. Standing in sullen silence, arms folded, Nattarra apparently studied the roses which climbed the wall of their house, as they did every property along the street. Until recently, the Lants (as with his hair regime, Patric had long dropped the 'O' from his surname to further conceal his Celtic background) had been a two-pony family. But to Nattarra's disgust and embarrassment, the second pony, *her* pony, had gone the way of their savings and every spare earned pebble. All put up as surety for men and materials for the huge contract her husband had just won. A contract which Patric assured her would set them up for life. Patric mounted, before leaning down and offering a hand to his wife.

'You comin or what?' he growled.

'S'pose so' came the petulant reply after a while, as Nattarra at last allowed herself to be hauled up into the saddle behind her husband.

'G'on boy' Patric urged the mount into a walk out onto the lane.

'Mornin brother' came a greeting from over the fence.

'Mornin brother' Patric responded to his neighbour, a fellow mason who was lovingly tending his lawn with a small flint sickle. Everyone along the well-manicured lane was of course a mason.

'People-'ll' think we're fackin-common!' Nattarra bitterly-complained short minutes later, pulling the cloak about her and the hood down to conceal her features. She had been hugely upset at the loss of her little Gwillum, a three-year-old grey run-around. Her loss of apparent prestige and independence had led Patric to suffer greatly in the ear and bed department ever since.

'When we were courting Natti, you used to love a backy on mi pony, remember?' Patric's voice had mellowed with fond memories of moonlit teenage pony-back canoodling.

'Well, we were youngsters back then'. Though still with an edge, Nattarra's voice had softened somewhat. The journey continued through The-Big-Smoke in thoughtful silence.

'Look Nat' Patric's tone was that of the peacemaker, 'I know you've put up with a lot lately babe, but I swear it'll all be worth it! I know you woz gutted about Gwillum..'

'Bastard' Nattarra interjected.

'..But when this job's over you can ave as many ponies as yer bloody like! By Geezer! Yer servants can ave as many ponies as they bleedin like!'

'Servants?' Nattarra's voice was markedly more-friendly.

'Of course, a lady of standing needs servants! And a big drum to fit em all inta,' Patric added with a smile. The pony walked on through bustling streets toward the outskirts.

'Well in that case ginger-nuts' Nattarra's tone was now silken, her hand gliding beneath her husband's riding cloak, to his groin region. 'Maybe I can put up with yer a little longer'.

'Glad to ear it darlin' exhaled Patric, his smile intensifying.

Following his recovery after the marathon trek from Ireland, brother Patric had applied himself to becoming the most hardworking and dedicated of brother Baldor's employees. As a matter of necessity, Patric's eager young mind had picked up the language quickly, and it was not long before he could swear with the best of them on the building-site. Following several black-eyes, he also soon learned that it would be a wise move indeed, to do away with the distinctive Celtic red-mane that apparently marked him a northerner, even though he came from an island to the west...

Brother Baldor's group had shortened their gofer's uncouth Celtic name to Ric, and in a further effort to fit in amongst the southerners, Patric had soon adopted the title.

Every night the pining lad would go out under the stars. The very same stars which could be seen from his homeland. He would then assure his beloved Enixam that he was labouring in earnest to make his fortune, so he might return to her at the earliest opportunity. Patric would also warn his father that he looked forward to rubbing his nose in his son's success.

173

However, the naïve lad would soon further learn that an apprenticeship in one of the lower Masonic-orders would not see him amass a fortune any time soon. Though all the Masonic trades were well paid in comparison to the non-stone-based careers, and though Patric was certainly earning far more than he could have in his homeland, he soon found much of what he earned was swallowed by the high cost of living in The-Big-Smoke. As the seasons toiled passed, the ambitious lad had therefore given more and more thought to a change of field within the industry.

At the top of the Masonic pecking order were the dealers in stone, the stone-smiths of weapons and the makers of beakers. Yet Patric knew that it took a lot of time, brown-nosing and bribing, to gain admittance into the highest echelons of the trade. On the next rung-down of Masonic hierarchy were the Masonic-builders and users of stone-weapons, the warriors. Just below them, the stone-herders. Below these were a thousand increasingly-obscure and quirky apparently-masonic roles. However, Patric had no wish to take up a career of violence, having seen quite enough of it already in his short lifetime, and yet neither did the nomadic lifestyle of the stone-herd appeal.

So it was, that by the end of his first year amongst the southern beaker-people, Patric had at last decided upon his future niche within the stone-world. It was a calling just below that of the stone-herders. A job upon which all the other major-stone-construction roles relied. A job which was extremely well paid, yet relatively easy to get into. Patric would become a stone-scaffolder.

Given Allen's earlier scepticism concerning the stone-circle in the Lake district, and Alex's comments that he should see a little more of the story before passing judgement, Allen had chuckled at Patric's career-choice. By the close of his second year in the south-east, the determined Celtic lad had indeed found employment within his chosen area of the trade, and had said an emotional farewell to brother Baldor's band.

During this same period, something else had also happened to the hormone-driven teenager away from home, and that of course had been the local female population. For the first year, the young lad had admirably rejected numerous advances from many an amorous lass. For all the girls it seemed, liked a boy in a Masonic-apron. Yet irrespective of their many charms, Patric had initially found it easy to say no, for he bathed in the radiance of the light of his life, Enixam, and needed on other. Yet as he grew ever nearer to the age Enixam had been when he'd departed his homeland, it began to dawn on an embarrassed Patric that the

174

object of his affections must have perceived him as a child at the time, and therefore it was no wonder Enixam had never actually told him she loved him in *that* way.

Surely the beauteous, charming and intelligent girl would by now be wedded to someone worthy of her.

By the outset of his third year in The Big Smoke, Patric found himself feeling increasingly at home within the beaker-people's culture, which he'd originally regarded simply as a means to an end. He also felt increasingly less-inspired to blow-out the local talent. In the end, he felt more horny than guilty about breaking what was after all, an oath concerning a childhood crush.

Patric had been initially intimidated by the sprawling riverside settlement, as it was far greater in size than any of his previous experience. Yet the impressionable lad soon became beguiled and intoxicated by its infinite cosmopolitan sights, sounds and smells, and began to think of his own birthplace as an ignorant backwater by comparison.

By the end of that second year in The-Big-Smoke, the sixteen-year-old Patric was still intent upon making a fortune, but was in no hurry to return home with it. For the most part, Patric's income was going on girls, clothes, ponies, and enjoying himself in general, rather than being ferreted away for the future.

However, by nineteen the hard-working, hard-playing, fiery 'Ric' ran a scaffolding team of his own, had a tidy sum of stone stashed away, and a nice little drum in the mason's quarter of the large-settlement. The circular, domed-roofed properties of the The-Big-Smoke had the appearance of an overturned kettle-drum, and were indeed referred to by their owners as 'drums', as many people of the region still do so to this day.

After five years of playing the field, the successful young geezer had attracted the attentions of the delectable and equally-ambitious Nattarra, two years Patric's junior, and the couple were wed in the following year. The year after Patric's marriage, upon his twenty-first birthday, a great proclamation was issued by the druids to all the masons of the land. Apparently passing on a message from Geezer the great, the holy brotherhood announced that a vast and most holy stone-building project was to be undertaken, and that all interested devout members of the Masonic brotherhood should attend the chosen hallowed building-site, to tender for the equally vast contracts.

Patric recognized a rare opportunity to truly become an extremely wealthy and influential man in one fell swoop, for these vast contracts would command rewards of equal scale. In an effort to keep Geezer, Domi, and any other gods with an interest on their side, each and every Masonic lodge, as every clan, paid a portion of their income to the druids, and the holy-brotherhood were well and truly loaded. It was therefore with a grim resolve that Patric pursued and secured the desired contract, against strenuous competition.

However, the particular task which the Celt was to undertake was of such a scale that his every worldly possession was required to stand as surety, to attain just the first instalment for the men and materials necessary. Yet Patric worried little, for was his fortune not tied up in dependable stone? and therefore as safe as houses?

So it was, seven days before the summer-solstice, the Lants had set out on their last-remaining pony to return to the holy building-site, and gain the ceremonial blessing and permission of the druids to begin work.

'Aren't we going after them?' asked Allen. The two still stood outside Patric's house, whilst the young couple had now disappeared from view down the lane.

'In a moment mate' replied Alex, before gesturing to the domed-abode 'I just wondered if you recognized the place at all?'

'What do you mean, Recognized the place?' Allen's expression and tone were confused.

'No feelings of deja-vu perhaps?' Alex asked, raising his eyebrows in apparent disappointment.

'What *are* you going on about now Alex?'

'Well you bloody should' said Alex, taking Allen's hand. Allen felt the ground shift beneath his feet, and the scene before him blurred. Seemingly it was fast-forward time yet again.

'Fuck!' exhaled Allen, shaking his head, 'I'm back'. It was now night-time, yet a night-time lit by the amber halo of electric street lights. Allen was standing on the uneven pavement in front of the scaffold-clad, turn-of-the-century drab semi where he rented a damp room. Alex was once more attired in an ever-changing business-suit.

'You see Allen' commented Alex, 'different era, different incarnation, same address'.

'Oh bollocks-to-yer!' giggled Allen.

176

'I shit-you-not Allen mate, Patric's house stood exactly where you live now'.

'Yeah right Alex'.

'And I've been here before when I was alive too chap' continued Alex, ignoring his companion's cynical tone. 'In fact, the last time I was here in body was on the day I died..'

'Corse you were' Allen smiled glibly.

'Yep! The last sale I ever made in fact!'

'Were you *really*?' Allen responded in mock-serious tone. Alex remained silent, but began to look increasingly uncomfortable.

'It's the very fact of what I did that day Allen, which is the reason you live here now in this-life mate!' Alex confessed at last, his tone sheepish.

'The bloody reason I live here Alex *is*, it's the best I can piggin afford at the moment!' laughed Allen.

'No' Alex's tone was emphatic. 'The reason you live here, is that I sold this pile-o-shite to a young couple in nineteen-eighty-seven, knowing it had subsidence. I even made the mortgage-interview appointment for them, and pre-warned the dodgy-surveyor on the mobile before the viewing was even over' Alex grimaced.

'Subsidence?' Allen commented thoughtfully, looking up at his own bedroom window with concern. Even though he knew he was dreaming, Allen wouldn't have put anything past 'fat' Mehmet, his highly-debateable Turkish landlord. When he'd moved in, some eighteen months earlier, Allen had asked about the scaffolding. Hairy as a bear, beer-belly poorly-restrained by string-vest, and constantly chewing the stub of a cigar, 'Fat' Mehmet had owned up to being far too kind for his own good. As a caring landlord, he was apparently having the building completely refurbished for the good of his tenants.

No builders had ever materialised. The scaffolding had remained. The jowly, moustachioed-Mehmet reminded Allen of a Mexican bandit from a spaghetti-western.

Due to the cheapness of the rent, Allen had never queried the matter.

'It's due to what the poor bastards who I sold it to, went through after they moved in..' Alex continued, '..which meant my next incarnation would have to come and live here themselves. Balance the ol' spiritual-books of atonement so-to-speak.' Alex fell silent, looking down at his shuffling feet. After a while, Allen burst into laughter.

177

'It's a friggin good job I know this whole load of bull is just a dream Alex! Coz if that were true I'd feel highly justified in giving you a good kick in the balls!'

'I wouldn't blame you mate!' chuckled Alex wryly, before adding, 'but the reason we've both been to this address begins with Patric'.

'How so?' asked Allen, disappointed in himself for even entering into the insane conversation.

'Well, the reason the place had subsidence in the first place was down to Pat's greed..'

'Pat's greed?'

'Yep, him and that poxy cellar of his!' Alex responded.

'The cellar?' Allen echoed. In the blurring history of Patric's first seven years with the beaker-people, He'd seen the young Celt have an ever-deepening cellar excavated beneath his property, as many of the day did. It was in this vault, roofed over by stout oak beams, Patric stored away an ever-increasing wealth in stone. The successful mason's vault had nearly been full-to-brimming when he married. Yet it had of course been completely emptied shortly-after, with the initial outlay for the masonic-bribes required in order to get him in front of the druids, and the first down-payment on manpower and materials just to start the ground-works required in the huge construction-contract. Patric hadn't worried, because he knew that he would never need the vault again. His next vault would be far-larger, and dug under a far-larger property.

'Yes indeed' continued Alex, 'between Pat's time and that of the Victorians and Edwardians, when this lot all went up' Alex gestured up and down the shabby, bay-fronted properties of the run-down street, 'soil levels obviously rose, as each culture built on the remains of those that went before it. However, in the nineteen-hundreds builders didn't go down very far foundation wise, and the buggers had no idea they'd plonked your home-to-be on top of Pat's still-collapsing vault. In the right soil-conditions, oak can last for thousands of years. When the oak finally gave up the ghost, the house above subsided.'

'Are you quite finished?' Allen asked.

'I think so'.

'Well then, if it's all the same to you, I'll just pop back upstairs and get me-ed-down shall I? I've got work in the morning!' Allen was about to step forward when again he felt the ground shift beneath him, the scene blurring, and daylight returned. Patric's white-washed house stood before him once more.

178

'Shall we catch up with Pat then?' asked Alex innocently, before striding off in the direction the young couple had gone.

'Right fuckin-behind yer!' Allen growled to himself, before following.

Just after midday, on the fourth day since they'd set out from The-Big-Smoke, Patric and a constantly-complaining Nattarra arrived at their destination, some eighty miles west of modern-day London. Here it was, set amid a wide and windswept barren plain, that the druids had ordained this holiest of building-projects would take place.

As with many stone-age monuments, the site had already been considered hallowed ground since the wood-age. Narrow holes of about an arm's depth ringed the site, forming a great circle. Those wishing to please Geezer and the other gods of rock and soil would make pilgrimage here, to place votive offerings in the holes.

Patric dismounted and strode purposefully to the centre of the great ring, which was marked by a single great timber post rising some four-men's height skyward. He stared about him, breathing in the sweet summer breeze and the peaceful serenity of the isolated spot. Feeling the sun on his face, eyes closed, arms outstretched and smiling widely, he could almost taste the wealth which would soon be his.

'I tell you fackin-what!' Nattarra's piercing voice echoed across the open plain, shattering the silence. 'This had better bloody be worth it Ricky! For your sake! Look at the bleedin state-o-me!'

'Oh, it'll be *more* than worth it luv!' Patric crooned. 'By Domi, more than worth it!'

'So where are the ol-buggers then!' his wife spat angrily, staring about the empty plain.

'That's no way to talk about our beloved druids!' Patric sniggered, before squinting up at the sun under the shade of his palm. 'We're a little early, they'll be along in a while'. Patric paced back toward to his shapely wife. Despite being just about to meet holy-men, Nattarra was still attired for the beach.

'Natti-luv' the buoyant Patric cooed.

'What?'

'How d'yer fancy a naughty quick one eh? There's time..'

Apparently, according to his wife there wasn't. Not even if they had all the 'fackin' time in the world.

CH 18: HOLY SMOKE

From *The* Book, Allen knew the druids believed themselves to be apart from others, for they bore a heavy burden. A secret handed down through generations uncounted. A secret the flock were not quite ready for yet.
In an age when most never left their village of birth, the druids often made long journeys not only all around the country attending to the congregation, but also abroad to consult with their foreign counterparts, with whom they were in secret alliance, and with whom they shared their dark secret.
When not on the road, the druids of the beaker-people and Celts dwelt apart from all others in remote communes. In the north, this was upon the remote isles later to be known as the Orkneys. In the west, on the island later to be called Mona, and then Holyhead, just off the coast of Anglesey. Whilst in the south, the druids dwelt within a natural inland island-fortress. An isle surrounded by treacherous bog and marshland, four day's march west of The-Big-Smoke. It was a pleasant wooded isle of oak, elm, beech and sycamore, bordered to the west by high hills.
Druids were chosen generally in their early teenage years. In any community, there would always be those who had a natural talent for hard manual-labour, making and fixing things, agriculture, hunting, fighting, or organizing. Yet there would always be those who seemed to serve no practical purpose whatsoever, and who spent most of their time asking why things were the way they were. These were to be the next generation of druids. On their constant rounds, the druids would ask the village headman if there was anyone they could do without, and would leave with the most feckless teenager available.
Novices would be taken to the northern home of the druids in the Orkneys, where they would remain until early middle-age. Here they would live a hard life, sleeping on hard cots in tiny stone cells. They would live on gruel and water. They would endure the howling, storm-wracked elements and the sub-zero temperatures. Dawn till dusk would be spent in solitary meditation, and memorising the vast array of deities of their stone-age world. They would live a chaste existence and were allowed no alcohol or any other stimulant.
When it was deemed that they had attained a suitable level of wisdom through endurance, abstinence and inner reflection, the acolytes would then be sent to the far-more-pleasant forested isle in the south. Following rites and ritual, they would then be told the dark secret.

180

They would then be taught about drugs.

In herb-lore, the ancient priesthood was unrivalled. Indeed, the druids had chosen their southern island home not only for its inaccessible nature, but also due a small bush which grew only in the wetland surrounding the isle, and nowhere else. The Gla Bush.

It was the small dark berries of this inconspicuous plant, which appeared just before midsummer, in which the druids were most interested. If the ripened fruit was squeezed, the flat, circular, almost pill-shaped stone was easily popped into the mouth and swallowed. The berry flesh was then eaten. After a short a period, the potent berries acted as an intense-stimulant to the senses. However, the druids knew only the wise who shared their dark secret should attempt to take the berry in this form. For its intense mind-expanding effects could also lead to insanity for the naïve and ignorant, who were generally unprepared for its visions. After being stored and dried however, the berry had a soothing and mellowing effect. It was for this reason the druids harvested them and handed them out to all spectators at the extremely emotive Domi-Knows and foot-ball contests, to prevent violence amongst the crowds.

None except the druids were allowed to set foot upon the hallowed isle in the south. This was apparently due to the fact the very gods walked that sacred soil, and those who had not had druidic training would have their very minds burned away should they behold them in the waking world. In truth, it was to keep the population away from the Gla-berries.

However, upon the summer solstice, the longest day, people were apparently relinquished from any obligation to their gods, who ruled every aspect of their lives throughout the rest of the year. This ancient custom had originally been intended by the druids to act as a pressure valve, allowing the flock to let off steam. However, annoyingly enough to the holy order, it also meant they were powerless to prevent the annual invasion of their isle from an army of those intent on picking the fresh berries and having one hell of a party. Indeed, the fresh-berries were so strong that their effect lasted for three days, as did the party. Each year, due to the sheer mayhem, weirdness, and general outrageousness of the wild festivities, those southern druids not off on their travels would retreat to the safety of a solitary high hill, on the eastern side of the island. The steep slopes of the hill were ringed by four concentric timber palisades, behind which were terraced vegetable and herb gardens, and storage halls

181

for the dried berries. So, each year the druids would stoically withstand the annual siege, whilst their flock got up to the-gods-only-knew-what below. It was the stone of the Gla bush fruit which gave the long-lasting high, rather than the flesh, and being under its influence was therefore referred to as being 'stoned'. Another attraction to party-goers was a readily available source of food. For scavenger birds, such as ravens would also eat the berries, and in their stoned state the carrion birds littered the ground. An occurrence known as 'the-stoning-of-the-crows'. The birds could then be picked up and roasted, a drug-and-munchies in one.

In later ages, due to climate change and land reclamation, the unique wetland habitat of the Gla bush would dry up, and the island become no more than a hillock, so that the bush became extinct and was lost to botanic history.

The druids also partook of a strong hallucinogenic mushroom which appeared in the late Autumn upon their isle, known as the Lon mushroom. The ignorant and lost who wandered onto the isle and witnessed secret druidic rituals not for their eyes, would be given the mushroom. They would then be hard-put to recall what was real or not, after the event.

As well as spiritual-guides, the Druids were also the healers of their time. Like the doctors of today, they thought a lot-of-problems could be remedied by handing out a lot-of-drugs.

Amongst other narcotic weeds, the druids had also brought back the seeds of the cannabis plant from their distant travels. They grew a rich crop of pot on the sunny, terraced slopes of their fortified hill, sheltered from both the elements and solstice festival-goers by high, spiky timber-walls.

The reason for the druids' interest in all-things-druggy, stemmed from their dark secret. For the priesthood were weighed-down by the elaborate and continuous lies they had to concoct for their people's own good, and ensure their secret remained undiscovered. The druids were generally under the influence of mellowing substances giving rise to many wondrous theories and ideas far beyond the mundane, if of little practical use. This assisted their imagination in creating further far-fetched but plausible lies. Or they were on stimulating, euphoric substances, to deal with the guilt of telling so many lies, to so many people, over such a long period of time. Mainly, it helped them deal with the dark knowledge they shielded their people from.

From *The* Book's history of the beaker-people, Allen had seen that although the masons liked to believe they controlled their stone-age society, they themselves were unknowingly manipulated by the ancient priesthood of the elder gods.

From the Stone-Way, to the Domi-Knows stadium and foot-ball, and indeed to their latest proposed colossal stone-building-project to the gods, the druids had only one purpose in mind for the masons, and that was to keep the dangerous-buggers busy. Left to their own devices, the druids knew that any all-powerful group soon grew bored. This generally led to conquest, warfare, repression, and mistaken ideas of divinity and grandeur. In short, a lot of aggravation for everyone else concerned.

Due to their unique position as spokesmen for the gods, whom all men feared, even the influential masons dared not openly go against the will of the druids. Yet over the long passage of the stone-age, the power of the Masonic order had increased to such an extent that the druids had grown ever-more anxious, and ever-more annoyed at the stone-wrights' ever-growing arrogance and self-importance. The druids' greatest fear was that the more powerful and controlling the masons became, the greater chance their dark-secret would be revealed.

Therefore, nothing was more amusing to the druids after a good puff, than dreaming up new Herculean ridiculous-tasks to keep the masons occupied. So it had been, in the obscenely-early hours following one such smoke-entwined gathering, the idea for the 'great-door' had been born. The druids had verily pissed themselves. As far as the masons and the rest of the population were to be concerned, the vast stone doorway would allegedly act as a portal to the spirit-world. This would allegedly allow their holy-men easier access to the gods, and thereby gain on behalf of the people, their greater divine favour. In truth, the idea for a doorway leading to the 'other-side' had come about by the druids' lamenting the fact that due to a cooler-climate, their home-grown brownish-green hash, was not as powerful as the deeper-green plant which they had sampled in hotter countries abroad. Therefore Deliars, the high-druid (though in truth all the brotherhood were as high as kites) had reflected that it would be great if there was indeed a portal to the 'other-side', because it was a well-known fact that the *grass* was greener there.

In an effort to ensure the masons would be occupied for many generations to come, the druids agreed the stone-doorway must indeed be of huge dimensions, as of course befitting to the gods. So it was, the eager army of masons wishing to be immortalised by taking part in this career-making feat of holy-construction, had been interviewed. It was the most ambitious, and therefore most dangerous to the druids' minds, who were to be given the sought-after lucrative contracts. The biggest liars went to the front of the queue, and no one exaggerated their experience, list of satisfied customers, size of operation and sound financial-backing as much as Patric. The liars were most-feared by the druids of course, and it was they who must be kept most busy for as long as possible. For the deceitful had the greatest chance of recognising the brotherhood as fellow liars. For indeed, it takes one to know one.

So it had been later that same year, two senior-druids had set out from the marsh-bound isle some days before the summer solstice, to meet Patric; He who was to have the great honour of beginning the epic task, and erect the stone-scaffolding which would eventually support the bottom hinge of the great-stone-door.

Their holy-brothers had watched them go, each hoping this next great undertaking would ensure (for the next few generations at least) that the population would be very busy indeed, and that the great secret would remain protected, for they loved their people. Deliars did have a side bet down as to how else the Masons might be dealt with, but only he and a close-knit circle of senior druids were aware it. But until that came to fruition, which was by no means certain, it was better to have a long-term plan in place. *The* Book had not hinted as to what this alternative ruse might be.

The dark secret of the druids was that they knew there weren't any gods, and the druids should know, because it was they who'd made them up in the first place..

CH 19: BE CAREFUL WHAT YOU WISH FOR

'Can yer still see em?' Nattarra asked through the gritted teeth of a wide set smile, as she waved enthusiastically. The girl stood on tiptoe, squinting into the distance as she waved.

'No, that's them just about gone I'd say' replied Patric out of the corner of his mouth, waving and smiling in similar fashion. He could no longer see the two white specks on the near horizon. The couple stopped waving, but continued grinning.

The two druids had arrived at the site shortly after Patric and his wife. They had completed a hasty ceremony (which had included the handing over of the stone-seal of the druids, and formal reconfirmation of the fee for the works being undertaken) and had promptly left. The druids had been keen to get the forty-mile return-journey to their isle underway as soon as possible, for the summer solstice was in three days. The holy-men wished to be safely within the walls of their hill-fort with time to spare, before the first festival goers arrived on their island.

'Well' said Patric in a calm, measured tone, still gazing along the track upon which the druids had departed under the hazy, afternoon sunshine.

'Well indeed' said Nattarra, standing next to her husband, arms at her sides. Minutes passed in silence. 'How much did he say they were going to pay you again?' Nattarra asked at last, her tone seemingly only of mild interest. Patric repeated the price woodenly.

'R-right' his wife responded quietly.

The black pony whinnied nervously, pulling against his tether, and startled birds took to the air all around, as the calm silence of the plain was suddenly shattered by screams and howls of hysterical delight. After many minutes of cries, shrieks, oaths, and general running and jumping about, Patric and Nattarra collapsed on their backs, breathlessly staring up at the summer sky. They giggled.

'Well darlin, we'd better be gettin on our way if we're gonna get the pick of the berries at the festival' Patric chuckled hoarsely, reaching out to take Nattarra's hand in his.

'What's the hurry my clever boy?' Nattarra purred seductively in answer, 'surely there's time for a *naughty-quick-one* isn't there?' she added, rolling on top of her husband. Patric's answer was stifled by her lips.

'Do you think we should turn around or something?' Allen asked guiltily, though of course neither he or Alex did.

Obviously without the slightest trace of shame, Alex didn't fast-forward time again until the flushed couple were readying to set off westward toward the island festival. He also didn't warn his companion that it would be four-and-a-half years later, before time would slow to the pace Allen was used to living with.

Following his recovery from that year's festival, Patric had commenced the task immediately. He'd already hired the services of an army of the Masonic, including scaffolders, herders and general labourers, all of whom set to work with the religious fervour of he who is on a fat bonus if the job is completed in time. The workforce was of such a scale that a bustling, tented settlement sprang up about the site overnight. The first urgent task to be undertaken upon any building site of the beaker-people, where workers were big meat eaters and entitled to six beer-breaks a day, was the digging of the toilet-ditch. Due to the vast number of workers, and the length of time construction was expected to take, the ditch had to be of immense proportions indeed. It ringed the entire building site, and was very wide and very deep. The excavated earth formed an inner bank, as high as a man, and would be tipped back into the fouled ditch when work was completed.
A minor tributary of the Stone-way which ran from Wales in the west, eastward towards the main Em-Wun, passed someway to the north of the building site, and stone was diverted from it, to supply the vast amount which would be required in the project. Firstly, a great flotilla of giant rafts brought the stone southward, where it was disembarked about a mile and a half from the building site. From the river bank to the construction-site, a wide avenue of flattened earth was prepared, and as the greatest stones were each landed, a legion of herders added them to the lines, whilst smaller stones took the fast-track route of being dragged on rollers. Once on site, the scaffolding erectors and joiners would then begin to manoeuvre the stones into place. So, the great army laboured on through the cycles of the seasons, overseen by a nervous Patric, and a gleeful wife, turned-on by the fact that her husband commanded the entire sweating, straining host before her. This would indeed become an extremely-saucy stage of Patric's marriage, and Allen was a little disappointed that he and Alex had to view this part of the Celt's story in fast-forward mode. However, there was soon to be little time for such carnal distractions as stress levels increased, and Patric wondered more than once if he'd taken

on a task too great for his own abilities. For the truth of the matter was that Patric was flying by the seat of his pants. Little did he know that the druids were more than aware of this. If he were to make a mess of the work, that was fine with the brotherhood. The longer the works took, the longer it would be before they had to dream up another ridiculous task to keep the masons busy.

The years that followed were to be filled with incessant worry, toil, and uncounted curses concerning the fact that the foreign Welsh blue-stone was a real bastard to work with. There were to be endless negotiations with the workforce, for if anyone knew their rights, it was a mason. In the end, there would also be quite a lot of violence. Many were the set-backs and unforeseen obstacles, yet all were overcome. Four years after work began, the giant stone-scaffolding was nearly complete. Patric yet had six months to spare before the advent of the fifth winter-solstice, the date by which the job was to be finished. He was ahead of schedule.

As the finishing touches were added, an extremely weary Patric at last found himself in a calmer state of mind, and dared to look forward to a golden future. Throughout the build, Patric had received staged payments from the druids, and he'd already made a sizable down-payment on a chalk-hill in the sought-after druid-belt, which he intended to be his future pension-fund. Patric was an astute business man, and though heavily invested in harder rock, knew that it was wise to have your finger in more than one strata.

Patric had also secured land within the most expensive section of the Masonic quarter of The-Big-Smoke, and had plans drawn up for a lavish residence to be built upon it. The seal of the druids guaranteed the best line of credit possible, and Nattarra was already in possession of several new wardrobes, ponies to match certain outfits, and hand-maidens to help her dress in those outfits. All in all, as Autumn approached, all looked exceedingly rosy.

However, as the attainment of his long-wished-for goal approached, and Patric found himself with less and less to do or organize, his thoughts had unexpectedly turned to his past. More and more, Patric had begun to think of his father.

He'd realised that without Hatric having been an utter bastard, he would never have ended up where he was.

Mainly he'd realised you only get one dad.

The fiery anger which had once burned fiercely within him for Hatric, had cooled and mellowed with the passing of time, for Patric had now been in the lands of the beaker-people for nearly twelve years. The twenty-five-year old Celt still wished for his father to be aware of his own son's great accomplishment, but wanted Hatric (if he still lived) to be proud rather than bitter. He wanted his father to be comforted by the news rather than having his nose rubbed in it. He wanted his da to know he was safe and making his way in the world, rather than being enraged at having been disproved and abandoned by his first-born. So it was, Patric had dispatched riders northward to journey to his birthplace, to inform Hatric that he was alive and well, and loaded. The riders would also bear an invitation for Hatric to join his son if he so wished, so that he might witness Patric's good-fortune for himself at first hand, and spend his last years being well cared for. The riders also went with enough spare ponies to bear Patric's younger brothers, should they still dwell with their father, and the promise of employment within the Masonic brotherhood for them both.

Cover stories would of course be required for all concerned, as except for brother Baldor's band, the beaker-people world in general thought Ric to be a true blooded east-end-Geezer. This would be no problem. The O'Lants could tell tall-tales with the best of them, and Ric certainly had the resources to set the family up in new lives.

As a child, Patric had been utterly ignorant of his clan's dramatic history, and simply thought his father to be an uncaring and useless excuse for a man. However, following his talk with the ferryman concerning the O'Lants, and his long and arduous journey to manhood, Patric increasingly realised his damaged father had simply done the best he could. After all of course, without Hatric, he himself could never have been born.

Patric had therefore also found himself feeling increasingly guilty, both for the hatred he had directed toward his father for so many years, and for running out on his family in the first place. Yet Patric had now carved a place for himself in the world, and was finally able to fulfil his role as the clan's first-born son. He was now in a position to look after the O'Lants, and could settle the debt he felt he owed at last.

As winter settled upon the land, Patric's heart felt lightened as he watched the riders set off, hoping they would return in time for the winter-solstice, the shortest day. For then his family would share in Patric's great triumph. The Celt had also not forgotten his debt to the ferryman, and hoped he'd found a worthier apprentice. He would now be aged indeed, but should he yet live, then the riders were instructed to formally apologise on Patric's behalf, and inform him of the rich reward which would follow. However, given his trade, and Patric's one-time experience of sea travel, it seemed highly likely the ferryman had long been with Tides, god of the sea. Then of course there was Enixam, to whom he also owed his very life. Enixam.

She would now be twenty-nine, and no doubt wife, mother and assuredly something special in the world. The riders were charged to enquire concerning her wellbeing. Should she require assistance in anyway, then it was to be provided. Should she be content, then Patric's heart-felt gratitude was to be respectfully delivered, and oath concerning the life-debt owed. Should ever she be in need, Enixam need but send word.

Thanks to a gut-spilling, berry-fuelled first summer-solstice festival on the isle of the druids the year before, Nattarra knew of Patric's true origins, and life-story. Tellingly, though Ric was now a grown-up happily-married man, a life-story with a greatly down-played role for Enixam, though silly childhood-crush it had of course been.

Nattarra would rather die, than her catty social-circle discover her husband was a Celtic-ginge. Her silence was therefore assured. From her point of view, though she loved her husband dearly of course, Nattarra also thought the information useful, should Ric ever dream of trading her in for a younger model in the future.

Patric kept the existence of this mission strictly to himself, and the riders had departed in absolute secrecy, only to report directly to him alone. Each having been paid a small fortune, to ensure their future silence.

Nattarra therefore remained blissfully unaware of Patric's plan concerning his family. For her advice concerning Hatric, had always been to let sleeping-bastards-lie. The thought of a ragged bunch of Celts turning up on the doorstep of their soon-to-be-built mansion, in full view of their well-to-do neighbours would have mortified her.

Four days before the solstice, Patric set out with Nattarra at the head of his jubilant Masonic army, to make the twenty-mile journey northward to the Domi-Knows stadium. The Celtic-lad-made-good was to be the star of the climax of that year's winter-solstice contest. For a great ceremony would take place after the match, when the druids would proclaim Patric to be blessed by the gods before the vast crowd. On the following day, the druids would hand over the bulk of the equally vast payment for his work. Though Patric's breast swelled with pride at the holy labour he had accomplished, and though he was soon to be both wealthy and famous, his mood was not as exuberant as might be supposed. For the riders sent to his father were now long-overdue.

'Yer see Allen mate! I told you to watch this lad! What a blagger! What a grafter!' Alex cried from the air above the marching ranks of beer-swilling, singing men below. Allen didn't answer immediately as he was once again dealing with the after effects of firstly having travelled through a number of years' worth of time at an accelerated pace, and then having the breaks whacked on without warning. He now knew better than to look for any sympathy from his guide.

'Yeah, he's a real diamond-geezer Alex' Allen replied at last without much enthusiasm, still feeling a little groggy.

'Learn from him Allen-buddy, learn from him!' Alex gestured toward the Celt and his wife, who rode at the head of the procession.

'Oh yeah Alex, I have to learn from Patric!' Allen replied sarcastically, 'So first I've gotta find a *really* nice girl, promise her I'll come back for her, but then never do…'

'What like with Maxine you mean?' interjected Alex in innocent tone.

'Up yours Alex!' spat Allen, 'that's completely different!'

'Corse it is mate, corse it is' Alex replied quietly, avoiding eye contact.

'*As* I was saying, before I was so rudely-interrupted.' Allen growled, before continuing 'Then I've got to pretend to be someone else and take up with some money-grabbing-bimbo, and lie my arse off to earn enough money just to keep her happy…'

'Bimbo is a nasty word Allen, everyone's got their own way of getting through the life-thing. It often pays not to be too judgemental!' Alex warned, before adding, 'and I think *Extremely-horny* money-grabbing-bimbo is a more fitting description'.

'Huh! She's not a scrap on Enix' Allen retorted, defending the girl, but thinking of Maxine.

'Is it me Allen-mate, or did our lovely Enix get married the day after Pat left?' Alex smiled, knowing his companion wouldn't have a word said against the girl that was Maxine's double.

'Yeah, but *he* didn't know that!' Allen angrily gestured toward Patric below, before adding 'and anyway the poor-cow didn't have any choice, did she!'

'Come on Allen, give Pat a break! We've all had teenage crushes! This isn't some fairy-tale, it's real! How many people end up with their first-childhood crush eh?'

'Not some fairy-tale?' Allen chuckled in incredulous manner, reflecting on the story so far, and looking back at the diminishing great-stone-construction behind them upon the plain. 'Not some fairy-tale!' he repeated, 'what? A culture where the entire religion revolves around beer? and stone is money?' He laughed, shaking his head in disbelief.

Alex looked at his companion evenly 'And? What's so hard to believe about blokes worshipping beer?' A silence followed.

'Point-taken' Allen admitted at last.

'Don't get me wrong' Alex said after a while, 'my spirit knows that getting drunk is just a short-term remedy, a false remedy, but the bit of me that remembers what it was like to be wrapped in meat..'

'Wrapped in meat?' Allen interrupted.

'Yeah, wearing a body I mean'.

'Oh.'

'Well the bit of me that remembers what it's like to wear a body, knows that when I'm next wrapped in meat, having a few beers will feel great!' Alex chuckled.

'What do you mean? When you're *next* wrapped in meat?' Allen asked, confused.

'Well like all spirits, at some point I'll go back into a body, I've still got loads to learn, loads to contribute mate! It's not just our next reincarnation who will walk the earth again. Each individual spirit of a lifetime returns as well, how do you think we get population growth on the planet for Christ's-sake? The more lives-lived, the more spirits there are, we multiply like bacteria chap! Hell, you might even meet me one day in your life when you wake up, though of course you wouldn't recognize me, coz who knows who or what I'll come back as! And I'll be the last one to remember who I was!'

'Oh Fuck-off Alex!' Allen giggled in reply.

'You might even end up shagging me if you're not careful!' Alex added evilly, 'It happens all the time on earth! People are surrounded by their own previous incarnations and never know it!' In reply, Allen only grimaced, wishing he could bleach his mind after the mental picture which had just flashed through it. A long silence followed, below the procession marched on.

'And as for stone being of great value, what's the problem with that?' Alex asked eventually.

'Well it's ridiculous, the stuff's everywhere! If this were true, everyone would be a millionaire! They could just pick it up off the ground!' Allen replied, glad the previous head-bending subject had been changed.

'That's crap Allen, a handful of tribal-chieftains own the whole land, and they employ enough people to make sure it stays that way!'

'No I'm sorry Alex, the whole stone-is-money part of this story is one of the most unbelievable bits! It's one of the main things keeping me sane, coz it confirms this is all most-definitely a dream!'

'Oh, unbelievable, is it?' Well sunshine, in our time I believe precious stones are pretty valuable? And in this very same land in your time, about 0.6 percent of the population own over 30% percent of the land itself, and that's before you get into what the corporations own. That's the underlying-rock, the stone we're talking about. It's been handed down through many generations and it keeps the landed gentry and now the corporations mega rich, and keeps everyone else working for a living! Stone-means-wealth, in our era as well as theirs! Check it out when you get back to our time if you don't believe me, I think you'll find it's the same or worse in most countries'.

'I'll still be looking for a more meaningful relationship than one based on just sex and money' Allen said haughtily some miles on.

'Well that's a good job Allen-mate, seeing how you're generally too beered-up or too shy when you meet the birds, and broke as arse-oles' chuckled Alex as they strode along through the air.

Allen refused to take the bait, and continued unperturbed 'I'm looking for something a little bit more-worthy than a relationship based on just shaggin 'n' dosh!'

'Very well-spoken Allen, but hey! shaggin 'n' dosh makes the world go around!'

By the close of the first day's march, the Masonic column had completed the greater part of the twenty-mile northward journey, and as a frosty dusk fell they made camp. In the morning, they would march triumphantly into the winter festival site bedecked in their finest clothes and best aprons, each wearing a crown of holly. Their arrival would herald the kick-off of the first foot-ball match, and the beginning of the marathon three-day beer-and-footy fest, culminating in the great Domi-Knows competition. To stone-age man, it didn't get any better than that.

'Shit!' Allen exhaled, poor bloody Pat!' he added in sympathy. It was now midnight, and Allen and Alex stood next to Patric on the frost-spiked grass, just beyond the firelight of the encampment. Above, a cloudless black heaven was bejewelled with bright stars. Patric's mournful upturned face was streaked with tears. Earlier that evening, amidst the singing and revelry, Patric had been called from the fireside. The overdue riders who had been sent north at the beginning of the season had at last returned. The reason for the delay in their return had also now become clear.

Patric was no fool, for his hard life had made him a realist. Before he'd even sent his emissaries to his homeland, the Celt had considered the fact that his father may well already be dead. For Hatric hardly looked after himself, and by now would be quite an age for that era. However, it was not the fact that the messengers sadly confirmed Patric's father was indeed now with Domi, but rather it was the nature of Hatric's death which had frozen his son's heart, and left him feeling broken and empty, upon the very eve of the realization of all his dreams.

Though the messengers had indeed at last found Patric's fetid birthplace, they had suffered serious delay upon both the outward and return journeys. After following the Celt's careful directions, they had quickly found the small fisher-village on the western coast of Scotland, but had been informed that the ferryman no longer sailed from there, due to long-term unrest on the further shore. Not only had Pat's emissaries had to travel some distance southward before finding another ferryman to carry them to Ireland, but also therefore landed many days march of the village of the Bird's-eye. The ferryman concerned had been much younger than he who had rescued Patric, and so it could only be assumed that the old man now plied his trade elsewhere or had indeed crossed to the *other* side.

Having arrived in Pat's homeland, it soon became clear to the riders as they journeyed northward, that they were entering a war-zone. According to the ever-more emaciated, furtive and fearful locals, the entire northern half of the isle had been locked in bitter inter-tribal strife for not far off twelve cycles of the seasons, so that the lands through which they travelled became ever-more sparsely-populated, barren and desolate, punctuated increasingly with burnt-out homesteads, villages and evidence of terrible-atrocity.

By travelling only at night, and being well armed and trained, the party remained unmolested and avoided confrontation. But even when they arrived in the far north-east of the isle, the locals refused to guide any who searched for the hated O'Lants.

However, they did at last reach journey's end, and there had discovered a lowly and foul-smelling despicable pair of wretches, who cowered at their feet, begging not to be slain. When at last Patric's cringing younger-brothers seemed to grasp that the messengers meant them no harm, and after they had greedily consumed the meat and a large amount of beer the riders offered in order to gain their trust, they had been more inclined to talk.

When questioned, the brothers had cried into their beer, saying that their father had been long dead. Indeed, he had died the very same season their elder brother had disappeared. Hatric had fallen to his death from the great cliff, joining his ancestors in their watery grave. But their father hadn't tripped, rather he'd been pushed, or more to the point, butted...

Apparently, the family goat had been extremely skittish and bad tempered ever since Patric had left. One day she had slipped her leash and charged at Hatric, as he stood taking a leak over the side of the cliff....

The goat had then escaped to freedom, disappearing inland.

Upon hearing the news, Patric had instantly been transported back to a teenage boy, about to set Adwi free. Though at the time it had broken his heart, he'd not released his beloved-pet to ensure his father's wellbeing. Yet in a cruel twist of fate, his actions had ensured Hatric's death. In Patric's mind, he'd killed his own father.

'Be careful what you wish for..' quoted Alex, '..because you just might get it'.

Patric had desperately wished for Adwi to have her freedom, and his wish had been granted, at the cost of his father's life. Alex raised his eyebrows 'If I recall correctly Allen, at the time you said it was a real-shame about leaving the goat to a certain death'.

'Well y-yeah..' Allen stammered, raising his hands, 'but how was I to know?' he added, his tone defensive.

'You weren't' replied Alex, 'it's just a good lesson in the intricacies of the world mate'.

The riders had also failed to return with Peeta and Porl, for when they had awoken the following morning, the messengers had found that the rancid brothers had disappeared, along with most of their provisions and ponies. Meaning they all had to double-up, thus delaying their return still further.

And then there had been the news concerning Enixam.

The handful of riders had been unable to reach the village of the Bird's-Eye, as they had been informed it was presently encircled by the besieging forces of the powerful O'Hoohalarahan clan. No one was getting in or out. Apparently the current civil-strife had erupted some eleven years previously, when rumour had reached the ears of the O'Hoohalarahans that one of their number had fairly-and-squarely won that year's Onni-Okki competition, only to be the cruelly chased into the sea in the dead of night by the Bird's-Eye and surrounding clans, clearly out of envy, and to cheat the victor of his prize.

The clan's fury doubled when those concerned cowardly attempted to insult their intelligence, by fobbing their envoy off with far-fetched tales of the now-extinct O'Lants being responsible. The outcome of the resulting tribal-war had hung in the balance over the years, with one side first gaining the upper hand, and then the other. Recently things had gone badly for the Bird's-eye and their allies, so that they'd been pushed back against the coastline, and local opinion seemed to be that the O'Hoohalarahan's were not far off final victory.

So it was, Patric had received the news that his actions had not only killed his father, but had also sealed the fate of his childhood sweetheart.

CH 20: A DREAM FULFILLED

The circular Domi-Knows festival site was vast, over four miles across, with the stadium set at its centre, like the hub of a wheel. Radiating outwards, like the spokes of a wheel, foot-ball pitches marked out in chalk, surrounded the stadium, which were in turn encircled by the barrows of long-dead heroes and generous sponsors of both games. Marked by standing stones, encircling these sporting-grounds were the clan encampments. The northern half of the site was occupied by the invading army of northerners, whose faces were painted with blue-woad, and the southern half was occupied by the southerners, whose faces were painted with red ochre. Each half of this outer ring was subdivided into fields for each of the different occupational clans, with the Masonic camping-site occupying the largest area, and having the best view.

Indeed, the masons of the south had built a huge forty-metre high man-made hill within their campsite, which gave an unparalleled view of the entire, otherwise flat surrounding area, and underlined that the masons were truly above all others. Upon this great hill was set the polished rock throne of the leader of the southern masons, a man with more titles than the credits of a Hollywood block-buster, and who was referred to as 'The-Most-Grand-High-Worshipful-Master' for short.

Each winter, many-many thousands would descend upon the winter solstice festival to witness and take part in the spectacular event. Indeed, so great were the crowds, that their cheers could be heard from afar, and at night time it would appear as if the very stars had fallen to earth, for so numerous were the camp-fires.

Though the whole event had been their idea, the druids detested the raucous often-violent festival, for they hated sport in general. Thousands of years earlier, the druids had introduced sport in an effort to reduce the number of people being killed within their volatile culture. The holy-brotherhood had no problem with those who took part in any sporting event for it allowed people to let off steam, work as a team, and gain satisfaction from the honing of their own skills. However, the druids had failed to foresee the phenomenon of 'supporters'. For the druids believed it was a nonsense for any soul to base their own individual happiness on how their team were doing. Also. the violence which had been reduced by getting people to take part in a contest had been replaced by the violence amongst opposing supporters.

Yet due to their unique status within their society, the druids' presence was required at each such sporting gathering, to act as referees. So it was that each winter solstice, the druids from all around the land would also descend upon the site. Yet they dwelt in a number of timber-walled hill-forts which ringed the festival site, half a mile so distant. Inside the walls of these forts were stored enough dried berries to keep the huge crowd sedated for three days.

'Jesus!' Allen gasped, from high above the sea of red and blue tents, and make-shift timber shacks. The bright morning air was woven with plumes of smoke, and the heady aroma of herbs, spices and roasting meat and fish. Drum-beats, horn-calls, and differing chants and cheers arose high into the chilly air, echoing backward and forward across the sprawling encampment, like an ebbing and flowing tide, even though the games had not yet begun.

Below, like a returning conquering army, Patric's column snaked its way into the southern Masonic encampment, winding about the base of the great hill, to the adulation and wild cries of their brethren. From his lofty throne, surrounded by the highest of the Masonic order and his guards, The-Most-Grand-High-Worshipful-Master raised his clenched-fist in salute to those who had accomplished the first phase of the great doorway to the 'other-side'.

'Wow!' exhaled Allen, impressed by the spectacle and vast numbers below.

Despite being the hero of the day, Patric was understandably subdued, and had spoken little to his wife or subordinates since the riders had returned from the north, the night before. However, none seemed to notice, as all, especially Nattarra, were too caught up in the glorious moment. The head of the column halted at last before the great hill, and Patric dismounted amid the deafening cries of the crowd.

Naked save for a leather apron and jock-strap, huge, shaven-headed warriors, painted head-to-foot in deepest red, ringed the hill. These were the masonic guard. Hard as rock. Painted red so their blood never showed in battle, for all knew you couldn't get blood out of a stone. Two stood aside, and with his wife and management team following at a respectful distance, Patric began the assent of the white chalk path which coiled upwards about the hill, until at last he stepped out onto the flattened, circular summit. Even-huger red-painted guards bowed low, before stepping backward, allowing Patric admittance into the Masonic inner circle.

The ring of warriors closed behind the Celt, and Patric's entourage waited obediently upon the path, just below and out of sight of the hill-top. Alex and Allen stepped onto the ground behind Pat.

Morbrix, the leader of the Masonic order, sat upon his throne of polished stone before them, swathed in a black bear-pelt. He was a balding, heavy-set man in his mid-fifties, with paunch spilling out of his richly patterned apron; piggy-yet-quick eyes, and sweaty, pallid features.

Patric halted some paces from the throne, before sinking to one knee. 'GEEZER-MOST-SORTED! THOU ART TRULY A ROCK LEGEND' came the cry from all those gathered upon the hill-top. Patric inclined his head in acknowledgment of the accolade, before rising. There then followed an elaborate and prolonged ritual involving the rolling up of sleeves, trouser legs, numerous funny handshakes, and a barrage of odd questions from the gathered Masonic dignitaries, to which Patric responded with equally odd answers. All then formed a circle, and recited well-rehearsed, yet seemingly meaningless verses, whilst scratching the back of the man in front of them.

'Tossers!' said Alex and Allen in unison, shaking their heads at the antics of the grown men before them. When the annoying ceremony was finally over, Morbrix arose from his throne.

'Ah, young brother Lant!' he greeted Patric enthusiastically, 'I can see we're going to have to watch out for you!' Polite laughter rippled around those gathered about the throne.

'Come' Morbrix beckoned to the Celt with podgy finger, as he slowly strode to the edge of the hill. The towering guards stepped back as The-Most-Grand-High-Worshipful-Master reached the brink, to be met by the roar of the masses below. Patric joined Morbrix, and was himself greeted by fresh cries of adulation from the crowd. Morbrix took Patric's hand in a sweaty palm, and raised it high. The guards flanking the pair put rams' horns to their lips and sent up a great fanfare. The vast crowd below obediently fell silent.

'GEEZER!' cried Morbrix.

'**GEEZER!**' cried the crowd. Following several roaring encores which echoed across the plain, Morbrix placed a fatherly arm about Patric's shoulders and led the Celt to his great tent, which stood just beyond the throne. The pair were joined by Morbrix's most trusted advisor, an elderly and bowed man, named Ballast, whose many titles were shortened to

'The-Venerated-Keeper-Of-The-Left-Handed-Secret-Trowel'. Allen and Alex followed.

The interior of the huge hide tent was opulent in the extreme. The floor was thick with deep furs, and heavy pelts stretched over high timber frames divided the cavernous interior into separate chambers. The billowing ceiling was richly decorated with interlinking Masonic devices, and a fire of coal, the recently discovered fire-stone, crackled within a hearth of beautifully-squared stones, set at the centre of the outer reception area.

Morbrix settled himself in an intricately-carved, high-backed chair set before the fire, whilst Ballast shuffled to take his place at his master's right-hand. Patric stood before the pair. The muffled noise of frivolity and celebration could be heard from below, and from somewhere inside the tent came the sound of giggling females.

'Well lad, you've done well' exhaled Morbrix, as he accepted a beaker of steaming warmed beer from a scantily-clad serving girl, who then retreated behind the curtain from where she had silently emerged, moments before. 'Though of course..' Morbrix continued between slurps, '..the way of the stone-scaffolder... is a noble calling, we must see about elevating.... your status somewhat, after having served Geezer-the-great so well, young Ric'.

'My thanks Most-Worshipful-master' Patric responded gratefully, smiling, though his mind was still utterly filled with the dark vision of his father falling from the great cliff, and rape and pillage in the village of the Bird's-eye.

'Yes indeed' Morbrix said quietly, staring into the flames as he warmed his feet. 'Come' he said kindly, 'sit with me and tell me of yourself and your kin'. The Masonic ruler gestured to the furs at his feet, for The-Most-Grand-High-Worshipful-Master looked up to no man, except the High-druid, and only then begrudgingly.

And perhaps not even him for much longer...

So, the interview commenced. Patric repeated his well-rehearsed, completely- fictitious family history, which put his ancestral-home and birthplace not only on the mainland, but also in the very bosom of the south. Patric was well versed indeed in the counter-history of himself and his clan, and was extremely proud of it. It was an elaborate and entertaining yarn. Constructed and added-to over the many years to cloak his Celtic origin, and designed to appeal to his betters, the opposite sex, and potential-customers alike. Patric had become so immersed in this false background, that for a long while he'd almost come to believe it himself. Indeed, it had only been recently, when thinking of his father, that he'd dwelt on his true identity.

As he recounted the lengthy and dramatic tale, Patric was glad that it appeared to be the fire which caused him to sweat. The Celt knew his well-informed Masonic master would already know all there was to know about him, for the spies of The-MGHWM were legion, and indeed, within the envious and competitive ranks of the Masonic order, tale-telling was compulsory. It was not by chance the wily and ruthless Morbrix had long sat upon the much-coveted stone-throne of the Masons. Many had attempted to wrest the Masonic crown from his head, all had disappeared or met extremely nasty, *accidental* deaths. The largest symbol on Morbrix's apron was the eye of the bull, denoting that he saw all, remembered all, and like a bull, was a terrible enemy.

It was said amongst the masons that those whom feared death, worshipped the High-druid, yet those who did not fear life, worshipped The-MGHWM; A man who could make anything possible for those who pleased him. A wise-man would rightly fear Morbrix, and strive to be perceived as a resourceful servant, rather than a possible threat.

'Lyin-bugger!' commented Ballast at last, after Patric had left the tent.

'Yep!' agreed Morbrix, 'he'll do well that one! See that he is closely watched'.

It was only with a cursory explanation and celebratory embrace that Patric re-joined his wife, before once again descending to the plain where mere mortals crawled.

'Cheers for that!' chuckled Allen.

'Well mate, that's the first time you've thanked me after I've speeded time up!' laughed Alex in answer. To Allen's relief, Alex had once more accelerated time, so that brief minutes after Patric's audience with Morbrix had ended, he and his guide floated above the packed Domi-knows stadium in the late-afternoon of the final day of the festival. Sunset and the beginning of the great match would not be long off. Alex was well aware of his companion's adverse opinion of sport in general, and hadn't thought Allen would have appreciated three solid days of foot-ball experienced in 'real-time'.

Though the agile Patric was an accomplished player of the game himself, and though he'd gone to see many a match with his Masonic mates in his younger days, the Celt had rather felt he'd outgrown the bravado of the game somehow in recent years. However, Patric had attended each and every foot-ball match of this year's festival, so that lost amongst the seething, deafening crowds, he could scream himself stupid. He was oblivious to all that took place upon the field, lost as he was in the tortures and anguish of his own mind. He'd laughed and wept hysterically in equal measure, had embraced and sworn at those around him, and he'd enthusiastically dived into the centre of any crowd violence. Each night, Patric had spent alone upon the plain, with only the stars, a large amount of beer, and as many berries as he could lay his hands on, for company. All his life, Patric had been absolutely-sure he'd be happy if he attained his dream of making it in the lands of opportunity, how could he not be? Yet here he was, his childhood ambition achieved, famous, and upon the ending of the festival also extremely wealthy, a broken man. Patric believed he was responsible for his father's death, and probably Enixam's also, not to mention those slain in eleven years of warfare. He felt empty and cold, bereft of any pleasure or satisfaction from that which he'd accomplished, which seemed tawdry by comparison.

Patric believed the gods had given him an opportunity to free Adwi and save his father, yet even though his actions had been with the best intentions, Patric felt he'd thrown away this gift from the gods, and had failed Hatric. Perhaps Hatric was doomed from the start. As a hated O'Lant, perhaps Hatric had indeed been cursed, to be given such a son as Patric. For it was said amongst the Celts *'If a man is slain by his own son, has he truly not been his own worst enemy?'* And if Hatric was doomed to be slain by the actions of his own son, then his son was doomed to live out a life knowing that his actions had slain his own father. As for Enixam, she had risked all for him, yet how had Patric repaid her?

'What were you saying about me *learning* from Pat?' Allen's voice dripped double-sarcasm.

'The story is far from over'. There was no hint of apology in Alex's tone.

'He can't really blame himself for his dad and Enix can he?' Allen asked. 'I mean, Christ! It wasn't his fault, was it? How was he to know the bleedin-goat was gonna kill his dad, or that dressing-up would cause a war!'

'That's the real-world Allen-mate!' Alex chuckled wryly, 'a million people can come up to you and tell you not to blame yourself for something, but it won't make any difference until you're ready to see it yourself! We've all got our own little things like that!'

'Yeah, but he did what he did with the best intentions!' Allen replied, exasperated.

'Oh yes mate, and it has been said that the best intentions pave the way to hell!' Alex smiled in response.

'You're just full of bloody-annoying little phrases like that aren't you?' Allen sighed.

'One for every-occasion matey!' Alex chuckled.

So it had been in the afternoon of the third day, physically and emotionally spent, the dishevelled, vomit and blood-covered hero of the festival had staggered to the great stadium unnoticed. Ranks of druids lined either side of the path, crying 'Av-a-berry!' as they handed out the dried Gla-berries to the passing crowds. Ric blearily wandered in and out of the broad entrance, until he'd had ten, before finally taking his seat. He and his wife were due to be seated upon the crest of the bank, within the most exclusive section of the southern embankment, reserved only for the highest-ranked and born bottoms. Yet the lurching Celt had settled himself upon the bottom of the bank, just above the toilet-trench, an area for the lower orders. Due to his tramp-like, begrimed appearance, the hero of the day remained unnoticed by the chanting crowd, which given his state of mind, was just how he liked it.

For her part, Nattarra had seemed not to notice her husband's absence during the festival, loving whole-heartedly as she was, the role of the celebrity wife. She had done the rounds of all the dignitaries' tents, attended a number of high-society parties, and had received a procession of the wealthy and influential at her own palatial encampment. Wooed by social-climbers wishing to be seen with the 'it' couple of the day, and a number of handsome gigolos who'd heard the spouse was absent, Nattarra had been far too busy enjoying herself to miss her husband. Only upon the day of the Domi-knows match, had she begun to become concerned for Ric. For it would be extremely embarrassing for her, should he not turn up for the ceremony which was to take place after the contest. Nattarra couldn't bear the thought of not being introduced to the high druid, and all the famous Domi-knows players in front of so many thousands. Therefore, as the third day progressed, she had sent as many of her husband's employees lucid enough to stand, to go in search of him.

'Right' said Alex in mid-air, high above the stadium 'follow me.'

'Aren't we going to watch the big-match then?' asked Allen.

'We'll be popping back in a minute, firstly there's something you need to see.' Alex turned away, and began to jog toward The-MGHWM's hill. Allen followed.

CH 21: POINTED NEGOTIATIONS

'They have arrived most-worshipful-master' Ballast whispered, standing as ever behind his master's chair, under the high canopy of the great tent. 'Good, good' replied Morbrix, looking up from the meat-laden platter held before him by a curvaceous serving-girl. The-MGHWM wiped juices from the side of his podgy mouth with a cloth, before dropping it onto the remains of his dinner. He rinsed his greasy fingers in a bowl of scented warm water held by another, equally-stunning girl, before wiping them dry on his bear-skin, and belching deeply. Ballast clicked his fingers and the serving girls hurried from the chamber. A chill draft of air, and brighter daylight entered the worshipful master's temporary hall, as a pair of red-painted guards stepped within holding back the billowing flaps of the doorway.

Ballast clicked his fingers once more, and a dozen or so further warriors filed from behind the hide-covered screens either side of the chamber. They jogged into position forming a beefy avenue from the doorway to their master's chair, each holding a flint-headed axe or spear at the ready. Morbrix settled himself in his carved, high-backed chair, before grinning and nodding to his advisor.

'Bid them enter!' intoned Ballast in a loud, commanding voice, despite his wizened frame.

Three large men entered through the outer doorway, followed by Alex and Allen. Each of the three was clean shaven. Two were dark-haired, in their twenties, whilst the man in the middle was older and slightly shorter, perhaps fifty or so, with greying hair, but strong features and smouldering eyes. Each wore a heavy leather long-sleeved vest, and trousers. The face of each man was ceremonially blackened with soot. The Three muscular men halted some paces before Morbrix's chair. The surrounding crimson-painted guards growled and menacingly patted their weapons into their palms.

'Well-met Prill, fellow master of a great and worthy clan!' chuckled Morbrix, spreading his arms wide in welcome, and smiling broadly at the oldest of the three men before him. The older man inclined his head in respectful greeting.

'Welcome fellow artisans of a valuable and great art!' Morbrix gestured to Prill's companions. There was a ripple of contemptuous laughter from the surrounding guards. Morbrix held up a palm for the laughter to cease, a look of mock-disgust on his face. 'Men!' he cried, 'stay your laughter, where is your respect? Do you not know that you are in the presence of another mighty clan leader?' gesturing to Prill, before giggling himself. The expressions of the three newcomers were set and unreadable.

'Most-worshipful-master..' Prill began in a cordial tone, ignoring the masons' derisive reception.

'That's Most-*Grand-High*-Worshipful-Master to you sonny!' growled Ballast sternly, the surrounding guards scowled and flexed their red-painted, oiled muscles.

'Of course, pray forgive my impertinence and ignorance, Most-*Grandest-Highest*-Worshipful-Master!' smiled Prill, bowing deeply, as did his fellows.

From the three-hundred-and-sixty-degree-history of the beaker-people in *The* Book, Allen knew that Prill was leader of the newest of the occupational-clans. A clan despised and ridiculed by the ancient and all-powerful masons. Though the druids had ordained Prill's clan-occupation to be a true and genuine calling some generations earlier, the masons believed the new group to be a mickey-mouse organization, with a ridiculous and pointless trade. The useless snotty-green globules which were the end-result and product of this bunch of upstarts enraged the masons, and they believed that unlike themselves, the wet-behind-the-ears, cowboy-outfit made no useful contribution to beaker-people society whatsoever. Though of course they dared not speak of it openly, the masons believed the druids to have obviously been overdoing it in the herb and berry department for some time. For the holy-brotherhood must be losing their grip, to grant this excuse-for-a-job, clan rights.

If the druids had become incapable of deciphering the god's wishes, as they so clearly had in the case of Prill's clan, then who would?

Morbrix would not allow the people to remain so spiritually-unprotected. It was his masonic duty. He owed it to Geezer.

The masons were at the top of the clan tree, yet they were not complacent. It had taken many, many generations for the Masonic-brotherhood to construct their elaborate power-hold over their society. Different clans required different forms of control. New clans, who would have a voice at the great-council, and be able to trade, only made things complicated. The masons' main worry was that if the druids were prepared to hand out clan-status to the likes of these green-snot-makers, then it wouldn't be long before they'd be handing it out to every Tal, Drem or Heri. If several new 'unknown-quantity' clans suddenly popped-up, it could endanger the

Masonic subtle balance of power, and that simply could not be allowed to happen.

Initially, Morbrix's indignant predecessors had hoped the flash-in-the-pan, fad clan would die out quickly. Yet to the growing annoyance of successive generations of masons, not only had this bunch of jokers stood the test of time, but they also appeared to be slowly growing in numbers. The Masonic spies also reported that oddly there seemed to be no animosity between those of the north and south who practised this ridiculous trade, rather they appeared to be in close alliance.

Yet the green snotty-shit they made was of no use to man or beast. The self-righteous masons saw this clan as nothing but a refuge for wasters and the lazy, a symptom of moral decline within their culture; For they were mystified as to why any decent person should wish to waste their life in such an occupation. The masons, who saw themselves as the moral champions of their civilization, therefore began a bitter and only thinly-veiled hate-campaign against the new clan, in an effort to utterly stamp it out.

The powerful masons let it be known that any of the lesser clans who assisted the newcomers would regret it, and ordained that in trade, the snotty-green product of the new clan was to be held as near worthless. Though the new clan had the right of their own encampment at the winter-solstice site, the masons saw to it that it was outside the circle of existing clan campsites, rightly reflecting the fact that these low-lifes were outside the sphere of decent society. Indeed, it was a lowly site befitting such worthless wretches and was positioned to the rear of the Masonic camp-site's cess-pit. Close enough so the masons could keep an eye on the cheeky upstarts, and with the great hill of The-MGHWM blocking the new-clan's view of the sporting grounds.

Each and every year Morbrix would press Deliars as to what service this worthless group performed for their culture or gods, and each year the High-Druid would rebuke him, warning it was not wise to question those who spoke on behalf of Domi and Geezer. Annoyingly enough to the masons, the druids would also point out that the new clan indeed performed a worthy task, for as the lowest of the low, they gave all the other clans someone to look down their noses at, thus making the lower clans feel a little bit better about themselves.

So the bitterness of the masons grew, until at last an opportunity arose which Morbrix believed would allow him to utterly destroy both the hated new clan, and the meddling druids in one fell swoop. The year before

Patric completed his scaffolding, it was reported to Morbrix that members of the accursed group had enraged a number of his masons, by having attempted to place orders for works to be done. Up and down the land, irate and infuriated masons had beaten the hated snot-producing scoundrels from their stone-smithies. For it was obvious to all that this was some sort of taunt, or practical joke meant to further enrage the goodly Masonic. All the beaker-people knew the new clan to be pot-less, and that they could not possibly pay for the large and obscure orders they were attempting to place. To their surprise and fury however, the masons were instructed by their high leader not only to refrain from going on the rampage and slaying those of the obviously-suicidal new clan, but to also accept these orders.

Though Morbrix was instructed by the druids to leave the new clan alone, he knew that not even the holy-brotherhood could save those who knowingly ordered goods which they could not pay for. In clan law, such miscreants had their clan-rights revoked and were banished, but in extreme cases such as this, where an entire clan appeared to be involved, it would mean death to all concerned, and the masons would be only too happy to carry out sentence.

Morbrix would have his masons complete the huge, obviously joke-orders. Delivery would be made as requested the following summer, and he would give a reasonable period for settlement of their account thereafter, so that when upon the cheeky-snot-making-buggers where unable to come up with payment, the masons would be seen to have been more than fair, and rightly aggrieved. So it had been that the orders had been fulfilled, delivery had been made, and the same winter-solstice upon which Patric was due to get paid, was also set as the date for the new clan to settle their huge debt with Morbrix.

Morbrix had seldom looked forward to the winter-solstice festival so much, and he'd wondered at the great stupidity of the new clan, hardly believing that they could provoke the masons, and then think they could hide behind the robes of the druids. For the new clan were about to find out there was no escape from the vengeance of the masonic. Morbrix had smiled to himself, it had all been so easy.

'So Prill, I trust the work of my brethren was to your satisfaction?' Morbrix asked in friendly manner, as if he were talking to a normal customer who would actually be in a position to pay.

207

'Oh yes my lord, we are hugely satisfied' replied Prill, once again bowing low.

'Good, good, then all is well' grinned the Masonic leader, enjoying the game, as the cat enjoys playing with the mouse. 'And the goods fulfilled their required need I trust?' Morbrix only just managed to prevent himself from giggling, for he had seen at first hand the ridiculous stone-goods which the new-clan had ordered. Goods to their own exact specification; Goods which all the masons agreed could serve no useful purpose.

'Admirably my lord, admirably!' replied Prill enthusiastically.

'Excellent, excellent!' smiled Morbrix, clapping his hands together, 'then all that remains, is for the small matter of payment to be settled...' Morbrix still smiled, but there was now a growing fire in his eyes, and his knuckles whitened upon the carved arm of his chair. A thin sliver of saliva escaped the side of his mouth, as animal anticipation of the blood-letting to come grew.

'But of course my lord' smiled Prill, seemingly at ease. 'I shall have it brought in, if I may?'

'Yes indeed..' responded Morbrix, only just keeping the surprise out of his voice, and wondering where this was all leading to. One of Prill's men turned, and waved a hand toward the open doorway. The Masonic guards looked to their master, and Alex and Allen stepped out of the way, as a further nine members of the hated blackened-faced clan marched into the chamber in ranks of three. Each bore a slender flattened tablet of stone, about the length of an arm, and the width of a hand.

Morbrix gestured for his men to relax, for he felt little concern at the arrival of the newcomers. After all, he had one-hundred-and-eighty hand-picked Masonic warriors upon the hill. Also, Morbrix had a far larger group of warriors currently poised upon the plain, to slay all those of Prill's clan within their encampment at his signal. Indeed, the very reason the Masonic leader had chosen this festival day to be that upon which he'd deal with the hated-clan once and for all, was that all the despicable-buggers would be in the same place at the same time. Also, everyone else would get to witness exactly what happened to those who displeased the Masonic order, which could only be to the good. It would also show the so-called holy-brotherhood who was the real power in the land.

Indeed, it was a sad fact that whenever events of mass-violence took place involving thousands of combatants, innocent bystanders always fell in the confusion and mayhem. In this case bystanding druids.

Morbrix believed his actions to be wholly righteous, and though he would truly upset the druids, the mason doubted that he would annoy their bosses, the gods. Morbrix was also comforted and reassured by the knowledge that the Masonic-brotherhood had paid more than enough to the worthy causes of the druids over the many generations, to off-set any dodgy moral behaviour on their part. After all, why else would the masons pay so much to charity?

'Er, you'll forgive me..' Morbrix smiled, feeling relieved and pointing to the stone-rods which the newcomers bore '..but are these not examples of the very same goods we supplied to you? Surely Prill, you do not seek to evade payment by attempting to return them I trust?'

'No my lord!' chuckled Prill, holding up placating hands. 'You misunderstand, I bring you payment in full, payment for *all* that you and your kindred have done, if you'll allow me to demonstrate?'

Morbrix's eyes narrowed for an instant, before once again his flabby, sweating features broke into a wide grin. 'Of course my good Prill,' he chuckled. Ballast placed a tentative hand on his master's shoulder, eager for the charade to be brought to an end, but Morbrix angrily shook him off, and gestured for Prill to proceed.

'My thanks most noble lord' Prill purred before turning to his kinsmen. One of the slender, flat stone tablets was passed forward, and he took it in his large, calloused and scarred hands. On closer inspection, it could now be seen the tablet was actually made up of two plates, bound together with leather thongs.

'For many generations my lord, we have sought to conquer our art..' Prill began.

'Art?' Ballast chuckled scornfully. There was a ripple of derisive laughter from the red-painted warriors.

'Ballast' Morbrix warned gently, holding up a palm to silence his advisor, 'do not interrupt our guest'. Behind his master's throne, Ballast scowled but wisely remained silent.

'We have had many failures, and pursued many dead-ends' Prill continued, seemingly oblivious to the aggressive nature of his audience. 'As I'm sure you're aware great lord, we have long-worked with the gifts of the earth.'

'Too-long' smiled Morbrix. Though he had no interest in the ramblings of the work-dodgers, the Masonic leader was still enjoying his game, and thought it best to make an effort to appear interested at least. The longer

Prill bored him to death, the longer Morbrix intended to take in torturing him to death.

'But I think it's fair to say, after all these generations m 'lord, we've cracked it at last!'

'Have you indeed?' enquired Morbrix, 'well-done-you!' he added amiably, whilst thinking the only thing which would soon be cracking was Prill's skull.

'Yes my lord, we've discovered a couple of cool things over the generations and have knocked up some fairly-decent bits-and-pieces.'

'Have you really? That really is most gratifying to hear' Morbrix replied, fighting the urge to reach under his robe for his ceremonial flint-knife.

'But now we've come up with something truly-special..' continued Prill, his voice climbing with growing excitement, '..and it was under our noses all the time!'

'Was it really?' gasped Morbrix with mock surprise.

'Oh yes my lord!' replied Prill, his voice almost ecstatic. 'We'd found one thing that was really-cool, and then another, but we'd never thought of mixing them together till recently!'

'Hadn't you indeed' sighed Morbrix, beginning to wonder if his own patience was deserting him.

'No great lord' confirmed Prill, before turning to his fellows. 'We felt right plonkers didn't we lads!'

'Fuckin-plonkers' agreed one of his men sheepishly.

'What are we like?' chuckled another.

'It is this break-through in our ground-breaking-work which places us in a position to truly pay you back my lord'.

'How so?' asked Morbrix, impressed at least with Prill's animated performance.

'If I may make so bold as to borrow the knife of one of your brave, illustrious men?' Prill enquired, gesturing to the leather thongs tying the two slender stone plates together. None were allowed to bear weapons on the hill The-MGHWM.

'Why certainly' replied Morbrix, gesturing to the nearest guard, and ignoring Ballast's nervous whispers concerning the prudence of handing a weapon over.

'My thanks.' Prill bowed gratefully, accepting the flint-blade from a grim-faced bear of a man. He cut through the bonds easily, before returning the knife. 'Before I continue with the demonstration' Prill continued, 'I feel I really must thank the masons on behalf of my clan, and indeed the whole of our nation. For without these..' he gestured to the stone tablet now resting against his knee, '..our latest creation simply would not have been possible!' Prill turned once more to his men, there was a chorus of 'aye' and 'well-done'.

'Think nothing of it' replied Morbrix humbly, raising a palm. The Masonic guards growled like hunting dogs, straining to be released.

'Indeed, without *these*' Prill emphasized this last word with a hand gesture, 'we simply couldn't have made *this*..' He then pulled the two flat stone plates apart, revealing a dull glimmer from inside.

'What *is* that?' Morbrix asked with suddenly-genuine interest. Leaning forward from his chair, he stared at the odd object held within the hollow of one of the stone panels. Ballast and the guards craned their necks in an effort to get a better look.

'Well it has to be said,..' continued Prill, lifting the stone plate holding the odd object, '..of all that we've fashioned over the passing of the generations, all that we've made, we are verily the most chuffed with *this*!'

'Fuckin-chuffed', added one of his men.

'Yes, but what *is* it?' asked Morbrix, enthralled by the glinting, tapering object held within the stone, a material unlike any of his previous experience.

'*This* will change *everything*' Prill's voice was a hushed rapture. As he prised the object from the mould, dropping the stone tablet to the floor, his face split into the widest of grins. He reverently held the thing aloft in the firelight, and a shimmering patina of light played over the gleaming surface, causing the masons to catch their breath in wonder. They had never seen such a thing.

Open-mouthed, Morbrix appeared utterly mesmerised and beguiled by the beautiful object in Prill's hand, as he paced slowly toward him.

'*This*..' Prill breathed, staring at the wondrous thing in his hand with great affection and pride, 'is what we lovingly-refer to in the trade as a *sword.*' Once again Prill emphasized the last word with a hand gesture. 'That's *sword*' he repeated.

'If you've ever wondered where the legend of a sword in a stone began, now you know!' Alex whispered to Allen. Allen giggled.

'Oh yes! What a fool I am' exclaimed Prill suddenly, slapping his cheek and laughing, as he stood before the entranced Morbrix. 'I almost forgot in all the excitement!' he added, shaking his head, 'I bear a message for you from Deliars, the High-Druid..'

211

He then thrust the sword to its hilt into Morbrix's belly, straight through the centre of the bull's-eye emblem upon the Masonic-apron.

'..The age of stone is over, welcome to the Bronze-age!' he said calmly into the dying man's eyes. Allen abruptly stopped giggling.

Ballast and the guards had also been so completely captivated by the gleaming blade, that they had appeared not to notice the other metal-smiths slip the loose thongs off the other stone-moulds.

The moulds which the masons had been duped into making. The moulds into which the metal-smiths had poured the molten bronze.

A further eight swords were drawn. The killing began.

'C'mon, let's get you out of here Allen-mate, I don't think you wanna see this.' Alex grabbed Allen under the arms, rising swiftly into the air. A shocked and sickened Allen was glad indeed, when the bloody scene of carnage below was hidden from site by the roof of the tent. However, as they rose higher, Allen could see that things were no better outside, in fact they were worse.

The metal-smiths of the north and the south had smuggled large numbers of swords into their encampment, inside the inconspicuous-looking stone moulds. They had also covered their bronze-tipped arrows, axes and spear-heads in clay, cloaking their true deadly nature. The slaying of Morbrix had been the signal for the long-planned otherthrow of the tyrannical-masons to begin.

Nearly all the Masons were within the Domi-knows stadium. From their conveniently placed encampment, the metal-smiths entered the deserted Masonic camp, surrounded the hill, and poured volley after volley of arrows onto it, until all one-hundred-and-eighty of Morbrix's body-guard lay dead or dying. In later years, to commemorate this glorious act, bronze-age beaker-people society would adopt a game named 'Dats' in the north, and 'Arrers' in the south, where metal-tipped darts were thrown at a circular-board, representing the circular-hill of the MGHWM. At the centre of the board would be the red bull's eye, denoting Morbrix and his blood-stained emblem. The highest possible score in this game would be one-hundred-and-eighty, recalling the number of Masonic guards slain. This game would eventually merge with Onni-Okki which had also involved a bull's eye, giving us the cry that is taken up when a player makes ready to throw their darts; 'On-the-oche' or 'Onni-Okki' if it's a Geordie commentator.

To their surprise, the drunken Masonic warriors upon the plain, who were expecting an easy slaughter, a bit of plunder and a spot of rape, found themselves not only confronting a strong force readied for battle which issued from the metal-smiths encampment, but also assailed by a larger force from the forest to their rear. Due to the superiority of their bronze-weaponry, the smiths of metal were quickly victorious and the plain ran red with Masonic blood.

Even as Prill had begun his audience with Morbrix, emissaries of the metal-smiths had presented themselves to each and every clan-leader, proclaiming the dawning of a new age, the Bronze-age. All the clans, from the weavers to the dyers, from the carpenters to the fishermen, had little love for the leeching stone-masons, and were happy to stay out of the fray as advised.

Messengers had not been sent to the high-druid, for Deliars was all too aware as to what was transpiring. Indeed, it had been the druids who had created and nurtured the metal-smiths. It was the druids who had first directed the fledgling clan in the extraction and use of copper and tin, and it was they who had dropped endless hints concerning mixing the two ores together to create bronze. For with bronze the sword could be made, and it was the druids who'd pointed out that as a cutting edge of technology, bronze had a far sharper edge than flint. This was knowledge the holy-brotherhood had been directed to pass on from their druidic-brethren on the continent, where the Bronze-age was already well underway. Bearing in mind the number of hints they'd dropped concerning the forging of this superior metal, the druids had begun to fear the bronze-penny was never going to drop with the metal-smiths. Thankfully it had at last.

Deliars had decided that the time of Geezer was over, for he had served his purpose. His arrogant followers had become far too powerful, and far too dangerous. It was time for Geezer the great to move over, and join the ranks with rest of the gods. Morbrix and his lodges had underestimated the 'old-stoners' to their cost.

The winter-solstice was a major turning point of the year. It marked the passing of mid-winter, when at last there would be less time to endure till Spring arrived, than had passed since Autumn ended. It was a time of optimism, and hope for the future. It was a time for inspiration and new ideas. Upon the winter-solstice, the beaker-people gave thanks to their god of progress, Invoe-g. Deliars therefore felt that this festival was indeed a fitting time for a change of god and ruling clan, and knew that it would be easy to persuade the flock that Invoe-g approved, for he was the god of the-latest-greatest-thing. Indeed, during this period of the year, or

Christmas as we know it, Invoe-g remains the god of the marketing departments of toy and gadget manufacturers especially.

Morbrix's choice of demanding payment from the metal-smiths upon the winter-solstice had made it all very convenient indeed for Deliars. Doubtless, one day the metal-smiths would also get too big for their boots, but that would be a problem for a future generation of druids. Until then, the holy-brotherhood would do as they always had, they would keep the new ruling-clan busy. The flock weren't ready for the fact that there *weren't* any gods.

At the close of the foot-ball tournament, Deliars and his brothers had secretly departed from the festival, and withdrawn to the safety of their surrounding hill-forts.

So it was, that due to the diminishing daylight and the noise of the screaming, chanting crowd, the masons within the Domi-knows stadium remained blissfully unaware of all that took place outside. Upon the summit of the starting-hill, surrounded by the vast crowd which stretched all the way along the mile-and-a-half course to the stadium, the Domi-knows team captains were wondering where the hell the druids had got to.

CH 22: VICTIMS OF PROGRESS

'You alright Allen-mate?' Alex enquired with concern, as the two hovered some feet above the stadium and Patric's head. Though he wasn't in possession of his body, Allen was instinctively retching at the gruesome sights he'd witnessed in Morbrix's tent and upon the hill. Thankfully the battle on the plain had been at a sufficient distance so that Allen hadn't been able to see any of the grisly details.

'I..I'll be f-fine in a moment' Allen croaked before going through the motions of being sick once again, though of course nothing actually came out of his mouth. After a while, the very-green-looking clerk straightened, 'Christ Alex! A warning would've been nice! I could've shut my eyes or turned away at least!' The vision of the bronze-blade sinking into Morbrix's fat belly returned once more, and Allen turned away again, coughing and spluttering.

'Unfortunately mate, in big-matters, there's no getting away from gruesome stuff like that. In our time or theirs' Alex replied, matter-of-factly.

'For a while there I was thinking this was a good dream, but I'm sure it's a bloody nightmare now!' Allen grimaced at last, when he felt he'd gained control of his stomach, the stomach that wasn't actually there. Alexander didn't answer, as both men's attention was drawn by the sudden hush which had fallen on the crowd. In the west, the sun was setting, and fittingly enough, it was blood-red.

Fashioned from tree-trunks, split-logs and wicker-work, four timber giants towered above the spectators and the great stones within the arena; each standing with its hands outstretched to the heavens; Each representing a season of the year. Two were male, two female. Each faced a point of the compass. As the crimson disk suddenly winked-out upon the darkening horizon and inky blackness descended, torches were thrust into the kindling about each giant's feet, and each burst into roaring flame, for their timbers were smeared with pitch and animal fat, and their stomachs were packed with hay and dried bracken. As the huge burning-figures joined the torchlight in illuminating the arena, the crowd once more erupted into wild cheers and cries, for any moment now there would be the tell-tale and growing rumble of falling great-stones. The Masonic spectators on either side of the embankment screamed as loud as they could, willing it to be their stones which toppled fastest. All eyes were on

215

the breach in the bank and ditch, where the two lines of standing-stones entered the arena. By contrast, an oblivious Patric sat staring into his beer. However, after some time the raucous screams and chants began to wane and diminish, until after many minutes since sunset, they dwindled to the buzz of confused, annoyed conversation, and wry laughter. There was the odd cry concerning the organizers, and obvious inability to arrange a piss-up in a brewery. From outside the arena there came no crash of falling stone, no cries from the vast crowd lining the course. From somewhere on the embankment came a melodic cry which was taken up by more and more of the crowd, until the arena rang to the chords of *'why-are-we-waiting?'*

At first, no one seemed to notice the solitary figure who entered the stadium via the breach in the embankment, emerging from between the two lines of great stones, and striding purposefully toward the centre of the arena. However, as the lone figure stepped into the brighter light of the burning-giants, more and more of the onlookers pointed or nudged their neighbours. Jeers and taunts broke out amongst the crowd, directed at he who had obviously been sent to offer the organisers' excuses. When at last the figure stood at the heart of the arena, between the ancient winning-stone, and the smaller flat-topped ceremonial rock, upon which rested the Grrrr-ale, the greater part of the crowd had fallen silent. The solitary man appeared to be a southern Masonic warrior, for his face and limbs glistened red with crimson paint. He held up a hand to bring the last sporadic cat-calls and mocking cries to a halt.

'I BRING NEWS TO THE MASONIC!' the figure cried before giggling, the acoustics of the circular stadium carrying his manic-voice to all. 'He's enjoying his moment' Alex said quietly gesturing to the blood-covered Prill, who was now pacing in a circle around the Grrrr-ale stone, staring out at his audience through wild eyes. After a number of circuits, Prill halted before the holy cup, 'YOUR TIME IS AT AN END! WE WEAR THE FUCKIN-APRONS NOW!' he cried loudly, swinging his crimson sword in a wide arc and sending the stone-beaker flying into the shadows amid a shower of sparks. An audible sigh went up from the appalled crowd at this act of blasphemy, which was quickly followed by a deafening roar of anger and outrage. Prevented from lynching the obvious madman by the deep sewage and vomit-filled ditch, they leapt to their feet, baying for his blood. In response, Prill simply smiled, and leaning against the Grrrr-ale stone, rested the blood-spattered blade against his shoulder. A number of enraged masons seated near the break in the ditch ran screaming into the arena, intent on murder. However, all were quickly cut down by hundreds of sword-bearing warriors, who streamed into the stadium from between the two lines of stones. The warriors split into two running columns, which quickly encompassed the circular Domi-knows field, until the blood-drenched men stood in an unbroken circle, facing the infuriated crowd across the foul-smelling ditch.

Angry cries for the Masonic guard, and vengeful oaths to Geezer, became cries of fear, bewilderment and anguish, as the wicker-fencing which crowned the outer crest of the embankment, disintegrated under the blows of a thousand swords, and the horrified crowd turned from the arena to find themselves surrounded by an army. It took a few-hundred of the most aggressive and arrogant of the Masonic audience to be butchered, before the remainder became somewhat more subdued and submissive.

'THE GAME HAS BEEN CANCELLED!' Prill informed the now-quiet crowd, 'AND THERE SHALL NEVER BE ANOTHER!' he added.

'He's coming-to' Allen said with a look of absolute disgust, 'and boy! Does he smell like shit or what?'

'It *is* shit Allen, what do you expect?' Alex chuckled in reply, wrinkling his nose. He and Allen squatted either side of Patric, who lay on his back upon the lowest edge of the embankment, submersed up to his waist in the excrement of the toilet-ditch. In the east, night sky was turning to a charcoal-grey, heralding the approach of dawn. Except for the corpses, the darkened stadium was now deserted, and the four great timber giants had reduced to glowing piles of embers.

'Nasty bruise!' Allen commented, wincing, whilst gesturing to the purple welt on Patric's mud and blood-smeared forehead. Alex only nodded in answer.

The night before, it had taken quite a while for it to register with the extremely-spaced-out Patric, that the sporting event wasn't going quite as it should. Lost in maudlin thoughts, Prill's arrival had apparently gone unnoticed by the Celt, and it had only been the screams of the women about him which had finally caused Patric's head to rise from his knees. He had groggily risen, only to be buffeted and jostled by a horrified, frantic crowd. Blearily peering about himself, Patric had begun to grasp the fact that people were dying.

217

Thinking of his wife, the Celt had looked toward the crest of the bank above, where he should have been seated with Nattarra and the Masonic-elite, but his view was blocked by the tightly packed, panicking throng. An intoxicated Patric ineffectually attempted to battle his way through the crowd toward his beloved, but was soon knocked to the floor by those attempting to escape their attackers. However, on his hands and knees, the Celt had gradually worked his way up the embankment, alternately being trodden on, or cursed by those who tripped over him. Eventually Patric emerged from the stricken crowd at the waist-height wicker fence which enclosed the restricted seating-area for the highest of the Masonic.

As in any coup however, it had been the occupants of this area in which Prill had been most interested, and as Patric tumbled over the low fence and staggered drunkenly back to his feet, he found himself confronting a wall of blood-soaked warriors, holding shiny and very pointy objects in their crimson hands. All around lay the slain, staring with sightless eyes in envy at the living. The VIP area had become more of an RIP area.

However, it was not the surrounding carnage which appalled Patric the most. It was the fact that his very-alive wife, Nattarra, was draped over an extremely large warrior, seemingly a captain of the enemy, and appeared to be cooing and whispering sweet nothings into his ear.

The Celt screamed his wife's name, and above the din, Nattarra had heard him, turning her head in his direction. The huge warrior holding the girl had also looked inquisitively toward Patric, as the lion looks inquisitively at the antelope.

'Be gone stone-lover or join your fellows!' growled the nearest warrior to Patric, gesturing about him.

'NATTARRA!' Patric had screamed again, ignoring the threat. The last memory the Celt had before the warrior raised his sword and brought the hilt down on his head, was Nattarra, his wife, looking straight into his eyes, and then looking straight through him, as though pretending not to recognize him. She had then turned back to the warrior, kissing him passionately on the mouth.

The Celt had been flung backward by the powerful blow, pitching over the wicker fence, and tumbling down the embankment beyond, to lay unconscious at its foot, half submerged in the toilet-ditch.

'What an absolute slag!' Allen had spat with contempt and hatred, gesturing angrily toward Nattarra.

'She's a survivor. Live-or-die Al, what'd you do, eh mate?' Alex had replied calmly.

Patric had lain unmoving throughout the night, and hadn't stirred until just before dawn.

'Ughh!' The Celt grunted with pain and exertion as he dragged himself hand over fist out of the sucking stench of the mire, until he lay panting and bedraggled further up the bank, his hands clamped to his aching head. After some time he unsteadily arose, bloodshot eyes surveying the awful scene about him. A whimper broke from his lips, and tears sprang to his eyes, running down his begrimed face as realization hit him that unfortunately the events of the previous night hadn't been a beer and berry induced nightmare as he'd hoped. Patric woodenly trudged back up to the wicker enclosure on the crest of embankment, and spent long minutes studying the entangled mass of humanity within. Patric wasn't completely sure if he was relieved or not that Nattarra was indeed not amongst the dead.

'I must be watching too much violence on the net 'n' telly!' Allen grimaced quietly, averting his eyes from the macabre scene.

'I've gotta sort my life out when I wake up for sure' he added, gesturing around at the massacre, 'coz I'm a fuckin-sicko to be coming up with this shit in a dream'.

'Yes, you do need to sort your shit out when you wake up. As I've been saying all along', Alex responded, 'You need a proper job.'

'Get-screwed.' Even though Allen accompanied the expletive by flipping Alex the finger, his heart wasn't really in it, too caught up as he was in the all-surrounding death. He was truly worried about himself to have conjured such a grim scene from his own mind. The deceased were of all ages, and both sexes.

'Alex mate.' Allen's voice was a fearful whisper.

'Yes, Allen-buddy'.

'I'm not dead, or-or maybe in a coma am I? I mean, all of this, you... I'm not in some hospital bed somewhere after an over-dose or whatever...am I? The uneasy feeling had been growing within Allen that this 'dream' seemed to be going on and on, and was getting worse and worse. He'd had enough now, and desperately wanted to wake up, no matter how-shit his real life was.

'No Allen-mate.' Alex replied gently, 'You're not in a coma, and you're not dead. I am though, remember?

'I should know better than to ask you', Allen chided himself. 'You're no friggin help! This is all so fucked-up, and therefore so must I be!'

'Don't be so hard on yourself Allen. If you believe this is all a dream, then really you should be pleased at least with the scope of your imagination, and you always did want to be a story-teller didn't you?'

'Then I'm clearly shit at that as well!' Allen spat dejectedly.

'How-so?'

'Well I can't even come up with a believable tale! It's like with Prill and his mates for example. The metal age didn't just pop-up overnight did it? It gradually came in and replaced stone slowly over generations for-fuck's sake. There wasn't some Mafia-massacre or Nazi night-of-the-long-knives type takeover was there, like this?'

'Why not?' Alex enquired, 'When Cortez and the Spanish turned up in South-America, they bought the metal age to a stone-age world in one day. And huge sea-changes happen almost overnight in your time, so why not in Patric's?'

'Like?'

'Well, for a century you got your gas from the gas company, and your electric from the electric company, all very normal. They'd spent ages in setting up thousands of miles of underground pipes and cables, overhead wires and pylons; lots of infrastructure; meters, power-stations, specialists in their fields as you'd expect. Then one day you wake up and you can buy your gas from the electric company, and vice versa, and Spec-Savers are selling fuckin-hearing-aids! Or like how for thousands of years, those of special-skill, merit and great-achievement, the best of us, have been rightly-celebrated. And how for decades, TV-licence and then network-subscription payers expected their entertainment providers to be spending their money and time on working hard in coming up with quality, imaginative, entertaining and diverse programming; They're meant to be the arty-fuckers after-all. *Then* out of bleedin-nowhere Big-Brother begins a shit-slide ending up with people watching other people watching TV on Goggle-Box. People who are famous for watching TV; Joining the endless ranks of apparent-celebrities, celebrated for being famous for doing sod-all! I mean, how fucked is that? From a species who're always banging on about how much progress they've made. What do we think we're playing at? You see? There's loads of things that happen, which if you'd been asked about just before they happened, you'd have said no-fucking-way; and then overnight, it's happened and is apparently normal.

'You've certainly got a point there!' conceded Allen with a grin, despite his sombre mood.

'Listen Allen, I know this is all very gruelling and hard-going to witness. But what if I said that by bearing with Patric's tale, not only will it help you in life when you wake up, but will also help you find Maxine, or her find you, as well?

'Then I would say both you and I are certainly dreaming.'

'Well then, if we're back to believing this is a dream, we're all back to normal then'.

'Oh-fucking-kay' Allen chuckled, 'let's get back on with it then shall we..'

As the enormity of what had transpired began to sink into Patric's hung-over and battered senses, he sank to his knees and let out an anguished howl, as the wolf who returns to its den to find its mate and young slain. Alex and Allen stood quietly nearby.

At last, Patric's head rose from the ground, and dragging himself back to his feet, he wiped a ragged sleeve across his eyes.

The young man's world had been turned upside-down overnight, a world which had already been shaken to its foundations by the news of his father and Enix. Patric's groggy memory told him that impossible as it might seem, it had been the lowly and despised metal-smiths who had butchered his brethren, using some mystical weapon of the gods, a weapon which shone like Domi himself.

Which clearly meant Domi must have had a hand in it.

Where had Geezer the great been last night? How could all-knowing-Domi let such a thing come to pass? Just at that moment, the first rays of the winter-sun crept over the top of the embankment as morning grew.

'WHY DID YE LET IT HAPPEN?!' Patric screamed at the rising disk, before turning his back on the sun-god, and furiously stomping off along the bank. The Celt stopped a number of times, painfully stooping to pick up the broken remnants of beer-beakers which littered the ground everywhere. He repeatedly swore loudly upon finding all devoid of beer. Patric's head was having a hard time indeed dealing with what it was being asked to accept. The Celt needed a damn-good drink.

Allen and Alex followed Patric to the breach in the embankment, and then to the centre of the arena. Allen tried unsuccessfully to ignore the bodies. Upon reaching the Grrrr-ale stone, Patric placed his hands either side of the flat-slab laying atop it, and shoved. There was the sound of grating stone as the slab moved slowly, followed by a dull-thud as it fell to the earth. Beneath, as Patric had known there would be, was a hollowed trough in the waist-height stone. The trough was filled with beer, as Patric knew it would be. This was the very ale blessed by Geezer, from which the Grrrr-ale was filled, and offered to the victorious Domi-knows captain by the high druid at the end of the match. Some years earlier, as many a teenager of his time, Patric had dreamt of being a triumphant Domi-knows captain, and drinking the blessed-beer. Of course, he hadn't dreamed it would be quite like this. With a grim smile the Celt submersed his head in the frothing liquid, only rising for air long moments afterward. Following two further prolonged such baptisms of beer, the panting Celt slid to the ground, leaning back against the stone.

'And this is really what you're advising me to do is it?' Allen asked angrily, 'get myself mixed up in something that's gonna go tits-up!'

'Allen, Allen, calm down buddy, it's still early days! Just show a little patience, Pat's tale has got a long way to go yet! Treat this more as an example of if you want something out of life, don't expect an easy ride!' Alex responded. Allen sank into a sullen silence, looking up at the sky so he didn't have to look at the bodies.

After a good while of staring about himself in a state of disbelief, Patric dragged himself back to his feet. He strode a few paces to the remains of what had obviously been a huge bonfire. He kicked aside the traces, realising that as he'd suspected, he looked upon the charred remains and ashes of what had been a fire of piled Masonic-aprons, thousands of them.

Though at the time, Patric had been unconscious, and literally in the shit, Allen had heard Prill's speech to the defeated masonic. After having proclaimed the Bronze-age as having officially begun, and having introduced the god of his clan, Hallmark, as the new most-powerful deity in the land under Domi, Prill had called for calm amongst his terrified audience. The metal-smiths he said, wished for no further bloodshed, for indeed all knew the way of the stone-mason to be a proud calling. A good number of those who quarried, transported or sculpted stone would remain valued members of their society, for people would always need stone.

However, all those involved in the numerous stone-related jobs which were nothing more than an excuse for an occupation, of which there were many indeed, could now consider themselves redundant. They were to be a burden to their society no longer.

Prill further stated the rates of exchange for stone were from this night vastly reduced, and that of course metal was now to be the highest-prized commodity. In weaponry and tool-making, metal would now replace stone. In short, Prill was announcing that the bottom had just fallen out of the stone-market. The great-stone-crash had begun. Prill further proclaimed that the now-surplus-to-requirement Stone-way was to fall silent forever, and the giant Domi-knows games which had taken place in its honour were to cease.

Each mason had to proclaim the exact nature of their work to the metal-smiths, who decided if their particular calling had a viable future. The greater part of the crowd, whose occupations were deemed either vastly over-manned, a waste of time, or redundant due to the introduction of metal, had to hand over their coveted aprons for burning, before being allowed to leave the stadium.

Patric looked down at his own excrement-stained apron, before untying the chords at his back, pulling the strap over his head, and flinging the once-prized piece of leather onto the charred pile. He then looked around for a while, before his eyes fell on the object he sought. Patric dusted off the Grrrr-ale with his hand as he picked it up, before submersing the once much-coveted stone-cup in the ale-font, placing it to his lips, and draining it in greedy gulps. He then refilled the cup and made for the exit. His invisible companions followed behind.

Patric found himself in a more or less deserted festival site, but soon learned of all that had befallen his once-proud industry from the few remaining celebratory non-stone-based-clansmen, or apron-less fellow ex-masons, intent on fleeing the revenge of those who had lived under Masonic-tyranny for so long. Now the violence was over, the druids had returned to proclaim the many virtues of Hallmark-the-shiny.

Patric learned from one such holy-man that any deals made before the new age began were now null and void, for indeed, only works fashioned from the new fashionable-metal were deemed to be worthy of the gods. As most of his fellow clansmen, Patric was destitute, a victim of progress.

CH 23: THE BIG PICTURE

Only in her dying moments did the winter sun at last break free of the sullen cloud-canopy, behind whose shroud her dazzling radiance had remained cloaked all that long, brooding day. A crimson tide suffused the ragged slate-grey line that was the horizon in moments, and laced the dark heavens with rivulets of fire. Blood-red waves swept outward across the cold plain, each gnarled rocky outcrop and wind-stunted plant outlined in a stark and brazen relief, until they broke upon the rock-hewn edifice in a roaring crescendo beyond mortal hearing.

In contrast to the flat, featureless landscape, the megalithic structure drove arrogant rock fingers skyward, as a regal crown might rest with disdain upon an unworthy head. A simplistic majesty born of sheer scale spoke almost of the hands of the gods rather than mere mortal men, and as each of the great standing stones was washed in lurid light, they appeared almost as if lit from within. Yet in brief moments the angry red disk sank beyond the rim of the world, the light receded, flecked the underbelly of the sky for a heartbeat, and then winked out as if it had never been. The chill embrace of moonless eve descended to reclaim the now darkened earth, and all creation appeared stilled.

And yet still he remained.

He knew the place of each and every great stone within that vast construction, and further, its position in relation to any of its counterparts. He knew the weight and dimensions of every chisel-scarred giant, where each had been quarried, and by what route and which means each had been brought to this, its final resting place. For he who stood dwarfed amidst those towering pillars, was both author and owner. He was therefore aware as to the exact value of all that stood before him.

As of two days ago, it was *all* worth bugger-all.

'YER-BASHTURDS-YE!' Patric cried drunkenly to gods he no longer had any faith in, before draining the stone-cup of beer in his hand. Bumping into more than one of the huge rock-pillars, he then unsteadily weaved his way between the towering stones. Leaving his stone-scaffolding behind, he staggered off into the rolling night fog.

'Progress is a wondrous thing..' commented Alex, watching the Celt go. He and Allen remained standing within the stone-circle, '..unless of course you're its victim!' he added.

'So let me get this absolutely clear Alex-mate' chuckled Allen, grinning in disbelief. 'You're saying Patric built Stone-henge?' The two stood at the centre of the inner circle, formed of six pairs of great-standing-blue-stones, each topped with a gigantic lintel-stone. There was an outer circle formed of slightly shorter sarsen-stones, which were also topped by a continuous row of lintels. The surrounding circular sewage-ditch and its inner bank of soil still ringed the site, awaiting the toiletry-needs of the builders of phase two, who were to build the huge bottom stone-hinge for the giant-doorway-to-the-other-side within the scaffolding circle.

However, the builders would never come, for with the dawning of the metal-age, stone-monuments were now of course considered passé and old-hat, and all such old-age projects had been cancelled.

'Stone-Henge? Don't you mean, Patric built the scaffolding for the *stone-hinge*?'

'Sod-off-Alex.'

'You've been bloody watching him build it haven't you?'

'This is just getting silly now!' laughed Allen, 'Stone-bloody-henge indeed! Built by a paddy-builder in under five years? What a dream!' he added, shaking his head.

'So what exactly is your problem with that then mate?' asked Alex sincerely.

'You're serious?' asked Allen in reply, his tone incredulous, 'Well for a bloody start, it's well-known that this lot took hundreds of years to build!' he said pointing to the stones about them.

'Oh, and that would be *well known* by the likes of the ever-so-bloody-clever archaeologists, scientists and historians, would it?' Chuckled Alex, before adding, 'I'd rather hoped that what you'd seen so far, would've taught you better than that Allen-mate'. It was now Alex's turn to shake his head in disbelief.

'Oh for Christ's-sake Alex! All of this, the society, everything here..' Allen gestured about himself '…it's just all too sophisticated and well organized for Britain four-and-a-half-thousand years ago!' Allen stood with his hands outstretched in exasperation, as if expecting that at any moment Alex would start to laugh, and admit that the whole thing was indeed a wind up, just part of a silly dream.

'Too sophisticated?' Alex replied, almost angrily, before adding, 'That's the bloody living for you! So bleedin impressed with themselves! It's not a case that it's hard to believe that this lot were cleverer than modern-people think Allen, it's more of a case that it's hard to believe that we haven't

226

become much cleverer since. That's why modern generations are so patronising about their ancestors, they're unconsciously embarrassed about what a short way they've come over the millennia!' Alex tutted, before falling silent.

'Under-five-years indeed!' Allen giggled, looking about the great stones of Stone-henge.

'Yeah, well mister-clever-scientist doesn't know about the stone-way or the fat-bonuses does he?' Alex piped in an annoying voice.

'Alex, if something as big as the stone-way really existed, I'm sure they'd be some sort of archaeological-evidence remaining, yeah?' replied Allen in an annoying voice of his own.

'Give-me-strength! There bloody is Allen! All over the bleedin-country and most of Europe!' replied Alex in frustration.

'You what?'

'Look Allen, how much of this lot remains by our time eh?' Alex gestured to the stones about them.

'Well, not much..' Allen replied, everyone knew what stone-henge looked like, a few stones still stood, some were tumbled, but most had disappeared.

'Exactly mate, and it's the same with the stone-way, for generation upon generation stones are dragged off and broken up by the locals for building purposes, they end up in churches and cathedrals, dry-stone-walls, cow-sheds, cottages and castles mate, and when you're nicking something you don't publicise it! Religion after religion, and especially Christianity topple the stones or have them buried, believing them to be evil sites of worship, but one of the major reasons that our scientific lot don't know anything about the stone-way is those thieving-bastard Romans!'

'The Romans?' Allen asked suspiciously.

'Oh yes, the *oh-what-a-lot-we've-done-for-civilization* Romans!' Alex spat.

'Er, how-so?'

'Look Allen, the Romans nicked their gods and most of their cultural philosophies from the Greeks, they nicked their business empire and economic ideas from the Carthaginians in north-Africa, not to mention they nicked a lot of other peoples' entire countries, so it wasn't much of a problem for their consciences when they claimed the historical glory for their roads!'

'You-bloody-what?' Allen chuckled.

227

'For god's sake Allen, the Romans inherited hundreds and hundreds of miles of straight avenues of standing stones all over Britain and Europe. These routes had developed over tens-of-thousands of years, the most straight-forward routes from A-to-B. All the bloody-Romans did was break the stone down on site, turning it into roads, they then claimed that not only had they come up with the routes, but also that they'd quarried and transported the stone as well!'

'Oh piss-off Alex!' Allen laughed.

'It's bloody true Allen! Obviously it didn't get much press, because the Romans were certainly bloody good at propaganda and killing! They didn't nick that off anyone! They were the ones recording history in writing. Many of the peoples they subjugated were illiterate. He who writes, records history. It is always wise to recall it's just *his-story*.

'Yeah-yeah' chuckled Allen sarcastically, having heard the pun before.

'Honestly mate! Alex continued, 'so that's why now, all over our countryside and Europe, there's only the odd solitary standing stone, or part of a marooned avenue or a circle..'

'Sod-off Alex!'

'Have it your way then Allen-mate!' chuckled Alex, before adding, 'the one that makes me chuckle the most though, about the scientific explanation for why there's stone all over the place which doesn't belong there, is that it was dropped by melting glaciers at the end of the ice-age!' Alex giggled to himself. Allen ignored him.

'Stone-scaffolding indeed!' Allen said at last sarcastically, looking around at the stones of the universally-known monument about him, a monument he'd learnt about at school, and about which he'd read quite a lot as a teenager. 'I mean, this was the great cathedral of its time, one of the arches is aligned so that the sun rises through it at midsummer, and another so the sun sets through it at mid-winter! It's one of the ancient bloody wonders of the world for Christ's sake!'

'Hey! I'm not having a pop at Patric!' Alex replied, 'he did a bloody-great job, this scaffolding was a forerunner in design mate, but the reason for the alignment of the stones was to maximise the hours of sunlight within the stone-circle. You saw what those bloody work-shy-masons were like! Patric knew that the Masonic-unions would look for any excuse to down tools, poor light being one of them!'

'Oh leave it out will you!' Allen giggled.

'The really funny thing is though, I have to say, in our time all the hippies, new-age-druids, and other misguided pilgrims turn up at Stone-henge on the solstices and equinoxes or other pagan festivals, like Beltane or Samhain bless-em, when in Patric's time, that's exactly when everyone stopped work and buggered off! Because after all, they were religious holidays!' Alex sniggered. Allen was too busy staring about himself, a fixed grin on his face.

'I must say though, it's cool to be standing *in* Stone-henge, and seeing what it looked like when it was first built'. He assumed this part of his dream to be generated from some digital recreation, or artist's impression from a book.

'Yeah, there's certainly a lot more to see than when you were here last in your waking-life' agreed Alex. Allen looked at his companion quizzically.

'Er, I've never been here.' Allen knew that as a child, his parents had never taken him to the world-famous stone-circle, and although he'd always meant to visit the place, he'd never gotten around to it.

'Oh yes you have.' Replied Alex flatly.

'I bloody-well-haven't' retorted Allen, raising his voice, 'and I know my mum and dad didn't bring me here when I was tiny, because I asked!'

'You've been here before Allen' insisted Alex.

'No I ha..' Allen began, before his sentence was interrupted by a blurring before his eyes, a shifting beneath his feet, and the sudden light of day bursting before his eyes.

'Oh here we soddin-go again!' complained Allen indignantly, squinting under the early evening summer sun. The clerk now found himself standing at the centre of the much more familiar rocky-jumble most modern-day people would recognize as Stone-henge. The once-deep surrounding toilet-ditch was now no more than a faint impression in the ground, only visible here and there. Similarly, the six-foot-high circular bank of earth had all but disappeared. Faint conversation wafted to Allen's ears on the evening breeze from the last handful of tourists slowly pacing around the encircling viewing-path of the monument. There was the odd swish of passing traffic from the two roads driven unsympathetically straight through the allegedly revered site, either side of the ancient ring.

'Is that noise what I think it is?' Allen asked Alex suddenly, a naughty grin spreading across his face. Alex only raised his eyebrows and smiled-wolfishly in answer.

From behind a large tumbled stone within the inner circle, a few paces ahead of the pair, came the unmistakable soft female whimpering, and the deeper male groans of lovemaking.

'Wa-hey!' chuckled Allen, 'good on em!'

'Do you wanna look first or shall I?' enquired Alex.

'We shouldn't really, should we?' smirked Allen.

'Where's the harm?' asked Alex, 'it's your dream after all' he added, smiling mischievously.

Even though he was invisible and could not be heard, Allen tiptoed to the fallen stone, before edging around it. His grin broadened as he was confronted by the well-toned gyrating bottom and shapely bare-back of a young woman. She sat astride the hairy legs of her male partner, who lay on his back in the grass, feet toward Allen. The girl's hair was long and dark, and flowed down her back. She wore what appeared to be from the back, only a bikini top, and a pair of denim shorts hung from one ankle. The man, whose upper body was hidden from Allen, wore black trainers, his jeans and boxer-shorts were around his ankles.

'Enjoying the show ye mucky-git!' laughed Alex, who remained standing beyond the stone. Allen looked up, grinning guiltily, before returning his gaze back to the intensifying sighs and moans which were now increasing in urgency and volume.

Rather than joining his companion in watching the show, Alex appeared to be watching Allen's lustfully mesmerised expression with interest.

Within minutes, judging by the frantic bestial sounds now emanating from behind the rock, the couple were nearing the sweaty crescendo of their physical union. However, the wicked smile growing on Alex's features was not due to the carnal overture, but rather due to the sudden change in Allen's own expression, from one of obvious arousal, to one of absolute horror. In their frenzied thrashings about, Allen had just seen the faces of the lovers.

'YOU FUCKIN-SICK SHIT-BAG ALEX!' Allen screamed hysterically as he sprinted past his companion and out of the encircling ring of stones. The ex-estate agent turned and followed, walking at a relaxed pace with hands in pockets, and miserably failing in the attempt to keep the wicked grin off his face. Behind the rock, Allen's very-young-looking mum and dad lay in a satiated heap.

'It's just gone six o'clock, on the sixth of June, nineteen eighty-seven, and you've just been conceived Allen mate' said Alex, as he joined the very-freaked-out clerk atop one of the barrows dotting Salisbury plain, all around Stone-henge. Allen remained squatting in silence, staring out over the rolling summer landscape, wondering if a full-frontal lobotomy was the only way he could remove the last few minutes from his mind.

'Hey! I don't know what you're so upset about, I just died mate!' said Alex, raising his hands defensively.

'You need help' Allen growled.

'I need help? I thought this was *your* dream?' Alex replied. Allen's face paled, and he shuddered.

'You see, I told you you've been here before!' said Alex at last.

'You could've just bloody told me.'

'Seeing is believing.'

'Most people don't even want to think about their parents shagging Alex! They certainly don't want to bloody *see* it!' Allen hissed, hoping beyond hope he wouldn't remember this part of the dream when he woke up.

'You really are an ungrateful git Allen; how many people get to witness their very own conception eh? It's a magical moment! C'mon, we'd best get after Pat'.

The scenery once again blurred, and foggy night returned. Before them, a drunken Patric at last managed to climb into the saddle of his pony, before urging it on into the winter mist.

After having emerged from the Domi-knows stadium two mornings before, a drunken Patric had stumbled to the body-strewn Masonic camp, under the shadow of the hill, to find it looted and burned. However, the Celt had managed to find some scraps of food and a near-full beer-skin within the folds of a trampled tent. His livelihood, wife and possessions having all disappeared, Patric took to the road and left the festival-site, never to return.

Back at the stadium, though the painted white dots denoting weight and rock-type, would soon be weathered away, many of the great-stones, still standing in the two-concentric circles of that last cancelled game of Domi-knows, would remain standing across the millennia, and can even be viewed to this day. The huge bank upon which the screaming-crowds used to stand still rings the site, as does the inner toilet trench. Two avenues of stones can still be seen, exiting the arena through a single breach in the embankment and ditch, leading up a gentle-rise for a mile-and-a-half from it. To prove Alex's point concerning the monoliths being reused by later generations, a medieval village now sits within the stone-circle, and it has been proven that many of the cottages and the church are built of stone taken from the ring. In its time, the Domi-Knows stadium was known as the 'Av-a-berry' circle after the cries of the druids at its entrance, as they handed out the dried Gla-berries. Three and a half thousand years later, the French-speaking Normans would pronounce it 'Av-e-bury'. The Avebury

231

Stone Circle can be found about twenty miles north of Stone-henge. As with Stone-henge, both the spiritual and scientific communities would have a lot to say about the significance and meaning behind the Avebury-stones, never guessing that in fact, they were the origin of the very popular pub-game, played with white-dotted little bricks. The usual 'tomb' or 'site-of-worship' label would be attached to The-GMHWM's hill, which is now known as Silbury Hill, and overlooks the Avebury circle. When in fact as the reader has seen, it was nothing more than a platform, enabling someone to look down on someone else. As has been stated, the hill was also the source of the other popular pub-game, darts. In the true spirit of their roots, an awful lot of people over the years would be stabbed in the pub by a dart, in a drunken dispute over a game of dominoes.

The berries of the Gla bush would also give their name to another nearby world-renowned site, known to this day. The sacred southern isle of the druids was known for the berry-stones which got the people of the era stoned. It was known to all that it was highly important to swallow the stone first, for it counteracted the adverse effects of the berry-flesh. If the flesh was eaten first, it induced immediate violent-vomiting the moment it hit the stomach. Yet for the berry-stone to take effect, the chemical-reaction of the berry-flesh was also needed. So all knew the phrase 'Gla-stone-berry'.

As in Patric's time, thousands still flock to the site for a three-day festival around the time of the summer solstice, involving outlandish-behaviour and the ingestion of a number of substances. Further, it has been proven by geological study, that at one time Glastonbury was an isle surrounded by wetland. The high hill on the eastern side of Glastonbury, known as 'The Tor', still bears the banks and ditches of the druids' hill-fort.

Those researching the Arthurian legend have also named Glastonbury as a potential site for a mystical isle mentioned in the tale, and they are correct. Indeed, the name is in fact derived from the Lon mushroom, which the druids handed out to those who'd stumbled onto their isle and saw for themselves that the druids were just a bunch of stoners, and that there were no deities in residence. For they would say 'Av-a-Lon' as they handed over the disorientating fungi.

So it had been, after two days of drunken trudging, Patric had arrived back at the site of his great stone-scaffolding, later to be known as Stone-henge, and had found it deserted. Understandably, his mood was even more depressed than when he'd set out from there a few days earlier. The Celt's humble origins had always instilled within him an air of caution and preparedness. Therefore, shortly after his arrival, Patric had led Alex and Allen to a nearby tightly-packed copse of trees. The young man had then sunk to his knees in the dense undergrowth, and after having cleared away a layer of leaves and mulch, had pulled open the small timber trap-door hidden beneath. The Celt had emerged from the waist-depth hole with fresh travelling clothes, a flint-tipped knife and spear, provisions in a leather saddle-bag, and most importantly to his mind, a number of bulging beer-skins. Patric had then moved aside a wicker screen, woven with leaves and bracken, and led out a stocky brown pony from the depths of the copse. Having nearly-emptied one of the beer-skins, the mumbling ex-mason had then walked the loaded beast back to the stone circle.

As evening descended, Patric had sat alone at the centre of his few-hundred tonnes of now worthless stone. Such was his mood, he hadn't even changed into clean attire, but had simply thrown a heavy cloak about his shoulders, and though he hadn't eaten properly for two days, he'd been unable to stomach the thought of food. So he sat, morose and dejected, repeatedly refilling the Grrrr-ale whilst darkly reflecting on the cruel betrayal of his wife, gods, society, and most of all, progress.

Progress was a bastard.

By sunset, the very inebriated and embittered Celt had reached a grim resolve. He would leave behind this evil land, and its fickle worshipers of progress. He would not return to the place of his birth, for there was nothing there for him, but he would go somewhere beyond the uncaring reach of progress and all who worshipped it; Somewhere far-flung and remote. Patric despised progress above all things, for had it not destroyed his life? Indeed, the very world as he had known it? He had lost his faith in stone, the bedrock of his life, and also the belief that hard honest work could achieve anything. Before leaving, he had screamed verbal abuse up at the heavens, to gods he wasn't even sure were there to hear him. He then staggered off and after a number of attempts, finally managed to get on his pony.

However, rather than heading south-east to seek out a ferryman on the coast, the drunken Patric had headed south-west. Before he left the lands of the beaker-people, the Celt had a last task to perform.

'What the bloody-hell is he up to?' asked Allen, under the moonlit, cloudless sky.

'Wait and see' replied Alex. The three stood upon the crest of a domed, solitary hill, which rose above a surrounding landscape of gentle wooded valleys and smaller undulating hillocks. The hill lay about forty miles south-west of Stone-henge, and having set out from the stone-circle, Patric had reached it after three days of drunken riding. Allen knew that this chalk hill belonged to Patric. Indeed, this was the very hill which had been intended to be the pension-fund assuring the Celt's financial well-being in old age. Of course, as with all of Patric's other stone-based-investments, his chalk-hill pension-fund was now worthless, its value destroyed by the all-devouring and hated progress.

Unlike the hills and escarpments owned by tribes and clans, who could afford the manpower to guard them, individuals of the stone-age who owned a rocky-hill, did not advertise their ownership with huge chalk murals, but tended to camouflage them with a covering of grassy security turf, hiding the valuable nature of the underlying stone. Patric's mountain of chalk was similarly covered in grass. Yet for reasons best known to himself, the pissed-up Celt was now removing rolls of this security turf, something which would have been unthinkable in the Stone-age, whilst a mystified Allen looked on. All that cold winter night, Patric toiled on, either mumbling incoherently to himself, or bursting into wild verbal-outbursts in turn. He shook his fists at the deities above, and spat and stamped on the ground at those below.

As the eastern sky paled with the approach of morning, Patric briefly viewed his night's labour by torchlight, and then hastily departed, before Domi arose to view the Celt's handiwork. Alex and Allen remained behind at the foot of the hill, apparently awaiting the sunrise.

'You've got to be kidding!' chuckled Allen, as sunlight at last weakly illuminated the hillside before him.

'You've got to hand it to Pat, he's got quite an artistic eye!' giggled Alex in reply. Upon the hill, there now lay a huge mural of a naked man, a giant. The big picture was executed in crisp white lines, fashioned from where Pat had removed the turf, to expose the chalk beneath. The vast figure held a great club above his head, and his huge manhood stood stiffly to attention.

'It's Patric's rendering of Domi' explained Alex, 'and he wants to make sure the sun god sees it as he arises, hence the size. After all, he feels that he's been both hugely *shafted* up the arse by Domi ..' Alex gestured to the figure's groin, '...and that he's been cruelly *clubbed* into submission' he added, pointing to the giant figure's other huge weapon.

234

'It's the bloody Cerne-Abbas Giant is what it is!' replied Allen with a snigger, as daylight grew.

'Yep, we're in Cerne-Abbas, Dorset. It's well-famous mate as you know' agreed Alex, 'It soon gets overgrown though, but the heavy-metal-louts of the iron age later uncover it, thinking it suits their virile, hard-man image, and for thousands of years after, including in our time, courting couples like to shag on it, thinking it to be some sort of fertility symbol.'

Though he didn't believe a word he was hearing, Allen still smiled, before following after Alex. Patric now headed eastward along the coastal paths, and the nearest ferryman who could carry him out of the land he despised. Nine days later he arrived just to the west of modern day Dover, where it required both his pony and nearly all that he carried with him, to pay the fare to cross the channel to modern-day France. The ferryman hadn't been interested in the old-age stone cup, and therefore when Patric arrived in the new land, apart from the clothes he wore on his back, the Grrrr-ale was his only possession.

Patric had been in no position to barter with the boatman, for he was extremely keen to exit the country, not only due to his feelings concerning that land, but also due to an unfortunate chance-meeting he'd had on the coastal path; A chance-meeting about which the local-authorities would be very keen to interview the Celt.

The utterly depressed ex-mason had met a man travelling in the opposite direction, who had appeared so annoyingly smug and happy with himself and the world in general, that the embittered Patric couldn't help but belligerently ask what the hell the man was so pleased about.

The smiling man, an ex-lowly-paid thatcher apparently, had happily informed Patric that thanks to progress, he'd just landed a well-paid job-for-life. He had gained employ within the newly-born coal industry. He and his distant descendants would apparently never be out of work.

Alexander had laughingly informed a disbelieving Allen that four and a half thousand years later, this man's reincarnation would seal the fate of the British coalminers, a reincarnation which would also bear the name Thatcher.

The enraged Patric, thinking that the fates were truly rubbing salt into the wound, to place such a man in his path, had turned violent. He was now wanted for an assault on a miner.

The Cerne Abbas Giant, Dorset, England.

Patric left behind him a land where the real masons, such as those who skilfully fashioned building blocks, or sculpted wondrous statues from the living rock, remained in work, as do their descendants to this day. However, the vast number of those involved in the Masonic trades which had simply been taking advantage of the stone-age, became unemployed en masse. Of these superfluous freeloaders, some were retrained, many starved to death, but a few, not accepting their time was over, carried on the numerous secretive Masonic ceremonies, even though they no longer carried out the obscure jobs that went with them. In an effort to keep their former trades alive, these masons even offered their frivolous services without charge, yet no one took them up on their offer, for it was as true then as it is now, no matter what the explanation, there's something just *not quite right* about free-masons. Unfortunately, the descendants of these back-scratching, secret-ceremonial-types are still very much with us to this day.

The other legacy from this age which also remains with us to the current day would of course be foot-ball. Though of course the game has become a far-more gentle pursuit with the passage of the millennia, the spirit of the original game still lives on. For it should be noted that many modern-day supporters, after having spent a fortune on seasons tickets and ever-changing strips, having sat through all-weathers, and having further invested a huge amount of optimism, perseverance and emotion in their beloved team, often come away after a poor result, feeling like they've had a good kick in the balls.

CH 24: A WALK ON THE WILD SIDE

Here the breath of creation burned the hottest, for this was a land reserved by nature for herself. An unspoilt sanctuary purified by a searing heat and free of noisome beings. A land where cloudless heavens merged with marching sand-dunes, seemingly welded together by a broiling, ever rippling river.

And yet still he lived.

The flickering dot grew until at last a single ragged figure emerged from the shimmering, oily veil that was day's seething air. A tortured and bowed body was driven ever onward by an equally tortured soul, without purpose or destination, other than an overwhelming desire for solitude and escape. Yet escape from what, the man's fevered mind could only recall erratically, which was in-itself a welcome blessing.

'Woah! That's a tad-warm I must say!' Alex exclaimed, fanning his face with a hand. After just having sped through a further seven years of Patric's life in a fast-forward mode, Allen remained silent, waiting for the rest of him to catch up with himself. The two now stood under a blistering sun, amid the towering dunes of a great desert. Before them, with matted copper beard and hair to his emaciated waist, a skeletal, thirty-two year old Patric staggered on through the inferno.

'I really wish you'd start making less of a fuss every single time we need to speed things up a bit!' complained Alex, 'it's getting a bit irritating if you don't mind me saying!'

'Oh don't you bloody mind me!' replied Allen angrily, kneading his throbbing head.

'Oh for Christ's sake Allen! Stop being such a tart will-you! It's not as though it's an unusual human experience!' Alex sounded genuinely annoyed.

'Come a-friggin-gain!' growled Allen, 'I'm only used to experiencing time at one pace!' he added, grimacing against the pounding within his skull.

'Allen mate, the living's perception of the passage of time has always been all over the bloody place! Even you can't deny that!' Alex's tone was incredulous, his hands raised in exasperation.

'Oh will you utterly-fuck-off-please!' exclaimed Allen, in no mood for his companion's annoying mind games.

'What? So you've never had the feeling of something you've done recently feeling like it was ages ago? Or something you did ages ago suddenly feeling like it happened yesterday?' Alex stared into Allen's eyes as he added 'You're saying you've never had the feeling of the longer you live, the faster time appears to pass? Or that the weekend passes faster than the working week?'

'Yeah, but all that's a little bit different to flying through seven odd years in a few minutes!' Allen retorted.

'But I thought you felt like the last thirteen years of your own life has passed in blur, from when you left school, to your current very-mediocre station in the world?' Alex's voice was matter of fact. Allen didn't answer, but angrily turned from his companion to follow after Patric, who had just disappeared over the crest of the huge sand dune ahead.

'Oh by the way!', the clerk said over his shoulder half way up the slope, 'you look a right ponce in yer new frock!' Alex was now arrayed in a fine robe of shimmering white, edged with golden thread and fashioned from a single sheet, which wound about his waist and draped over one shoulder. Upon his wrists and ankles were golden bands, and an intricate necklace of precious stones hung about his neck. Upon his feet were supple, sandals with thongs that wound about the ankles, and under his sunglasses, his eyes were ringed with dark make-up.

'Jealousy will get our next incarnation nowhere!' Alex peevishly replied, before quickly checking his reflection in a full-length mirror which appeared for a moment before him, before vanishing. Seemingly reassured by his appearance, the ex-estate agent whistled a tune to himself as he followed-after his other two less-glamorous incarnations.

Upon his arrival on the continent, the Celt had immediately set out on foot eastward, toward the rising sun. For the beered-up and belligerent Patric intended to travel to the place where Domi arose at the edge of the world each day, to ask the sun-god what the bloody-hell he thought he was playing at. As all his kindred, Patric further believed that the world was flat, and though it wasn't within his nature to take his own life, he'd half hoped that if he ventured far enough, he might well inadvertently wonder off the edge of it, and into restful oblivion.

On mainland Europe, the metal-smiths had already conducted their unfriendly business take-overs of the masonic monopolies at the point of the sword, some generations earlier. Having therefore found himself in an equally advanced culture to the one he'd just left behind, Patric had set off at a blistering pace, to embark upon what would be an epic yet unrecorded journey. This journey would encompass many lands and cultures, a path which would reveal wonders and sights before undreamt of by the Celt. However, Patric's heart would be untouched by all that he beheld, for he was driven simply by the all-consuming desire to escape the cruel march of progress and all its worshippers, and his soul had become a dark thing, gnawed by bitterness. Patric survived on that which he could forage, and (when sober enough) hunt. At each settlement crossing his path, the once-proud ex-mason undertook all and any lowly task in exchange for whatever passed for the local brew. Though he travelled alone through the lands of often-hostile and vicious tribes, Patric's intoxicated state, ever worsening appearance and odour protected him. For he was taken to be some wandering shaman or madman, both of which were believed to be unlucky to slay by the superstitious folk of the time.

Intermittently, Patric's marathon journey was broken by brief halts as he found himself in some isolated spot or other, such as at the heart of a dense forest or cavern atop some lonely hill. At each such haven, Patric hoped to have at last given progress the slip. However, to his consternation the Celt found himself unerringly pursued by his nemesis, and it would never be long before someone showed up to start clearing the trees or quarry the stone. So Patric's drunken quest, to both find Domi-the-bastard-of-bastards, and to escape from progress, from *change*, had continued, the passing seasons growing into years.

The almost-familiar Celtic tribes of modern-day France, Belgium, Germany and Poland, gave way to the unfamiliar-looking inhabitants and cultures of modern-day Ukraine, and the Caucasus. Patric found his eastward march at last blocked by what we now call the Caspian-sea, and the north gripped by the impassable snows of icy winter. He had then turned southward, initially with the intent of returning to his original eastward march, after he'd found a landward route around the watery obstacle. However, having reached the southern edge of the inland sea, the annoyed Celt found that the east was now walled off by mountainous terrain marching ever-southward. Yet to his fury, even when at last Patric reached the southern tip of this natural barrier, he found his eastward route still blocked by what we call the Persian Gulf.

Patric had ranted and raved at the insecure sun-god, who was clearly scared of mortals turning up to tell him what they thought of his unfair and crap-world, to his face. The Celt's anger was also increased by the fact that though his intention was to flee progress, the further he travelled, the greater the grip of progress appeared to be. For he now found himself within a land of large, walled-settlements and well-tended fields.

After much swearing and inebriated deliberation, Patric had at last decided that perhaps he'd now head westward, toward the setting sun, for the Celt hoped not only to catch the sun-god at the other end of the world, but also that if he travelled toward where Domi died each day, then perhaps the grip of progress might also diminish.

So it was, that Patric had staggered westward on into the arid Middle-East. Due to the long years of solitary travel, alcohol and drug abuse, and being unused to the tipples and narcotics of these strange eastern lands, Patric had grown somewhat reticent by this stage. Increasingly, the Celt's mind and feet wandered without purpose, so that often he forgot why he was even making the meandering journey. Apart from the fetid rags clinging to his back, Patric's only possession remained the once-precious ancient stone-cup. To the Celt's addled senses, the vessel had become a trusted companion, and he muttered to it incessantly as he journeyed on, lovingly stroking and caressing the once-priceless, now-worthless beaker. Patric had come to believe that sooner or later, everyone would let you down, however he knew he would always be able to rely on the container from which he drank liquid-oblivion. He and the cup were very intimate, indeed on dire occasions when Patric had run out of strong-drink, he'd even drunk his own urine from the Grrrr-ale. Patric's own water had an extremely high alcohol-content after all.

However, one dark day, as the befuddled Patric neared what would later be called the Mediterranean Sea, he'd stumbled and the beloved cup had been dashed against a boulder. Worn thin by the passage of the centuries, the cup had been holed. Betrayed by his last and only friend, a distraught Patric had flung the useless beaker from him, and stumbled on alone.

At this point Alex had briefly halted time. He'd then turned to an extremely disorientated Allen and reached into the clerk's raincoat pocket. Alex had quickly retrieved *The* Book, which now appeared to be an engraved bronze plaque, before thrusting it in front of the groggy clerk's eyes.

According to The Book, the holed stone cup had in fact lay where an infuriated Patric had hurled it for nearly two and a half thousand years, under a deepening covering of soil and debris. Apparently, it would eventually be unearthed when the foundations for a tavern were excavated above it. The cup which at one time had been worth more than the life of a man, from which men had dreamed of drinking, became in turn a door-stop, a missile to be thrown at stray-dogs, and a club to deal with the more-rowdy drunkards.

However, upon one extremely busy night, when the downstairs common-room was heaving, and a party of thirteen had suddenly turned up without a booking, wanting to use the upstairs function room, the innkeeper had found himself short of drinking vessels. The landlord had briefly rinsed out the ancient cup, and plugged the hole with resin, before sending it upstairs to be used by the party. Allen had witnessed a terribly polite, bearded man in his early thirties drink from the cup. A man who had until recently been a carpenter. A man whose last supper this was. The holey-Grrrr-ale, had become the Holy Grail.

'Jesus Christ!' Allen had sworn at the time, as the vision of the *The* Book had ended.

'Yeah it was, wasn't it' Alex had replied, before speeding time up.

Having been unable to travel further westward due to the Mediterranean, Patric had been forced ever southward, until at last he'd entered a great desert. Unexpectedly as it might seem, it was within this hell-on-earth that Patric's low mood had at last began to rise. For here at last amid the endless dunes, the Celt believed he'd finally escaped progress, and with a sense of relief, believed that here also he would surely perish, leaving behind the uncaring and cruel world. Following a few days of the intensive heat, he no longer cared where he was going or why.

As an ever-more incoherent Patric trudged on across the shifting sands, Alex had at last slowed time once again to its regular pace, seven years to the day since they'd set out from Stone-henge. After having recovered his senses following the whirl-wind journey, Allen had again given thought to his last unexpected reading of *The* Book, as he and Alex followed Patric under the burning sun.

'You could've given me chance to recover before you shoved *The* Book in me face mate!' he complained. Alex ignored him.

'Though I must say, I liked the bit about what happened to the cup in *The* Book!' Allen continued with a chuckle, 'Nice-touch! This is certainly one dream I'm going to remember!' he said, not for the first or last time.

'I don't see how Pat's gonna get out of this one' Allen said darkly, as he and Alex passed Patric's discarded empty water skin. Above them, the Celt was nearing the crest of the latest high dune. Alex didn't reply. 'Who's he talking to this time?' Allen asked amid the oven-like temperature of mid-afternoon. Patric was once again babbling to himself. 'Who knows?' replied Alex.

Though Patric appeared to be the only living being in all that vast and inhospitable landscape, he was seldom alone, for the desert's heat conjured many companions for him. Hatric had returned briefly from the houses of the ancestors, to berate his errant son for abandoning him, and to say thanks-a-lot for the business with the goat. Before returning to the other side, Hatric had shaken his head at his son's lowly and pathetic state, and with great satisfaction reminded Patric that he'd always foretold it. Nattarra had appeared, her laughter cold and mocking, as she rebuked herself for ever having allowed such a vagabond to touch her delectable body. She'd haughtily informed Patric that she was now with a real man who could provide for her every need, and that yes, she'd faked every one of her orgasms whilst with the Celt.

Enixam had put in an appearance to ask why he had never returned to her, and where had he been when those O'Hooly-bastards had fought their way into the village. The ferryman's dark shade had also materialised to curse Patric as an oath breaker. Each visitation arrived and departed in cruel procession, until the lone traveller knew not whether he witnessed mirages of the blistering inferno, or indeed if it was his tormentors who were the living, and he who was now dead. The visions appeared so real, yet they answered him not. However, as Patric reached the crest of the great dune, and looked out from its height, a final apparition would confirm to the disappointed Celt that it was he who lived, for the vision he now beheld could not have existed in the real world.

It was clearly a mirage, he was disappointingly therefore alive.

Patric stood, the searing heat forgotten, jaw slack, eyes wide in disbelief. For below him, seemingly out of the very desert there arose wide and tended fields of the deepest green and gold. He turned woodenly to survey the hellish, sun-blasted terrain he'd traversed, and only returned his gaze to the lush crops beyond after long thoughtful moments. A barking, rasping chuckle issued from the Celt's cracked and broken lips. Yet the cause of his grim mirth was that which lay beyond the rich pastures, for there sprawled a vast settlement, a city. Yet this was a settlement surely beyond the wit of mere mortal hands, for in scale and beauty it was undoubtedly without rival. Here there were only straight lines and edges, dressed stone and the despised yet cunningly fashioned metal. Here there was only purpose and method, indeed the very streams and waterways which interwove the encircling fields did so in regimented fashion. Broad, evenly-paved stone avenues spanned a metropolis which bestrode either bank of a great and ponderous river, upon which there was a busy traffic of sails. Towering above the ordered stone streets were mighty temples, ringed by a silent and menacing legion of rock-hewn giant guardians, their obsidian eyes of jet ever watchful. About all was a halo of white, glimmering light, so intense it caused Patric to squint. No defensive bank, palisade, nor even ditch was there, indeed no fortification of any kind. For as in all else this was a settlement unlike any of Patric's experience, which was indeed great. Patric collapsed to the burning sands in hoarse, hysterical laughter.

After some moments, the bedraggled and emaciated Celt arose unsteadily, released at last from the cruel choking embrace of wracking, humourless sobs. He cried out in manic glee for the vision to be gone, yet still it remained.

When after some moments he was still not freed of the bewitchment, the cackling Patric charged forward, down to the foot of the dune, gait crab-like, toward the imagined embodiment of his nemesis, progress. Hardly would any have suspected this to be one who had wandered without shelter of nourishment for many days in the fiery wilderness, as in agile manner he bounded with great merriment along a wide, raised causeway he knew did not exist, toward a city that simply wasn't there. Patric knew himself to be in truth upon the road to nowhere.

And yet still he ran.

The outer limits of the phantom city were marked by a ring of great stone pillars, set at regular intervals, and one such mighty sentinel stood at the centre of the road upon which the Celtic-tramp capered. Patric's laughter grew in volume and intensity, as increasing his pace, he headed directly for the pillar, to symbolically banish the foul spells of his own mind.

The thud of self-propelled human hitting immovable stone was sickeningly audible.

'Ouch, that's gotta hurt!' grimaced Allen from atop the dune, 'hey, nice place' he added, staring out at the great city before he and Alex.

'Yeah!' agreed Alex, before adding in dramatic tone, 'and inside its walls is written the secret of the meaning of life!'

'No shit!' exhaled Allen doubtfully.

To be continued…….

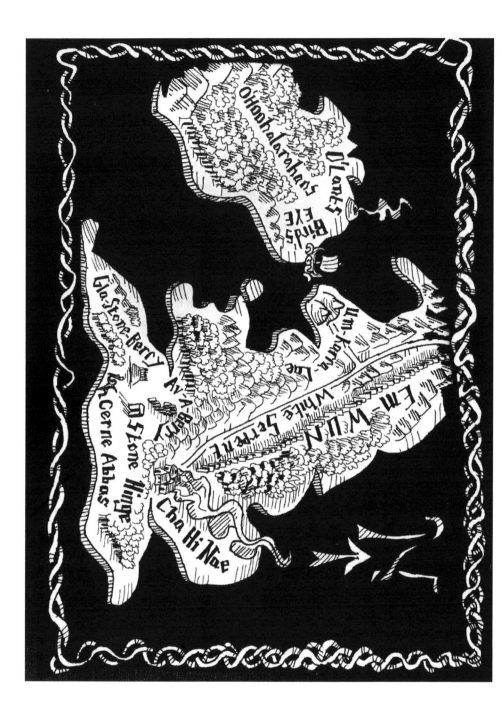

Printed in Great Britain
by Amazon